BROKEN RESTORATION

BOOK 3: ARMOUR OF LIGHT SERIES

DONITA BUNDY

JOURNEY
PRESS

ISBN
Print: 978-0-6487823-6-0
Ebook: 978-0-6487823-7-7
Editor: Belinda Pollard
Proofreader: Alix Kwan
Cover design: Donita Bundy

Cover images copyright ©
Envato Elements:
Characters: fxquadro
Background: martinm303

❀ Created with Vellum

For Simon

CONTENT WARNING

Dear Reader,

I want to alert you to some of the topics covered in this book that might influence your decision whether or not to read it.

Child prostitution and sexual violence:

The work of the young British woman, Amy Carmichael (1867–1951), inspired some of the context and characters in this book. She worked in India to rescue children sold to the temples and forced into child prostitution. Amy rescued, housed, educated and cared for over a thousand girls. In my teens I was inspired by her, and a number of years ago I came across Destiny Rescue, a not-for-profit organisation currently working around the world pursuing the same goal. This is still a prevalent reality in the world today.

Reasoning:

My goal is not to glorify these issues or to use them gratuitously. As a writer, I marry my life experiences to the fiction in order to create a three-dimensional work. And it has been my experience and prayer that when the grace, hope and love of our Lord meets with pain—physical, emotional and psychological—it is transformational. He has the answers. His is the way, the truth, the life and the Light. And He is for all.

Sincerely,
db

TO THE CHURCH IN LAODICEA

"Those whom I love I rebuke and discipline. So be earnest and repent. Here I am! I stand at the door and knock. If anyone hears my voice and opens the door, I will come in and eat with that person, and they with me.

"To the one who is victorious, I will give the right to sit with me on my throne, just as I was victorious and sat down with my Father on his throne. Whoever has ears, let them hear what the Spirit says to the churches."

Revelation 3:19–22 (NIV)

PROLOGUE

MARCUS: UP TO SPEED

And why exactly, you may very well ask, were we in our current predicament? Out on the street, at night, with only the bare essentials packed in the truck? For that we had Laodicea's Overseer to thank. Actually, I was sure there was more to it. But truth be, right now, I was mustard to throw all blame for our current situation on the single individual who had made me life hell for the past six months. I was sad to farewell me friends, Felix in particular, but happy to see the back of the hot air balloon who had an unhealthily attachment to his title and entitlements. Even if it did leave us in a prickly—homeless, jobless, hopeless—pickle. So, for now we found ourselves cruising the streets of this white-washed tomb of a city: all lickety split on the outside, dead as a dodo on the innards, one eye focused on finding a hint of a home for the night. The other on guard for the enemy.

Yesterday, at the twins' birthday party, we'd had confirmation there were, in fact, demons in Laodicea, despite all posturing and declaration to the contrary from the Community. Of course, this was not news—the hordes of hell had thrown out their version of the welcome mat six months ago. But since then, we'd not seen hair nor ugly butt of them... of sorts. Val'd had a run in. As had Dan... apparently. I'll admit I'd dropped me guard. Not me Warrior Guard or me training—I'm not that daft—but I'd stopped looking for the enemy where I'd expect to see the krets lurking. But when a collection of crud-eating, nose-hair-burning vermin decided to join us for the twins' celebration last night, they were well and truly outed and back on the menu.

Our time working with the Community here had left us at sixes and sevens with each other, and we had a fair bit of work to do to get back in the same boat. For me, first up was shoring up me place with me wife, Kait. From there we'd all be looking to reclaim the common ground we'd lost since leaving Sodom. Especially me poor girl, Tessa. But thank the Light, He had us and knew what He was doing. Because, sure as taxes, we didn't.

TONIGHT, on the streets, our optimism was running on the fumes of hope by the time we decided to check out an abandoned factory. Dan and Val had come across the place before on their hunt for the "black and white" girl who tormented Dan in his dreams, relentlessly crying for help. They'd always found the gates locked, but we'd been as successful at finding a place to camp tonight as they had been at finding Dan's elusive spectre, so it was worth a try.

WE WERE SHOCKED and as delighted as pigs invited into the veggie patch to have access to shelter for the night. And possibly longer. But a sign on the gate said this particular veggie patch was contaminated —which explained why such a huge compound butting up against the CBD had been left to die a slow and lonely death. Trying to choose which side of the "hopefull-dreadfull" pendulum to cling to was tipsing me turvy.

WE ROLLED into the deserted factory and hid the truck under the rising arch of a bridge that rose above the car park. The common consensus was to let Tessa and the twins hide out in the cab for as long as possible, in relative safety, to rest, as the four of us—Kait and Val, Dan and me—paired up to scope the scene on a reconnoitre.

We sensed we were not alone here. The place was occupied. By whom—or what—we were yet to discern. Me pendulum was hiking further away from "happy dance" towards "hitch your wagons and draw your swords".

But you can bet your bippy there was still a hint of jig left when I saw Dan *not* scrunching his face like he'd just licked a lemon and the hairs on the back of me neck were inert. Our company was not of the demonic variety.

Truth be, after our run-in with the Overseer this afternoon I wouldn't have been too upset at the prospect of some actively hostile confrontation. For, as we all knew, there was nothing like a bit of "justified defence" to work out your ticks and skitches. Just the thought of it had me pendulum hiked another notch toward excited.

But then I thought of me family and especially the kids. Raph was tap-dancing along the edge of an anxiety attack. Tessa had been away from home and out of condition and was presently running as taut as a loaded clothesline, flying off the handle at the slightest twitch of a wisp. An all-out attack at this point might very well push them to waltzing each other over the edge.

Dan and I discovered there were people in the demountables just off the tarmac. They didn't answer the door, so we left them in peace. Meeting Val and Kait back at the truck, they confirmed they'd been followed. But even though they'd provided an invitation, their tail had not wagged. They suggested we approach the neat-as-a-pin cabin set in the middle of the open area. Either someone was in there—and we'd force an introduction—or we could "borrow" it for the night.

We gathered the kids from the truck and like black cats in the dead of night, made our way through the shadows edging along the walls of the monstrous buildings. Once Dan and Val had scouted the scene and given us the all clear, we hustled across the open tarmac and joined them at the porch of this odd little building. We were out in the open so everyone stayed on guard, making way for Dan to climb the ramp and knock. But at Riah's prompting, he drew his sword and ran it down the crack in the door and the lock released. It was a Soteria House. Me tension leaked away, even more convinced we were in the right of it.

But as the door swung open, a beast on wheels barrelled out of the house. As broad as an ox and with a roar of a lion he slammed Dan into the tarmac and fairly well got stuck in. Before I could throw off me gloves and join in the excitement, Tessa was all over the bloke like a rash. Val and I grabbed the fella, but Tessa was still swinging away. Kait did her best to restrain our girl, but it was the shock reveal that stilled her.

"Indy?"

"Dan?"

"What the frack?"

Turned out the beast in the wheelchair was Indigo, Dan's long-lost friend.

ACT 1: TRACTION

RAPHAEL: HEALING IZA

A warrior stepped out of the darkness and brought the shadows with her. She stood in front of Dan's friend, Indy, and blocked him from entering the hut. The wheels of his chair weren't fully on the flat of the veranda and she made him hold the chair on the incline, blocking him and the rest of us from entering the house.

There was a cry from inside, a woman's voice. "Indy?" I could feel her pain through the goosebumps spiralling throughout my body. Her voice drew me like a magnet.

The weight of Indy's tiredness blanketed the air as he spoke. "Move aside, Amina." It made me realise how exhausted I was. This day had lasted a year and we had been under its thumb since yesterday.

Yesterday had been our birthday. Sariah and I turned eleven. We had a full day of adventure, exploring the city, going to the zoo and ending up with a party for dinner at our house—the Community's house—which they took away from us. But, last night at our party, the demons came. We survived the battle, but first thing this morning we were thrown out. The Overseer whittled the day away as we were trapped, waiting in his tower. We could have been looking for somewhere to live. To move to. To be safe. But he stopped us. He even sent Uncle Felix away so he couldn't help.

Now it was night-time and Dan and Val had led us to this place where Dan's long-lost friend lived. In a wheelchair. The two of them —Dan and Indy—had fought, before they realised who they were facing. Tessa joined in too. But for now, she had calmed down. Dan was still burning. He had only just learned his friend was living without the use of his legs and his anger danced over his armour in dark flames.

Indy tried to explain, but there was a woman inside, in pain, calling for him. I was sure he would tell Dan his story. But inside. After he had taken care of the lady. But the shadow-woman would not let us in. I was sure I could help. But I had to get inside.

Indy groaned, "Amina, please. Let me in. Iza needs me."

"They do not come in here." The woman, Amina, spat words seasoned with venom.

"Dan is family." Indy's words grew a steel skeleton and all hints of weariness had evaporated into a growl.

Amina's eyes flashed to Dan. Somehow, he had caused her great offence. I do not know how. We had only just arrived, and he had not even spoken to her yet. She then looked at Marcus the same way. Her eyes narrowed and her nostrils flared even more when she looked at me. Sariah moved to my side and put her shoulder in front of mine. The pressure was building like oppressive humidity before a summer storm. I did not know what the problem was or how to help. So, I smiled. "Hello." I held my hand up to her over the porch railing, using manners like Abbot had taught me. "I'm Raphael."

She tilted her head, squinted her eyes and looked at me like I was a stain on the kitchen bench. I was surprised when she decided to shake my hand. But she stopped, her head turning to look at each of us through squinty eyes. Then she saw Val and her eyes grew to be like those of the little dogs with googly eyes some of the Laodicean ladies carry around with them. They almost popped out of her head. Her eyes, that is, not googly-eyed dogs.

She stepped out of the way and allowed Indy up onto the porch. "What is it, Mina?" It seemed the sharp edges of their hostility at each other had merged to be a common fortress against us.

"What is this? Who... *what* are they?" She took a step forward and drew two knives from nowhere.

Indy turned to look at us in the light of the doorway. His eyes also became daggers. He manoeuvred his chair beside Amina. None of us missed his inspection. Finally, he examined Dan. "What the frack is that?"

Dan was quiet and calm. "What are you talking about, Indy?"

"You see it?" Amina edged her way closer to Indy so the two of them completely barricaded the door.

"Dan?" Indy's voice dropped to a growl. "What. The frack. Is that?" His finger pointed to the sword hilt poking up over Dan's shoulder.

Val moved into the light. "What exactly can you see?"

Amina took another step forward to meet her. She now stood more clearly in the light of the open door. Dull grey scales coated the left-hand side of her body. They slithered up her neck and covered part of her face. Light was absorbed into their dead surface. The contrast highlighted the richness and glow of her dark skin. A Greyscale. I had never seen one before. It was my turn to have little-dog-bulgy-eyes.

"Indy..." the voice from inside wavered. Whoever it was, was in need... or pain. Indy's eyes locked with Amina's. His own dark skin paled.

Dan extended his hand, palm out, pleading with his friend. "Trust me. We are no danger to you and yours. You know that. We may even be able to help."

I looked around the group. Everyone's attention was bouncing between Indy and Dan. I was shocked that they could see our armour. I guess everyone else was too. It was really important what happened next. Amina and Indy were now Potentials.

But there was someone inside, suffering.

I felt the shift. This wasn't just about finding a shelter for the night.

In fact, that seemed to be off the agenda altogether. The sky closed in and the weight of the universe focused itself on the small space we occupied. I knew we stood on a knife's edge, so I did not move or say a word. But my heart, attention and soul were being pulled through the door to the woman inside. She needed help. My help.

Please help them trust us so we can help. You have brought us here for this.

Dan tried again. "I promise, we will explain everything. You are safe. You can trust me... us. Please Indy, let us help."

The man's eyes softened as his shoulders dropped. He was going to agree.

But the grey-scaled woman would not stand down. "No. You will not enter." She turned to face Indy and she lashed him with her words. "You swore to protect her. You promised. But she has only just survived this last attack, and now you want to let these... men"—again she spat the words with acid—"enter? You don't deserve her. You worthless pi—"

"Yes, Amina, I am a kret, a no-good man who is the scum of the earth, just like all the other no-good, kret, scum-of-the-earth men." His voice tripped along in a monotone-bored manner as he turned to face her fully.

Val edged backward and placed her hand on my shoulder. With a squeeze and a slight nudge towards the door, I understood immediately. Val knew my heart. Whilst Amina and Indy's argument heated up, no one was thinking about the door. Riah slipped her hand in mine to give it a quick squeeze and together we slid under the railing, up onto the porch, into the shadows and through the unprotected door.

An open room, neatly and sparsely decorated, greeted us. Against the far wall was a wide bed. A person lay curled up facing away from us. White-blonde hair water-falled over the edge and washed onto the floor. Riah and I crept across the space and approached the body.

"Um... hello?" I could hardly hear my own voice, so I am not sure if she could. I was about to repeat myself when she rolled over gingerly and faced us.

I turned to a block of concrete.

I could not move.

I could not speak.

No thoughts passed through my head except for the exceptional beauty I was confronted with. I could not pull my eyes away from her perfect face. The left-hand side twined with the goddess colours of blue, purple and gold.

Even though pain veiled her face, she smiled. Riah elbowed me in the ribs. Shaking myself like a wet bird, I came back to the moment. Outside, Indy and Amina still argued and ranted.

"Why, hello." Her voice was a whisper. "We don't often have visitors. Well, ones as lovely as you two." She looked over the two of us, not missing our entwined hands. "My name is Izabaal. Welcome to our home." A slender hand also coated in the goddess's scales emerged from the blankets, froze as she grimaced, then extended in greeting.

Riah elbowed me again and spurred me into action. "H-hello, I'm Raphael, and this is my sister, Sariah." I took her hand and gasped. I was expecting it to be cold and metallic. But it was warm and smooth, the scales seemed to move or… breathe with a life of their own. With wide eyes we each studied the other's hands. She ran long, porcelain fingers over my scars. I ran my thumb over her scales. Our eyes met with greater understanding.

"Pleased to meet you, Raphael and Sariah"—her eyes crinkled—"my friends call me Iza. I'd be pleased if you would too."

She went to remove her hand. But I held firm. I had begun to sense her pain and suffering. A picture of her injuries was forming. I shut my eyes to focus. She allowed her hand to relax into mine. I opened my eyes to thank her and saw that Riah had laid her hand on Iza's shoulder. She held Iza's eyes with her own. I went to work as they shared a moment.

"Miss Izabaal?" She broke away from Riah's gaze and gave me her attention. "I think I know what ails you, and I think I can help. May I please have your permission to try?"

Her head moved to sit at the back of her neck, even though she allowed me to keep her hand in mine. Her face scrunched. "What do you mean?"

"Please, Miss Izabaal, just let me help."

The woman looked between me and Riah, and rolled her lips in.

Riah clenched her jaw and nodded. Her eyes sharp and serious.

"Sure, I guess so. What do I—"

I took her hand in both of mine and shut my eyes. I had already gained a sense that she had suffered internal injuries. I did not know what internal organs were supposed to look like, but all I did was picture her whole and healthy.

You have given me this gift for a reason. I do not know if you want to heal Izabaal, but I think you have a purpose here. If you want her better, use this Badge you have given me.

I then pictured her whole and well and happy. I focused as hard as I could on the image in my mind. All else faded. I heard nothing but my heartbeat thumping in my ears. I saw nothing but the image in my mind. Much like when the angry red haze takes me. But this time it was not heavy and suffocating, rather it was lightweight and transported me deeper into the vision. I could breathe, I was not scared, I was able to focus on the Light and the image I received.

Izabaal was surrounded in darkness. And I had to get the Light to her. I pushed through. I held tight onto her hand and to the vision in my mind. It was like pushing back the tide. It had never been like this before. Even when I clung to our birthday demon. That had been blazes of white lightning in a vicious electrical storm. This was also a great strain, but darkness clung to the image in my mind like golden syrup. I fought on. I stood my ground and waited for the change. I would not give up. I had come to learn the lesson of hanging on and not letting go. So, I stood, strained and strived, until there was nothing left.

The Darkness swirled and gathered. I was a pinpoint of light anchored to the image of this beautiful woman and her suffering. I tried to find a way to surround her with the fire and warmth of the Light and burn away the darkness that clung to her, that threaded through her and held her bound. I was so intent on my purpose, I did not see the wave until it picked me up and tried to roll me away.

But I was used to riding the tide. I knew how to fight that battle. Waves would come. Just like when I rode the Dragon through the red haze. When I fought it, I had to cling on and withstand his terror rolling over me and drawing me out. But if I waited, and hung on, I would survive. Fighting the Dragon had taught me waves *had* to pass. They could not remain. The Light would remain. And if I hung on, and waited, *I* would remain too.

I remembered the library in Sodom. I remembered the Light telling me to hang on to the hilt of my sword and not let go. I remembered the burning pain and the torture. And I remembered that, too, had passed.

I remembered my last battle. All I had to do was hang on and I knew—in the depths of my soul—that I would remain. I found the anchor and clung to it with all my might. And breathed. Light in... Darkness out... breathe in... two... three... out. Out.

I was a firefly caught in a stormy sea at night.

Focus. Stand. And do not let go.

It became a circle that spun endlessly in my mind. I focused on the repetition and my job. I allowed the pain to retreat into the background until, eventually, the darkness ebbed.

In the shallows of the storm, I made ground and I pushed on. The tide turned. Buoyed by the dawn breaking, I surged on. Night's darkness dissolved like mist in the morning sun. I saw Izabaal in my mind's eye standing happy next to Dan's friend Indy. Izabaal, her scales silver but ablaze in all colours, and Indy standing at her side, both bathed in pure radiant Light. I did not know what this meant, but I kept pushing till all the darkness had faded.

"Enough. It is finished. You have done well, Raphael."

I smiled and opened my eyes. Kneeling on the floor, I looked up at Izabaal. Her eyes were wide, and she was crying.

"Are you hurt?" Surely, she should be happy, not sad, I thought it had worked. Maybe I was mistaken.

"Get away from her." The voices outside were now inside.

I could not see her, but I knew Riah stood at my back. She would not let Amina get to me. I let everyone else deal with the angry woman and returned my attention to Izabaal. "Did that help?"

Her mouth opened and closed but no sound came out. She looked at her legs and went to lift herself up on her elbow. We still held hands: I was not in a hurry to break the link. I tried to help her sit. She stared at me, her summer's-day, blue-sky eyes unblinking. She slowly nodded. "Yes." She mouthed the word but still, no sound came out.

"Yes!" I leaped up. I could not help it. It had worked. I had done it. My legs may have jumped, and I may have pumped my arms... a lot. Sunshine exploded in my heart.

Thank you, thank you, thank you.

Iza had finished arranging herself on the bed when I'd finished my happy dance. I looked back at her perfect face, the light from the dim light bulb catching on her wet cheeks. I was surprised that her scales were still only tricoloured. I had expected them to have turned into a silvery rainbow.

She pulled me to sit on the bed next to her. "Who are you? What have you done?" Wonder danced through her words.

"What? What has happened?" Amina lunged towards us.

I tore my eyes from Izabaal's beauty to Amina's rage.

Riah stood between us. Not moving. Grounded. Centred. Ready for a fight. My sister would not back down. Ever.

The room shrunk and I realised a war had started in my absence.

Amina raised her hand to strike my twin. I sprang from the bed to put myself between them with my hands raised, palms out. I may not be the warrior my sister is. But I was allowed to defend.

"Stop. Do not touch the child." Val demanded obedience.

And got it.

Amina stilled and turned.

No one could ignore Val when she had her warrior on.

The room shrunk even more when Dan, Tessa, Marcus and Kait all loomed, ready to rip apart anyone who touched Riah. Just like Riah would rip apart anyone who threatened me.

What a mess.

I noticed Indy trying to get through the wall of anger. His chair bumping and crashing through the forest of legs. "Iza!" Like a wild animal he roared. "Damn it. Let me through." Ramming his chair into the back of Dan, he made a gap and shot across the space and put himself between Riah—who had pushed me on to the bed behind her —and Amina. "Stand down, woman. For crying out loud." He swore. A lot. "They're just kids." He turned to Izabaal. "I am so sorry for the disturbance." It was then he really looked at her. "Why are you sitting up? How are you sitting up?" He looked at her face. "What's wrong? What's happened? For frack's sake, would someone fracking tell me what the frack is going on!" A wild bear trapped in a chair, the whites of his eyes matching his clenched white teeth, bared in a grimace.

Time stopped.

Izabaal, awash with wonder, stood and took a step, closing the gap that separated them. Taking hold of his tortured, twisted face in her perfect hands she looked at Indy like he was the most precious of gems. She kissed his forehead, each cheek and then his lips. "Peace, my love. I am well."

"What the frack..."

"Peace." Her thumb caressed the scarred mess of his cheek. "He has made me well. The little one has healed me." She then turned to me, and I was hit once again by a wall of overwhelming beauty. I could not breathe.

Riah came to sit on the bed next to me and kicked my foot.

"Oh. Oh no, Miss Izabaal. I have not made you well. The Light has." Both Indy and Izabaal stared at me. Her, the essence of beauty: perfect, pure, and graceful. Him, the definition of ugly: scarred, torn, and tortured.

Amina pushed her way through and ran her hands over Iza's face and arms. "What...? How...?" Grey scales, black hands, on white skin. Like lightning she turned to me and struck me with a glare full of hostility.

I looked to Val. What should I say? I knew this was really important. I did not want to make a mistake. Val smiled and nodded her head.

I widened my eyes at her, pleading not to have to be the one to explain. I did not want to mess this up. I knew how important it was. I begged for help. For an intervention.

Val nodded again. But not in the way that said, "Yes, I'm going to help you," but rather, "Go on, off you go."

So, set adrift with no idea of where I was going or how to get there, I threw my paddle in the water and started paddling like the lost child I was. Needing to stand so I was not at such a disadvantage, I began. "Well, you see… the Light brought us here. To you. And the Light gave me this Badge. To heal." I held up my hands so the three of them could see my scars. "When we heard the pain in Izabaal's voice, Val suggested we come in and help. So, we did."

I looked back at Val. She smiled. So I continued. "And now Izabaal is better, because the Light brought us. And the Light enabled us. And the Light showed me what to do." I nodded my head to my sister. "Sariah helped too. Her badge is Peace." I was not sure if that helped.

No one said anything. So I added, "I did not know if it would work, but I am very happy it did." My stomach was still in knots, but the memory of helping Izabaal flooded back, and I could not help but smile.

"The Light?" Amina spat.

She did not seem to be a happy woman.

"Yes."

"Like the Light of the Community?" Her top lip actually curled as she spoke of them.

"Oh, gosh no." I could not help but think of the Community's college. I really did not know what to say now. It was like someone had ruined a perfect dessert with soured cream. I may have screwed up my face.

I looked around the group for help. My eyes finally rested on Riah still slumped on the bed. She rolled her eyes and pretended to gag. "You said it, Riah." She summed up our opinion of the Community perfectly.

When the strangers looked at us like we were speaking a different language, I explained. "We have had a very big disagreement with the

Community College, and the Community gathering, and the Community Overseer... which is why we are here. It seems the Light in Laodicea is very different to the Light in Sodom."

I think that was the wrong thing to say. We took cover as a new war broke out.

2

KAITLYN: THE MORNING AFTER

There was an eruption when both Indy and Amina exploded at the same time.

"Sodom?"

"You were in Sodom?" Indy dragged his eyes from Raph and sought Dan.

"When? How long have you been here? Sodom fell six months ago." Amina seemed to enjoy an argument as much as rational folk enjoyed chocolate. Everything she said came out as an accusation.

Dan took over the storytelling and recapped our time here as Raph, still a blazing ball of joy, slipped back into the shadows beside Riah. Once again, she placed her shoulder in front of his as they huddled on the bed next to Izabaal. Riah's eyes did not leave the woman, Amina.

When Dan came to the end of his brief summary and shared how we'd parted company with the Overseer, Amina bared her teeth and growled like a panther. No love lost there, then. Now *that* would be an interesting story, but not one we would be privileged to hear anytime soon, I was guessing.

"Come on everyone, it's late. We can talk about this in the morning." Izabaal rose from the edge of the bed where she had perched, one hand resting on Indy's shoulder. "We need to get you all settled for the night. I'm thinking the office of Warehouse One might be suitable for now. What do you both think?" The young woman stood and glided between the scarred man and the scaled woman, calming each of them with a touch of her graceful hands, bless her. Both exhaled and nodded.

"Lovely. Amina, we'd best let everyone know. The lockdown is still in place, but please tell them about our guests. I don't want them to be upset or shocked. And please, let Lottie know of my recovery. I know she'll be pleased."

"You think they do not know of this intrusion? They have been aware since that ugly bus first arrived."

"Yes, of course. But it might help if you explained to them that they are friends…"—she looked to Dan, then Indy—"family. That our visitors are no threat, and they are not to be concerned." Izabaal gently corralled Amina to the door.

"I do not trust them." Her chin stabbed at each of us. "We still do not know what this"—her hand sliced the air towards Dan's armour and her lips puckered like she'd just sucked a grapefruit—"shimmering is. How did"—her dismissive yet accusatory hand now slashed toward Raph—"he cure you? It is trickery."

A tinkling of gentle laughter fell from Izabaal. "Amina, if this is a trap we've been tricked into, I am immensely grateful and, at the very least, we should offer them a place to stay for tonight." She placed both hands on her guard dog's shoulders. "Please trust me. I love you, need you and appreciate you. But I am asking you to, please, let the ladies and boys know they're not to be concerned. I can't bear to think they might be uneasy."

The dark woman huffed and stomped out of the hut, mumbling, "I am not happy, my girl." Before Iza could reply, Amina had been swallowed by the night and, praise the Light, the tension dissolved in her absence.

The walls stretched and it became easier to breathe. For the first time since we'd entered the cabin, I took the time to look around. It was small, but neat and functional, clean, and well loved. An old double bed was tucked into the corner, taking up almost a quarter of the floor space. It was butted up against a dividing wall which hid another small room cloaked in darkness. Two chairs and a small, battered desk, decorated with a jar holding an eclectic collection of flowering weeds, sat in the opposite corner.

The twins had inched their way to the middle of the bed now that the threat had left the building. Out of the limelight, they'd curled up and were zoning out. It had been a jam-packed, adrenaline-filled forty-eight hours, and my chicks were done in and overdue for bed. Riah's hazy eyes tracked everything. Raph was miles away, his smile still flickering in place. Tessa slumped against the wall next to them, lids heavy and shoulders drooping. Marcus exhaled and rolled his shoulders, still on high alert for threats. Val stood by the door watching everyone's back, with a clear line of sight to our Warriors of Light on guard outside.

And Dan could not pull his eyes off his long-lost friend. "I cannot believe you're alive. That you're here. That you're"—his eyes searched his friend's broken body and the chair that held him—"here."

"We've got a lot of catching up to do, but first, let's get your guys settled." Indy took in Raph, Riah and Tessa. "And then, Dan, we talk, yeh?"

After we grabbed our essentials, cots and bedding from the truck, Indy and Iza led us through the compound to one of the many huge sheds. The warehouse was not too far from their own hut. The mammoth doors across its yawning mouth were chained shut but there was a smaller, normal-sized entrance to the side. We filed through, every footstep, scrape and whisper echoing around the empty tomb like a gunshot.

"Cosy place you got here, bro." Dan waited till we were all through and shut the door behind us, walking at the rear with his friend. Izabaal led us off to the side where a shoebox—in comparison to the size of the warehouse—of office space had been installed in the corner of the cavern. We followed her through, once she'd flicked on a light. The first room was a square space with two desks pushed up against one wall, carpeted in beige with white-painted walls. The oppression of the void outside was removed by a ceiling that insulated, making it a safe, hospitable space.

Iza pointed to a door on the other side of the room. "Through there is the rest of the old staff utilities: a locker room, men's and women's bathroom, a dining room and three back offices. There's also a separate toilet equipped with a shower which accommodates Indy's chair, so that is his bathroom area. But my sisters have a bathroom in their cabins. There is power and water, so please feel free to help yourselves. Although we don't have towels and linen. Or much food I'm afraid."

My husband wrapped his arm around my shoulders and cleared his throat. "Izabaal, your two mites are a far greater treasure than all the Overseer's wealth. When I allow myself to imagine where we might've ended up tonight..." Marcus was quiet for a moment. "Thank you."

I moved to take the young woman's hand in gratitude. "We have everything we need, thank you both again for your hospitality." I would have hugged her if I thought she'd let me. Behind me, Val, Marcus and Dan made quick work of the beds and bedding. Then Dan followed Indy and Izabaal through the opposite door as we put everyone to bed.

We didn't expect to see Dan again this side of dawn. He had much ground to cover. But as I prepared to sleep, I had to wonder at the Light and his plans for us here. Not just in Laodicea, but more specifically here in this abandoned factory. I did not wonder for long before sleep took me. It had been a big day and tomorrow, I expected, would be bigger still.

3

CONTESSA: TESSA'S DEMON

I woke with a start. But the ringing of silence and the beating of my heart were the only things I could hear. I squinted my eyes, straining to hear what had woken me. Which was silly, I know, but the more I strained my ears, the louder my pumping blood became.

Breathing deeply, I worked on relaxing and convincing myself that the first night in a new place there were bound to be unusual noises to get used to. Right? I tried opening my eyes wide in an attempt to study every shadow. Even though it was dark, the light of the moon came through the office windows and a huge length of see-through panelling along the spine of the warehouse roof. I was able to make out the bodies sleeping on the cots around me.

Nothing moved.

Well, apart from the sleeping bodies breathing.

There were no unusual noises.

Except for the warehouse adjusting to the night temperatures.

I chided myself for being silly. Of course. That was it.

Even though we were insulated in this compartment of a room inside a ginormous shed, the creaks and cracks boomed and echoed like the inside of a hollow drum. It must have been the upheaval, the exhaustion, and the all kinds of crazy I'd been dealing with over the last twenty-four-ish hours. I could not believe it was only the night before the night before it had been business as usual at Kari's. My world had completely imploded.

And last night.

Oh. My. Word.

Being at the twins' party with an all-out demon attack.

And me with no armour.

I'd been so busy trying to fulfil everyone's expectations, do my job, keep Kari and the Community happy so that the others could stay in the big, beautiful house, wearing glorious new clothes, eating scrummy food, I'd let my armour fade.

Well, it was a bit more than that. It was kind of… gone. As in, I was all kinds of naked, or I may as well have been. When it really mattered, I was blind and defenceless.

Thank you for welcoming me back and forgiving me for going AWOL. Like, straight away. Without any kind of probation. One minute nada armour. The next? Bang. Back in the game. I know it might take a while for my family…

Well, that wasn't completely true. Val, Kait and Marcus had already forgiven me… and Raph, I think. I couldn't help but smile at the memory—all my memories—of that special kid. I'm not sure where I stood with Riah. But Dan? We had a way to go.

Thank you for my family and that most of them, and you, were so quick to welcome me back. Thanks for providing this place and possibly a way to help these people? Even though they're kind of perfect, and gorgeous—even Amina in her scary pants. But maybe not Indy. I mean, I suspect he's really nice and all, but, you know… not quite gorgeous-ish. Anyway, it seems like they've been here, and doing okay all by themselves for… ages, but… maybe they need some help? So, thanks.

I settled back on my cot and exhaled. Surrounded by all of my family and knowing, outside somewhere, Dan and Indy were sure to still be awake and talking, I was safe and at peace. Remembering how tonight had played out, I knew Dan and I still weren't on the best of terms, but there was hope.

Definitely hope.

I couldn't stop my smile.

I know I stuffed up with him, but in you all things are possible, right? Even salvaging my friendship with Dan... right?

"Did you see that woman?"

My heart stopped.

I mean, literally. Stopped.

A whisper of stench wafted through the air and out of the shadows as a woman stalked her way through the obstacle course of my sleeping family and perched on the edge of my cot. Cold sweat broke out... everywhere. Tingly, nasty snakes slid across my skin. Now the tang of sulphur singed my nose. "My goddess, she is beautiful. Did you see the scales? Full body. You know what that means, don't you?"

The form of Izabaal filled my mind, and my peace and confidence bled away.

And I mean like, haemorrhaged, with a severed artery.

Out of the darkness a perfect porcelain face emerged and leaned close to my ear. She whispered loudly, "Fully covered, means fully proficient." I knew she was talking about Izabaal's beautiful scales. "There's not one thing that woman doesn't have going for her." An icy hand reached out and stroked the hair from my clammy face.

I froze.

Except my heart.

That took off like a speedy, gallopy, painfully out-of-control flappy thing.

My Guard stood at the end of my bed in my line of sight. He locked eyes with me. And I noted he didn't have his sword drawn.

I tried to slow my breathing.

I was not in mortal danger.

I mean, my heart might literally explode. And if I didn't calm down, I would hyperventilate from lack of oxygen. But apart from that...

Breathe.

"She is exquisite." The demon ran her eyes over me critically. "But you"—she tilted her head—"aren't ugly. I mean, you're presentable, aren't you?" She lifted a lock of my hair and rolled it between her fingers. "Kari seemed to see something in you. Well, for a while. Before she threw you out." She sighed. "But Izabaal is stunning. You've got to agree. Even in a sack, Achilles would snap her up—no armour required there."

That hit scored a bullseye to my pride. Turned out the only reason I was interesting—the new flavour of the moment with Kari—was my armour. One of the big-time designers had seen it and decided I was his new muse. But when I'd worked so hard to be what she... they... wanted me to be, I'd neglected the Light. And lost my armour. The only thing of any value to them.

It shook its head and tsked. "Poor little"—her eyes flicked to my chest—"Tessa, you're never going to shine in her brilliance. He will never notice you or want you after what you did." She ran the back of her frigid fingers over my cheek. "I guess Raphael and Sariah still like you. Well, Raphael does at least. You will always have a place with the children." She made a point of running her eyes over my stick-figure shape not doing much to make an impression in the blankets.

I hugged them closer to me.

It didn't help.

I was naked under her inspection.

"You fit in perfectly with the children." She feigned brightness. "You always have, and you always will. A sweet little child who has all these wonderful grown-ups to take care of you."

My pulse throbbed furiously. I knew she could sense my fear. But with each barb, my soul sank deeper. I had no way of fighting back because she was telling the truth. How could I argue? Just because she was a demon didn't mean everything she said was a lie.

It wasn't long before my depression drowned out my fear.

I rolled over, exposing my back.

I didn't even try to stop or hide the tears.

4

MARCUS: NEW BEGINNINGS

W as that woman never satisfied? A bulldog chewing a wasp she was. Arms flying, face raging, she marched over to us. "Get out of sight. Now. You cannot be here."

"Mina, what's happening?" Izabaal, the white-haired angel, flew out of the hut and intersected the Amazon's approach.

"These fools stand here in clear sight of the bridge doing... doing..."—for the first time since we'd met her, it seemed the woman was finally lost for words—"whatever they do. Plus, with these men..." —again with the spitting. It was a skill to spit words, to fire them like weapons. And this one was a markswoman of the highest order. With this particular bullet I felt ashamed, I didn't know what for yet, but I was sure to soon find out—"...strutting around like peacocks, the girls will not come out. Arrogant. Ignorant..."

"Mina, please. They are our guests and are unaware." Izabaal laid a hand on the Amazon's shoulder, white on black, calm on fury. "Let me explain to them while you finish the rounds and get ready to lock up."

With nostrils flaring like a raging bull—and eyes just as red— Amina clenched her fists and, without taking her eyes from us, nodded her head and marched off in the opposite direction.

Thank you for Izabaal!

"Please forgive sweet Mina. She cares a great deal for us here and takes her responsibility for our care very seriously."

Sweet Mina? There was nothing sweet about that woman, she was as mad as a bag of spanners.

Izabaal glided towards us and lifted her left hand, indicating the warehouse we'd just left, and used her right to usher us forward. "If you would be so kind as to come with me, I will explain."

I watched the dark woman storm off and head onto the porch of the front demountable. "Interesting lot you got here, Izabaal." I waited till everyone had filed in, then followed.

Her eyes lit up like the sun. "Indeed, Marcus. Indeed." She shut the door behind us with an ominous crash. We waited till she took the lead and once again followed her, back through our sleep room, down a dark hallway to an open, well-lit kitchenette/dining area. We'd already made use of the space earlier this morning. I assumed it had been the factory workers' lunchroom. "I'm so glad you've made yourselves at home. How did you sleep?"

We all settled around "our table" and Tessa started preparing a second brew. We were going to need it.

"Again, I beg your patience with Mina. But we really must be careful here. Our security is in secrecy. Within these tall walls we provide shelter for the women who have been abused and abandoned by the Temple."

"Greyscales?" Raph's eyes were moths to Izabaal's flame. I'm surprised there was no drool stringing from his chin. The kid had it bad. Although, I couldn't blame him. She was an exquisite sight. Not that I was drawn or tempted in any way, but I could appreciate a perfect sunrise, a fine piece of art, and a beautiful woman. It just so happened, Izabaal was all three in one.

"Darling Raphael, yes, Greyscales. However, we choose not to use that term here as it refers to our sisters as outcasts. And they are not. Each is a beautiful individual who is brave and resourceful; a survivor." She smiled at him and the poor boy almost swooned.

But then, like he'd been shocked with a small shot of electricity, his body jerked. He looked to Sariah sitting by his side, then nodded at Izabaal. "We understand what that is like."

Her whole face softened. "I'm quite sure you do, young one." She smiled again. "We are all, each one of us"—she looked around the group like she was reading us—"survivors."

Tessa passed round the drinks and the first serve of toast Kait had prepared. The combination of freshly brewed caffeine and toasted bread were the original comfort food for our crew. So, we inhaled the calm and I passed Iza a piece of toast as Tessa, who wouldn't look Iza in the eye, handed her a coffee. "I... um... don't know how you like it, but there is milk and sugar." Tessa turned away and placed the condiments on the table then came and settled under me left wing.

"Thank you, Tessa." She tilted her head trying to see our girl, but Tessa would not come out of hiding.

"So, to explain..." Izabaal looked at Dan. "Forgive me if you have heard all of this last night, but it will help."

The lad could barely keep his eyes open or hold himself up. Kait ran a hand over his rough cheek. "Do you want to go get some sleep, sweetheart."

"Nah, all good. Thanks, Kait." He smiled, wrapped his hands around his cup and leaned his head back into the corner behind him.

"I have heard so much about you, Dan. It's both an honour and a privilege to meet you."

Both his eyebrows bounced into his brow. "If it was good stuff, don't believe a word of it."

"You sacrificed your freedom, and we have no idea what else, to save him." Her words were whispered and heavy with emotion. "That debt can never be repaid."

"He's my brother... there is no debt." Dan struggled to get the words out. His exhaustion momentarily hidden behind fierce and glassy eyes.

"To him, maybe not. But to me, I owe you the world. Ask anything. And if it is in my power, it's yours." The soft, gracious facade dropped, and steel sealed her vow. A deep, slow breath, and her composure settled around her once again.

Very impressive.

"Now, let me share some of our story. Just over seven years ago I met Indigo." She stopped, a small impish smile wavered. "But that is not the story I will share... for now. By and by, we found ourselves in need of shelter, much like you were last night." She stopped again, thoughtful. "Actually, exactly like you were last night. In fact, at our wits' end after being kicked out and moved on. I had been looking for something for weeks. And just before we found ourselves homeless, I discovered this place and our cabin."

She was lost to us for a moment, then returned. "I could not believe my luck. I didn't know what we were going to do on the streets without shelter. With Indy new to his chair and me completely useless. I had only known life inside the Temple since I was an infant. And here it was, waiting, unlocked... well, almost." Another impish grin broke out.

Looking around at us again, she beamed her trademark smile. "Then, as we made our home here, Mina discovered more and more sisters and brought them home and offered them and their children shelter. No one is compelled to stay but, as of yet, no one has turned us down. We don't have much"—she shook her head—"we have so little, but what we have we share.

"Lottie does what she can to care for us when we're sick. Shauna cares for the babies and little ones. Vashti and Aiko help keep everything in order. Amina and Indy watch over us and Indy provides for us. He also teaches us self-defence, our letters and numbers, and does what he can—with the younger ones' help—to maintain the place. I take what he supplies and provide very meagre meals, clothing and medicine to those who need it most." Pride and joy shone out of her.

Me eyes were drawn to Kait and Val. Me heart beating a tattoo of triumph. Both looking to each other and me. Hunger and excitement. This was it. This is where we were supposed to be. This was our call in Laodicea.

Squeals and laughter pulled us up short. There was some bashing and crashing and low grunts making their way through our new domain. I looked to Iza to see if we should be concerned, but it was obvious that either Lightmas had come early, or good news had just entered the building

"Darling. You're home." She rose and made a space beside her chair.

The doorway was full to overflowing with life, noise and limbs. Indy was propelled by a navigator—a lad about the size of Raph and the colour of Amina. He had two passengers in his lap—one about seven, the colour of bronzed gold, the other a few years younger with porcelain-like skin. All were clothed in seconds and beatific joy. But when they realised they had guests, the smiles slid, the laughter stilled and the lads clung like baby possums as Indy came into the room.

"It's okay guys, come and meet some friends of mine, yeh?"

Wary eyes flicked between Iza and the rest of us. Fear. Intrigue. Accusation.

Iza's voice was like a balm to a burn. "Don't be scared. Jordan, Hiro, come and join me." The bigger, golden boy peeled himself away from Indigo, edged his way around the outside of the room and climbed onto Iza's lap. But the littl'un stayed. Turning, he buried his face in Indy's broad chest. That left the driver with his hands locked on to the handles of the wheelchair.

"All good, Joko. Take me to Iza, yeh?" The lad, the spitting image of his mum—minus the spitting—walked Indy's chair around the table, giving us all a wide birth. None of us escaped his inspection. Once he'd locked Indy's brakes in the space Izabaal had made, he stood on guard behind them both.

When everyone was settled, Tessa stood and made more coffee for Indy, hot chocolate for the kids and toast for everyone.

Izabaal rested her hand on Indy's leg. "How did you go this morning, my love?"

"Sweet-as. Tried to bargain a few more things into the deal, considering our swollen numbers."

He tried to brush it off. But in the light of day, it was easier to see the strain on the lad's face.

Val started negotiating. "Thank you both for taking us in. First thing we want to do is to make sure you realise how grateful we are. Second, we need to assure you that we are not here to be a burden. We can not only provide for ourselves, we think we might be able to help you do the same." Her lifted chin indicated the group. "We feel we have skills and abilities that you guys may be able to make use of. We can help out with supplies and skills. But we will need to hear from you what, and how, we can fit in to what you're doing, and what you would like help with." She looked to Indy. "You have both taken on a great responsibility here. And we applaud you. But please hear me, we are not here to add to your burden. We're here to help."

Raph piped up. "If you would like us to help, that is." He nodded to Val, mustard to show he knew the rules.

Indy's facade deflated and about ten years of worry sluiced from his face. Izabaal's eyes overflowed. "You have no idea how good that is to hear. We will not lie. Things have been... are... tough. Any help you can offer we will gratefully receive." Iza looked to Indy. She took his hand. "It may take the others time to come to appreciate what you offer and how you can help. They have been hurt badly and trust rarely. But if you are prepared to be patient, I know we can find a way to make this work."

Indy kept his head bowed, buried in the blond head of the child nestled against his chest. But the nod of agreement was not lost.

I think we caught this one in the nick of time.

Thank you. Help us fit in and build trust here. Show us how to proceed.

"If I may make a suggestion?" Tactful as ever—when she had a mind to—Val pushed on at Izabaal's nod. "With the supplies we brought with us, we have enough food for a few days to cover our needs, so we don't need to go into the city today. How about Dan, Indy, you boys go and rest. We'll do sets in the warehouse out of sight. Would it suit you if we set up camp in this building?" Again, Val sought Izabaal's approval. "Then we'll spend the rest of the morning setting up for the short term."

Val raised a hand to placate the protest that was about to erupt from Raph. I suspect he wasn't keen on the prospect of "short term".

"This afternoon, when everyone is rested and fed, if it suits, we could meet with you both and... Amina? And any others who need to be there." Val waited again for the nod of approval. "You may want to call your Heads in first without us, to explain the situation and to get them to start thinking of how we may help.

"Don't censor your imaginations. Don't limit your ideas. What do you need? What would you like? Start everyone thinking, and this afternoon we'll meet and start discussions."

Light and possibly hope lifted Indy's shoulders. With his free hand he rubbed the back of the child on his lap. His left hand still clasped Iza's.

"If it's agreeable to your family, we will set up more permanently. If not, we ask that we may stay here short term until we can find somewhere else. We will not be a burden to you and the work you are doing here." Val looked to me, me wife, then to the rest of our family. "I think it's fair to say that we would like to help you in any way we can. We believe that we are here for a purpose. And I promise you, we *can* help."

By this stage rivers were running down Iza's face. The child in her lap was cupping her cheek, attempting to stem the tide.

"Thank you," Iza sniffed and laughed, "thank you." She and Indy had a silent conversation.

"Sounds like a plan, Legend." Indy swivelled his head and winked at Dan. "Later, guys. I'm gonna head out and crash. Come on you crazy kids, lets blow this popsicle stand, yeh?" There were a few light giggles as the dark-haired child stepped from Iza's lap back into the arms of the boy in Indy's. The older lad took control of the driving and bumped Indy and his passengers back out of the building.

Unable to stem the tide of tears, Iza stood as well. "I'll leave you to it. But again, thank you. I'll meet with the others then let you know the time we are to meet here this afternoon. Thank you." And with that, she drifted out of the room and left us to our own brewing excitement.

"Right. Dan, bed. The rest of you, warehouse. Now." Val dealt out the orders.

"What happened to the gracious, polite Val from a few moments ago?" Dan didn't... couldn't even open his eyes.

"Sleep well, Daniel." The warmth in her voice erased the rough bark. She was just as excited as the rest of us. But we couldn't afford to hitch our wagons to the stars... yet.

5

RAPHAEL: THE GO-BETWEEN

The sun swam in a tall pool of weeds in the open shed next to ours. With the roof removed, and the concrete floor taken away, nature had bloomed in the middle of the warehouse. An oasis of weeds, flowers and seeds flourished in the sunshine. I could see why Izabaal called this their sunroom. She had heard the owners took a piece out of the roof to remove some machinery by crane, which is when they must have damaged an underlying pipe that caused the contamination. At some point the wall had also been removed between our warehouse and this one to maybe make a bigger work-space. The exposed area lit by natural sunlight was the first thing I had seen this morning. But it wasn't until now that we'd had a chance to explore.

I looked to Riah. Her eyes were as happy as mine. She didn't even bother looking at me before using her hands to tell me of her plans for the garden.

"First we have to see if we can stay."

She rolled her eyes at me.

"Yes, I suspect you are right and the Light has brought us here. But, even so, we have to see if they would be happy with us ripping up their garden."

At this she turned, hands on hips, with "you have got to be kidding" plastered over her face.

"We might think it is helpful and a good idea, but remember, we have to ask if people want help. We can't just—" I stopped when my sister's face shut down, she crossed her arms, and glared over my shoulder.

"Hello. We heard you arrive in the night." I turned to face the boy who had driven Indigo's wheelchair this morning, his skin as dark as night. I thought he might be about the same age as us. "I am Banjoko, this is Hiro." He indicated a golden boy, a bit younger, with straight black hair and dark eyes. "And this is Jordan." A little boy with the palest of skin and wheat-coloured hair was holding Hiro's hand.

"It is wonderful to officially meet you and see your wonderful home. My name is Raphael, and this is Sariah, my sister. We're twins." Sariah gently shoved me in the back. She knew I rambled when I got nervous. Whereas Sariah became hostile when she was unsure of the situation. Even so, normally we would have been better than this. But we had learned our lesson about trusting easily at the Community's school. Now we did not trust other children to be nice, or as well behaved as we had been taught to be. I could feel Sariah's tension build behind me and I knew she was preparing for a fight.

The boys had stopped watching me and were now totally focused on my sister.

Oh dear, oh dear, oh dear.

I raced forward and stuck my hand out to shake Banjoko's. It had worked last night—sort of—with his mother. Well, I suspected she was his mum. It was worth a try. "It is very nice to meet you." He was on guard and took a while to shake my hand in return. I then offered the same greeting to Hiro. "So, how long have you lived here?"

Both older boys played tennis with their focus, bouncing their attention between Sariah and me. She was obviously a threat, but I did not think they knew how to respond to me. I was trying to be polite and let them know they had nothing to worry about. Until I also turned and looked at Sariah. Then readjusted my thinking.

Oh dear, oh dear, oh dear.

Frantically, using our hand language, I pleaded with her to stand down. To give them a chance. If we were going to make a home here, we had to make an effort and try to get on. She was not happy but agreed to put her hostile away. Sometimes I wish I had my sister's badge of Peace so I could use it on her.

After that I managed to melt the ice that had crept through the sunny garden room, and I started to share some of our story with our hosts. In turn they gave us a bit of their history. When the temperature was almost back to normal, I told them that we had a beautiful garden back in Sodom in which we grew lots of our own food. And maybe, if it was alright with them, and if we stayed, and if they were happy, and if we could get the things we needed, and if it was okay, that perhaps we might be able to use a bit of their garden to grow some food here too.

Sariah had given up on me and my attempt to make peace and had started exploring the garden, squatting down and looking at the soil. The little boy, Jordan, was following her around picking flowers and giving them to her.

Thank you.

I am not sure if anything could have broken through her barrier as well as this little child, with his openness and natural ways of welcoming her. She smiled and the tension washed from my body. No fights today.

"What kind of food can you grow?" Banjoko was intrigued. Hiro's eyes stayed on Jordan and Sariah. I wanted to tell him, if Sariah was smiling the baby was not in danger. But I also did not want to let them know that Sariah was actually dangerous. They may not be so welcoming.

Instead, I used this as an opening to try to bring my sister into the conversation. "Riah, what do you think we could grow here?" We had already discussed it. And she knew what I was doing. She was not happy but agreed to play along.

She shrugged, looked around and then started listing using her hands. "Tomatoes, potatoes, onions, herbs, possibly fruit, lettuce, peas, beans, etc, etc." She finished with a lazy twirl of her fingers above her head. She was not really interested but had made an effort. So I decided to let her be. She then sat in the middle of the dandelions and started teaching Jordan how to make a flower chain.

"You can grow all of that... here?" It was Hiro's turn to speak.

Now I knew I had their attention because they felt Jordan was safe with Riah, and I could start to get to know them and tell them all the things we could do, and the meals we could cook, if we were allowed to stay, and we were allowed to use their garden to grow food. We would need a few supplies, but I knew the Light would take care of things if it was supposed to happen.

It was very nice to meet people our own age who were not interested in making our lives difficult. Or being rude. It would take a little while, but I thought it would not be too long before we could drop our walls altogether and be ourselves around each other. Them and us. It had not happened before and I began to hope, maybe a little bit too much, that perhaps we might be able to stay. There was so much to do. And I rather think I would like some friends my own age.

6

DANIEL: MAKING A START

Bone-weary-exhausted but buzzed, I couldn't sleep. I was comfortable, safe, away from the Community freak show, but still I couldn't shut down. Indy was alive... in a wheelchair. It was impossible and wrong all smashed up together. My constant stream of thanks hadn't stopped flooding the Light. But how could he be confined to a chair? He was so strong, active, capable. So alive and agile.

How... why?

Well, he'd told me how. All last night we'd talked. He'd escaped Gomorrah, unknowingly on the same train as Abraham. During the trek across the continent they'd bumped into each other and reconnected. I was... happy wasn't a strong enough word. Relieved? Still not enough to describe how I felt about Indy making his peace with his dad.

But then they'd landed in Laodicea. Seems like the good folk from Gomorrah received a similar welcome as us kids from Sodom. "Frazzle off. You're. Not. Welcome." So, under the cover of darkness, a horde against two, they'd been "welcomed". Abraham had forced Indy to run before he went down. Alone. Beaten.

Indy had run into the night before his conscience turned him round. He'd just had time to find Abraham and get him to the hospital before he died. There, he'd received the same message. "Might be best if you just kept on moving... right on out of our nice city." Too tired and wrung out from the whole skrat-show, he'd taken to one of the multiple bridges to hideout. Just so happened to be the same bridge Izabaal was using to get a breather from Temple life.

He'd met her on the edge but, apparently, she wasn't a jumper. She was a teaser; teased the edges between far and too far. She'd grown up in the Temple alongside sisters of all race and colour. Seems the men of Laodicea did not like to mix socially with other nationalities, but they were keen to taste and sample any, and as many, colours they could.

Indy felt like he was forced to live. Like he owed a debt to his dad and me. And Iza was sick of the life she'd been sold into as a baby. But up on the ledge they'd pledged to help each other make a go of survival. Seems they'd not only done a decent job at their own survival, they'd pulled others along with them, improving the lot of women kicked to the curb as Temple waste.

But the blanket of hope had been ripped out from underneath them as Indy lay in hospital, treatable but not treated. They had the tech and know-how to repair his spine and give him his legs back. But instead, he was left alive but half the man. Iza's parents, bigwigs at the hospital, argued. Her dad wanted him dead; her mum wanted him sainted. They met in the middle and granted him life.

Scoping the city at night, hidden from public eyes, Iza had found this place. But she couldn't read. So she didn't know it was contaminated. But, since they were short on options, not welcomed anywhere, nor socially acceptable to anyone, they'd given it a go. And seven years later they were still here with no ill effects from the advertised poison. And they'd made a home for themselves and the Greyscales.

Using some freaky tech, the scales that the priestesses were scarred with started out in blue, purple and gold. An acolyte would only have her left hand and foot marred to begin with. Then, as they progressed up the ladder of service to the goddess and humanity, the more scales they'd earn. A full left-hand side of scales equalled a high priestess of pleasure. And of course, "meeting with the goddess" through these priestesses required a far greater offering to the temple.

Didn't matter how they disguised it, it was prostitution plain and simple. Girls of all ages, but not too old, mind you, were brought in and sold to the Temples. Not only were they given an education in "pleasure", they were fed a cocktail of hormones to ensure they each over-reached their potential in proportions and usage. However, pregnancies were not acceptable.

If a girl was careless enough to fall pregnant, despite the pills, their freaky teched-out scales measured the level of whatever hormone was triggered. At the earliest sign, the scales started losing colour. There was no hiding it or escaping it. Even after miscarriages, the scales never returned to their original colour. So, the girls were evicted without even a "thank you for your service". Definitely no gold watch or retirement plan with benefits... of any kind.

Now I understood why Amina hated the Community. Seems they didn't care for ex-Temple priestesses. Or "out of towners"—especially those escaping Sodom and Gomorrah—like the rest of this fracked city. It didn't suit the Community's shiny image... or look good for business.

So, over the past seven years or so Indy and Iza had set up this place as a haven for the ones no one else would care for. The tough thing was, they had so little to give. Indy made do from daily visits picking up supplies from his "contact". He hadn't given me more information on that... yet. Iza had to remain hidden. It wasn't safe for her to go out. She was constantly being accosted by men who saw her full-body of full-coloured scales and expected full treatment when "communing" with the goddess.

But each morning before first light, Indy went out. He never told anyone where, but came back with a trolley full of supplies. He couldn't have stolen it. I knew he was good—not as good as me, mind you—but passable. But with a trolley? In a chair? He'd be too conspicuous. He told me he'd made a vow not to reveal his source—and vowed to Iza that it was all above board—and I respected that, so didn't push.

Because it was tough to supply their constantly changing family—especially one with three growing boys—one of the girls went out each night to earn what she could the old way. That's why we'd found the gates unlocked last night unlike other times we'd come past during the day.

There were enough men out there who were happy to pay for what she offered. Not top dollar—she was damaged goods, after all. But some scumbag decided he could make a regular buck from her services and set himself up as her pimp.

Each morning, Lily came in off the streets and found shelter here —minus the scumbag.

This morning after Lily and Indy came in, Amina checked the grounds to make sure the place was secure, then locked up for the day, guaranteeing everyone could rest in peace.

I get why we needed to stay hidden, and if I hadn't been so brain-dead and in shock, I would have warned the others. This was an abandoned factory shut down over a decade ago because of contamination. People didn't come here or want to use this space because they were scared of being poisoned. But if life here was detected, developers would be in here lickety-split making the most of this prime piece of realty.

It was a skrat-load of canal-front land directly opposite the CBD, easily accessible by the bridge. What they were doing here was amazing. But they had limited resources, little help and no inspiration. I knew we could make a difference. I wanted to help them make a real go of it.

But first they'd have to accept help—from us. For a group of vulnerable people who had been abused by the city and neglected by those who were supposed to help, there was not a lot of trust. I got that. I'd been in the same place. But how could we make them see we were trustworthy?

Could you sort that bit out? Do what you do to get them to see that we're okay. Surely you've got something up your sleeve, especially since Amina and Indy can see the armour and all. That's all you, isn't it? And using Raph to heal Iza was way awesome. So, you know, you do your bit and when

41

you're ready, let us do our bit... and tell us what that looks like? Cool. Cheers.

And thanks again for finding Indy and making him okay. Despite the chair. Thanks for keeping him alive and making it so we could meet up again. Thanks. I really mean it. Please let us help them.

"Come on sleeping beauty, time to rise and face the music."

"Val, I thought you wanted me to sleep?" My body ached.

"We're meeting with the group in about twenty minutes, and I thought you might want to join us."

I managed a grunt in response.

"Clean up, then come back here. Tessa threw you together a sandwich, but we had to clear out of the Common Room. That's where the meeting is."

"Lunch? Bit early don't you think?" I rolled off my bunk and looked out the window into the warehouse where my family were gathered.

"It's after twelve, snoozy. Move it."

I navigated the hallway to the bathroom, then on to the locker room and changed my shirt, then bumped my way back to our sleep room, which I guess was the old office. Once again it was empty except a plate of sandwiches, a coffee and a tall glass of water in a clearing on one of the tables we'd stored our stuff on. I stumbled my way over and froze. "Oh. Hey."

I hadn't seen Tessa squatting in the corner going through one of the equipment boxes. But by the way she kept her head buried in the pile, I guess she hadn't wanted to be seen. This was the first time I'd been alone with her or had the opportunity to talk with her since she'd come back. My stomach churned, my pulse quickened and my heart hurt. "Morning. Thanks for lunch." I continued over to the table and got stuck in.

"You're welcome," she mumbled as she ducked through the door to stand on the outer of the group gathered in the cavern of Warehouse One.

Obviously, she was as ready to talk as I was. I figured I could just share space, create respectful boundaries, be polite and not set her off... unless I was really bored and needed entertainment. Speaking of which, remembering Tessa taking on that demon at the twins' party brought a smile to my face. In her element, she was a small, willowy ball of fire-cracking sunshine. I did miss her, but I was hungry. I scoffed the sandwiches and washed them down with my bitter coffee. Taking my water with me I locked all that emotional skrat away and went to meet up with the others. We had work to do.

"Dan, Dan, you will not believe what we found." Raph was whisper-yelling inside the door to our warehouse. Everyone was milling around waiting... for me, I guess.

"What's that, LM?" I grabbed him in a neck hold and ruffled his hair as I reached them.

"A warehouse..." Raph's voice squeaked, and he coughed.

"Now that's a surprise. In a factory?"

Riah punched my shoulder and pursed her lips, shaking her head.

I released him. "Sorry mate, what's so special about this warehouse of yours?"

Unfazed and full of beans, Raph rolled on. "In the next building, through there." He bounced and pointed to a large opening in the southern wall of the cavern we stood in. The sun beamed down through the opening in the roof. "There's a garden... inside. A huge garden... inside the warehouse. Just through there." At this point his body was shaking like a nervous dog in a thunderstorm.

"Well, if that don't beat all. After our meeting, do you guys want to show me?" I couldn't believe what a sweet deal these guys had going here. Maybe they didn't need our help after all.

Raph's face shone like a polished wheel-hub. And Riah was doing her best not to look even more excited, especially when Raph started talking about compost. It was then they lost me and thankfully it was time for us to move on.

"Apart from finding Indy, that's about the best news ever, mate. I can't wait to see it and help." I threw my arm back around his shoulders as the others made signs that we were ready to go. Riah took my other hand, energy buzzing through her. She could barely keep still—despite her efforts to play it cool.

"Okay guys, before we head in, let's petition the Light for guidance"—Val's smile enveloped the twins—"and ask that a space will be open for us here. That we may be of use and find a home in this community. There's heaps we can do to help, but it won't do a jot of good if they don't want us." With respect for their wishes for us to stay out of sight, we re-entered the office and made our way down the dark hallway to the Common Room.

"We do not need them. They are a burden we do not want." Amina's argument was a fine welcome to the meeting. We hadn't even made it past the bathroom when her words carried to us.

"Yeah, nah." Indy's calm voice, deep and mellow, was harder to pick out but we could still hear his counter argument. "Dan has told me about the work they have done and the skills they have. He has promised me they won't be a burden on our resources, and better yet, they could genuinely help us out here."

Marcus clapped me on the back and gave me a nod.

"Men are not welcome here," Amina countered.

A softer voice that we could not discern—I'm guessing Iza—said something we couldn't hear.

Then Mina jumped back in. "He is no man. And we all know it." A tide of contempt flowed out to us, followed by a wash of soft words.

Amina rebutted, "He is half a man. Impotent."

"What about Joko, Mina." Indy's low voice re-entered the conversation. "When he gets a bit bigger, you gonna throw him out too?"

"That is not the same." Like drops of water on a red-hot iron, her words sizzled. "And you know it."

"No Mina, he is not different. He's a fine boy, and he'll be a great man. But a man, nonetheless. And what about Hiro, and Jordan, what of them, eh?" Indy's growl raised hackles.

We weren't exactly dawdling. But we weren't rushing down the hall either. Staying out of sight, we slowed our pace and "just happened" to be listening to their conversation as we approached. If they were expecting us, it wasn't really eavesdropping, was it?

"Enough." This time Iza's words were as clear as a cast iron bell. "Amina, thank you for your opinion. It has been noted. As has Lottie's,

Shauna's, Vashti's and Aiko's. Everyone has had their say." A pause. We all stopped and waited. "But do not forget the final say is Indy's and mine. You are the mother of my heart. You know I love you. But in this I believe you are wrong. Our boys are good boys, and it is right for them to see us welcome good men. Like Ben. Like Kerm. And. Like. Indy."

We all crept another step closer, not wanting to miss a word.

"Every decision we make is based on the welfare and care of our whole family. Everyone. If we feel that it is in our best interest, we will proceed. If we feel it is not, then after they have had time to find their feet and another place to stay, they will go."

We were almost at the door; I knew from last night this hallway echoed. Any second, they'd know we were here. We couldn't really delay any longer. But I just wanted to hear the outcome of this argument unfiltered.

Iza still held the floor. "I am following your instructions and example Mina. This is me mothering-up. This is me caring and being responsible for my family. Do you doubt me, Mina?" Who'd a thought the chick had a hidden junk-yard dog within her. But her words were met with silence. "*You* trained me for this. Do you doubt me, Mina?" The challenge was softer but there was a steel fist inside of it.

An animal growled and the partially-closed door between us and those inside flew away from us into the Common Room and ricocheted off the inside wall. I for one was glad it didn't open outward or we would have been currently splattered like bugs on a windscreen. Amina caught it on the rebound, easily, and looked ready to slam it shut behind her, but when she saw us crowding her path, she paused. Her lip curled and daggers flew from her eyes. "I vote no."

Val met her glare, held it, nodded once, then led us into the Common Room after Amina stormed down the hallway. "Good afternoon everyone. I trust this isn't a bad time?"

7

CONTESSA: LIGHT OF DAY

I stood at the back of the group as we filed into the meeting. Two large tables pushed together sat in the middle of the group, with cups littered over the top. Indy was positioned in the far corner closest to the external wall. I could see the trees lining the boundary wall through the filmy-curtained window near where he sat with Izabaal at his side.

I tried not to stare, but it was seriously impossible.

She was all kinds of perfect. Standing in front of the window as she was, she even had a flopping halo.

Every square millimetre of her was exquisite.

Nothing was wasted on the ordinary. Every strand of perfectly straight, golden hair. Every spectacularly proportioned curve, subtle, provocative... perfect. Even the scales that glided their way up her body added to her allure and mystery. Her eyes faded from fire to warm chocolate—all in different shades of blue, that is—in a heartbeat as she welcomed us into the room. She wore rags, for crying out loud. But Izabaal made them look classical and stylish. She moved like water, acted with grace, and carried herself like royalty... or how I thought royalty would move.

I felt like a frump. Even on a good day... my best day ever... with heaps of work and time… I'd never pull that off. I was a small, skeletal stick with bad hair. Hanging around Kari and the fashion scene had all been about image and looks. I'd been swept away by their gifts of tips, clothes and make up. Even Achilles had designed and draped women with style, yet none… not one, came even close to the aching beauty of Izabaal in rags.

She had already been standing when we entered. Her flawless, pale hand resting on Indy's slumped shoulder. While I couldn't look at her for her beauty, I could barely tear my eyes away from the chaos of his scars.

His body was a mess.

His face especially.

He looked like a jigsaw put back together all wrong. Like trying to pull a 3D picture into focus, I couldn't look away. The suffering and pain he must have endured to cause such scars would have been ridiculous.

His eyes found mine. I felt the fire climb my neck and engulf my whole head. I'm sure even my scalp shrieked like a foghorn. Quickly I looked away and checked out who else was in the room.

A husky old woman's laugh rattled. "Come on then. Let's get a good look at y'all." She reminded me of a wrinkled elephant, over-flowing from a chair in the corner on the other side of Indy. With a meaty mitt—a dead cigarette butt lodged between two fingers—and a hacking cough, she welcomed us in. Grey scales sat over the top of pale layers of wrinkled fat and excess skin. But even yet, you could tell in her day she would have been pretty.

I flicked my eyes to Izabaal. Another contrast to her over-whelming beauty. I was surprised to see—although I shouldn't have been, as I was coming to understand that this was her thing—warmth and love as she looked to the old whale. "May I introduce sweet Lottie. She is our nurse and cares for all of us no matter what we throw at her."

"Ha"—phlegm caught in the whale's throat—"honey, I've not been sweet a day in me damned life. But glad to finally find out what all this fuss is about." She grinned at Indy, and I noticed she was missing a few teeth. He gave her a wink. She guffawed and hacked up another fur ball.

I slipped in further behind Marcus.

"And this is Shauna, who takes such wonderful care of our little ones." Iza indicated a woman sitting next to Lottie. Silver-streaked dreadlocks were gathered in a topknot and a newborn slept in her arms. She had a full side of grey scales. Well, as far as I could see. But they did not reach her face.

I had no idea babies could sleep through the angry storm that had swirled through here earlier. The beautiful bundle was wrapped up like a bean pod. The first hint I had of its gravitational pull was when I was close enough to touch it without memory of moving. I squatted down so I could get a closer look.

Kait's hand rested on my shoulder. "So beautiful." Her words hardly a whisper.

Shauna looked up and studied Kait, who was oblivious to every-thing but the baby. Without a spoken word, she stood and handed Kait the bundle. And from that point on Kait and Marcus were lost to the conversation. Marcus held Kait as Kait held the baby in their own special, secret place. I hadn't noticed that the room had fallen silent until Izabaal continued gently. It seemed no one wanted to break the spell.

"And Aiko, who was our first mum to have her baby, Hiro, onsite. Seven years ago, now." Izabaal nodded to a beautiful young woman with straight black hair and dark eyes. I couldn't help my mini gasp as I realised she looked about my age. I could not even begin to think of having. A seven. Year. Old. Child.

My vision swam but I thought it best not to drop my head between my knees to steady my quaking equilibrium. So, I just shuffled even closer to Marcus, hoping I could hide in his shadow.

"Carley and Lily have been with us for a few years now." She looked to the two drop-dead gorgeous girls—a brunette and a blonde —in the opposite corner. "Then there's Vashti, our other long-term member. But she's with Amber and together they're helping Genni— our newest mum. You'll meet them all later." Izabaal's smiled cloaked the five women in the room, her hand still on Indy's shoulder. "We were just hearing what our family had to say about the idea of you joining us. We believe from what we've heard that you have skills and, more importantly, a desire to help?" She dropped her eyes to the floor. "Mina's made her vote and"—rallying, she looked up and attempted a smile—"so has everyone else." Izabaal raised a perfect eyebrow to the room and invited the others to share their verdicts.

"If you prove useful, I've voted you stay. If you're a pain in the butt, I vote we show you the door," Lottie rasped before inhaling from the dead stub submerged between her fingers.

Aiko nodded her head. Sheets of glossy black hair shimmered with her movement. But it was Shauna who spoke and gave me the encouragement I craved. "We have always said we'd never turn anyone away. We literally have rubber walls here and can make space for as many as need sanctuary. You may not have been rejected from the Temple, but you have been rejected by the Community, and as far as I can see, it's just the same. I am happy to share what we have and will be grateful for any help you can offer. I voted yes." Her alto voice was soft and soothing. I bet the babies loved it. Right now, I knew I did.

Tension I had been unaware of started seeping from my shoulders. And all of a sudden, I was so very tired. But then I watched as the two girls, Lily and Carley, gave Dan the once-over. The brunette's smile warmed as the blonde's eyes gleamed. And equally quickly, I wasn't quite so tired. Or relaxed.

Izabaal was waiting for them to share their vote, her expression of benevolence unchanged as the two looked to each other and grinned. But she positively beamed when the two girls looked back at her and nodded. "Well then, without further fuss, we are very happy to offer you shelter and a place in our home. But may I suggest we agree to a three-month trial. You may not like it here. Or"—she stopped and looked around at her sisters and squeezed Indy's shoulder—"it may prove too much of a strain." With her shoulders back and chin set she morphed into business mode. "You've now met most of our family. As I mentioned, Amber is with Vashti helping with Genni. But let's give it a go and see what happens." Four women nodded and smiled, Lottie gave us all an extra squint-eye of appraisal, and Indy dropped his head.

Thank you! Amina scares me. And Lottie. Actually, so does Indy. And Izabaal intimidates me. But I think this is a good place to be. I'm not sure what I can do to help. But if you can use me, I'd be really so very happy to help. Please give me an oar to pull here. Oh, and please help me find my way back to Dan. I miss him so much. And maybe, could you please put some kind of blindness, or barrier, a brick wall maybe... really, really high... and wide... between those two girls and him. Please?

"Can we start on the veggie garden now?" Raph was bouncing on his toes. Riah tapped him repeatedly on the shoulder until he looked at her. "Oh yes, and chickens. How many people do you have here?" Raph had everyone's attention.

"Pardon?" Izabaal voiced the communal confusion.

"Well, before we decide the size of the plot and how many chickens we get, I think it is best if we work out how many people we will be feeding." Riah was at him again and they broke into silent twin speak. "Great idea, Riah." He turned back to the group. "Fruit trees. It will take a while before they fruit, but the sooner we get them in the better." Raph was on a freight train that wasn't stopping for anyone. "How much money do we have left over, Dan? Maybe we should go back out this afternoon and make some more. Marcus"—the man lifted his eyes from the baby still wrapped in Kait's arms—"can you build a chicken coop?"

Marcus came back to us then and re-joined the conversation. He didn't answer immediately but narrowed his eyes and considered the question. "I reckon we could, mate. I saw some old pallets lying around the warehouse this morning. All I need is some wire, or mesh, and some ground... earth, for them to scratch in."

"Great. Then first thing we will need to do is start a compost. Unless you already have one?" Raph paused long enough for his audience to catch up.

The whale hacked. I think it may have been a laugh. "Steady on there, young fella, what the hell are you on about?"

"If you do not have a compost already, that is okay—I will start one today." Again, Sariah attacked his shoulder. "Yes, of course. Good thinking, Riah. Worms. Do you have worms?" He was on fire, his nerves twitching every limb, his hands flying wide and high as he spoke, punctuating and accentuating every word and idea.

The loose skin on Lottie's face went taut at Raph's question. "We may not be doing too well, mate, but we don't have worms."

"Raph, take a breath." Val stepped in. "As always you have great ideas. But first things first." She stepped forward clapped him on the shoulder and addressed the room. "Would it be okay if we started growing some food?"

"You can do that?" Even shocked, Izabaal was beautiful.

"Yes, Raph's pretty much nailed it in what he's just said. But first we need to ask if you are happy with this. They"—she tilted her head to indicate Raph and Riah bursting at her side—"have found a place that seems perfect and out of sight. And he's also right in asking about numbers so we can determine how many we're providing for." She looked down at the bursting kids under her wings. "Good thinking, guys."

Raph beamed and his chest swelled.

"And we'd also like to hear of any other needs we can help with." The room went silent under the weight of Val's invitation.

I snuck a peek around to the seven of them. Iza was crying, Indy held his head in his hands, Aiko put her hand on Shauna's shoulder as they both closed in around the baby Kait had returned. Lottie's eyes bored into Val. "You could really do this? Provide food for us?"

Val shrugged and nodded. "Yes, of course. With a bit of work, some space and time, we should be able to make a start and have some food growing in about six to eight weeks."

"Lass, one of our biggest burdens is providing food. That and protection."

"We can help with that too," Marcus joined in. "We can help patrol and teach self-defence."

"We'd be happy to help with the kids as well." Kait's eyes strayed back to the sleeping child, then flicked to her own chicks. "Any you have here can join Raph and Riah in school. Which reminds me"—she eyeballed the twins—"don't think I haven't noticed you've missed school two days in a row. Before you two run off saving the world, you've got lessons first."

"We've got a few young ones we try to help with the basics. But we'd appreciate any help you're offering." This came from Aiko, Hiro's mum.

Val slipped back into her bossy pants. "Sounds like we've got a plan. Dan and I will hit the streets with his guitar. Kait, you take the twins for lessons and you two can help if any other kids come along" —she nodded toward Raph and Riah. "Marcus, Tessa, could you try unpacking a few more things from the truck? If it's too hard to stay hidden, we'll do it tonight. Take a good look at that place the kids found and see if it's suitable for chooks and veggies. Also check out any other resources or building materials you can find around the place." I looked to Marcus, he winked, and we both nodded at Val. She then turned to the others. "Anything else for now?"

Dumb and awestruck, they just shook their heads.

"Um… before we go, can I ask"—everyone looked at Dan—"do you have a voiceless, black-and-white girl in your crew?"

Aiko and Shauna looked at each other and shook their heads. Carley and Lily raised their perfectly sculpted eyebrows at him like he'd lost some marbles.

Good move. Thank you.

Indy and Izabaal considered his question and also shook their heads. But then Lottie barked, "Not unless you mean every single one of us, lad." We all stared at her. "Well, look at us. She held up her grey-scaled arm and used it to sweep the room. They all looked at their own scales. "Black and white… grey. And look at how we live. In hiding, no support, no rights… no voice. We're discarded, invisible waste." Fire had stirred in her and she became even more scary. "I feel pretty voiceless. Have most of me life. Before that, I was a voiceless white girl. Now I'm just an angry, invisible, voiceless grey woman."

Oh. My. Goodness.

She was right.

Maybe this was what the Light had meant.

"Well, Lottie, right now you're looking mighty beautiful to me. I've been searching this city for over six months trying to find you." Dan's joy was like an injection of caffeine on a cloudy morning.

Lottie lolled her head back and held her rolling stomach as she coughed and spat out a laugh. Pointing her stubby finger at Dan she looked to Indy. "I'm starting to like this one even more."

He returned her grin. "He's always had good taste in women, Lot."

Val grinned and nodded. "So incredibly glad to finally meet you all. Now we can stop searching and get to work."

"Well, I for one don't know what the hell y'all are on about, but I think I'm gonna like having you round for a spell, for entertainment at least." Lottie lost a bit of her lightness and went back to scary... er. "I'll be seeing how the usefulness goes first before I roll out the welcome mat fully, though." She heaved a sigh and threw her hands to her knees. "We done here?" She didn't wait for anyone to respond before she heaved herself to her feet.

Iza stepped up to dismiss the gathering. "Thank you all for your time this morning. Ladies"—she turned to the others—"thank you for sharing your opinions. Probably best if we get the kids to come over and meet everyone officially."

We watched as Lottie rolled out the door, but she stopped and leaned back in. "Just a warning to y'all. Never enter one of the cabins uninvited. I am armed and I take the care of my girls very seriously. Under my watch they are safe, and they can rest."

"But we almost tried that door last night." Raph was as pale as I felt.

"I know, boy. And I was ready. Thank whatever god you pray to that you didn't enter. Because you would'na been walking out. Ever." With another disturbing rattling cough, she squeezed through the door and stuck to the edges of the bitumen under the shade of the tree-lined wall, making her way to the cabins.

Yep. That was a definite. I was very, very scared.

8

DANIEL: REUNION

We'd… I'd… had another successful session at Serendipity, the cafe that held an open mic for me under their front awning. Val always headed out with me but didn't stick around. She used to say she was hunting for the "black and white" girl while I played. But I'd always suspected she was actually hunting some hidden demon action to scratch her fight-itch. But now she didn't have that excuse. Not that she told me anything as she left me to set up, then came back a couple of hours later to help me pack up.

Missy, the owner and head chef of the cafe had always been generous with giving us "leftovers" for the kids. And now that I explained our changed situation, she made sure there was even more to go round. We came back to the Factory with pockets full of change and bags of baking to contribute to dinner.

I dumped the bags in the Common Room, dropped the cash into the kitty, then went to wash up and get ready for dinner.

Raph was in the washroom dripping with water. "Dan, you will not believe what we have found." The white sink was streaked with mud and his clothes were covered in dirt.

"A tunnel out of here?" Obviously, the kid had been either digging in the dirt or rolling around in it.

"Why would we want to tunnel out when we have everything we need right here?" His eyes drifted to a corner of the ceiling. "Except seeds. And chickens."

I reached over and turned the tap on in the shower and turned Raph's shoulder so he was facing the water. "Sink's not going to cut it mate. How about you have a proper wash, then tell me all about it at dinner." Raph blinked a couple times. "I'll save you a seat." I left the room and waited to hear he was with-it enough to lock the door before heading back to the Common Room.

"How long have you had this…" Indy was accosting a tall, graceful lady standing at the sink up to her elbows in sudsy water, fitted out in solid, aqua armour. "This…" Indy turned as I entered the room and accused me. "Did you know about this… this…"

"Armour?" I suggested, hoping to help him out.

"Yes. Armour." He turned back to the woman, who didn't seem at all phased by Indy's rant. She took a cloth, wiped away the suds and glided across the room extending her hand toward me.

"Good evening, my name is Vashti, it is a pleasure to meet you."

"Vashti, what is going on?" Indy was a terrier after a rat.

"Nothing is 'going on' Indigo. I have been in the Light since shortly before I arrived. Helen helped me find The Way. And I have been wearing my armour ever since."

"Helen? What has Helen got to do with this?"

Indy didn't get his answer. Raph—still mostly wet—came in and leaned against me. I wrapped my arm over his shoulder and waited for the show to continue. I wasn't the only one. The two girls who'd been at the meeting earlier were setting the tables. Their job paused as they tried to figure out what was going on. Obviously not having the sight, they couldn't see what Indy and Vashti were… discussing.

Right on cue, the outside door opened and the three kids who'd accompanied Indy this morning came in, with a red-headed girl not much older than the twins.

Raph raised his hand in greeting. "Hi guys." The boys responded but didn't stop as they made their way to the table for dinner.

"Mummy," the youngest kid yelled, and launched himself at the brunette who'd been setting the table. She did not look old enough to have a pinball-running, semi-talking kid.

But she swept him up and blew raspberries on his neck as he squealed with laughter. "Hey, buddy."

I looked from the blonde chick to the white-headed kid in the brunette's arms. Huh, thought they'd have been a match. Not that it was a bad thing they weren't—the blonde looked even younger than the brunette.

But that particular head-fruddle, and the kids' reunion, was drowned out by Raph who was pulling on my arm and jumping up and down. "Amber! Dan, it is Amber." He started madly looking around and as soon as Val entered the room to join the dinner crowd, he was off again. "Val, it is Amber."

The whole room was now focused on Raph and the redhead he seemed to know. Raph looked like he was at war with himself. Half young colt wanting to run and buck around the paddock, yelling. The other half, a pubescent tween, had those reins held in a firm grip. But nothing could stop his legs jumping or his arms twitching. He didn't know what to do with himself. But both the colt and the boy looked like they wanted to hug the girl.

She was a good-looking kid, but then again, she was an acolyte as her tri-coloured hand and foot revealed. I pulled Raph in tight to my side before he did anything to land himself in hot water. "Looks like the two of you have met?"

Amber's face went from fear, to curiosity, to liquid warmth. She solved Raph's problem in three quick steps as she engulfed my little brother in a hug. I'm pretty sure I heard a purr vibrate through Raph's chest.

Good ol' Amina threw her bucket of ice water over the room. I had been so caught up in Raph, I hadn't seen her enter. "What is this? What has this boy done now?

"This is *the* boy." Amber looked to her family. "The one I told you about. The one I met in the square just before you came and got me, Amina." Her face radiated joy. "This is the boy who healed me."

Amina's dagger-eyes raked over Amber, then flew to Izabaal. "What magic is this? Last night and now this?"

Anyone would think she wanted her family pinned to the mat suffering and in hardship. Stuck-up twik. But I had to hand it to Raph, he was getting better at wading into a fight. "Oh no, it is not magic. I told you; it is the Light."

"IGNORANT, BLIND, INSOLENT, SON OF A..." The rest of Amina's insult was lost in mumbling.

It didn't stop Raph. "I am sorry Amina, you may not want to know about the Light, but you have to know it was the Light that healed Izabaal"—he looked over at Iza and beamed—"and the Light who healed Amber. And you have to know it is because He loves yo—"

Amina's next insult punched Raph's explanation. "Do not dare to speak to me of such things. You are an intrusive, impudent child."

Full credit to the kid though, he ploughed on. "You might not like Him, but He loves you. You may insult Him, but He is faithful to you. You may reject Him, but He will still welcome you. And that is why He has healed those you love and the only reason why you can see our armour. Because He has let you see."

Electricity filled the room until we could hardly breathe. No one moved except Riah, who edged her way forward to stand at her brother's side and threw her own laser-eye-daggers back at Amina. The girl was unsettled and spoiling for a fight. Even a fight with the skat-scary Amazonian.

Amina pulled her eyes away from the twins and noted everyone in the room staring at her. Her nostrils flared when she looked at Vashti. Then she stormed out, slamming the door behind her. Hopefully there wasn't anyone walking the streets nearby because the woman had just broken her own rule. Even though it was dark out, she'd just alerted the whole neighbourhood something was going down at the Factory.

9

RAPHAEL: BREAKING OUT

How could the world change completely in three days? Three days ago, Val and Dan had taken Sariah and me to the zoo for our birthday. Surely it was weeks... months ago. When we were at the zoo, we watched a tiger pace the perimeter of its enclosure. We had watched as its huge, padded feet ate up the path in a slow, pounding rhythm. Over time it had gouged a crevice into the earth as it circled again and again.

Riah's fingers trailed along the concrete wall surrounding the Factory. Her feet, slow yet rhythmic, paced our new enclosure. I was sure, in time, she too would wear a rut into the earth.

An air of excitement was stirring throughout the Factory. Not just from our family but from the Greyscales as well. We had finally found what we were supposed to be doing here whilst we were in Laodicea. Everyone was happy. Except my sister. You see, when we were little, we had the run of the streets. The markets had been our playground and even though we were to perform for our owner, he allowed us this freedom. As long as we came when we were called.

Then we were sold and put on a ship making its way to Sodom. When we arrived, we lived in a huge house where we were not allowed out. We had thought our world had closed down. But then we were sold again, and our world ended.

After we were rescued, Riah chose to stay close to our protectors. Her debilitating fear of the Darkness kept her bound indoors. We knew the enemy could come into the house, but we also knew that was where she was safest. So that is where she chose to stay, for two years. During that time, she transformed the barren concrete box of a home and desolate backyard into a world of colour: a living art gallery.

But then it was time to leave. Sodom was going to fall, and the Light called His children out. It was there, in the midst of hell and chaos, that Sariah had awoken and found her claws. And they were sharp. This ignited a fire within her. She was alive and consumed with the desire to make up for all the lost time when she had hidden and surrendered to her fear. Now she was on a mission to take back all that she had sacrificed, with force.

We had struggled at the Community's college because we had been obliged to squeeze into their ill-fitting box in order to live in our house, to be fed, clothed and controlled by the Community. But to do this we had to stay quiet, sheath our claws and suffer the harassment, bullying and taunts of our fellow students—and some teachers—at the prestigious school.

But then we had been freed, allowed out, to explore the city with Val and Dan looking for... here. This place. And now that we had found it, once again we were locked up. Enclosed in a cage. We did not know how long the Light would keep us here, but I petitioned Him on behalf of my sister. Because Sariah was not going to survive another entrapment. And it was only day three.

I followed along behind her in the pre-dawn light, hoping my mere presence would offer comfort and support. I did not know if it was working. I did not think she even knew I was there. But as I trailed behind, I remembered all the times she had stood by me and protected me. My sister was a fiery storm of fierce love. To see her passion doused broke me. The concrete walls surrounding us had created a concrete box inside her mind, shutting her down. I think this was the only reason she did not see the movement in the trees before I did. She did not react to the girl dropping from the branches until she landed on the ground in front of us, facing away from us.

Recognition untangled my shock. "Amber. What are you doing? Where have you been?"

She spun. Horror and fear masked her pale skin. She looked around, noting we were alone, and a small smile pushed the fear from her face. "Um... hi."

Sariah's eyes were busy bouncing between Amber and the tree she'd jumped from. So, I repeated my questions. Amber explained how the whale woman—Lottie—liked cigarettes, but Indy refused to bring any home in his daily supplies. So, she went out in the early hours of the morning—after Indy had gone—and scoured the foot-paths in front of the pubs and bus stops looking for stubs. It was her offering to her family. She opened up her hand to reveal a disgusting collection.

Riah's eyes lit with excitement and life, and it was not because of the stubs. Her hands a whirlwind of activity, flicking and twirling with questions, ideas and commands.

So, I translated. "Do you think you could show us? Take us with you?"

Amber looked around. "Sure? Maybe... tomorrow?"

Sariah's hands flew. "Do you think you could take us now?"

Amber looked to the sky. The sun was rising above the lower buildings across the canal. She examined the factory again. "Now is not safe." Flicking her gaze to both of us, she dropped her eyes to the ground and ran her hand over her stomach. "Tomorrow?"

Once more Sariah's fingers flew. "Now?"

Two channels furrowed Amber's brow, and she chewed her bottom lip. Again, her hand ran over her stomach. "Okay. But really quickly." She thrust the stubs back in her pocket and pulled back some branches of a shrub to reveal two old milk crates, one stacked on top of the other, and scrambled to the top of the wall. We followed her and, just like that, we were out.

Amber scurried along a narrow, well-worn path beside the factory wall, hidden by a hedge of trees. As we walked around the block, Amber kept her focus on the ground, her face well hidden behind the wall of her red hair under her hoodie, her hands tucked into the pouch of her jumper. In contrast, Riah's eyes drank in every detail.

It seemed we were only going to go around the block as every turn was right. I was not too upset as I was very aware of Amber's great discomfort. At least if we got lost, it would be easy to get back. All of this thinking flew out of my mind when we walked past a large building that reeked of the cigarette stubs, a stale, sweet stench, and sulphur. From her path along the gutter edge of the road Amber urged us to hurry. Riah was not dawdling, but she was taking her time looking in every window, nook and cranny. Obviously not watching where she was putting her feet.

"What the frack? Watch it."

Sariah leapt back in surprise as Amber gasped and froze, her pale skin turning a sickly green. A body had been curled up in a doorway next to the hotel. But now it unfurled and, when it saw us, unsteadily rose to its feet. And stumbled. The man looked at each of us but doubled back to Amber, staring at her through bloodshot pools of black. His face was swollen; large patches of purple merging into red marred his features.

His squinty eyes opened wide, and the man grinned and scratched his belly, lifting his shirt to reveal a toned, muscular tummy. "You come back for more, sweet thing?"

It took me a while to realise that everything had grown darker and colder. And it was not just because we were in the shadow of the building. At first, the sulphur had been weak under the cover of the yucky smell of the hotel. But when ice pinched the nerves down my spine, I realised the Dark was among us.

"Amber, run."

Oh dear, oh dear, oh dear. Please help us.

Other men rose from doorways and hidden places. Demons emerged from the buildings. Just like in the playground when we were confronted by the bullies, Riah shifted around until we stood back-to-back. Our guards stood beside us with weapons drawn. I did not know what to do. Who did we fight? How did we fight when we had two types of opponents?

Feeling Riah draw her sword, I followed her lead and raised my hands, palms out, getting ready for the Others' approach. The more significant of our two hostiles. I gulped and kept a petition to the Light on repetition circling through my mind, focusing on passages of *The Way*. But felt slightly better when I saw Amber, after a momentary hesitation, run back the way we had come.

This left us as the centre of attention and the source of their entertainment. "What have we got here, lads?" Creepy guy laughed.

In some part of my brain—the part not panicking—I realised that for someone who did not have the sight, we would look... odd. But it was enough to halt the human's approach. Even if they could not see Sariah's sword, or the Warriors at our sides, in our "ready" stance it did look like we might know how to fight.

However, the part of my brain that was feeding my fear noted the demon's laughter, and sickness swirled in my stomach, my mouth went dry and my saliva turned to paste. Thankfully I was not holding a sword because it would have slipped through my sweaty palms. Although, the rational part of my mind informed me, this would make for a better conductor of my zappy-Light-palm-defence.

Sariah's shoulder nudged my back softly but with intent. *Breathe.*

So, I did. And it helped.

I knew we were mice to their cat claws as the demons came at us, poking and prodding, laughing and insulting us. The sight of us defending ourselves against the Unseen was enough to keep the human danger at bay. And entertained. I suspect they thought we were mad, as Sariah and I stood back to back, making a stand against the demons' taunts. I knew they were not really trying. We were just entertainment to them, too.

Our Warriors had backed up, and kept the bulk of the attack from us. We did have to deal with those who came through, but it was minimal compared to the horde that was building. I did not have enough capacity to focus on anything other than those who stood in front of me. But when they stilled, tilted their heads and stepped back, I was puzzled but mostly relieved.

The three who had held me hostage leered then retreated into the shadows. I turned to see the rest doing the same. Our Warrior's weapons were still unsheathed, so Riah and I remained alert. However, our stillness was the invitation our human audience had been waiting for. They gathered around us in a rough circle and moved in. I felt Riah sheath her sword and reposition herself, ready to defend hand-to-hand against our Seen foes. I did the same.

Thank you for scaring the demons away. Please help us. Again. Please.

Once more, briefly, Sariah sent me her message. This time her heel tapped mine. *Breathe.*

I pushed the panic out and breathed in the Light. I was a tree with roots reaching to the centre of the earth. I was solid, firm, unmovable. My body was a river, flexible—

My mantra and preparation were interrupted by feet pounding the pavement and an earth-quaking battle cry.

Val was here.

And just like that, the street was swept clean of opponents.

"For goodness' sake woman, for once in your life could you at least leave us a few? Or even one? Is that too much to ask?" Marcus and Kait were here as well.

I almost collapsed with relief until I saw Val's face and then all calm thoughts of mountains, trees and rivers were eaten by my sheer panic. We were in so much trouble. It was made even worse when she didn't speak. With my heart stuttering more than when I faced the enemy, I quickly looked to Marcus and Kait for reassurance.

Once again, my mouth went dry and sweat coated my body.

Oh dear, oh dear, oh dear. Help? Please?

No one said a word as we were led—Val's hand resting at the back of Sariah's neck, Kait's hand on mine—back to the Factory for our prosecution and sentencing.

* * *

The three of us were seated in a row, with hot chocolates going cold on the table in front of us.

"What were you thinking, Amber? Three days ago, someone broke in here to assault you. And now you go out looking for more trouble? How could you endanger not only yourself and our home, but our guests as well?" Iza's cranky voice did not hold much steel. I was so very glad she had not yet had a chance to learn from Kait. Or Val.

Amber did not respond. Apart from a quick glance at me and a mouthed "sorry" she had not looked up from her lap since we came in to join her for our trial. She sat like a sack, unmoving. Tears flowed down her face and she made no attempt to wipe them away.

It was now our turn as Val began. "I think now would be a good time for you to explain what happened."

I gulped and started with the truth. "I knew it was the wrong thing to do." I looked each of them in the face—Val, Kait, Marcus, Izabaal, and Indy. One by one. "It was not fair to pressure Amber. She did not want to do it. It is not her fault. But even as I knew this, I still chose to do it." I breathed deeply and exposed my shame. "I am very grateful to the Light for bringing us here. But I love my sister." Sariah took my hand. "She was feeling trapped and I could feel her spiralling back to where she was in Sodom." I looked to Val, Kait and Marcus, surely they could see. "Being allowed out here in Laodicea and then being trapped again. It was drowning her." Sariah squeezed my hand twice. I pumped it back. "I had to help her get out and I abused my leverage with Amber to do it. It was wrong to manipulate my friend. It was wrong to endanger the Factory. I am sorry I put her in danger." I looked back to Val. "Thank you for coming to get us."

Silence returned to the room, but it was a little less steely. There was just enough room to hope.

The adults all looked at each other and spoke their silent talk. They still did not know we could read them, and I tried to hold my relief in until they had pronounced their verdict.

Amber had been grounded, and we would be on shared kitchen duty for a week. Sariah would go with Val on her daily outings to the city with Dan.

Maybe they thought that our scary experience was punishment enough.

Thank you!

10

CONTESSA: DEMONIC ENCORE

The nerves at the back of my neck shivered and the skin on my arms puckered into gooseflesh around about the same time my eyes watered and my nose tingled from sulphur.

"My, my, young Riah is starting to develop, isn't she?"

Damn it. What did she want now?

"That's not a nice welcome."

I flicked my eyes to my guard. He was at ease. I mean, he was tense, but he didn't have his sword in his hand. It had taken me a while to get used to living under the eyes of a... watcher who watched... everything.

And I mean every thing.

Every.

Thing.

To start with it was all kinds of creepy. Until I realised, he... it... they... weren't into anything weird. And since I knew attacks could come at any time, and that these guys were there to protect us—and they did—it didn't seem creepy anymore.

The demon on the other hand was a totally different kettle of rank-stinky fish.

We hadn't really settled in yet. We weren't sure if we should go to all the trouble when we didn't know if were staying. Setting up camp properly was like planting hope. So I, for one, was completely happy living out of boxes for the rest of our probation.

We kept most of our gear from the truck in an old locker room off the hallway of our living quarters in Warehouse One. It was between the office where we spent our first night and the Common Room— the large room with a kitchen and enough... more than enough tables and chairs. In the in-between of making a decision, we were using the locker room as a change room.

Well, not all at the same time.

The guys would go through and then we—the girls—would.

Riah had just left, and I was finishing off a few things before meeting everyone out in the main warehouse for morning sets.

"Good to see you fitting right back into your old role of *servant*."

Wait, what? I'm not a servant.

"Sorry, I meant to say, waiting on people, cleaning up after them and... serving them." She nodded to Dan's shirt I'd just picked up off the floor. "I mean, it's good to know that even though you didn't make it in the real world—like you'd dreamed—you still had this to fall back on." Her eyes grew wide and she nodded her head as she looked around and ended up focusing on the clothes basket in my arms. "It must be a huge comfort knowing that after your failed attempt to be a success, you could pick up where you left off... as the maid." She jerked her finger up. "No, wait, what did you call it? Serving? That's right. It's your Badge." She patronised me with a mock smile. "The Light is so gracious, giving out all these Badges and gifting you with being. A. Servant. What a blessing."

Twik.

"Come now, Tessa, that's not nice. I'm here to help. Well, not to do the laundry and the dishes and wipe people's backsides, like you seem to love doing, but to give you some advice."

"Thanks, but no thanks. I have to go now." I collected the rest of our washing and left the room.

"Oh Tessa." I stopped and turned. "You forgot these." A pair of men's boxer undies were levitating behind me. Dan's. I knew he was still adjusting to not living on the streets and, like, actually having stuff to take care of. But seriously, could the boy not see mess? I snatched them out of the air and threw them in the basket with all the other dirty washing.

Her raucous laughter followed me down the hall. I left the tub of dirty washing by the door to be taken to the laundry afterwards, then joined the others in the open space for sets.

I could really use the calm that came with the routine right now. I mean, sadly, she was right. She was always right. I had failed in the outside world. I had come back into my family's embrace. I was, once again, cleaning up after everyone. And one of my badges was Serving.

Help me out here, please? I'm happy to be back. I'm happy to be with my family. And I'm happy to have a purpose. So why do I feel so... useless... worthless... hopeless...

I mean, it used to give me joy.

What had changed?

How could I get that back?

"Oi, Tessa. Leave the fairies to sort their own way out of Dodge and get your buttooshie over here. We're ready to start." Marcus's bark was enough to scatter my pondering and pin me back into the here and now.

Right.

Sets.

A new day.

A fresh start.

A new load of dirty washing to deal with.

11

CONTESSA: MEET AND GREET

"Oh. Sorry, I didn't mean to interrupt. I can come back later." I'd carried our dirty washing to the laundry. Yep. You heard me. The. Laundry. If you had asked me a few days ago when we were heading to life on the streets if I thought I would have access to a laundry? I would have sat you down and called you silly.

But here we were, in the end room of the second row of demountables, in the "laundry".

Sariah came with me, with a small boy wrapped around her finger. Or maybe it was the other way around. She seemed pretty taken with the little guy. The older boys had been playing a game in Warehouse One after we'd finished up, but this one kept getting underfoot.

We had been told we could use the Factory's facilities, and it would be good to finally have a proper clean. But there was a woman already using the space. I'd seen her in the meeting on our first day. She'd not said anything nasty or negative. And I remembered her warm smile.

"Please"—her thick glossy curtain of hair shimmied around her shoulders as she smiled and held out her hand—"my name is Aiko, we haven't officially met yet."

Both Riah and I stared for a while, but Jordan—the little boy—squealed and raced to her, wrapped his arms around her legs and attempted to climb her skirt. Rather than being frustrated, she laughed—even though her skirt was elastic waisted, if you know what I mean... Elastic. Waist—and bent down and picked him up.

"I can see Jordan has made himself known. Put your washing down and come round and meet the others. You can put your load through when this one is finished." She turned sideways to slide past us to leave the room. Riah and I just stared at each other, then followed.

Keeping to the shelter of the overhanging trees, Aiko led us to the veranda, on the front row of demountables. Honestly, I thought I'd walked into one of those paintings. You know the ones with beautiful women all sitting around in flowy skirts and dresses, braiding each other's hair, leaning over each other, whispering in each other's ears?

Yeah, well... that.

"Hey there Tessa. Riah. Welcome." Izabaal unfolded herself from the floor where she had been doing something to someone's feet. "Carley, shuffle over and make room." The brunette who'd been at the "let them stay:kick them out" meeting complied. She was definitely a teen, but when Jordan sprang out of Aiko's arms and threw himself at her with a cry of, "Mummy!" I kind of found it hard to think of her as a girl.

I recognised Amber—she was the one Raph had met at the Temple. She couldn't have been too much older than Riah, but with the drugs she'd been fed, her body had accelerated past the age of her face. It was all kinds of weird. I didn't know how to take her either. Was she a kid? A woman?

There was the dreadlock lady. Shauna? She was one of the older crew. But definitely not as old as Lottie.

And not as scary.

No one was as scary as Lottie.

Except Amina.

And Val.

Actually, in fight mode, no one was scarier than Val. Just reminding myself of that, and knowing she was on my side, kind of made me feel a bit better. Safer. No one could do anything to me here, because Val had my back. And the Light had hers.

Thank you for putting me on the same side as Val. And Kait... and Marcus... and the rest of them.

I recognised Vashti from before. More than the rest of them, she was a regally-porcelain-ghost of a woman. Where Izabaal was other-worldly beautiful, Vashti oozed subtle dignity. The woman was a riddle; a beautiful, soulful puzzle. Even in our short time here, I'd noticed she and Aiko were always hovering around the kitchen prepping and serving meals. And, since we'd run into Aiko in the laundry, I suspected the two of them were responsible for "keeping house" at the Factory.

Vashti was possibly around Kait's age—fortyish, or a bit younger—again, it was hard to tell. All these women had lived hard lives on the streets before they had arrived at the Factory. I just couldn't make sense of it. How—after surviving so much horribleness and having so little—could they be so composed and graceful? Next to them I was extravagantly blessed, but still I felt like a failure. Inadequate.

I squeezed in beside Carley on an old two-seater couch. Jordan was talking to Riah using a very serious little boy tone, so I grabbed Riah and pulled her onto my lap. The old cane seat creaked but held. Riah didn't resist, even though she was getting bigger and almost dwarfed me. Sitting sideways, she continued to listen and engage with the little boy as I hid behind her back.

Aiko took her place on the floor next to Izabaal and looked up at us. "So, tell us a bit about yourselves."

Riah and I froze. Obviously, Vashti could see our armour. But I wasn't too sure about how much to share. I took a breath, ready to give a recap of our time here in Laodicea, when another woman stepped out of the shadows. "Wait, don't start till I get there." The newcomer, who could have been Aiko's twin, but older, snuck from the shadows, around the veranda and up the stairs.

"Tomiko." Everyone smiled and as a whole gave off a totally joyous vibe. Izabaal was the one who rose to embrace her.

Tomiko then squeezed between Izabaal and Aiko on the floor and threw her hand out to my knee. "Sorry to interrupt, I didn't want to miss anything."

Iza explained. "Tomiko, Ben and Kazi live at a cafe a few blocks away." I could see from the extensive grey scales down one arm and leg that she was one with the others. "It was Ben who found Tomiko, and helped my sisters, until we could bring everyone here, to the Factory." Izabaal's smile swept over the woman sitting to her right. "She doesn't live with us, but her family is part of our family." An extra warmth like hot cocoa on a cool evening filled Iza's eyes as she addressed Tomiko. "Where's Kazi? With the boys?"

Tomiko laughed. "Yes. She has just had an upgrade on her chair and is ready to take them all on—with Indy by her side, of course. But enough of that, what have I missed?" Tomiko seemed keen to get the focus off herself and Kazi. Or maybe she just really wanted to know our story.

I told them that we'd moved from Sodom to Laodicea about six months ago and had been offered a house and jobs by the Community. When I mentioned that, some drew back, others shook their heads, someone actually hissed. That may have been Shauna.

When I explained how we ended up here, at the Factory, there was more nodding, and understanding of being shunted. But they wanted to know more. What had we been doing in Sodom? How had such an odd group of people met?

Again, I didn't know how much to tell. I mean, I was free to tell my story, but the stories of the others? Not so much.

"Well, just over a year before Sodom fell, I had been living with one of the gangs that ruled the city. I hated it. But both my parents had become victims of the Temple. And died."

It was just so horrid to repeat. So I decided to skip over all the gory details and just give the dot points. But then I looked around the group and realised, there wasn't one person there who had suffered less than me. Each of them was a victim of the Temple. So, I told them. "The clientele of the Temple in Sodom was different to what it's like here." I couldn't stop the shudder. "I found their bodies in the street outside the overflowing building. Lying among other bodies. Some still breathing, some comatose, some still showing outward signs of life."

But not my parents.

They were cold.

And still.

So still.

I hadn't known what to do.

I was seventeen.

But up until the time my parents had become seduced, we had been a tight-knit family who did most things together. They'd both worked and, whilst we weren't filthy rich, we were comfortable. But when they died, I was lost. And homeless.

"They'd given everything to their addiction. Our house... car... savings... belongings. Everything. The State took the smidgen that was left to pay for the cost of disposing of their bodies. It was deemed that I was old enough to not need 'care'. But I had nothing. No one. And was incapable of looking after myself. I couldn't get a job because I didn't have an address. And without money...

"It was only my second night on the streets when I was picked up by a spotter for one of the minor gangs. I was offered shelter, food and 'protection'... for a price. I was the bottom of the pecking order and didn't have much to offer. To start with, I just cleaned up after everyone. And cooked a bit. I was also sent out on errands and deliveries. I wasn't told what I was carrying and didn't want to know. I didn't like it, but I grew used to it. Until they wanted more.

"After a while the culture on the streets changed. There were mergers and takeovers. Always, it was survival of the strongest. And to be stronger, you had to be bigger. As our leadership continued to change, so did the roles... and the rules. It didn't take too long before my housekeeping wasn't enough.

"For six years I stayed at the bottom of the ladder. Used by every new member, walked over by every new mule.

"Until Val, Kait and Abbot came for me. Then everything changed. They took me to their home where I met Marcus and this terror and her twin." I hugged Riah and she snuggled into me. I had really missed her over the past six months. I was glad we were rebuilding.

"And what about you, little firecracker?" Tomiko leaned over and ran her hand over Riah's shin. These women were all, very, touchy-feely.

Again, Riah froze. I think they'd picked up my sister's peculiarity. If they hadn't, they were about to. "Um… Riah doesn't speak."

Shauna paused braiding Carley's hair. "Why can't she talk?"

"Riah *can* talk. She chooses not to." I squeezed her extra tight, letting her know I had her back, and I would stand by her always. "And that's okay by us. When she's ready she will. But. Oh. My. Word. When she does, look out. My little sister has the most agonisingly beautiful voice on the planet. Her singing makes the Warriors of Light weep—from delight, that is, not because it's bad or anything. The opposite. She's unbelievably talented."

"But why doesn't she want to speak?" Again, Shauna asked, her hands still frozen in Carley's hair. Carley didn't seem to mind… or notice. She was staring at Riah who was still holding Jordan's hands.

"Um… I'm not sure I can tell you that. It's Raph and Riah's story." But before I could go on, Riah nodded. Using my hands on her shoulders I pushed her back and twisted her a little bit so I could see her face. "Are you sure?" Her huge dark eyes stared unblinking back at me and she nodded. "I've only heard this once—from Raph—let me know if I get it wrong?"

She nodded again then she shuffled down a bit and snuggled against my chest. She went back to playing with Jordan's hands as he sat curled up in his mum's lap next to us.

"Sariah and Raphael were babies when they were first sold. As they grew, their owner noticed they were pretty special. Raph can make people feel better by placing his hands on them. Back then, he couldn't do what he does now. But it was still pretty spectacular. And Sariah's voice would stop people in their tracks. This guy—their owner—would take them to the markets and Riah would sing, and Raph would 'cure all'. Apparently, he made pretty good money from them."

I ducked my head and spoke softly, "Is that right so far?" Riah nodded. "You want me to go on?" She nodded again, but now she dropped Jordan's hands and hugged herself.

"Then, when they were about seven, a man from Sodom travelled to South America, and when he saw Riah, he offered to buy them. They ended up in our city in his 'private collection' as entertainment. It was pretty dodge, but it didn't cross the line. If you know what I mean. I mean, seriously, she was just a kid." I looked around the group and then wanted to eat my words. Of course they knew. These women had exactly the same experience. I burned with shame at my ignorance and serious case of foot-in-mouth.

Izabaal came to my rescue. "We understand, Tessa. Even at the Temple, we are allowed our innocence till about that age. Seven, actually." She then nodded for me to continue. All of the women were silent and focused on my story.

"One night at a party, both twins had performed and been sent to bed. But the next thing they knew the staff were packing their things and getting them ready to leave. One of the men at the party had bought them. But as always, thank the Light, they were sent together."

I rubbed Riah's shoulder and held her closer. I ducked my head again and whispered in her hair, "Okay?" She nodded. "More?" I asked. Again, she nodded.

"But when they arrived at their new home, things turned ugly, very fast." I looked around the group and locked eyes with Vashti. "The twins were coming into the Light. These men were of the Dark. They took her and used her. Raph was going berserk fighting to save her. They pinned him down and made him watch." I paused to get my emotions under control. A lump the size of Warehouse One was blocking the words in my throat, and rage like an inferno was eating me up. I wanted to hug Riah and never let her go. To protect her from all harm from her past, present and future, for the rest of my life. But her hand on my cheek brought me back to the present. She nodded, so I continued.

"When the twins had both screamed themselves hoarse, they knocked Raph out and... I don't know after that. I've only heard the story from him. But he told us when he regained consciousness, she was curled in a ball in their cell. He clung to her and wouldn't let anyone near her. He suffers PTSD pretty badly, and Riah has chosen not to speak.

"Shortly after that, Val, Marcus, Kait and Abbot stormed the building, killed them all and brought the twins home. I arrived about a year after them. And Dan about a year after me. He'd escaped some seriously..." I had to stop. I'd only had a glimpse of the torture he'd endured. I swallowed my tears again and tried to continue, "...scary stuff in Gomorrah, made his way to Sodom, and had been living on the streets, fighting off the gangs and managing to survive as a loner for seven years. Which in itself is pretty unbelievable. It was harsh. Really harsh. So, we all ended up in the family and left Sodom the night it fell."

Riah hit my arm and gave me her "puh-lease" look. I huffed a chuckle. "Yeah, it was a bit more difficult than that. But that story can wait. Oh! Except to say, this one"—I looked down at Riah—"played a big part in saving the day by choosing to release her gift of singing into the world. Seriously, it changed the tide of the battle."

Her olive skin darkened in a beautiful blush, but the two of us shared a smile. A sad smile as we both remembered Abbot.

She collapsed back into my arms and we were both lost to our memories. I had kind of forgotten we were sitting in among a group of near-strangers. Until, as one, they all came over and started to stroke, embrace and adore Riah... and me too. Some had tears in their eyes. Whether it was from our story or a memory of their own, I couldn't tell. But still, as freaky as it sounds... it wasn't.

Izabaal kneeled at our feet. "Sisters, welcome to our family. Our refuge is yours. Our heart is one. Our bond is strong and never breaking." Riah was taken from my lap and embraced, just as Vashti, Aiko and Tomiko pulled me to my feet and drew me into their arms.

I knew Riah was silently releasing more of her pain through her tears. Not that I could see or hear her. It's just that's what I was doing and I knew she'd be doing the same. I knew we had found our family in the Light. But here among the refuse of Laodicea, we had found our tribe.

"What the frack?" We all snapped apart as the blonde appeared on the veranda, glaring at Sariah and me. She looked like she'd just woken up.

"Calm down, Lily. We're just getting to know the new girls." Carley winked at me. "Our new sisters."

I smiled, so incredibly grateful for the lifeline. Lily was another one who kind of scared me. She too was a teen, but her permanent hostility threw me off-kilter. I just didn't know how to handle her. But I was dealt a reprieve when a young dark-haired girl coasted silently out of the shadows, whisper-yelling, "We won. Indy and me smashed 'em, Mum, and—" She came to an abrupt halt, staring at Riah and me.

We began to return to our seats, making room for Kazi to join us. Riah and she were locked in a staring, glaring, weighing-up contest, all thoughts of Riah's previous sentence—and victory—apparently forgotten. But then we were all distracted when the door from the cabin behind us opened. Lottie stood there, her sharp investigation taking us all in, including the multiple red-rimmed eyes. Then Kait walked out. I went to say hi, but she didn't see us, or anything, except the baby in her arms.

KAITLYN: FORCES CONVERGE

W e'd been here four days already, but were still unable to lock down a routine. We were going to be late... again. Because shortly after first light, when Indy got back, Val took Dan and Riah into the city for their gigs at Serendipity. Not only was Dan playing, but since the day was fine and warm—promising to pull folks from their homes early before the heat took hold—we had decided it was best for everyone if Sariah was encouraged to get back into her music and art.

But now they were back, and it was time for us to practise some disciplines. After brunch—thanks to Serendipity—had been put away, we gathered in the warehouse.

Perspex panels running lengthways along the roof, and the gaping hole from the absent roof over the veggie garden, splashed enough light into the space that we didn't need lights. Hopefully it would also send some cooling breezes through. We'd not yet been here a week and already we'd experienced a sample of the stifling heat these cavernous steel buildings could generate. Thankfully, whirly-birds constantly spun in the ceiling, extracting the worst of it. And the peak of summer had passed when we were back in the Community's luxury.

This was our time to focus on the Light. I knew I was not going to be able to stop thinking about Dawn, Genni's baby, and all the challenges and the potential end result of the garden shed and the hope it represented were sitting there like a blank canvas, right in my line of sight. So, we turned and faced a blank, dark wall.

As we drew to a close and moved apart, ready for sparring, I became aware of an audience. Each day they had become a little braver, emerging from the shadows. Faces peeked around the corner of the gap between the sheds. I suspected they'd come to inspect what we were up to, then stayed to watch the show. We made an effort to ignore them. Let them watch. Let them learn that we were not a threat. Although, watching us fight each other may not be the best way to prove that point.

Now that Marcus was back with us on a permanent basis and not driving Felix and the Overseer all over the continent, he retook the training reins. The twins had done well under Val and Dan, but Val had insisted they return to Marcus's care and ministrations.

But he wasn't the only one who'd been absent.

Tessa had been drawn away and absorbed into her role as P.A. to Kari—Event Coordinator for the Community in Laodicea.

Just as I had been working with Georgie—filmmaker extraordinaire—for the informational/promotional series, "Face of Laodicea".

Our job had been to report on the amazing technological advancements the medical scientists and specialists were achieving in this city. I had been surprised how much I'd loved it… and Georgie. I had made sure that my morning routine always included sets with the family. But Val and I had needed to reschedule my training around my new job.

Now I could re-join the group and watch how everyone was doing. I'd been seriously impressed with how they'd handled themselves at the twins' birthday battle. And so very proud.

Raphael was still taking his direct orders from the Light not to kill —anything—very seriously. Marcus had been trying to convince him that maiming the enemy was not the same as killing them. He could still attack and injure our opposition without eliminating them. This would slow them down and enable someone else to take them out. Raph was unsure and undecided. So, until he was confident and had made up his mind on the matter, Marcus worked with our boy mostly on self-defence.

Sariah, however, was a totally different kettle of fish. Since her awakening in the battle of Sodom, her strengthening through the trials at the Community College, and her exposed vulnerability at the birthday battle, she had grown to be formidable.

A flashback to the day we rescued them from their torture at the hands of the Dark Lord and his minions in Sodom three years ago settled like a concrete slab of nausea in my stomach. But to see how far they had come—how much they had grown—had me bursting with pride and joy.

Thank you for my little cubs.

As the morning progressed, our observers had grown in confidence, sneaking in and sitting in the shadows around the walls. Silently watching as Marcus took each of us through our training. Considering our audience, we left out our sword work and stuck to hand-to-hand. After our one-on-one training with Marcus, we each paired up and faced off.

Raph and Riah went toe-to-toe. Then Marcus paired Dan and Val. I suspected Tessa would be put with Dan after a break, but waited to see how Marcus would handle *that* sticky situation, glad it wasn't my call. They were both hurting. But, if they had a future together, they had to figure out how to navigate the struggles. I would offer a listening ear, a soft shoulder or a word of advice if asked, but until that time I would stay back and petition the Light on their behalf. For now, though, it was my turn for hand-to-hand training, so all of my attention was focused on taking my husband down.

"What is going on here?" The bark broke my concentration and I landed on my butt, tangled in among Marcus's legs.

He leaned down and whispered in my ear, "Focus, *Kaity*," then kissed my sweaty lips. I scissored my legs around, threw him off-balance, flipped him and pinned him to the floor, his waist squeezed between my thighs and his shoulder locked. Bending low I whispered,

"Good advice," and nibbled his ear lobe. "Now what?" The heat wasn't just from a good work out.

A cough brought me back to our current situation. I looked up to see Val's legs. "I'd say you guys are obviously overdue for a date night, but right now we have more pressing matters."

My husband's chest rumbled beneath me. "Pressing. Ha. Good one, Val."

"Mind out of the gutter, Marcus." Val helped me up and, when Marcus was up off the floor, the three of us turned to face an irate Amina. I was starting to wonder if this woman had any other settings.

"How can we help you this morning, Amina?" Val smiled and greeted the woman amicably.

"What are you doing here?"

There was a pause. How to answer this one? I mean, it was pretty obvious. I tried to think what her real question might be. What her real *concern* was. Then maybe we could help her be at ease.

Help us here, please.

"Good morning, Amina." I stepped forward to stop Marcus opening his mouth and inserting a fist. "Since we were out earlier this morning, we decided to change our schedule. But we have taken your advice"—I thought flattery might help—"and are inside and not making any noise. The doors are shut and no one can see us."

Indy's wheels were almost silent as he made his way over. Iza glided by his side.

I continued to try to bring the woman down from her arctic cliff before more tension was created in their leadership team. "We thought it would be okay. Especially since none of you normally use this shed." She was definitely a "handle with care" package. But, unfortunately for her, the woman didn't have a leg to stand on in this current argument.

And she knew it. She didn't have a comeback. The silence became more volatile the longer she failed to find an argument to defend her interruptive outburst.

"Would you like to join us, Amina?" Marcus's voice was gentle. "There's always room for one more."

He meant well. He really did, and I loved him for it. But it was the spark that ignited the explosion.

"You. You…" Her ebony skin darkened to acidic crimson.

Marcus threw his arms up in surrender, turned to me and raised his shoulders. *What was wrong with that? Seriously.*

My heart broke for him. He really was trying. *Nothing. You did good. I love you.*

He shook his head. *Love you too.* We both turned back to face the firing squad.

"How dare you come in here and… and …" She was a hissing, spitting wild cat, her hair on end and claws extended. "You have brought nothing but trouble."

"Amina, stop." Iza came forward and pleaded with the woman. "That's not true and you know it. They have done nothing but help us. Look at what they have done so far." Iza turned and could not hide the glow of pleasure when she gazed at the start of our work with the veggie garden in the neighbouring shed.

"Then what? What will they do then? We do not need men here."

"They have offered to help train us. So we can protect ourselves, Mina." Iza's voice was cool water over the heated coals of her friend, but it did little to dampen the fire.

"What can he teach me?" She looked to Dan and snarled. "They have nothing to offer me. I can protect you all."

Marcus, bless him, had had enough. "Amina, we rescued Sariah, Raphael and Tessa from horrendous circumstances. We can possibly understand, in part, why you hate men. But why all men?" He stepped into the fray. I recognised that tone and knew there was no stopping him now. At that point I decided to just support him and do what I could to clean up the fallout later. "Can't you acknowledge at least Indy's loyalty? He has gone way above and beyond what has been asked of him. Why do you hate him… men… us, so much?"

Lord, help her. You've allowed her to see our armour. You have brought us to this place. You have prepared her for a reason. Help her over this barbed-wire fence so she can begin her healing.

The fury buzzing inside her built until it burst. Keeping her burning eyes drilling through my husband, her finger jabbed toward Indy. "Because he lived."

"What?" Marcus was as perplexed as I was.

"He lived." She turned her head to Indy and didn't quite spit, but it looked like she wanted to.

Iza stepped forward. "I don't understand."

"No. You do not. You cannot." It looked like she wanted to say more. Or I should say, her will to say more was overridden, trampled over and shut down by a herd of stampeding elephants. The rage fairly bubbled under her skin. I am sure the woman was close to splitting at the seams, considering all the anger she kept inside. The Light had an awful lot of work to do in that one. Not saying He didn't have lots to do in all of us, but… some seemed tougher nuts to crack than others. And Amina sure was one tough nut. But the Light had opened her eyes, so the Light would show her the way.

Iza sighed. It carried the weight of the world and was filled with her tears.

"May I make a suggestion?" Val's quiet voice bounced around the cavernous shed. She didn't wait for an answer. "Amina." Val stepped forward and placed her hand on the woman's shoulder. She flinched but didn't step out from under Val's touch. "Uriah was taken from you. Izabaal was taken from you. You have overcome unspeakable odds and horrors to raise, protect and provide for your son, Banjoko. You are a fierce warrior… a passionate protector. You are carrying the burden of these"—Val's free hand encompassed the community who'd gathered in the warehouse—"admirably. But you *don't* have to do this alone. You have been hurt, abused, abandoned, like everyone here. But you are *not* alone. You've had a lot taken from you, but you are strong, a wall, a defence. But you are not *alone*. We have not come to take from you. We have come to help, to walk alongside you. The love in your heart is a raging fire. I see it."

Amina's eyes widened and she gasped.

Val leaned forward and spoke quietly in the woman's ear. What she said, I would have given a month of sundaes—and I mean the ice cream, not the day—to hear. But none of us were privileged to receive that treat.

Amina swallowed deeply and her eyes were awash.

"You are not alone. Amina…" Val waited until the woman gathered herself and looked her in the eye. "The Light has sent us to you. To help you. You. Are not. Alone. You are seen. And you are loved."

At this, Amina brushed Val's hand off her shoulder and a snarl curled her top lip. Her wall had returned with a vengeance.

Val nodded once and narrowed her eyes. "I challenge you."

Amina, to her credit, didn't flinch, but a shadow crossed her face momentarily, nonetheless.

Squaring her shoulders, Val continued. "You think we have nothing long-term to offer. You believe that you are able to do a better job training and protecting your family. You think you are better equipped than Marcus and Dan?"

Amina looked to both the men, contempt dripping from her eyes, and nodded.

Dan looked uncomfortable.

Marcus raised his eyebrows.

"I suggest a"—Val tilted her head—"trial. If you win, we leave. We'll pack up and move on today." The collective gasp and protests were deafening. She held up her hand. "But if our contestant wins, we stay."

Amina squinted and looked around our group, immediately dismissing the twins and Tessa. Her gaze lingered on Dan briefly, swept over me, burned Marcus and came back to Val. She was worried about Val.

"Not me. I won't fight you, Amina," Val assured her. It was enough. Amina nodded once.

Dan shifted uneasily. He hated fighting women. Marcus started rolling his shoulders. But we all froze when Val continued. "Tessa, you haven't trained yet this morning. How about you come and spar with Amina?"

Pre-emptive triumph erupted from Amina. Her chest swelled and her chin rose as she set her sights on my darling girl. Then dismissed her with a wave of her hand. In one fell swoop, Val had allowed Amina her pride back. It was obvious that being emotional in front of everyone had cost her. But by offering her an opportunity to prove herself and restore a semblance of honour, Val had presented her with a gift, bless her. A gift too good to refuse.

However, I was not so confident it was worth sacrificing my precious girl's feelings—and body—to make Amina feel better.

Tessa agreed with me. "What? Val? Are you kidding?" Tessa spluttered. She was already trembling. I just hoped my sister knew what she was doing.

13

CONTESSA: DON'T PICK ON MY FRIENDS

Oh. My. Word. What was she thinking?
   I was going to lose.
Scratch that. I was going. To. Die.
This woman was going to eat me alive.

I looked to my family. Each one of them staring back at me. The twins were scared. Marcus and Kait looked quietly optimistic—shocked, but nodding encouragingly to me all the same. I didn't look at Dan. His lack of confidence would kill me. But Val's burning conviction was unnerving.

"You... ahh... know I'm out of condition? Right?"

Val nodded.

"You know I've not been in training for... months?

Val nodded again.

"Six. It's been six months, Val."

She just raised her eyebrow. Just the one.

I know she knew that. But I was just putting it out there. In case, because of all the excitement, she may have just forgotten? I asked her silently. *No?*

No.

What the hell was she thinking.

"Maybe Sariah would be a better choice?"

My little sister stepped forward beside me, nodding madly.

Strange girl.

Val shook her head.

Oh God. Oh God. Oh. My. Lord.

Help me.

My whole family is going to be back on the street because of me.

What is she thinking?

"Val, I really don't think this is such a good idea." She must be light-headed from compost fumes or being hit in the head or something.

"Great thinking, Tessa. Make her think you're scared." Dan's breath tickled my neck.

Oh, *that* I could do.

"You've so got this, Contessa. You have the advantage; she thinks you're weak. She underestimates you. It's perfect. Keep playing it up." Dan's whisper over my shoulder sent shivers down my spine. He gave me a small nudge in the back. "Go kick her crabby butt."

I tripped, then shook myself out.

Okay, okay.

Okay.

Breathe.

Okay.

Alright.

Okay, I could do this.

Just breathe.

Oh God, I'm going to die, aren't I? Is this my punishment?

Amina turned her back on me as I approached. "So, you trained this one?" She sneered at Marcus.

"Aye." The pride coming out of him bolstered me. I looked to him. He winked.

"I will not fight her. She is just a girl."

"Hey"—I gave her shoulder a shove—"don't call me a girl." How dare she dismiss me. She didn't even acknowledge my shove. "Hey—" She lifted her hand to silence me, not even turning around to face me.

The twik.

"I will fight that"—using her chin she indicated Dan—"or that."
And then Marcus.

The gall of the woman.

How dare she?

It was one thing to ignore me, but she was not going to insult my
family and get away with it.

I saw red and grew about ten foot tall.

My armour turned bulletproof.

I kicked out the back of her knee and she dropped to the floor.
While she was down, I stepped in, pulled the bulk of her weight back
so she was off-balance, and wrapped my arm around her neck, whispering in her ear, "Do *not* speak to my family like that."

I flexed my arm around her neck and held her head at an uncomfortable angle. She was my prisoner. And I was trying hard to figure
out just how much—or little—mercy to show. "I will spar with you."
More pressure. She tried to get me with her hands, so I dug my heel
into her calf muscle. It wouldn't do permanent damage, but it did
hurt. Especially since, by now, both her knees were digging into the
concrete. "But if you insult my family again, it will not. Be. Training."

I had already eased off and was stepping away when Val spoke.
"Tessa, enough."

"Right there. That's what I'm talking about. Bring it home Tessa." I
looked over to Dan. Surprised by his encouragement.

Raph was bouncing on his toes.

Riah's armour was on fire.

And Amina's fist was in my gut. Gah.

Twik.

I heaved in gasps of air and willed the red to fade from my vision.

"Focus." Marcus and Val barked at the same time.

I guess Amina and I had each other's attention now. I just wished I
could use my sword. Fighting demons was one thing, but hurting
humans was something completely different. I didn't want to hurt this
woman.

Well, not really.

Maybe just a little.

I mean, I was used to sparring with my family, but I didn't know her.

Help me do this right.

I knew I couldn't fight angry. I didn't hate her... much. But I did need to fight smart.

I straightened up and stepped back, shaking myself out. Amina was rubbing her neck and limped a circle around me. Was it wrong to be happy I'd hurt her? At least we were even.

I exhaled. Bounced a few times on my toes then dropped into low breath. Mentally, I was both a solid and a fluid. I could stand and receive her attack, or I could redirect it. She was taller. Stronger. Older. More experienced. And fitter. But I didn't have to take what she dished out. I didn't even have to give back as good as I got. All I had to do was alter its course away from me.

I inhaled the Light. I imagined I was a tree with roots reaching to the core of the earth. I was solid. But my body was the slender swaying branches of a willow, reeds in a river, clouds through the mountains. I could bend, sway and roll. I exhaled the anger. She was not my enemy; she was my partner in the dance.

She came, her rage hitting me before her fist.

Deflect, bow, give.

Her foot lashed out.

Step to the side, push, glide, pass.

Another fist.

Lift, curve, turn.

Amina's control was devoured by her anger. Before long, she lost all style and finesse. Desperation and frustration marred her thinking.

It was time.

The river became the mountain.

She had become used to me taking and redirecting, absorbing and deflecting, and she dropped her guard. This time when she came and swung her arm, I stepped into her embrace. Dipping my knees, I sunk my fist up into her diaphragm. All the air rushed out of her lungs. She wasn't really hurt; she just couldn't breathe. I held her as her arms dropped over my shoulders. And I lowered her gently to the ground and eased her into a foetal position to help her lungs recover.

From the corner of my eye, I saw Indy usher the children out of the warehouse and, at Iza's nod, the women followed. Marcus and Kait led our crew out till all that remained were Val, Iza, Amina and me. I rubbed the woman's back. I didn't hate her. I didn't understand her. But she wasn't the enemy.

Val gave me the nod, indicating I, too ,should leave. Iza squatted down next to her friend, taking my place, and I left the three of them to it.

I was walking on a cloud.

I had won.

I had beaten the Amazon.

We could stay.

Far. Flaming. Out.

Just as I made it to the office door of our sleep quarters, the heat of the fight drained out of me, leaving me cold and a little bit—okay, a lot —shaky. And I kind of lost it. I stumbled through the dark hallway and was hit by an octopus wrapping its long suctiony limbs around me. There may have been muffled cheering. I wasn't too sure.

"You were bleeding brilliant, me girl."

"Darling, I knew you could do it. We're so proud."

"Tessa, you were amazing."

I think I was sobbing by then. I had completely turned to jelly.

"She's in shock. Dan, bring her into the dining room. Raph, boil the kettle. Riah, get a blanket."

As their voices retreated down the corridor, a wall-like body closed around me, and I smelled... man-sweat, eucalyptus clothes detergent, coffee, home... Dan. I buried my face in his chest and sobbed.

Okay, so not my proudest moment.

In the darkened hallway I was transported back to Sodom. Back before the rift. Back where we knew where we stood in the chaos. Back when he was the centre of my world, and I was his.

"Frudge, I've missed you, Tessa."

"Miffed ou ooo."

He laughed. "I'm sorry I don't have a towel on hand, but"—he gently prised me off, leaned me up against the wall and ripped his shirt off in one swift movement—"you can use this?"

We may have been in a darkened hallway, but there was enough light for me to see that, while I may have been out of training, Dan had not been.

Oh. My. Word.

"You may want to start here." The horrible boy... man... dabbed my mouth with his shirt.

Okay, so I may have drooled... a little bit.

BUT HE DIDN'T HAVE to be a pig about it.

I grabbed his shirt and wiped my face clean from tears, snot and drool.

Then I hit him. Hard. In the shoulder.

He laughed and pulled me back into his embrace. His shirtless embrace. Then kissed the top of my head. "You were fracking amazing, Tessa," he purred. "So fracking proud right now." He kissed the top of my head... again, then steered me further down the hall to the Common Room. "If we don't show up soon, Papa Bear will send out a search party."

I clung to him. I am ashamed to say I was a bit desperate. I knew that as soon as we walked back into the light, things would go back to awkward. I didn't want awkward. I wanted Dan.

I miss you so much.

I just followed his lead back into our new ordinary... in our *new home.*

I had totally forgotten.

We could stay.

This was our new home.

A flush of excitement hit me just as we were greeted by the others.

"And why do you not have a shirt on?" Marcus roared across the room. "And why are you plum as a beetroot young lady?"

"Oh Marcus. We can stay." I broke away from Dan's hold and hugged Marcus.

"I know sweetheart. You did good. You did so bleeding good."

From under his wing, I winked at Dan.

Disaster averted.

He winked back.

"I saw that." Damn it. Marcus didn't miss a thing.

* * *

"Hey sweetie, you did really well today." I no longer felt goosebumps. Although the sulphur and dropped gut still accompanied her arrival.

"Thanks." I knew I had to be careful with her. But was it wrong to feel good about my victory today? I knew it was the Light who really did it. But I did play a part in it as well. I was the vessel. It was my context.

"You did alright. Frack me, I wish you could have seen her face when you dropped her. You ripped the bottom out of her world. It was perfect. And no. It's not wrong to feel good about it."

All of a sudden, I felt bad about it.

"Don't worry, the Light used it for good. It opened doors for conversation." She continued with a subject change that gave me whiplash. "So, tell me, what about Dan? Did you see that washboard? Hose me down and hand me a margarita, I could sit and look at *that* all day."

At first, I burred up. I didn't want anyone looking at Dan. But then the image of him standing in the dim hallway, without his shirt on, flashed bright in my mind. The memory of being held within the walls of his arms—of being safe, reconnected—flooded me and gooey, melting honey filled every crevice of my empty heart, warming me from the ends of my fingers to the tips of my toes. And I had to agree with her. He was fine. No doubt about that.

"Oh sweetie, 'fine' doesn't even come close. You know you want some of that."

Well, I'd be lying if I said I didn't. But mostly I wanted *him* back. I missed him so much. We'd been distant longer than we'd been close. Hell, we'd only been close for a few weeks. But they were the best few weeks of my twenty-three years.

"Pity he's moved on."

"What? What do you mean?" He'd hugged me, kissed me. Told me that he'd missed me.

"Yeah, like a sister." She huffed a half-hearted laugh. "He hangs out with the little kids here, every single day. And before that he was with Raphael and Sariah, every single day. From where I stand, I can't see any difference between how he is with them and... you. But, on the other hand, have you seen what he's like with Carley and Lily? Honey, you've been out of his life for months."

My heart dropped to the floor and shattered into a million pieces.

She put on a fake philosopher's voice. "A brief hug, and a peck on the head, a lover does not make."

And once again, even though I hated to admit it, she was right.

"And have you seen *all* the women here? No, not just Izabaal." She'd responded before the thought had finished forming. "Indy is the only one who can touch *her* heart. I'm talking about the others. They are all cut from the same Temple cloth—that very curvaceous, experienced, lonely-girls cloth—if you know what I mean."

"Yeah, I know."

"Don't worry sweetie, there's someone out there for you. Somewhere. Pity it's going to be hard to find them hidden away in *this* fortress."

I couldn't stop the sigh from crushing me.

ACT 2: BREAKING

DANIEL: LIE OF THE LAND

E*yes ahead. Eyes ahead. Eyes ahead.*
"Bro." Indy's elbow connected with my hip at the same time his voice broke through my litany.

"What?" Couldn't he see I was trying bleeding hard to focus?

"What's up with you?"

Was the guy a machine? How the hell didn't he notice? How did he do it? Maybe he lost his man-card when he lost his legs. I couldn't help it, my eyes flicked to his lap.

"You frecking weirdo. You checking me out?"

I now knew how Tessa felt every time the red comet swallowed her face in shame. "Nah. Just... how do you not look? I mean..." My eyes were drawn to the enticing mirage that surrounded us. Since we'd arrived two-and-a-half weeks ago, I had been trying really hard. But I was so frolcking warped that even the twik queen herself, Amina, half glorious black skin, half dead, grey scales—attitude aside —was a mouth-watering demonstration of... Woman. But then there was Carley, and Lily, and Aiko. And even Shauna and Vashti, despite their age, were stunning and... stirring. And, of course, there was Iza. Thank the Light for Lottie. There was nothing appealing about that woman. And I loved her for it.

"That's easy, bro." Indy addressed my unfinished question. "I know them. I see them when they come in. I've heard their stories and, believe me, when you get to know the human being under the dressed-up meat, it changes everything."

And I thought the shame racing around my face was bad. The shame lodged in my gut shrunk me to the size of a gnat. Of course. The reason they were here... they were all here because they had been used, abused, then made to disappear. Talk about feeling like a complete heel.

"So, you and Tessa huh?"

"What?"

"Pay attention, yeh? Tessa."

We both looked over to where Kait and Tessa were taking the girls... women, through some basic moves. The ex-priestesses moved awkwardly, giggling, and fumbling with the steps. Kait moved among them, helping here and there. Val and Amina watched from the sidelines. With all the scales and multi-toned skin it was like watching a pulsating rainbow. And right in the middle, leading the lot, was a ray of golden sunshine. Tessa. Confident, capable and taking charge.

I couldn't help but remember our short, wild history together. My gut travelled from lightness, joy and rightness, to pain, pride and confusion. "I don't know man. I thought so, but..." I couldn't watch her anymore, it just hurt too much. Thankfully, a distraction came in the form of Iza. She would not take part in the classes, much to Indy's frustration, but she hadn't stopped anyone else. She left the cabins across from us carrying the baby. The look on her face was radiant... angelic.

Shaking my head, I looked at my friend. "So, you and Iza, huh?"

He laughed from the belly and it drew Iza's attention. The look on her face relegated the rest of us to a black hole. There was only room for Indy. "Yeah bro, me and Iza. Who'd have fracking thought?"

"Indy." Even from the distance across the tarmac she'd heard him and admonished his choice of vocab, covering the ears of the newborn. Skirting her way through the shadows, Iza made her way to us and laid the babe in Indy's arms. Her hands now free, she cupped his scarred, ugly face and worshipped his lips with the gentlest of kisses. "Language, my love." Now empty handed, Iza made her way further round the shadows and joined the others in the warehouse.

As she entered the building it drew the attention of her sisters but soon that landed on us. The younger two, Carley and Lily, stopped their workout and started giggling behind their hands whilst making it bleeding obvious they were making eyes at me. I didn't quite know where to look.

Tessa's demonstration out the front halted. She coughed. But it wasn't nearly enough to get their attention. "Ladies, please. You have a lot to learn."

Kait continued her instruction with Shauna, Vashti, Aiko and another Temple survivor, Tomiko, who lived nearby. The four older women showed no interest in us at all. But Carley and Lily were not to be distracted from their… distraction. Amber just stood to the side and watched the show. Her eyes flicking between the darkening Tessa and the oblivious girls.

"Ladies." Tessa didn't quite stamp her foot, but her hands were on her hips and the predatory bird was out in force. They'd better look out, if my experience was worth anything at all. Val and Amina who'd been chatting in the shadows stopped to watch as well. But the straw that broke the camel's back was when… Lily? I still didn't know which was which. The blonde—the one who didn't have a kid—looked over her shoulder, ran her eyes over Tessa and dismissed her as nothing.

"Uh oh. Look ou—" I hadn't even finished my sentence when Tessa drew her sword and leapt, pirouetted, slashed one girl through the torso on an upward slash and completed the swing by cleaving the other girl's head.

Well, she would have if the sword worked on mortals. As it was an Unseen sword for Others, it didn't have any effect on them.

Much.

Although… that was odd.

One blinked and the other stood straight and shook her head a bit.

"Whoa. Mate. That was pretty impressive and uh… very scary." Indy's sight had given him a visual on the whole thing. Amina was less impressed. She stepped forward sharpening her claws, ready to eat Tessa's heart for morning tea. Kait stood motionless with her jaw hanging down around her knees.

"Tessa." Val barked. "Stand down. Walk it off."

Tessa slammed her sword home, glared at Val, Amina, then the girls. She seemed to dare Kait to say something before storming off to the gate heading to the outside world.

"Dan." My focus flew back to Val. All she did was jerk her head in Tessa's direction. But the message was clear as a bell. *Follow and keep her safe.*

I sprang to my feet and spoke over my shoulder on my way out. "Petition the Light for me and my... friend. This could be tricky."

I didn't bother to try to catch her as she took off at a run through the sheds and headed for the back gate onto the side street. I just made sure to keep her in sight. Which wasn't too hard, she was out of training. But she was skitched. And I wasn't a complete idiot. I'd wait till she'd burned off her prickles and, when she was exhausted and out of breath, I'd get closer.

Her sprint soon turned into a run, which inevitably rolled into an amble before collapsing into a folded body, hands on knees. "Why are you following me?" She didn't bother turning around.

But I still didn't get too close. "Orders." That got a spark. I knew she wasn't done-in yet.

See? Smart.

Keep your distance till they've got nothing left in the tank.

She didn't bother responding, but her back straightened and the predatory bird came out of hibernation, fluffed its feathers and flexed its talons.

Again, I'd learned quick. Best not speak at all in these situations. Guaranteed, I'd say the wrong thing anyway. Just wait till she let out enough rope to hang herself. Leave me well and truly out of the process.

She pretty much screamed at me. "What?"

So, it turns out that skitching Tessa off was still a whole world of fun. "Nothing. Just following orders."

"To babysit me?"

"Nah. To make sure you don't take your aggro out on any other poor, unsuspecting innocents."

"Innocents." I'm sure her screech broke some windows somewhere. "Those... girls are hardly innocent."

"Yeah well, neither am I. And..." I waited till I had her full attention, predator bird and all, "neither are you."

"What's that supposed to mean?"

"You know bleeding well what that means. *Friend*." I knew this was supposed to be about her losing her skrat back at the Factory. But pretty quick it became about us and what happened here in Laodicea. I knew what that word meant for Tessa. It carried a lot more weight than for most people.

For Tessa, *Friend* was seriously significant. Like Marcus and Kait were *lifetime Friends*. She said feeling a connection for someone due to attraction was dangerous. From her experience, physical appeal led to selfish abuse. But friendship meant trust, admiration and loyalty.

Before the skrat hit the fan royally in this warped city, she and I'd had an arrangement. We were *Friends*. She was wary of our mutual attraction, but if it was grounded in mutual trust, she'd allow it. But then, just as we were moving forward, testing the friendship out, she'd up and left me. Just like every other person in my life.

Talk about trust issues. I had them in spades. But it was a mutual failing. We'd both been done-over by life and neither trusted easily.

"For flopping sakes Dan, why can't you understand I was doing it all for you. Everything. It was for you. To make you happy." Her arms flailed and her colour intensified to a DEFCON-level red. "You'd been out on the streets for so long. I was doing what I could to give you a house, and food, and clothes, and... and... stuff. So you could be comfortable. And have someone look after you for a while. It was all. For. You."

"Did you ever think of asking me what I wanted? What would make me happy?" I couldn't help it. Our combined anger was a magnet pulling us closer together. I hadn't even realised until the heat radiating off her tiny, shaking body hit me like an open pizza oven.

"Because if you'd been around long enough to ask, Tessa, I would have told you. I would rather live on the street with nothing than live in a mausoleum without you. Haven't I done enough to prove I don't need that stuff? I don't want that stuff. I wanted you."

I could sense we were pulling a crowd, so I stepped back and drew a breath before I continued. "But I didn't have a chance to tell you that, because before we'd even set up our digs, you were gone. You let them transform you into a skeletal... clown... in drag. You became a stranger in every sense."

My description hit her like a tidal wave. Her face morphed from incredulous to volcanic in seconds. "Clown? In drag?" Each word was screeched in a higher octave. However, I noted she didn't disagree with "skeletal". "But what about me and what I wanted?"

"At last. The truth comes out."

"And what's wrong with that? Just for once I wanted to be the one who was up front, pulling their weight. Not always in the back picking up everyone's dirty laundry, cleaning up everyone's mess and sorting out everyone's skrat while the rest of you were out the front getting all the glory."

I didn't bother responding. But couldn't help hiking an eyebrow.

"Shut up."

I hitched the other. Like I said, I didn't have to say a word. Just allow her to let out enough rope to hang herself with no help from me.

Her eyes narrowed into a lethally focused glare.

"So, how'd that work for you, Tessa? How's that *glory* feeling now?" She was winding up for some epic response, but I'd had enough. I spun round and threw out over my shoulder, "You know the way back, try not to take out any more *innocents*." I couldn't help but throw weight at the word.

Her scream raised a smile. I made a point of sauntering back down the street toward our new home, grateful she didn't have any projec tiles on hand.

"I was loving you. You stupid... ignorant... blind... idiot."

Her yell stopped me in my tracks. *What?* I spun around to face her. "What?"

"I thought you were different."

"What?"

"But you're not. You're just like all the rest."

"What? Wait, back up. What did you say? What are you talking about?"

"Of course you wouldn't understand." It was her turn to storm off. And once again she had the last word.

Loving me? What the flick? Love? Did she say, love?

* * *

"Hey bro. You okay?" My blurry eyes cleared, revealing Indy's face.

"What?" I looked around and took in my surroundings. I was sitting on a park bench beside the canal. Indy had parked his chair on the grass beside me.

"Tessa came back ages ago in a state fit to be sedated. Not that she was, yeh, but you know the drill: duck, hide and look busy."

"What?" I shook my head again, trying to make sense of the impossible.

Please help me. I'm so flecking confused.

"Tessa. She came back ages ago, and since you were supposed to be keeping an eye on her, thought I'd come and find your carcass. Glad to see you still breathing, bro."

I looked around. The sun had shifted and was making long shadows of the trees across the canal. The heat of the day had faded to comfortable and the early evening streetlights had come on. "I don't understand."

"Women? I hear that. I've been living with a horde of them for the past seven years and I tell you, if it weren't for Ben and Kerm, I would have gone swimming with a lead chair. What's to understand, yeh? Weird as hell is chicks."

15

CONTESSA: POOR LITTLE FREE GIRL

"Poor little free girl. Having to do it rough in the gangs. Being used by multiple punters at the same time. How tough." The girl's snark was epic and laced with all kinds of nasty.

"Ease up, Lily, she doesn't know what it was like for us." Carley stood behind Lily, brushing out her hair. The girls were hidden under the verandah awning attached to their cabins.

I'd been waiting for Lily to return home from her night "doing her bit" for the family so I could fulfil my orders to share the Light with them. Since I'd carved them up with my sword, the Light had started seeping into their lives. Now, along with Indy and Amina, Carley and Lily had started to "see".

Apparently, this was not a normal response when a "Seen" came in contact with an "Unseen" blade. But instead of asking Vashti, or even Kerm or Helen who these girls knew well, Val had said I had to do it—something about sleeping in the bed I'd smashed. I baked scones to help ease my way into their inner circle.

So far it was working a treat.

Not.

"That's exactly my point, Carley. She doesn't know." Lily's eyes cut to and through me like I wasn't standing right in front of her. "But it doesn't stop her sitting up there on her high-and-mighty entitled throne looking down her nose at us. Judging us. She has no right." The bitterness was tangible.

I had tried to be positive and start a new leaf but, quite honestly, Lily intimidated me... and scared me silly. I was glad Carley had a hold of her as she started working an intricate braid, weaving ribbons through Lily's hair. It ensured she would stay put, but it also had a mesmerising effect on me as I watched Jordan's mum weave her magic.

I shook my head and returned my focus to Lily. "I'm not judging you."

She sneered. "No? I see you watching us... me. I go out and do what I can to help out here. We aren't taught a lot of skills at the Temple, you know. Well, skills that don't require us lying on our back or dancing on the end of a chain. We can't escape. If we try, we're either disciplined or made to conveniently 'disappear'. But if only it was that easy. Branded for life"—she raised her left arm encased in the tell-tale dull grey scales up to her elbow—"with a neon sign that screams 'cheap, desperate, and experienced'. With no life skills, we're fodder for the dogs.

"Our only family is within the walls of our jail. Not all of us have doting mothers who visit and bring gifts. Some of us are dropped off straight from the womb. Other girls are brought in when they're older, their 'trade' the answer to too many mouths to feed, or one too many bills, or 'how the hell am I gonna afford that dowry?'

"No. Our only way out is by committing the biggest crime of all and becoming impregnated by the scum who feed off us."

"Come on Lily, give her a break. She's here to try to help us understand this... this..." Carley stopped braiding, let go of one hand and stared at the scales on her arm that had once been a dead, light-absorbing grey, but which had now begun to lighten and reflect the dusky pink of her new armour. Her eyes came back to me in wonder as they roamed my yellow encasing. "And she brought scones." She winked at me.

It was hard to keep up and find my place between the two of them. Lily wanted to rip me apart and Carley kept throwing me a line.

Lily tilted her head away from me and spoke to her friend. "I want to know about this as much as you do, Carley, but I can't learn from someone who thinks I'm scum." She turned back to me. The edge of her anger had been replaced by a tinge of desperation. "I'm doing the only thing I can to help my family. You think I like the job? Chase it?" She paused.

But I kind of thought it was a rhetorical question? I was so confused, and I didn't want her to hate me. I just didn't know what to say, or do, to make it better.

"You. Know. Nothing. You have everything. So what? You had to do it tough for a while; so what? Now, you have a family, a job to do, and skills to do it. You have a decent guy who respects you, he doesn't beat you. Hell, he actually wants to hear you, listen to what you think and not see you for a Frankenstein body you have no control over. So, you can get off your high horse and stop judging us... me."

"What? Frankenstein? But you're"—my eyes flashed between the two of them and their beautiful faces and perfect bodies—"you're beautif—"

"You think this is beautiful?" Lily launched to her feet tearing her hair out of Carley's hands. I took a step back and held my scone plate up as a barrier between us. But she didn't attack me. She ripped her smock off and stood naked before me.

Oh. My. Word.

The girl—I called her a girl as she was four years younger than me. But she didn't act it. Or look it. And I couldn't help looking, because she. Was. Naked.

Yep. As in completely, stark. Naked. Not even wearing undies.

And perfect.

Her skin as pure as her name. She was completely and utterly, breathtakingly, beautiful. A work of art. Even though I was not attracted to the female form, I couldn't help but appreciate the perfec tion as she stood before me. The scales covering her left foot and leg up to her knee, and her left arm from hand to elbow had started to lighten and come to life, picking up the hue of her faint, lime-green armour.

"But"—again I looked at Carley for support and included her in my affirmation—"but, you're," the both of them were, "perfect."

"Perfect?" Lily stepped into my personal space, the scone plate pinned between our chests. "This is a prison of somebody else's making. This is not me. This is not who I am. And what's worse, within this prison, I am tattooed with the label 'whore'. Do you think this is power?" Her hand swept up and down her exquisite body. "No. This is bait.

"When you are on a leash you do not have power. You have just enough room to hope. But then, after a while, you realise that's just a joke—an illusion—you are the worm on the hook at the end of the line. This is not beautiful. This is not power. This is not me." The storm of desperation and anger had swept through and left tears sparkling in her eyes.

"You twik and whinge about your man because he doesn't understand you. Are you fracking serious? He *sees* you." Dan often accused me of having predator-bird eyes when I was angry. For the first time ever, I think I understood what it was to be on the receiving end of that look. And I didn't like it. Thankfully, she took a step back and I could breathe again. Short, sharp breaths. Because, to be honest, I was still a bit scared and weirded out being verbally attacked by a naked woman-girl.

"You think 'poor me' because you don't have what we have? I would kill for what you have." I believed her. I hugged my scone plate. "You're not permanently branded with an open invitation, held prisoner by the need to be safe. You're free to move. And not only are you safe from men you don't know, the men in your life see you and accept you for who you are. And I tell you what, any man who sees past this"—she waved her hands down her naked body—"and sees this"—she thumped her chest—"is a real man. And a man I give a free ticket to the whole package." She placed her hands on her hips, did a cobra-weave of her head and thrust her chin up to the side, one eyebrow raised.

Eeks.

"Hell yeah. That's truth right there, sister." Carley was nodding her head and grinning.

I looked between the two.

Double eeks.

Carley waved her comb and beckoned Lily. "Come on girl, put it away and let me finish your hair. You've made your point and I want scones."

Finally, Lily put her smock back on and a bit of the pressure in my brain eased. When her head was under the fabric, I quickly scanned the grounds to see if Dan was in the vicinity and had seen the show. I couldn't see him. It helped me feel a bit better. I mean, I heard what she was saying. And I honestly believed I was beginning to understand. But that didn't mean that I felt like I could compete with her.

Lily then plonked back onto the stool in front of Carley, who inspected the damage Lily's rant had done to her work. She unpicked a few lines of braid then continued.

So did Lily. "That's what makes Indy so special. He knows us. He doesn't see the scales. He doesn't see the body. He sees us. I've seen Dan and Marcus. I know they see the body, but they work hard at seeing more; seeing us." Held in place by Carley's hands threaded through her hair, Lily resorted to using her finger to stab the space in front of me. "But you don't. You judge us just like everybody else. You're as bad as the men on the street and the punters at the Temples."

I waited a few heartbeats. It seemed like she had finished and let all the hate out. She definitely looked more like a deflated doll than the raging bull I'd first encountered. "But why do you still do it? Go out there? When you don't have to anymore." I was scared it was the wrong thing to ask. But I really wanted to know. Lily had been right. I had only seen them skin deep. The outer image. And what I had seen was the mirror of my insecurities that echoed the taunts of my demon.

"Because when I use what I have when I want to use it, how I want to use it, that's power. That's choice. I've got nothing. Nothing! I know nothing about this." Her hand waved vaguely around the Factory.

"And, since I'm not tied to a child..." Her words were harsh and her sentence was left out there, unfinished, hanging. Carley leaned forward and softly kissed the top of her head.

Izabaal had told me how Lily's baby had miscarried and I, in my epic ignorance, had thought that had possibly been a good thing? Like, it wasn't another burden, or mouth to feed? Or child to bring up in poverty? I mean, I'd literally had a breakdown at the thought of being on the street—with a family to look after me. Let alone doing it whilst being responsible for an innocent, defenceless baby.

But again, I'd been so shamefully wrong.

And I was sure.

Absolutely.

Positively.

Sure.

I was not going to share *that* misconception along with all my others.

Lily raked in a watery breath and continued. "This is the only way I can pay my family back and do my bit to support them. It's the only thing I have. So, I choose to use it for my family. So, don't you dare judge me for doing exactly what you did. You said you chose to leave your family to work—to provide? Well, I choose to do exactly the same thing."

I couldn't argue with her because she was right. I had judged her, *and* I had sold myself to the machine to do what she, and Dan, accused me of.

What do I say now? How do I make this right? I need to work with these girls... women. I am so inadequate. And lost.

I was reminded of a time, back in Sodom, I had really stuffed up with Dan, making a big deal about a small thing. Again, I'd only seen the surface and not seen the bigger issue. I had thought he'd never forgive me. But he had. Maybe I had the same hope here. Struggling to find a way forward, it was the only answer coming to me, so it was worth a try.

"I'm sorry. You're right. I have always had issues about how I look… or don't look. When I arrived and met you all, all I could see was what I wasn't. And all the accusations and my insecurities were set on a loop. A loud, deafening loop." I dropped my head and took a huge calming breath. The scent of scones and the memories it wrapped around me helped me go on. I looked first Carley then Lily in the eye. "Please forgive me, and thank you for explaining the situation to me."

At this, Carley guffawed. "Yeah, our Lil has always been good at 'explaining'."

Lily half-turned and tried to whack Carley, but Carley jumped to the side and tugged Lily's hair, causing her hand to fall short of her target. Lily then turned back to me, a faint blush in her cheeks. "You're alright, Tessa. But I'm warning you. You better get your skrat sorted. A good sort or not, if that man"—she nodded to Dan who had just emerged from the doors of Warehouse One making his way around the perimeter on his way over—"is not nailed down soon, I'll take that as an open invitation to try my hand." She raised the hem of her smock and slowly lifted her bare right leg and laid it over her left, leaving a lot of skin on show. She tilted her chin and raised that perfect eyebrow again. And all I could think of was the image of Lily, completely naked under that smock.

Carley gave Lily's braid a final tug as she tied it off. "Give it a rest, girl."

Dan came around the corner. "Tessa, Val's looking for you." He shifted his focus and nodded at the two women beside me. I glanced at Lily's legs and caught her eye. *No undies.* Then stepped in front of them and shoved my scone plate at Dan's chest. "Scone?" I then took his elbow and led him back the way he'd come.

Both women cried out, "Hey, they're ours."

"I'll bake more for you later." Their laughter followed in our wake. And I couldn't help but smile at the lightness of the sound.

Thank you.

That barrier had started falling and the weight of the world was slowly rolling from my shoulders.

Munching on a now-cold scone, Dan glanced at me from the

corner of his eye, his body stiff, but he didn't pull his arm free from my grasp.

And thank you.

We were in a mess. No doubt. I didn't know my way out of this one. I wished I could ask Kait, but she was so tied up looking after Genni's baby, Dawn, she wasn't really available anymore. I missed her. But with or without her advice, one thing was for sure. I was not stepping aside and giving Lily—or anyone for that matter—an open invitation to make a move on my friend.

I may not have him just now.

But there was no way I was going to stand down from the dance.

16

DANIEL: GET OVER YOURSELF

"I'm just so confused." My gut was churning and my mind kept flipping head over butt, not knowing what to do.

"Why, what'd she do, bro?" Indy was playing with a blade of grass as he and I and Marcus sat with our backs to the outside wall of the Factory, watching the canal. A breeze caused the sun's speckles through the canopy around us to flicker and fade over our outstretched legs.

"She ditched me publicly in a room full of krets in our first week in Laodicea, not even a week after we'd come to an... arrangement, then left me for a lifestyle." It still burned.

"Harsh." I'd always have Indy's support, no matter what. "I wouldn've picked that, the way she defended your sorry butt the night you came, eh? All over me like a rash."

Marcus joined the laugh at my expense. "I think you're being a bit tough, lad. You know what she means by being 'Friends'. You know very well what she was saying that night."

He was right, frudge it. "Yeah, but they didn't."

"Irrelevant. You did." His words rubbed gravel into my wounds.

"But then she left and moved into Kari's. Couldn't get out fast enough."

Marcus took the time to breathe deeply and exhale. "It wasn't just you she left. And it wasn't just her who left you." This time he waited till I looked at him. "We all left. Well, everyone but Val."

"That's a bit tough, the twins didn't have a choice. Neither did you or Kait—"

"And neither did Tessa." Bleeding heck. I hated it when he was right. "Have you asked her what it was like? What she was doing? What was involved?"

My silence was answer enough.

"So, she left to go to work so you guys could live in a fancy house, yeh? She sounds like a real twik." Indy shook his head giving me a mock look of sympathy. "So, what else she do?"

"What do you mean? Isn't that enough?" I flicked my eyes between the both of them and landed on Indy. "And don't call her a twik."

Both Indy and Marcus laughed again. This time from the bottom of their guts. "Seriously, man, she didn't leave you for another guy, she left you for a job to try to help you?"

A football made of lead wedged itself inside my chest and I had trouble continuing. "Everybody fracking leaves." I made the effort to push the emotion down. "To date, the only person who has stuck by my side is Val." I looked over to my best friend, who sat broken in the grass next to me. "Even you. I just wanted her to be different. Someone who could... would *choose* to stay."

For a while, we sat silently as a group of walkers passed us on the bike path running along the canal.

Marcus broke our silence. "She is different. And... she's just like everyone else. Her personal baggage and scars set her feet a-dancing to her own tune, her Badges setting the beat and guiding her steps. Just like the rest of us, she's doing the best she can with what she's got in her arsenal."

I tried to stop the smile when a kaleidoscope of memories flashed: fighting with her by my side, watching her care for us all, her laughter and joy, her passion. And I couldn't stop the smile deepening when I remembered her confronting Amina. She'd been so skitched when the woman dismissed her, ignored her and—worst of all—called her a "girl". It was perfect. Just what she needed to get her thug on. Pride swelled at the memory of her dropping and incapacitating her opponent in the blink of an eye. This morphed to rage when I remembered Amina punching her in the gut. I'd wanted to kill the Amazonian twik.

But then, in utter amazement, I'd watched Tessa collect herself, calm down, size up the situation and defeat her superior. "She is fredging amazing," I sighed.

Indy must have been reading my mind. "Was pure gold the way she handed Amina her butt on a plate, yeh? Blew my mind. Sweet-as. Obviously, it's not something we talk about in my house." Indy was beaming. "I need to find some way to thank her for giving me a treasure that will sit with me for the rest of my life." But then he sobered. "Mina's not that bad though, eh. She hates anything with balls, but I get that." His eyes drifted to the canal. "Her life is all about protecting family—her sisters and her kids: Joko and Iza." He looked to his scarred hands and ran them along his useless legs. "We both love Iza. But I have her. So, I'm doubly hated." The hint of a smile didn't reach his eyes. "You speak about people leaving. But what about the ones who stay?"

"Indy, you weirdo. What are you talking about? You're skitched because that mirage of a woman stays with you?" I hated it, but I couldn't stop my eyes travelling down his broken body.

"Yeah bro, exactly that. I burn for Iza and not just because she's a... a mirage." A smile lit his whole face. "She's something, yeh?" Then the darkness returned. "The one thing that gives me hope is that she chose me. She saw me, who I was: black, ugly, homeless, lost and powerless... and she chose me. Before I lost my legs. *And* after. She cast her lot with me.

"It only lasted a second before it all ended. But for that, I would give her—have given her my life. She stays because she has to. She has nowhere and no one else. None of them do. But what if they... she... didn't need me? What if she wasn't a prisoner, reliant on me for everything. What then? Would she stay?"

The water flowing in the canal in front of us pulled time along with it into the afternoon. We'd taken a break from the world in the heat of the day to sit and be apart. Marcus had started the habit in our first week, just the four of us: him, me, Indy and Raph. It was only our sixth week here but already we'd seen the value in the habit and increased it to a couple of times a week. We carved out time and found space to sit and talk. To begin with, it had been about sharing the Light with Indy. At the start, he'd been quiet. He'd listened, taken his time and mulled it all over. We'd wait till he came back with questions. But today Marcus had used this opportunity to nail me about Tessa. And I admit I felt a bit guilty I was happy Raph had been too busy to join us.

A cyclist flew past, and we sat in the wake of her breeze. An elderly couple walking a dog passed, bringing hints of some expensive scent to us as we waited for a lull in pedestrian traffic.

"Women have the power to make the mighty, dullards and the weak, savage beasts." Marcus drew the conversation back on track... his track. "Seriously Dan, I hear what you are saying. I haven't even been able to unlock half your story—what you suffered in Gomorrah —but I hear your pain." He drew a slow steadying breath. "But we both know a lot of Tessa's journey. Just think, when was she ever the one in control, calling the shots, being the supporter rather than the supported, the rescuer not the victim? Used, abused, helpless, saved, doesn't look good on your resume. She wanted to be the one saving others."

"I get that. But couldn't she see what was happening? Man, couldn't she just draw a line?"

"Ah, since you put it that way, I can see you two were never going to work. So maybe this is for the best." Marcus's quiet words threw me for a six.

"What do you mean, it was never going work? Of course it was going to work." What the hell was he thinking.

"Dan, if you want her to be perfect, it can't work. She's not and never will be perfect, and neither are you. She has, is, and will continue to let you down. You have, are, and will continue to let her down. She cannot be your constant. She cannot be your insurance policy for happiness. She is fallible and human. And it isn't fair that you burden her with the load that only the Light can carry.

"He is your constant. He will never fail you or leave you. He is your investment. Not her, not me, not even Val. All of us have, are, and *will* let you down. Just like you will let us down." The man I had started to consider a father-figure pinned me with his frosty green eyes, challenging me. "So, if you want perfection, walk away. You're looking for pearls in pig skrat.

"If, however, you want company along the way. With someone who understands what it's like to survive the rat-race and face-plant, and who can help you get back up when you do the same—because they understand what failure is all about—then perhaps you'll have a chance with her." He then turned back to the canal in front of us in quiet contemplation.

The three of us sat in comfortable silence and I tried to let the gentle breeze drifting off the canal cool my frustration and the road-block doing my head in. We'd been out here for... "How long have we been here?" I slapped Indy in the leg. "Do we have to get back?" Then a more complex reality hit me. I looked Indy in the eye. "How are we going to get you back over the wall?"

"Fracked if I know. It was your bright idea to leave my chair behind this time, dimwit." We both looked up at the wall behind us. Sturdy branches of the trees sheltering us from view stretched over the top. But Indy couldn't climb trees. I looked to my best frie... brother and broke down laughing. "Sucks to be you." I stopped laughing when he launched himself on top of me and pinned me down. And he was doing a pretty good job of returning the compliment.

"When you two boys have finished skylarking..." Marcus tried to get our attention. "Hey." And tried again.

The tussling turned to laughter. I was remembering Abraham's exact same words over the exact same situation. Indy rolled off the top of me and wiped his face. We caught each other's eye and broke into laughter again.

"Children." Marcus stood and leapt into the nearest tree and disappeared over the wall.

Indy and I were back at it, rolling around in the grass, fighting, skitching ourselves laughing. We were brought up short though when the legs of the wooden ladder we had used to get over the wall in the first place landed by my head.

Marcus called from the top of the wall, "When you've finished being a chocolate teapot, you can help your brother up the ladder."

"Yeah, nah, bro. I got this."

I was once again completely gutted, shocked and impressed as I watched the muscles of Indy's upper body ripple and work as he pulled himself up the ladder. When he got to the top, he lay on his stomach and I skuttered up beside him. We then dropped the ladder over to the inside and I watched him descend and climb into his chair positioned by Iza.

"Thank you for coming back, I was starting to get worried. But now I need to see my man about a few things"—Iza bent down, whispered in Indy's ear and brushed her hand over his cheek, then looked at us—"if you'll excuse us." They moved towards their hut. Indy had placed her hand on his shoulder, and she kept it there, accompanying him to their home.

Marcus elbowed me in the side. "That there's not a relationship based on desperation and imprisonment."

I tried to see the two of them in the light of what Marcus had said. "No. And it doesn't seem to be just gratitude either." Not that I knew anything about relationships... obviously.

"Aye."

We watched as Izabaal waited for Indy to open the door for her, then she went inside, he followed and shut the rest of the world out.

"Excuse me Dan, I need to find me Kait. We need to... talk about... something." His vagueness swallowed his words and he disappeared into Warehouse One.

And I was left feeling like a sundry, wobbly fifth wheel with a huge hole in my gut that used to be the place Tessa lived. My defences were shaking, and my pride was looking pretty pathetic and legless right now.

Help me get this right. I want what they have. How do I do that? How do I get over this pain? How do I make things right? Do I want to make things right—wait, don't answer that. I kind of think I do. So, yeah, help? Please?

17

CONTESSA: GIRL TALK

Her laughter was like tinkling.
Seriously.

I know that sounds so... gah. But really, it was.

I had always thought those kinds of comments in books were a bit OTT.

Until I met Izabaal.

She *was* the fairy princess who chatted to birds, calmed dragons and recognised the beauty beneath the beast. Everywhere she went, small animals trailed in her wake.

Okay, so that was a bit rude, calling children animals, but... you know... perfect, much?

It would be really easy to hate her, but she was all kinds of lovely. So, I tried to ignore her extreme gorgeousness, and just play it cool.

Cucumber.

That was me.

Short, shapeless, yellow cucumber.

With crazy hair.

I had climbed the ladder and dropped over the external wall and was on lookout duty. Once I'd given the all-clear, Kait landed on the ground next to me. We both looked up and watched as Iza, balanced on the top layer of the concrete block edging, wrestled with her skirt.

Yep. The girl wore skirts All. The. Time.

I liked a nice skirt, or dress. But all the time?

"Why don't you wear pants?"

She stared down at me, uncomprehending. I then realised some people confused pants with undies.

Seriously, didn't they realise undies go *under* pants. That's why they're called underpants—undies. "You know, jeans. Or leggings?"

She smiled and the sun came out from behind a cloud somewhere... cloudy. "I don't own any... pants." She shuffled her butt forward, and kind of fell—in a graceful kind of way—off the wall.

Don't worry, we caught her.

"What do you mean you don't own pants?"

"I've never worn them." She straightened and checked everything was in place—hair around her face which was hidden under a hood, skirt down around her ankles which were covered in socks, and the ends of her gloves up under the sleeves of her jacket—then continued. "I was given to the Temple when I was three and left seven years ago when I was nineteen." She gave me a wry smile. "We weren't given *pants* to wear. They're not part of the uniform. Now it's just habit, I guess."

"How do you fight?" It was the most important question of all.

Kait gave us a nod. She was indicating the coast was clear. But I'm sure she was also agreeing with me. We sat down on the grass and continued our hushed conversation. We'd taken inspiration from Marcus bringing the boys to this spot for "chats".

Kait and I figured if they could get Indy over the wall, sit out here and talk without being detected, it was a good chance we could do the same with Izabaal.

Even though sweat dripped down her face and dark patches grew under her arms and around her neckline. We had promised we weren't going anywhere. We were just going to sit on the grass, under the trees, in the shadows. But she had insisted on the cover up.

Once we were settled and she'd arranged herself, Iza continued in a loud whisper, "I don't understand why that's relevant. Indy has taught us all how to defend ourselves. And it's not like we intentionally mix with people." Her eyes twitched and her head flicked constantly left to right watching the path on the other side of the shadows in front of us. "And besides, Kerm has taught us the basics of sewing, and skirts are easier to alter. Anyway, as we have well established"—she pointed her glove-encased hand to her hair-covered, sweat-slicked face—"we don't go out much, so, does it really matter?"

Kait came in swinging off the elephant in the room... on the grass... whatever. "Except when they come on site?"

Izabaal sighed. "People... men, see me and think I should be available to... *help* them meet the goddess." She rolled her eyes. "However, when any of my sisters go out in public, they're either beaten, scorned, or dragged off to be used." Her shoulders fell as she exhaled. "The lack of colour in their scales marks them as the Temple's seconds: unworthy and valueless.

"We're not fooling ourselves. The neighbourhood knows who we are and that we're here. It's the local ill-kept secret. Generally speaking, though, they turn their heads and let us be. However, they know if they're desperate to scratch their itch, Lily is available." Fire burned over her skin—as much of her skin as I could see under her disguise— and her body zinged with rage.

"There is a horrible man, Axel, who's taken it upon himself to 'help' Lily. He organises jobs for her. Picks her up, delivers her to the punters, then brings her home. For a cut of her earnings, of course. He's tried several times to come on site. But Indy and Amina always take care of him."

She shook her head. "He taunts us. Says he could do a great business with the rest of us. Could get us 'some real action'. I hate him." She swivelled her head to look at both of us sitting either side of her, her pale skin an angry red... or that could have been her roasting body temperature, but it was definitely prodded by her mood. "I've begged her not to go. She doesn't enjoy it. But... the money... she feels she doesn't have options... that *we* don't have options. I'm not in a position to tell her what to do. And I'm definitely not going to take away her right to choose. As much as I hate what she does, the last thing I'd do is evict family—family in need of shelter."

Confident there were no pedestrians on the path, or bad guys hiding in the trees, Izabaal exhaled and tucked her head further into the back of her hood, finishing the job of becoming invisible, but her hushed sigh gave her away. "The more she goes out and offers herself up, the more they come round looking for a piece of the rest of us. Not everyone is content to go through Axel, you see. Some would rather cut out the middleman."

"Is that what happened the night we arrived?" Kait asked.

"That wretched man started hassling Amber. She's a real target, poor thing. Her scales didn't finish losing their colour after Raphael... whatever that sweet boy did—and before Mina got her out. Quite frankly, I don't know which is worse: coloured or greyed scales. But now, it's the same as it is with me, people see her colours and try to take her. Of course, they throw money, thinking that will make it alright."

My heart broke for her. Once again, I was reminded that she wasn't some entitled princess. She'd been donated to the Temple, which was even suckier than being sold. It wasn't out of desperation that her parents gave her up, like some of the others. She was just... given... for nothing in return. How could you not grow up thinking that you simply weren't wanted? Then, from the age of seven, she was trained to be a tool for the pleasure of others.

The question wasn't why she was so nice. It was how was she not so jaded?

Her face fell even further. "I do worry about the little ones though. Especially when we get break-ins. But..." She sighed. "It's not just Lily. I knew Amber was sneaking out, hunting those disgusting cigarette stubs that Lottie is addicted to. And just like Lily, she is doing what she thinks will help." Izabaal stopped, breathed slowly and gently shook her head.

I held my breath. I was hooked on her story... their story. But I waited till the mother walking her kids had passed by on the canal path for Izabaal to go on.

"No one here is under pressure to do things they don't want to do. You know? To contribute? We appreciate every cent and supply that comes in, but we will... we have... made do with hardly anything. There's always enough." She shook her head again. "But, with Genni arriving, and now her baby"—she flicked her gaze to both Kait and me —"we are growing."

Perhaps the fact we hadn't been seen, or maybe it was her frustration, but whatever it was I definitely felt better when Iza pulled off her hoodie to reveal a sweat-slicked body. She used it to wipe herself down, then lifted her face, eyes closed to catch the gentle breeze. And smiled. "I don't know how he does it, but each day Indy comes home with a cart full of what we need. I'm not allowed to ask." She slid us a sly smile. "I tried following him once. Of course he knew. He promised me he wasn't stealing but asked that I trust him. He can't, or won't, tell me how he sources the supplies, but he always manages to get just what we need."

Again, she paused. But this time she looked up and stopped us with her radiant smile. She was still beautiful, even though her hair was plastered to her head and her face was beetroot red. "But now, with your help, we will have the means to support ourselves."

Another part of my wall against her fell, and my heart warmed another degree. Just like it had with Carley and Lily when Lily had explained... with illustrations.

"But you don't know how to protect yourselves? Do you have weapons?" I couldn't hide my astonishment.

"Don't be silly. Weapons? We'd be in more trouble with them than without. Indy always says"—she gave a very bad impression of Indy's voice—"'if you rock up to a fight with a weapon you can't use, you've just given your opponent another advantage and another weapon to use against you, yeh?'"

"But why won't you join us for morning sessions where we can teach you to protect yourself. This is not okay. The other women can see the value. We're even helping the kids."

"Oh, Tessa. My sisters are joining you because it is something different." I don't think she meant to be condescending, but I felt like a child nonetheless. "You have been with us for just over six weeks, but think what it would be like to live inside for years… your whole life. What you offer is new, interesting and gives them something else to do—to occupy their time. And something else to think about."

I tried very hard not to think about what they *were* thinking about. Especially Lily and Carley. Especially when it involved Dan. "Then why don't you join us? Don't you want to learn a new skill? Have some variety?"

And once again her look had me feeling like an ignorant toddler. And how well I fit in with the children.

"I may not see what Indy and Amina can see… and apparently what Vashti, Carley and Lily can see, but I know this has something to do with your god. And I do not want to be involved."

We were all silent for a while. I respected her viewpoint. I mean, I had to. But it still didn't sit well with me.

Please help her see you're different to what she's used to. How amazing you are and how you can make all things new.

"I think we need to go to a charity shop to see if we can find some suitable clothes for training." When Izabaal started to protest, Kait continued, "For the others. Those who want to learn." She threw her eyes over Izabaal, the wheels of her mind obviously churning. "Maybe we can organise a visit to your local shop? You'd have a pretty good idea of the others' sizes, wouldn't you?"

"Are you kidding? Of course. We swap clothes all the time. I can introduce you to Helen and Kerm—they are our adopted grandparents. Although Helen is far too young to be our grandmother, but the kids adore her. But not quite as much as they love Kerm. No one can hold a candle to him where the kids are concerned—except Indy." Her smile turned up to full wattage.

"It's not far from here, and they always give us good deals." She fiddled with the fabric pooled in her lap. "They know the truth about us, and what we've been doing here from the very beginning." She looked up, eyes wide. "I wasn't after charity, but from our very first day, they were in our lives and helping us out. And now, they're just as much a part of our family as… as… everyone." She laughed again. That princess-glitter-Tinkerbell laugh. And instead of making me want to vomit, a few more boulders fell from my wall.

"They were so nice and always asked about how things were going, what we needed and how the babies were growing. They got to know us and put things aside for us. It didn't take long for them to find excuses to visit us and meet everyone. I go to their shop pretty regularly to see what we can scavenge. We work in the evenings, after hours, when big loads come in, sorting the donations in return for goods. But I know it's not nearly enough to cover what they've given us." She returned to the knot she was tangling in her full, flowing skirt.

"I'm sure they do it to help you out. We'd love to go over there and meet them and check out their stock." Kait winked at me. "It's our favourite thing."

I snuck a glance at Izabaal from the corner of my eye. The girl looked amazing in rags. It left me feeling empty. I was still wearing the leftovers Kari had dressed me in. All of a sudden, I missed my old clothes… from Sodom.

Kait leaned across Izabaal's legs and tapped me on the thigh. "Right? Seriously Tessa, when was the last time we went shopping together?"

I pretended to think. But I didn't have to. It was when we first arrived in Laodicea. We'd been showered by the Community's gifts and money. We were each given a new wardrobe… and then the wheels fell off. "About seven and a bit months." My heart curled in on itself when I thought about all I had missed.

I missed Kait.

Our times together.

She wasn't my mum.

But she was the nearest thing to it.

It made me feel homesick, which was ridiculous, because she was sitting right there. But I will confess I felt a bit selfish… and happy I was getting to see her without that baby in her arms. To have her all to myself again… almost.

18

IZABAAL: SHOPPING SPREE

"Thank you for the invitation, but I simply can't go with you." It was so kind of them to ask. But they just didn't understand. Then again, how could they?

"But you go out, don't you? Like, to Good to Go, and"—Tessa looked between me and Indy —"you *do* go out, don't you?"

There was so much I admired about Tessa, but she still didn't understand. Even after two months and all our explaining and stressing how important it was not to be seen. If only I could make her see. "It's difficult to explain and... understand, I guess. People mean well—" Indy's grunt interrupted my response like a car speeding over the bridge. "I like to think that most of them mean well. But they do tend to get a bit carried away... and they like to take me with them."

I couldn't help the memories flooding back. And the pain: pain caused by others—physical, emotional and psychological. And self-inflicted pain in an attempt to release, manage and cope. I knew it had been a vicious cycle climbing to a vortex of the perfect storm that could not find release. And the bright silver blades that sliced the prison walls and rescued me from the chaos. That enabled me to breathe. To unleash the beast. To exist within the realm of the expected.

The pain of my knotted fingers brought me back to the knot of anxiety in my stomach. It helped pull me back from the dark, consuming spiral.

I ran my fingers up and down the raised, white ridges woven through my wrists.

That is who I was.

That is not who I am.

I escaped.

I survived.

I have options.

I have a voice.

I shook my head and looked to both Tessa and Kait in turn and tried again to explain. "The higher up the food chain one is at the Temple the less one sees of the outside. In my final years—as High Priestess—I wasn't even allowed out onto the portico. And even within the shadows I had two Keepers." Instinctively my eyes sought out Indy, my anchor. "That's why I started sneaking out in the early hours of the morning—to the bridge where I met Indy—I was not coping with the expectations of my role... and the tightening of my imprisonment."

"But aren't you in exactly the same situation here?" Tessa's voice climbed higher with disbelief.

"Well, yes. And no." My heart warmed at the truth of the haven we had found. "Here, I have the right to decide." I couldn't stop my smile even if I'd wanted to. "And I get to visit with Kerm and Helen. And I have my family around me. And"—again I looked to Indy and joy literally bubbled out of me at my good fortune—"others don't come in... often."

Again, Indy grunted and positively scowled. My poor man. I hadn't meant that as an insult or a reminder. It was just a fact of the lives we were lucky to live. Every silver lining had a dark thread.

Kait stepped forward. "What if Tessa and I acted like your Keepers. We're capable of protecting you—"

"And if we, like, covered you up again? And gave you a disguise? And looked really scary? Kait can be really scary. Surely that would work. Wouldn't it?" Tessa really was one of the most determined and bubbly people I'd ever met. It had only been two months and already she had become a vital part of our family. She was so generous with her emotions, never hiding what she felt. She was a breath of fresh air. Close to me in age and the only one who didn't feel compelled to defer to me. She didn't understand much of our way of life. But the upside of that was that she didn't understand the hierarchy. I had a sense she liked me because of me, not because of my role. I couldn't help but see her as a friend whom I didn't want to disappoint, even though I knew how this would end. Again, in my indecision, I looked to Indy.

He shrugged and shook his head. "I didn't get it until I saw it for myself, yeh? But it's up to you. Go if you want, stay if you'd rather. Always, Iza, the choice is yours. I'll support your decision."

* * *

KAIT DROVE Tessa and me from the Factory in the early hours of the morning. We pulled over on a quiet street not far from the place they had been coming to buy supplies for our wonderful garden. When a queue of people had started snaking their way into a nearby bakery, Kait popped over and brought us each a coffee and a selection of pastries for breakfast as we waited for the plant nursery to open.

To stop myself focusing on the approaching shopping nightmare, I took my time appreciating the absolute delight of the flaky treats and daydreamed about the gardens. So far, there were two long beds planted and growing food. I just couldn't believe it. Not only did I love the idea of being self-sufficient, I loved that my sisters and the children were learning new skills. Everyone was involved in some way, contributing any way they could. I was so absorbed in thinking about our new garden I had tuned out of the conversation Kait and Tessa were sharing.

But when they engaged in an extremely awkward embrace over

gearsticks, around the steering wheel and through seatbelts, my attention came back to the present. I studied the street and surroundings for life and movement. I was torn. Excited to see new things, but fearful of who would see me and what they would do. I knew these ladies were experienced in self-defence, but I couldn't stem the nervousness rumbling through my stomach threatening to eject my tasty treat.

Kait sat back and started the truck. "We're going to buy seedlings, shop for clothes, then go home and spar."

Whilst Tessa and Kait were nearly salivating at our plans for the day, I was less enthusiastic. However, I was looking forward to introducing them to Kerm and Helen and shopping for new things at Good to Go. Yet how anyone could get excited about being in public or fighting was beyond me.

Kait pulled into the nursery and already there were customers milling around displays in the carpark.

"Um... I really do think it best if I stay here." I didn't want to dampen their excitement. But they had no idea what they were in for. And I really didn't feel up to the horror that was guaranteed to unravel.

"Come on, you'll love it. Kait's the best shopping partner."

"No, that's okay, I'll wait till we get to Good to Go. You guys go ahead."

"Please, Iza, you can pick whatever seedlings you want. We can even get flowers..." Tessa left the word hanging like an enticement to treasures unknown. I couldn't hide the beginning of the smile that threatened to betray my determination.

I looked between the two of them. "You do know how to defend yourselves don't you? I mean"—I felt my cheeks heat in a blush—"you can take care of yourselves, can't you?" Was it at all possible that maybe this would work? "And me?"

"Are you serious?" Tessa had sensed her victory, and held her hand out to help me down from the cab. "Of course we can. I promise to keep any wildflowers under control and all seedlings will tremble before me."

I gently shook my cap-covered head, which was now covered by the hood of my jumper. "Well then, I'm game if you are. But don't say I didn't try to prepare you."

Kait whispered under her breath. "Well, bless my soul. She did warn us." I'm not sure who she was talking to, and I only just heard her over the rising, eager whispers. It started shortly after we entered the indoor section of the nursery. Even though I had my hood up, a cap on and my hair out. As soon as the first person caught sight of my scales it all got hot and nasty very quickly.

It started with the whispers. It usually did. But we ignored them and moved outside to where there were tables all set out under a shaded cover. Pots of various sizes were arranged on tiered shelves and trolleys. It was an overwhelming spectacle of greens, colours, shapes, shades and textures.

Kait led us over to a section under a large painted sign, "Vegetables". Instantly I recognised the little segmented containers they had brought home previously. I did my best to focus on the variety of plants and their labels, beginning to dream of the food we could grow. But all the same, I made sure my left shoulder was tucked behind Kait's right, and I could feel Tessa's left shoulder behind my right. I didn't look up and I didn't linger. I stuck to them like glue.

I sensed Kait's eyes were on the growing crowd. But Tessa was pointing out different varieties of seedlings we could possibly get. She was also suggesting some flowers, when a clawed hand pushed through, grabbed my shoulder and spun me around. I knew I should have kept my face tucked down, but the shock threw me. I was out of practise.

"I thought I saw your scales." The man kept his hand on my shoulder and yelled like a truck horn. "Hey everyone, a priestess"—he stripped me with his eyes—"a high priestess. Hey check this ou—"

Kait swung around and... accidentally? on purpose? bumped him out of the way. I think she may have also have stood? stomped? on his foot. But if anyone accused her of anything, I would be sure to say it was an accident. Especially when she followed it up with, "Oh, I am so very sorry. I didn't see you there." She gave him a beautiful smile, but her eyes were saying something completely different. He listened to her eyes and stepped back.

But the damage had been done. Like flies to a rotting corpse, they came. They crowded in on us, doing their best to shove Tessa and Kait out of the way.

Tessa began waving her arms around, indiscriminately hitting people. She started overemphasising her breathing and making an ungodly noise. "Back, everyone back, I can't breathe." To begin with, I was concerned for her. Guilt washed over me as I thought I had brought this on her. But when I caught Kait's wink, I relaxed. Tessa's act created a minute break in the crowd, but when the initial shock had faded, the swell came back, trying to swamp me.

Tessa started back up again. "Back. Now. I mean it. I can't breathe. I need space." The edge in her voice sharpened and her arms were a bit more intentional in their swings and hits.

This was simply horrible. My frustration quickly bled into memories of my previous life. Instantly I was back at the Temple. Then back on the streets, trying to find Indy and me a place to stay after we were kicked out of the Rehab unit, before it all began. I was aware of Kait's arm wrapping around me and she became my cocoon, turning her back on the crowd. And Tessa turned up her volume. "I mean it. If you don't get out of my face, someone is going to get hurt." I peeked over Kait's shoulder and watched as Tessa emphasised her point, by blindly swinging her tensed arm around. And by the grunts and curses, I believe she collected a few targets.

But it was all too much. Panic was only a breath away. I turned in to Kait and tried to slow my breathing. I attempted to make myself as small as possible. I pleaded, "Please." The crowd. The panic. The jostling. Everything was swallowing me whole, piece by painful piece.

Once again, the yawn of humanity's hunger and greed was consuming and deconstructing me. It didn't matter how hard I clung on; I was losing myself. I was going to fall into the darkness—my safe place—where I could wait until it passed. But not yet. First, I had to get out. "Please."

19

KAITLYN: EYE OPENER

With my back to the crowd, I looked over the tables and racks that spread out in front of me. The horde was growing, I suspect not just because of Iza, but because of the scene this relentless group was causing. And that's when I saw it. Its humanoid body, mostly blending in with the crowd, moved through the swelling numbers. Dead eyes locked onto mine, a slow sneer hinting a curl at the edge of its lip.

Leaning low, it brushed whispers through the gathered bodies. Fingers teasing. Words arousing. Emotions swelling. It did its job well. Not taking my eyes from it, I watched and considered my options as it slithered through the group. I suspected it wasn't alone when I heard Tessa draw her sword. She stood in front of us, but in my peripheral vision I saw she was looking off to the other side of the nursery. I didn't know how long we had before more arrived. But, trusting my guard and the Light to provide what we needed to keep Iza safe, it was time to move.

Releasing Iza to Tessa's care, I turned. "Enough." My bark was effective, for a moment. After a breath, the pushing began again. "Enough. Move back. Now." This was completely ridiculous. "Snap out of it. Have you never seen a priestess before? Get a grip."

"Priestesses don't mix with the common. Priestesses don't come to… nurseries." The man in front of me, the one who'd started the ruckus, argued.

Iza was aware enough of her surroundings to plead. "Stop it. Stop it. Stop. I am not a priestess. Leave me alone."

"Ha. So, what's with the scales?" A voice carried from the back of the group.

I'd had enough and more importantly, so had Iza. "Back off."

Please help.

"Hey, you're the woman from that show." Another disembodied voice carried through the crowd.

"We're leaving. And believe me, I will make it known far and wide that this establishment shows no respect for its patrons." To be perfectly honest, I had forgotten I was the medical team's "face" of Eye on Laodicea. That life was a world away. And quite frankly, if they hadn't figured out I was no longer part of the show, I wasn't going to tell them. However, it was enough to get the owners to intervene. The demon who'd been stirring up the crowd nodded its head to me. Then it and its companion dissolved.

"I told you," Iza whispered from the corner of the cab, her hands once again tangled in the mess of her skirt, her fingers trailing up and down the raised white scars on the inside of her wrist.

"Was it like that at the Temple?" Tessa was still outraged.

"No, we had Keepers that 'encouraged' the masses to behave. Pay up or hands off."

The conversation between the girls faded as my mind played over the events at the shop. I would never have understood what Iza was talking about until I saw it for myself. Even though she wore a hoodie over her cap and her hair down, gloves and socks, it was impossible for her to hide her scales.

By the time we left, everyone in the shop had been bowing and kowtowing—especially after the owners threatened to call the authorities, fearful of the bad publicity they thought I could inflict—and like an ocean parting before us, most of them shuffled out of the way as we flanked Iza to the car park.

Women tried to give her things: offerings, gifts and trinkets. Men tried to push past us to offer her money. Even though she was fully dressed and not for sale. They all saw her as something she wasn't and didn't see her for who she was.

Silently and politely, she declined them all.

It made me sick. And angry. I was consumed by a heat that ate away at my rational thought. I wanted to destroy the lot of them and burn the place to the ground. Yet I knew rage was not going to help her, or the situation. If only I could have gotten away with a tad more violence. But thank the Light He'd helped me keep my head.

Tessa and I had continued to edge people away. Oh, they had protested. But then I had, once again, tried to make it clear. "We're not here on Temple business, leave her be."

"But a high priestess in our shop?"

"Leave her be."

"Your holiness, please..." One was stupid enough to push past me to grab at her.

"Leave. Her. Be." I hadn't laid a hand on the guy, I hadn't kicked, pushed, or shoved. But I had walked through him, and all the others... enthusiastically... with knees and elbows. They grunted and stumbled out of our way.

We had made our way out to the truck.

"Your holiness, please forgive us." The manager's eyes flicked to mine. "Please forgive your treatment in our shop. Please accept our gifts and our humble apologies."

"Thank you." Iza's smile was sad. "Yes, of course."

She'd waited in the cab of the truck as the lavish gift was loaded into the back. If it had been an offering to the goddess, we wouldn't have accepted it. But since it was an apology to Iza—and an enticement for me to keep my mouth shut—we relented. And it was far more than we could have afforded with our meagre budget.

If that was wrong thinking, forgive me. If we've received these resources under false pretences, forgive me. If, however, we are free to use them please make that clear and... thank you.

The girls' conversation drifted back to me.

"Is it always like that? The gifts?"

"Mostly. I know they want to honour the goddess, but favours to your favourite were also common. Not that we got to keep them, mind you." She looked around Tessa to me. "I'm glad this time we can put them to good use. Almost makes it worth the effort to get them." The start of a smile crept across her face like the pre-dawn sun, bless her. "Finally, after all these years, working for the goddess paid off."

"But you don't work for her anymore," Tessa finished for her.

"No." Her smile vanished and her hands stilled. "There is no goddess. It's an economy established by men, trading in pleasure, perpetuating slavery." Not for the first time, I glimpsed passion. Angry, raw, passion.

"I can't wait for you to meet the Light." Tessa said it under her breath, but Iza heard.

"I don't believe in your Light."

"Fair enough." Tessa smiled brightly. "I'll tell Raph that, next time you, or one of yours, need healing."

Iza's eyes narrowed and her head tilted as she appeared to be chewing that over. Apart from Iza's quiet directions as we neared our destination, silence was our comfortable companion. I figured that, like me, the girls were tied up in their own reflections.

I pulled up outside Good to Go and the promise of shopping worked its sparkly miracle. Like glitter-glue all over one of Riah's early pictures. Delight dawned over both girls as their developing bond deepened through their—our—mutual love of the best pastime in the world... apart from sparring.

They were roughly the same age, and whilst they had come from different backgrounds, they had some shared experiences. This could be a mutually beneficial friendship.

Thank you.

Iza and Tessa looked at each other and laughed as with linked arms they dashed across the road. I followed, after locking up the truck and grabbing my—still full—wallet. Iza opened the door with a flourish and we entered, walking straight into a woman wearing full armour: full, shining, radiating, sit me down and shut me up, armour. Its golden glow filled the doorway. Tessa bounced off her and the three of us stared. The woman, with a twinkle in her eye and a warm smile. Tessa, with mouth wide open. And me, beaming.

Again, thank you.

"Welcome." She looked over Tessa and Iza's shoulders and nodded to me. "His peace we offer, our shelter we share, your presence is welcome."

Iza scrunched up her face. "Helen, what on earth are you talking about?"

The woman, Helen, wrapped Iza in an embrace. "Hello, my beautiful girl, so lovely to see you. Come, tell me, what have you been up to and why haven't you been by these past few weeks?" She released Iza. "Is that better? Now introduce me to your friends."

An older man encased in blazing violet ambled out from behind a rack of clothing. He smiled, nodded. "Peace," he said simply, then, "I'll put the kettle on, shall I? Nel, shut the shop love. Time for a break."

Thank you. Thank you... Thank you so very much.

* * *

Tessa and Kerm, Helen's husband, were bent over a blank piece of paper on a design table in the back of the charity shop, which just happened to be Helen and Kerm's house. Tessa was madly sketching a design. "So, I'm thinking something like this." Her hand flew across the page. "I saw something similar when we were working on the latest fashion show in the city. But if we modify this, like that..."

"Yes, excellent idea." Kerm was as enthralled as she was with their project.

Walking through the racks, Tessa had grabbed a few items and started playing with ideas. Kerm had watched her and it escalated from there. He was a "sewist". We weren't to call him a tailor as he wasn't a professional but a hobbyist, he insisted.

"And, if we leave an opening at the back of the cowl their hair could hang free and not get tangled up, and it would allow some ventilation in the heat." Tessa was alive with excitement, her brow intense but her body zinging with energy.

"Brilliant. And what if we made this a cross-over with stretch fabric, but made it a bolero. That way the sleeves and hood could be loose but the bodice…" Kerm's soft voice lilted with life.

"Exactly. And what about…" Tessa threw a few more lines across the page.

"Yes. And…"

The more time they spent together the less words they needed. Helen, Iza and I sat on the back deck, watching them through the large open doors. After they'd finished working on a design, Tessa had been lured in to Kerm's sewing room by the shelves of colours. Each level a carefully arranged assortment of fabrics of various textures, patterns and blends. A huge table took centrestage. Off to the side was a sewing machine, an overlocker, an ironing board with iron set up, a press, and another contraption I could not identify. The fabrics gave off their own distinct smell which blended with the fragrance of the tea we sipped—Tessa's and Kerm's gone cold—basting the midday in a sweet glaze of peace.

I wouldn't have been surprised if I had found Riah hiding behind a curtain somewhere, influencing us with her Badge. I was pulled up short as Kerm and Tessa dashed back into the front shop, then moments later returned with items of clothing. Sounds of cutting, ripping, laughter and enthusiastic muttering bubbled out of the sewing room.

Helen smiled at her older husband through the door. "I suspect they'll be a while; would you like me to show you around our garden?"

"I love your haven, Helen. We've just been to the nursery and have a truck full of supplies. When we've finished here, we're going home to add to the garden at the Factory." It was like the events at the nursery had never happened. Iza had completely moved on. I suspected she was used to it.

"Oh? I have yet to hear all about this." Helen leaned forward and raised her brows at Iza, then looked back to me. Genuine enthusiasm radiated off her.

Tessa leaned out the door and interrupted. "Iza, we need you." Then ducked back inside yelling, "Measurements."

"Um, do you mind if I leave you?" Iza was already standing and following the call.

"Of course, dear, off you go. I believe Kait and I can entertain ourselves for a while. Isn't that right Kait?"

"We'll be fine. Take your time, Iza." Helen and I exchanged a smile. *Again, thank you.*

"So, Kait, you and your family have moved into the Factory. I'd love to hear all about that."

We moved off the deck and into the shades, scents and secrets of Helen's spectacular garden. Huge green elephant-ear leaves were married with palm leaves, spreading jacaranda branches and a sea of ferns of every shape, size and variation of green. The sound of trickling water falling into a pool sounded from somewhere at the back of the garden. And a chorus of quiet chirps, tweets and chortles rose as Helen led me deeper into her magnificent creation. It was like walking through a portal to a cool, secret world. Instantly all worries of the shop, the girls and the Factory fell away. It was so good to talk to a sister and learn how the Light had been working in the lives of this Community before we arrived, and to hear of the work that had already been done.

As always, it was a reminder that we were not alone. The job wasn't ours alone. And the journey wasn't to be travelled alone. Yes, we had the Light. That was no small gift. But to meet a sister and brother in the Light and to hear their story was a treasure beyond words. And so very exciting to have more hands to row the boat.

"We have a cunning plan," I started, then had to chuckle as Helen bobbed her eyebrows and linked her arm through mine.

"Do tell, sister, do tell. I believe things are about to get very exciting. Tell me what we can do to help."

2 0

MARCUS: PARTY PLANNER

"You forget something, Kait?" We couldn't believe our eyes when me beautiful wife came home with a truckload of goods to get our garden from yesterday into next month. But without the girls. They weren't in the cab and, after a quick search, not in the back.

"Great news." Kait looked around at all the faces that had shown up to unload the truck. It was like Lightmas had come early if the buzz was anything to go by. "Iza took us to meet some friends of hers at a charity shop nearby."

"Helen and Kerm?" Indy asked. He had come looking for his partner and started sprouting a crop of ants in his nethers when he found her not returned.

"Yes. Well, after an incident at the nurs—"

"What? What happened? Where is she?" Indy's litany of accusations railroaded me fear. "I trusted you with her welfare!"

"Whoa, settle down and let me finish." She went on to explain that both Iza and Tessa were still with Helen and Kerm and that the four of them were going to come home later this afternoon. Kait had invited this couple to come for dinner.

"Do you think that was wise, Kait?" I mean, I trusted her, but it really wasn't our place to be inviting people into Fort Knox.

She gave me the look. *Would you please give me a bit of credit here? I'm just saying...*

Trust me. "Helen and Kerm know the crew here very well. Wouldn't you agree, Indy?"

The lad climbed back down out of the panic-rafters when he heard the couple's names. "Yeah, sweet-as. I stop in there most days and chat on my way home from getting supplies. Although, with you lot turning up with this bloke"—he slapped Dan's arm—"I've not been over there for weeks, yeh?"

"They said it was more like months."

"Yeah, nah. Kerm's getting on and he has a tendency to exaggerate... and forget. He's pretty old."

Kait argued, "Helen didn't look that old."

"Don't you tell them I said that, eh." Indy shot Kait a desperate look. "They help us out. A lot. Sometimes they come across crates of tinned or packet food near or passed its use-by date and drop it round." He looked me in the eye. "They're good people." The lad was cumquat-cool, his previous angst dissolved. A good sign, first, that he trusted these folk and also that he wasn't worried about Izabaal.

"Yes," Kait continued, "they took us through their house and made us a cup of tea. It's a lovely place"—she eyeballed me and tilted her head—"full of Light." *It's so exciting, they're genuine.*

Are you serious?

Yes. They are going to help us.

I tried to remain casual. "And they're coming to dinner, did you say?"

"They'll bring the girls home when they're finished."

Dan asked. "Finished? What are they doing?"

"An exciting new project. I won't spoil their fun. You'll just have to wait and see."

At that, Kait jumped up in the back of the truck and started delegating the unpacking. It was all hands on deck. Except Amina. She waited off to the side, her sulk a wet blanket on the excitement of the new produce.

She was a tough nut, with her baggage welded away in titanium suitcases. Val had taken the woman on, being around the same age—mid-thirties—and both mustard for a scrap. Val hoped it would help Amina drop her guard a bit with what she was beginning to see. And all she was yet to learn. She had miles to go, but the ice in her veins was starting to thaw.

Like now, for instance. Even though she wasn't actively lending a hand, she wasn't spitting and hissing like an electrified cat either. We weren't the only ones starting to breathe easier. Around us, the chatter was infectious and the mood was charged like a lithium battery. Shauna and Aiko had even convinced Genni to leave her room and join us.

Raph explained to everyone what he and Riah had done and what their plans were for the rest of the garden. I was proud as a speckled pup. The kids held the whole crowd in the palm of their hands, teaching and demonstrating how to plant out the seedlings, using what they had already achieved as an example. Then giving everyone a turn.

The beds were about fifteen metres long. With the gifts from the nursery, about half of the new bed would be filled with seedlings. The rest was planted with seeds, then the whole lot was watered in and covered with mulch.

Just as we were finishing, Tessa, Iza, Helen and Kerm arrived, bringing with them several kilos of flour that was almost out of date. The girls immediately disappeared in a whirlwind, taking Carley, Lily and Amber with them. Then Joko and Hiro kidnapped the older couple, showing them everything we had done in the garden. And Raph's mouth was trying to keep up with his brain and all the ideas for how he could use the flour. "Bread. I can make bread… and muffins… and pikelets. Cake. Pizza!" His feet hardly touched the ground and his muddy hands flew like a conductor as he led us through the office building into the Common Room. The rest of us mice followed after his piper enchantment, salivating at his enthusiasm.

"A party," I declared to the world and his dog. "We need a party, and we should invite Kerm and Helen." Abbot had always said it was important to celebrate our victories well and, as far as I could see, this was the biggest victory we'd had in eons and the first real celebration we'd had since the twins... I had a horrid thought. I whispered in Kait's ear, "What date is it?"

"Um, I think it's..." She paled.

"Did someone call my name?" The older man and his wife walked through the internal door. The woman encased in stunning golden-orange armour and the man in vibrant violet. Helen walked through the group to embrace Vashti. Kerm slapped Indy on the back in greeting. "Close your mouth, lad, you'll end up catching flies."

Indy's eyes were bugging out of his head. More of his long-time friends were wearing Armour. "Why didn't I know about this? How could I not know about this?"

Kerm gave Indy another pat on the back and went to embrace Vashti. "Because the Light, in His wisdom, has decided that now is the time you need to see."

"And Amina? What about her? Does she know?" Indy was grasping at straws as his eyes searched for the Amazon. She shook her head, as gobsmacked as him.

"Welcome to the Factory family. I'm Kerm"—after shaking me hand he held his arm out to indicate the woman—"and this is my wife, Helen. We run a charity shop, Good to Go, around the block, and have been journeying with this lot since day one, when it was just Indy and Iza. Pleased to meet you."

I was surprised by his strong grip. "It's the cat's whiskers to meet you both. I'm Marcus. I believe you met me wife, Kait, earlier?"—they nodded. "This is Raphael, Dan and—"

"Dan? Indy's Dan?" He flicked his eyes to Indy who was nodding. Kerm moved to Dan with his arms wide and embraced the lad in an obviously firm hold. "So glad to meet you. We've heard so much."

From their spot near the sink where they'd been washing their hands from the garden, the twins turned to statues. With their eyes as wide as saucepans they approached the older couple. Raph with his violet armour went straight to Kerm, not as old as Abbot but much older than any of us. He just stood and stared. "Can you heal too?"

Kerm laughed. "No, but I can sew? And I like to cook. Sounds like you do, too."

Raph laughed and sobbed and threw himself into the old man's arms. We really needed to talk to him about social appropriateness. Thankfully, Kerm didn't seem offended, he just chuckled and patted Raph on the back.

Riah edged closer to Helen and, I suspect without realising it, was leaning against the woman's hip as they both watched on. Helen looked down in mild surprise, but then slipped her arm around Riah's shoulders with a warm smile. "Come on love, let's see what we can find." Riah just nodded and climbed onto a chair to help Helen and Vashti unpack food, along with flour from boxes on the centre table.

With everyone as busy as drones, Kait and I took the older man aside and asked for his help to plan our way out of our pickle. With a stealthy word to his wife, the couple were on board. We would postpone tonight's dinner till tomorrow, and they would hold Tessa hostage for the day in his sewing room, whilst we made preparations to celebrate more than just the meeting of new family.

* * *

BY THE TIME the sun had dipped behind the Factory walls the following day, tables in the Common Room were arranged in a square with seats set around the outside. We'd struggled to find enough cutlery and plates, but Helen and Kerm had helped by bringing another box of supplies from their shop. As well as a packet of serviettes and some candles.

We didn't have much, but we made a meal out of what we could find after searching through the cupboards. Helen had added a pumpkin and cauliflower to the mix along with a bag of rice. It was enough. With everyone's help and quick thinking we'd managed to pull a solution, full of fuss and fancy, out of the hat.

Raph had been elbows-deep in the trove of flour all afternoon and now the dining room smelled a treat. Freshly baked bread lay under the sharper spices used to make the main meal. It was great to see him cooking again. But he'd never rustled up grub for this number before. Kait took him through some deep breathing to calm him down. Had to do a bit of it myself, mind you. But the three of us put our heads together and attempted to work out quantities.

We were praising the Light that the peaks of summer had passed and we were in the foothills of autumn. The dining room, instead of being an oven, was cosy and welcoming, brimming with a mishmash of mouth-watering scents. The tinted windows facing the bridge had to be kept closed when the lights were on, but the inner doors were open to encourage a fresh breeze into the kitchen from the warehouses.

Helen and Kerm returned, bringing bottles of juice—a luxury for us all. We'd kicked Raph and Riah out earlier to shower, change and get ready. They now returned with Dan and Indy. "I don't know what they're up to, but the girls will be along soon, yeh?" Indy wheeled over to one of the two spaces left for the wheelchairs. "Smells great. I can't wait to dig into this grub, mate."

In short order, the rest of the crew came in: the older women, Joko and Hiro, then Amber, Carley and Jordan. When Ben had arrived to pick up Aiko and Kazi earlier in the afternoon, they'd all been invited too. We weren't too sure whether Amina would leave us hanging but knew Val would be here shortly. Which only left Lily.

Iza and Tessa waited in the hallway, to make a grand entrance revealing what they had been working on most of yesterday and all of today. Kait and I were official welcomers and thanked everyone for their help this afternoon and for joining us for the meal. Just as we'd finished, Val ducked inside. She walked around the table, laid a kiss on each of the twin's heads then took a seat next to Dan.

"Before we begin tonight, Iza and Tessa have a surprise they'd like to show you." We had a packed room, and all eyes were on me. I was as comfortable as a piglet eating apples at a spit roast, but this wasn't about me. "And for that, we'd like to thank Kerm and Helen, not only for their generosity for providing some... most of the supplies for today, but for helping the girls out. This is just as much Kerm's surprise as it is Tessa's and Iza's. Apparently."

The elderly man nodded his head and smiled in recognition. His hand rested on the table, holding his wife's. Kait and I took our seats next to Val as Tessa walked into the room wearing a new get-up.

"Ladies… and gentlemen. Although this is mainly for the women, but I guess you too. Because, like, whatever helps the girls out, is really helping you too, so—"

"Get on with it, Tessa." The girl was nervous and rambling, but I was hungry.

She glared at me, but then looked out the door and nodded at something Iza must have said. "Yesterday it came to our attention just how hard it is for you guys to go out in public. As soon as people see your scales, it's… well, it's just horrible and not okay. And I wanted to do something to help. Thankfully, the Light led us to Kerm and Helen and we've had a wonderful two days. Kerm was so helpful, and he has great—"

"Tessa." I didn't mean to growl, but Raph, Kait and I hadn't spent the whole day sweating over this meal to have it ruined by her rambling. "Dinner."

"Okay, okay." She straightened herself. "I was recently able to work with some of the fashion houses in the city and saw the most recent styles. Today we modified some of those so you might be more comfortable, better covered up, and able to fight."

All the women in the room began to buzz. Since that was most of the room, it was electric. I'll admit I was a bit excited myself to see what they'd done.

Iza floated into the room. She wore a hood of lightweight fabric that covered her head and the sides of her face in a large cowl. It was attached to a short… very short… jacket with long sleeves that swelled into a bell-shape over her hands. The jacket wrapped around her chest and tied at the back.

She wore it over a T-shirt which was tucked into a skirt with a very wide waist band that was wrapped around her hips much like the jacket. It was made out of the same lightweight, flowing material.

The whole room was murmuring in appreciation. The girls moved to a stool and Tessa helped Iza stand on top. Holding Tessa's outstretched hand Iza lifted her leg out to the side and we saw her skirt was actually pants.

"Oh my clever girl, that is perfect. And beautiful," Kait cooed.

Iza then dropped the cowl to reveal her beaming face. "Tessa and Kerm designed everything and, today, we made four extra sets. One each for Amber, Genni, Carley and Lily. Tomorrow we're going to finish making a set for Aiko, Vashti, Amina, Shauna and Lottie. Tomiko and Kazi too." Her eyes dropped. "That is, if you want one."

The room erupted in cheers as every female swarmed the model and designer—except for Lottie and Val, of course.

"Can't see me getting into one of those contraptions," Lottie wheezed. "Don't think they'd have enough fabric." She then coughed up another fur ball as she laughed.

"You could not get your leg that high Lottie, even with help." Amina's soft voice made me jump.

I tried not to drop me jaw as I noticed a faint red hue coating her body. "Welcome Amina, I didn't see you come in, but we sure are glad you made it." I snapped me eyes to Val, who was grinning like a Cheshire. I looked back to the Amazon again and repeated myself. "Truly, Amina, welcome." I held out me hand.

She looked at it. She didn't move. Her eyes closed and her chest swelled, then sharp as glass she looked at me and took me hand. "Thank you, Marcus." Then dropped it like it was infected.

Right then. I guess it was a step in the right direction. A small step. "Now all we're missing is Lily."

"Did I hear someone say my girl's name?" Everyone froze as a demon walked into the room with his hand loosely laid around the back of Lily's neck.

21

CONTESSA: PARTY GAMES

The demon was disguised as a human. But there was no way he could hide his stink.

And did he come alone?

Of course not.

What was it with parties and attacks? Seriously. I knew we were in for trouble the moment our guards doubled in number and unsheathed their swords.

Goody.

At least I could try out my new outfit.

Izabaal was indignant. "Axel, what are you doing here? Lily, what's going on?"

Val didn't wait for explanations. She was already moving and ordering us about. Or trying to. The enemy had done a good job of dividing us up. Kait, Marcus and Vashti moved to herd some of our group behind them into a corner. Kerm and Helen stepped in front of another lot. Val was cut off from most of us, except Iza, Carley and Jordan whom she shielded. I stood with Dan, Riah and Raph. We did our best to protect the remaining group. Thankfully, the few who had Sight helped their family members follow the unspoken instructions and stand behind those who had thick armour and seriously large swords.

But some who couldn't see were not happy with our "overreacting" to one man interrupting dinner. And I could see their point. If it was just one man, right?

But it wasn't.

It was heaps.

However, at the tone of Val's barked order to move, they all jumped to obey.

"Oh, calm down, Valarie, we're just here for the party." Axel nodded towards Kerm and Helen, then Aiko and her family. "We heard guests were invited and Lily couldn't wait to ask me to join her." He shoved the crying girl. She fell near us, but before I could reach her, three demons appeared and stood around her, blocking me and everyone else from getting to her.

"Lily, come here darling," Aiko called softly.

The girl had landed sprawled on the floor, quietly sobbing, but slowly drew her legs up to her chest and sat motionless, surrounded by her captors whom Aiko couldn't see.

"Now, isn't this... pleasant?"

No one answered.

"Surely you can't be surprised. How long have you been in this game and you didn't expect a visit"—Axel turned his cat eyes to those who were still adjusting to life in armour—"and an introduction to the new targets? And retaliation for trying to take my girl from me."

Even though they couldn't see what was going on, the unseeing stayed silent.

Except Lottie. "What is all of this nonsense about?" She clutched Amber to her side. "He's as pleasant as an enema, but do we really need to go to this much trouble for Axel?"

"He is not alone, Lottie. Hush and stay back." Amina's whisper from behind me was desperate.

I couldn't have agreed more. I willed the woman to stay quiet and not draw attention to herself. Even though that was a bit hard. Because she was rather large.

And loud.

And, I would never say anything, but she did kind of stink of cigarettes.

Once again, I was all kinds of grateful that our guards watched our backs, the roof and the floor. We knew we only had to deal with the demons in the room: the ones who were currently confronting us and blocking our path to Lily. As well as keeping us pinned back in fear for those we protected.

"Girl, you been hit in the head? Of course he's alone. Can't one of you burly young men show him the doo—"

Lottie fell silent as more demons came and started moving around the room. She couldn't see them, but she could see chairs moving and cups being up-ended and juice spilling over the floor.

We all could.

If ruining dinner wasn't enough, they had to ruin our treat too. I hadn't had a chance to drink any of my juice yet. So now I was just plain cranky. And worried for Lily. And the rest of our guests who couldn't defend themselves.

Far. Flaming. Out. Lottie didn't seem to know when enough was enough. Or maybe firing off was her default response when she was scared. Whatever the case, the shock of seeing random items float around the room was not enough to keep the woman down... or quiet. "What the frack are you on about you ridiculous excuse for a man. You're not welcome here, so skitch off and—"

It was the straw that broke Axel's patience. "Oh, for frack's sake. Why do we have to put up with tiresome humans. Just shut up, woman."

AGAIN, Lottie fell silent. This time she could not open her mouth. Her eyes were wide and her nostrils flared as she desperately tried to breathe.

"Calm, Lottie." Val spoke quietly, not taking her eyes off the enemy that stood in front of her but speaking to the panicked woman in her periphery. "Breathe slowly and it will pass."

"Okay, I'm bored now, so let's just get this over with." Axel flicked his hand carelessly. "Time to negotiate."

No one spoke.

"Oh, come on, it's not complicated." He eyeballed Val then the rest of the room. Then spoke as if he was explaining the rules of a simple game to simple people. "What or who will you give me for Lily?" At our silence he continued. "Seriously, I don't care, old or new. Who's it going to be?" He leered at all the ones new to the Sight but stopped at Carley. "Although, that one has spawn. Could be a nuisance"—he tilted his head—"could be interesting."

Again no one spoke.

I didn't think I would ever get used to this. I *hated* it.

I tried very hard to keep one eye on Lily, one eye on Val, and everything leftover in my periphery on Dan and Sariah on my right. And, if I just kind of... turned a bit more to my right... I could just make out Raph. And Amina. And Indy. And oh. My. Word. I hadn't been aware of all the people we were defending.

Right.

Breathe.

Just stay focused. Do your job and grab Lily if you can.

Axel invaded my pep-talk.

"We could flip for them if that's easier." He waited a beat, then added, "Or I could take all the newbs?" He raised his eyebrows hopefully.

I looked at Lily trembling on the floor, and I was transported back to Sodom, watching Ebony lying on the carpet, a plaything, the brunt of sick demonic humour. Then my heart kind of hurt, really bad, as I was reminded of Abbot and his ultimate sacrifice. Then I remembered what my demon had been saying to me. Not the lies—not that there had been many, actually—but the truth in what she had said. That I wasn't as important as, or as important to, any of the people here as they were to me. Maybe I could make a dive for Lily. Cover her with my armour and trust the others might take the rest down?

"Oh, do hurry up. For frack's sake, this is killing me, you lot are so boring." The crowd of demons in the room snickered.

One humanoid leered. "We could make some fun?"

Axel huffed.

I saw Amina scope the room with wild eyes. She looked to her family behind her and Raph in front of her. A boy standing alone, with no sword, positioned between her and Riah, Dan and me. And I had to admit, that scary woman was all kinds of brave. She inhaled deeply and stepped forward to stand alongside Raph, and drew her faint red sword.

Indy rolled forward and joined them.

My poor sweet brother was trying to stay calm. The strain in his voice was obvious when he addressed Amina. "Please step back. We are under attack, and you do not yet have the knowledge of how to handle your weapon properly." He held his own empty hands up, palms out.

Everybody who could fight was confronted by their own mini hell-horde. But the only thing between the three of us and Lily, was three of them. Again, I contemplated a mad dash and cover. But there was not enough room. The moment I made a move, I'd reveal my hand.

"Too late for that, sweetie." My demon had entered the room. She whispered to Axel, then disappeared back to the pit she came from.

My snarl of frustration was met by her bodiless chilling laugh. I felt so useless. We seemed to be at an impasse.

Axel leered at me, then looked back to Val. "I'm going to count to five. Make a choice or I take Lily for good this time."

More cheers and chuckles from the enemy drowned out the cries and sobs from the room.

"One." He bent down and stroked her cheek. Lily forced her head away. All the demons in the room muscled up to make sure their opponents knew they were in for a fight if they tried to make a break to Lily.

"Two." He gripped her chin.

I inhaled and fractionally dropped my weight and came up on my toes.

Please help. Please help. Please help.

"Three." Axel removed a black blade from the back pocket of his jeans.

I felt Dan's muscles whisper in preparation.

"Four." He traced a line down her cheek, the blade leaving a thin trail of blood in its wake. It was enough. It drew the attention of the three now blocking our access to Lily. The whole room was entranced. All eyes were on Axel's blade and the fine hair of red thickening to a cord.

"Fiv—"

As one, the three of us, Dan, Riah and me, lunged, each taking one of those guarding Lily. The room erupted as the others engaged the demons holding them in check.

"Indy, I can't see. What's going on?" Iza yelled.

The ones who were without sight would have been confused by the one-sided battle. Those new to the Light, having a rude introduction to their new reality, were possibly the most confused of all.

I seriously didn't have the headspace to worry about the Unsighted. I was trying to distract Axel to get to Lily.

"Enough!" Axel roared. He stood gripping his hostage by the neck. It was all she could do to keep her toes on the ground. He was strangling her. "I guess that's your choice. Lily is mine." Dan threw a knife at him, but Axel's body had started to dissipate and the blade clattered against the far wall.

Sariah and I both lunged. But in his state of change—halfway between mortal and Other—all we could do was pin him in space. He could not fully dissolve, but he would not die either.

Then a violet streak flashed from behind us and Axel screamed. The shock of Raph's hands forced him to true form and with the twin blades through his body, he howled, cursed and dissolved into a pool of tar. The smell drew tears from my eyes and an involuntary gag reflex. Not my best moment... or look. But even those without the sight noticed the stench.

The unseeing scattered around the room were frozen. They hadn't seen the demons, but they'd seen the furniture fly and there was no denying the smoking, stinking holes in the lino. I guessed they couldn't see that it was over. That the enemy had been defeated and, for now, the threat was gone. But I guess it was pretty obvious when Vashti, Helen, Kait and I ran in to check on Lily.

"What the frack was that." Indy was on edge and wasn't coming down.

I was vaguely aware of Dan talking to him about the whole "Light vs Dark" thing. But I was mainly wanting to make sure Lily was okay. I didn't want to impose. I mean, Vashti and Helen knew her best. And Kait was a nurse. But for the past five weeks I had been trying to help her understand what the Light was all about. And how important it was to be prepared. And right about now, I was feeling like an epic failure. Not only had she not been able to defend herself, she hadn't even picked up that Axel was a demon.

Yay me.

But I was yanked out of my pity-party when Lily threw herself at me. Yep. The girl was giving me the whole octopus treatment. But, not in a bad way. She was, like... really happy. "Thank you so much. Thank you." She then started mumbling about not being a good listener, not giving me a chance, yada, yada, yada. But the main thing was, I don't think she hated me anymore. Oh, and that she was okay. A bit shaken up, but she wasn't really hurt or anything.

After a few moments of utter shock, I hugged her back. "It's okay. I know it's pretty hard to understand if you haven't seen it before. I mean"—I eased her off me a bit so I could breathe—"it's hard to take it seriously if you don't know how... serious it really is."

"It is truth. I saw it and I swear by it." Amina was holding her red sword in her hands, watching it glow and flicker with faint red flame.

Seemed we might have another one who wasn't so hostile towards us anymore.

Well, a girl could hope.

Riah went to Amina and beamed. She unsheathed her own sword and the two compared colours. Amina was speechless.

It was beautiful.

The bonding bit. Not the speechless bit.

Although, that bit didn't hurt.

"Raph, you okay?" Seeing that Lily was unharmed—well, apart from the scratch on her face—Val was checking in on those closest to home.

"Yes, thank you Val. I did not have to fight anyone today." He stood tall and called out over the growing confusion and relief in the corner. "Everyone here is okay, no one got past. But if anyone else is in need of healing, I am available."

Light and love burned from Val's eyes. I recognised it as the fire that was mirrored in mine. I could not possibly love that boy any more. He already swelled my heart to bursting.

Val then ran a critical eye over all those who had engaged in the battle and made her own assessment, as well as making each one of us verbally check in. Once she'd been given the all-clear by everyone, obviously it was time to move on. "Right, I believe we have a party to see to. Raph?" Val flicked her eyes to Lily, who was still kind of clinging to my side. Why me, I still wasn't sure, but I wasn't in a hurry to bat her away. I mean, she wasn't arguing with me or scaring me... in a bad way, so... I kind of hung on whilst Val encouraged everyone out of the post-battle crazy.

"Out of the way. Let me look at her." Lottie had rediscovered her bossiness... and her voice... and finally released Amber, leaving the poor girl to breathe again, and wheezed her way over to us. She was trying to get in to see her girl, Lily. But had to wait till Raph had finished his once-over. Lottie froze when she saw the effect of Raph laying his palm on Lily's cheek. She was going to have a scar, but it was clean, closed and well on the way to healed.

"She seems to be fine inside. I cannot feel anything wrong. I am giving her some warmth. But it might be helpful if Riah could help too?" Raph looked to Val who nodded.

Riah came over and laid her hands on Lily. From experience I knew that, right now, Lily was getting the full R and R treatment: comfort, pain relief and the total warm-fuzzy package. She'd be right in no time. And on cue, Lily released a gentle purr.

"Right, then. Well... right." For the second time this evening—and possibly her life—Lottie was lost for words.

"Perhaps you could help her find a seat and keep an eye on her?" Val offered Lottie a purpose and the woman grabbed it with both hands.

"Right you are. Come on my girl. Let's get y'all sorted." The old woman took Lily and escorted her to a chair, where she stayed well and truly pinned for the rest of the evening.

Val got back to her happy place, issuing orders to put the room right and clean up the mess. "But first, Tessa, could you grab some spare blankets, please? Kerm, Helen, Vashti?" I noticed she actually dropped the barky-order-voice and made an effort to sound like she was asking. When she had their attention she continued, "Would you mind checking in with the ladies and kids and see how everyone is travelling?"

I took Amber's hand and smiled at her. "Come on, let's see what we can do about dinner." The girl was shell-shocked but came with me without argument. Maybe she was just keen to get out of reach of Lottie's claws. But since Lily was in Lottie's clutches, I think Amber was safe… for a while. I left her with Kait and Raph, sorting dinner, whilst I popped outside to follow Val's request.

Everyone who had a job was moving, but the others were like startled sheep and wouldn't leave the corners. But we knew we were safe. The extra guards had left. Only ours remained.

And my demon.

22

CONTESSA: DEMON DEMISE

She met me in the corridor, on my way to the storeroom to get blankets.

"Hey sweetie, nice party."

"What do you want now? Shouldn't you have taken off with the rest of your mob?"

She eyed my new outfit. "Is that any way to greet a friend? I just came to wish you happy birthday and compliment you on your new... look. It really suits you." Her sneer and exaggeratedly-opened eyes kind of dumped a bucket of sarcasm on her compliment. "But you have to admit, it sits better on someone who's got something to put in it." She stripped my body with her eyes and gave me her sad smile. "Keep trying, sweetie, one day you'll—"

A gasp exploded from my lungs as her head partly left her body.

She dropped to her knees.

And crumbled to the floor.

"Twik," was all Dan said as he kicked at her body, watching it return to its natural form before it started dissolving. The explosion of sulphur in the enclosed room almost made me vomit... again. "You okay?"

I couldn't speak.

He killed her.

I mean, I could see that it wasn't a "she", it was an... "it". But I'd been so used to her presence, I had forgotten.

"Come on. You're needed." He threw an arm around my shoulders, placed the blankets I'd been sent to retrieve into my arms, then drew me in close.

I won't lie, I nestled.

It felt good.

He felt good.

But I felt a bit stupid in the clothes designed for the others. She'd been right. They didn't suit me and my stick-like figure. And right now, I felt like a little girl playing dress-ups in a woman's clothes. So, I nestled into Dan's side and hid behind the blankets clutched to my chest.

Also, I felt a bit stupid I hadn't done that myself—slayed my demon.

I didn't even know I could do that.

SHE HADN'T HAD her sword drawn. So I didn't think I'd been in mortal danger. I didn't even know I could do that. Not knowing made me feel even more stupid. And even if I had known, could I have just done it? Out of the blue?

I mean, in a fight, when I was angry, I could do almost anything. But cold-blooded?

I'd had to be saved.

Again.

I FELT about as useless as... my stupid outfit. I groaned.

"If it makes you feel better, I did exactly the same thing." Dan's voice rumbled next to my cheek. "But Val explained to me where I'd gone wrong."

I laughed... kind of. "She's good like that."

He huffed. "Yeah. But she told me: first, I'd not spoken, then spoken, then not spoken."

"What?"

"Yeah, classic Val. First, I'd *not* told people I was being tormented. Then I'd fallen into the trap of talking *with* my demon. And finally, I'd *not* called on the Light. They can't stand Him. If you speak to Him, or recall passages of *The Way*, they skitch off."

"Huh," was all I could say. I'd had no idea. Again, I felt like a fool. I'd been in the Light longer than Dan, but he knew more, and he'd come to my rescue.

"Yeah, I felt like such a fool, but I hadn't told anyone... well..."

Oh. My. Word.

He had told someone.

He'd told me and I hadn't believed him.

"Dan, I'm so sorry."

"All good, Tessa. Glad I could understand what was going on and lend you a hand." His arm came tighter around my shoulders, and he turned me to return to the Common Room.

Seriously, if I could just get through the rest of the night under the radar, everything would be fine. Or, even better, if I could sneak away and change into something more suitable—I mean, more suited to me —I would feel better able to cope.

By the time we made it back, everyone was seated around the table and conversation was slowly simmering up through the tension. In time, dinner was served and cleared. There was enough for everyone and some left over as well. Raph exploded with pride as the room congratulated him, Kait and Marcus for their efforts.

"Why do they always pick birthday parties?" Marcus was grumbling again.

Had he been hit in the head? "What do you mean? This is a thank-you and celebration party."

We finished clearing the table and Kait wrapped her arm around my shoulder. "Actually, Tessa, it's a birthday party." She led me back to the crowd seated around the tables.

I looked around at everyone. But Raph bursting at the seams was a dead giveaway. "What?"

Kait sat me down and Raph and Riah raced off but returned just as quickly carrying a cake. It was only the size of a dinner plate, but it was coated in pale yellow icing and the words "Happy Birthday to our Beautiful Tessa" were written in cursive script.

"Oh," was all I could say before the tears started flowing.

"Happy birthday, Tessa." Raph jiggled and wrapped his arms around me. Then Riah eased him out of the way so she too could give me a hug.

"Twenty-four today, darling girl. We were not going to let that go uncelebrated." Kait dropped a kiss on my cheek.

Raph and Riah then returned carrying two cakes each and delivered them around the tables so everyone could share.

"We got you something," Raph's voice squeaked. He coughed then repeated himself. "Show her, Dan."

"Um, I think Marcus and Kait are going first." Dan's face was red and I was confused.

Then Marcus presented me with a box roughly the size of a microwave with an envelope attached. "This is from Val, Kait and me." First, I was blown away that they had remembered my birthday. Because to be perfectly honest, I hadn't. I'd been so swept up by everything else I didn't even know what day it was, let alone what date.

I broke into the box and unearthed an old sewing machine. And that was about the end of me. Not only had they thought of me, they had, in a very short amount of time, seen what making these clothes had meant. A way to help others. To make a difference. What had started as a small leak of tears turned into a torrent. I could barely read the card which turned out to be a gift voucher of ten sewing lessons from Kerm.

Speech was well and truly gone.

I suspected breathing might be going next.

Helen rose and placed an oblong package in front of me wrapped in beautiful handmade paper. Very carefully I peeled back the tape and was rendered completely mindless as I gazed upon the most beautiful bolt of golden fabric.

It was at this point I may have started to sob. However, I did manage a "thank you," squeaky and breathless as it may have been.

Dan handed me a tea towel. I tried to smile my thanks, but I couldn't see him clearly through my blurry eyes. But I turned into him all the same and wiped my face as he wrapped his arms around my shoulders, allowing me the privacy to try to clean up. When I turned back, Raph and Riah placed a flat, rectangular, seriously-badly-wrapped package in front of me. I threw my arms around them and squeezed.

Okay, so maybe I clung a bit too.

I had been so unsure of where I stood with my family. Things were definitely improving, but to have them make this effort, and think of me, and make me feel special in front of everyone, and to actually have thought of presents... was a little bit overwhelming and an incredible relief. Maybe things would be... could be... made right. Maybe we could go back to the way we were.

By this stage, the twins were squirming and Raph insisted that I open their gift. Again, with great care—which drew an eye roll from Riah—I carefully peeled back the beautiful paper. Inside, old pallet-plank cut offs, sanded silky smooth, framed a lifelike hand-drawn picture of our family, including Abbot... and me.

"Riah drew the picture, Dan and I made the frame, and Dan helped us put it all together and wrapped it. In paper he bought. With money. From a shop. A real shop that sells paper."

It was then that I totally lost it.

I could not speak, breathe, or see a bleeding thing.

Arms pulled me to standing and wrapped around me. A muscular wall of eucalyptus and coffee.

He turned me away from the group and gave me a fresh tea towel so I could wipe my face again. "Do you need a bath towel, or would you prefer my shirt?"

I hit him. Although, he did laugh when I took him up on his offer and wiped my face on his shirt.

"I've got you, Contessa." He kissed the top of my head. "Happy birthday… beautiful."

I snorted.

"That's my girl."

I hit him again.

He laughed harder.

And, just maybe, his was the best birthday present of the lot.

Thank you.

23

RAPHAEL: LOVING THE RAIN

Thank you for the rain.

I loved our garden, and I loved our new home. And I especially loved that we got to do school with Kait again... when she was available. Which was not so much. But at least we did not have to go to the Community's school. And today I was very grateful for the rain. We now had six garden beds planted and four were at the stage where they were producing food. It had been very rewarding to not only teach everyone how to grow the food, but also to show them how to make meals using what we had grown. Marcus and Dan had finished building the chicken coop and we now had chickens living with us. A couple had started laying and I was sure it would not be long before we were getting ten eggs a day.

On days like this, it was hard work in the kitchen. We had our small oven going from morning to night. Not only were Aiko, Vashti, Shauna and I preparing meals for everyone, we were baking things to freeze and send with Tessa to the markets. Winter was knocking at the door, so we were doing our best to preserve the last of autumn's stock. With all the activity, the kitchen was a big sweaty oven. But I was grateful it acted like a funnel, drawing in the frigid, damp air from Warehouse One which swirled in together to make a lovely warm hug.

However, as much as I liked working with Aiko and Vashti, I could not stay here because there was still too much to do today. And I was extra glad we would not have to water tonight. Living next to the canal had been the answer to how to provide water for our gardens. Each night, Joko, Hiro, Amber, Riah and I went out with buckets to collect water for our plants. And now chickens. But the rain meant we got a night off. It also meant, with all the noise on the roof, we could play a bit louder in Warehouse One without alerting our neighbours.

The murmur of the ladies working behind me, clearing lunch and drying dishes, faded as my heartbeat hardened and the red mist swirled at the borders of my mind. I breathed slowly and deeply, trying to keep it at bay whilst I struggled with how I could get everything done.

Lately, it had been hard for me to get away to play with my new friends, even though today was the perfect opportunity. Riah had been spending more time with Lily, Carley and Amber. I was happy she had found people who understood what it was like for her. The ladies had quickly built a connection that went beyond needing her to speak. So I was happy to pick up the slack of her not doing her chores.

But it meant I had to do her work in the garden as well as helping the others learn the job. Then I had to be in the kitchen to help Vashti and Aiko learn how to cook the food we grew. But because Riah's other job was helping Tessa with the laundry, and Tessa was busy working on a sewing project with Iza, and also teaching Lily, Carley and Amber about the Light, and training the ladies in combat, I was also doing the laundry for my family. And today I didn't know how I would get it dry.

At least, lately, we had not been having as much school. But I felt it was very important that my friends knew how to read. So, after lunch I had been helping them, just a little bit, to learn their letters. Iza had given us some books that were easy to read, and Kazi, Joko and Hiro were very keen to learn. I found that I really enjoyed teaching them and watching them improve. It was not real school. But until Kait had more time, it was something.

Kait would want to know if I needed help, but it was hard to find her. And when I did, she was always busy caring for Dawn, because Genni, Dawn's mother, had been very sad when we arrived and not able to care for herself. Or Dawn. I think it would be very hard to be so young and be a mother too. She was only sixteen. That was five years older than me. I could not think of how hard that would be. I knew it was not good to be proud, but bubbles of pride-joy frothed inside me when I saw Genni pottering in the garden. Over the past few months, I had become used to and enjoyed her quiet company as she spent time walking through the garden beds, talking to the plants with her fingers.

I was grateful we had finished building the chicken pen. But now I was also responsible to make sure people knew how to care for our pets and ensure they got fed, were watered and had clean beds. Riah should be doing this; she had always been the one who took care of the chickens. But even this seemed too much for her lately.

Marcus and Dan could not take care of them because they were teaching Indy about the Light and developing strategies for sword fighting from his chair. They were also spending a bit of time away from the Factory with Kazi's dad, Ben. Plus, Dan went into the city each day to earn money for us to buy precious supplies, materials for the gardens and fabrics for clothing. He was also gifted with food treats from Serendipity for all of us.

And I was confident that if I were to ask Val for help, she would ask me why I needed it. This then would point the finger back at Riah. And anyway, Val was working with Amina, Shauna, Aiko and Lottie, teaching them about the Light. As well as the rest of us. She also took Riah with her most mornings after sets into the city with Dan to Serendipity. Riah either played her guitar or drew on specially painted walls inside the cafe and outside on the footpath whilst Dan played. They were both very popular. I sometimes wondered if art was a Badge. I would have to ask Val about it. But later, when I had more time.

We were like a flooded river. Everyone running and overflowing and barely contained between the banks. It was good to be using our Badges to help pull the oars in a family that was happy to have us. It was so different to the Community. So, despite being so busy, I was very happy. Except I could not think of a way to dry our clothes today after I had finished in the kitchen. Even though Tessa was busy with Iza making us all more clothes, there were still not enough that we could go without washing.

"I said, can I help with that?"

I almost dropped the dish I was drying with fright. The crash of the rain on the warehouse roof was very loud, even in the insulated kitchen. There would have been no way I could have heard her wheels approaching. But I had been buried so deep in my problem-solving and stemming the red tide, I had not even heard Kazi's greetings and offer of help the first time.

Out of everyone here, she was the most helpful of all… and she did not even live here. I felt a bit guilty in accepting because, like I said, she was a guest.

"Are you ignoring me again?"

I spluttered. "I never ignore you. In fact, I was just thinking how much I appreciate you."

"You were?" Kazi pulled a spare tea towel off the bench and started drying dishes.

"Yes. You are the only one who offers to help and…" I took the time to look her in the eye. It felt uncomfortable, but Abbot had always said, if you have something important to say, take the time to say it properly. "…you have become a good friend. Thank you, Kazi."

Her skin—a similar tone to mine—turned a little bit pink. She dropped her eyes and whispered her thanks.

"Now, do you know anything about drying clothes in wet weather?"

24

CONTESSA: COMING UP DAISIES

"**A**gain." The girls looked all kinds of gorgeous in their new wrap pants and gleaming armour. "One, two, one." They responded, throwing their fists out in the combination. "One, one, two." I instructed, they followed. "One, one, two, one." And on.

Over the previous months, following the party, each of the women had made the choice to come to the Light. Lily had shared her story and it seemed to make it all even more real for them.

Except for Iza.

Whilst she had finally accepted our invitation to join us for sets, she refused to have anything to do with training and *The Way*. But apart from that, life had really taken shape. We had found our groove to become a well-oiled machine. Vashti, Aiko and Shauna worked with Raph in the kitchen. Amber, Lily, Amina and sometimes Genni worked with Riah in the garden. And Carley, Iza and I worked in sewing and designing clothes for everyone.

Helen and Kerm were selling our clothes in their shop. I was So. Ridiculously. Excited. Helen and I had started taking them, and some of the things Raph was making, to the Canal Markets that met every month at the other end of the bikeway running alongside the Factory. The clothes were now raising enough money of their own to pay for new fabric and turn a small profit. I could not believe it. I was making money doing what I absolutely loved.

Thank you!

Life was really good. There was so much activity around the gardens it had the whole Factory buzzing. I didn't have much to do with it but was aware of a change of veggies being served at dinner and noted there were interesting creations sitting over some of the garden beds.

Not only had the guys built a moveable chicken pen, but there was now a moveable greenhouse... or hot house... or some kind of house that meant they could grow things like tomatoes all year. Gardening was not my thing. Seriously. But eating good food was. So, whatever they were doing I was happy for them.

There were now eight veggie beds up and functioning—with chickens—producing enough food to feed not only ourselves but Helen and Kerm too, as well as offering stock to Ben for his cafe. In fact, we were able to use our produce to barter for goods from other shops. We'd even started thinking of adding the excess produce to our market stall.

Since a significant debacle with overwatering the garden, everyone had been shuffled into teams. And the twenty-two of us—not that Dawn ate much—were slowly becoming self-sufficient. At one point, Riah had mentioned getting a goat. But thankfully that was put down before it got going. The idea. Not the goat. But on the whole, life was good. There were still hiccups along the way, but men had stopped coming round since Axel had been dealt with. And Lily had walked away from the old way of life. Now there was something else she could do to help. That she was interested in.

Marcus maintained training all of our family, Indy and the young boys. Kait, Val and I trained the eleven women. And it was seriously cool to see the twins hanging out with kids their own age. And finding interests separate from each other. It was the first time they'd been able to be... normal... ish. And both Dan and Indy continued to hang out with Marcus for "Secret Men's Business". Much like Iza and I were sitting under the shelter of Kait's experience.

But for now, the priority was the training. We knew that with so many coming to the Light we had to expect a major attack. So every day we trained, in both warfare and *The Way*. It was great to be fit again and back into the old routines. I had missed it all when I was working for the Community. I felt so much more... strong? Like, inside. In my head. Funny how getting back into the Light, physical fitness and getting better at my fighting made me feel better able to cope with other stuff. I just felt more... able? Confident? Anyway, Kait had told us that, just like in Sodom when Dan came to the Light, we had a time of grace; a window of protection that wouldn't stay open for too long.

"Damn it." Indy had thrown himself out of his chair... again. He was so frustrated fighting with his sword in the chair. And to be honest, none of us, not even Marcus, could give him tips. It was so different: different techniques, moves and balance.

"Leave me alone."

Dan dropped his hand as his offer of help was thrown back at him. "Come on, man, let me help you."

"No. I can do it myself."

"At least give me your sword so you can get up, you stubborn kret."

The abusive language seemed to do the trick. Indy handed his sword over, straightened his chair and hauled himself back in.

Everyone was busy looking elsewhere, trying not to stare and make things worse. Because we could all see, the more time Indy spent in the Light, the further he and Iza drifted apart. She felt he was choosing his old friends over his new family... and her.

And the more time Indy spent training... and flailing in his chair, the more frustrated he became. Obviously, we hadn't been here in the early days of his transition into the chair. It seemed there wasn't much he hadn't mastered. So much so, no one even noticed he wasn't just like the rest of us. That he didn't have legs. He was just... Indy. But now, the growing frustration and outbursts of anger had the kids who loved him beginning to keep their distance. This, of course, only made him angrier and more out-burst-ier. Which, in turn, drove the wedge between him and Iza even deeper.

As far as she could see from watching him, there was nothing inviting about the Light. At all. Which really wasn't fair. She had to acknowledge the change in the others. Amina was more approachable… well, she didn't spit anymore. And even Lottie was nicer. But then, Iza had never seen them the way most people saw them.

Please help Indy. I don't know what the problem is, I don't know what the answer is, but you do. I know it's killing Dan as well, as he watches on. Just… please help.

I kind of felt a bit guilty. Since Indy was spending less time with Iza, she had more free time for me. Most days, after training and chores, we spent hanging out at Kerm's or in our sewing room we'd set up in one of the spaces in Warehouse Two, near the veggie garden.

I watched Raph lead Val away and have a quiet word with her. Val listened and after a while nodded her head. Raph beamed and jiggled, shut his eyes and breathed deeply. Then made his way back across the open space to where Indy and Dan were having a drinks break. Everyone else had slid a safe distance away from Indy's anger.

"Indy?"

"Yeah mate?" It was more of a growl, but it sounded like he was making an effort to be polite at least.

"I was wondering if you would mind if I helped you?"

Indy's shoulders dropped and a smile ghosted his lips. "Thanks mate, I really appreciate that, but I'm good now, thanks."

"No. I mean… help you. With your legs."

"How do you mean?" Not only was Indy confused, everyone else standing in the vicinity was just as perplexed.

"Your legs. I would like to help you. But I am not supposed to help people without asking."

Oh my gosh.

My heart stopped.

Dan's eyes flew up and met mine. He then placed his hand on Raph's shoulder. "Whoa, mate."

"What does he mean?" Indy looked from Raph to Dan then back to Raph. "How can you help me, mate?" His question was gentle and genuinely confused.

Oh. My. Word. Is this the right thing? Oh. dear.

"Ummm, Raph. Is that such a good idea?" Dan asked the question that was invading my brain like a million wasp stings.

"What does he mean?" Indy asked Dan again.

But Raph answered, "I would like to help fix your legs. But I have to ask first."

And there it was.

We couldn't hide that.

Or explain it.

Or take it back.

"Pardon?" Indy's scarred face screwed up.

The crowd that had retreated at the angry awkwardness edged their way back like little kids to sticky bun.

"If it is alright with you, I was wondering if I may help you. I am not one hundred percent sure it will work." Raph's voice faded as his eyes drifted toward the ceiling and he tilted his head. Then he nodded and turned back to Indy. "When we first came to Laodicea, I wasn't sure how strong my new Badge was, but I was able to help Amber." He smiled at her, standing with a small gathering behind Indy's shoulder. "Then, when we came here, I was able to help Izabaal." He became very serious and looked Indy in the eye. "The same pressure is pulsing in my heart, pushing me to ask if I may help. But you must understand, if it works, it is not me healing, it is the Light. I only help. You *must* understand."

Silently, with his mouth open, Indy nodded his head.

"I have been speaking to the Light about you for seven months—since that first night. You see, I saw you standing next to Izabaal in my mind when I healed her." He beamed at Iza who had been easing her way over.

She now stood at Indy's side and laid her hand on his shoulder. Tears were brimming and threatening to spill. Her other hand shook as it covered her mouth.

"So today, when I saw you having a very hard time at practise, I asked the Light again if I could help you, and He said yes." Raph's smile was like a halogen lamp. "I checked with Val and she reminded me I had to ask you first." Again, he was serious. "Do you understand?"

Indy again nodded dumbly. Iza's eyes now flowed, and she dropped to her knees beside Indy's chair and clung to his hand.

No one moved.

Except me.

I snuck around and ducked under Dan's arm.

No one said a word.

Indy tried to speak; nothing came out. He coughed and tried again. "So, you are offering to heal—"

"Help. I don't heal, the Light does that. I just help," Raph corrected.

"You're offering to help me, and you just need me to say... yes?"

"Yes."

Indy looked to Iza, both of them crying now.

She nodded.

"But what if—"

Indy's words were cut off when Iza gently placed her fingers over his lips. "You have to give it a go." She dropped her hand and smiled at Raph through trembling mouth and watering eyes.

Indy coughed. "Yes please, Raph, I'd like it very much if you could try to hea... help me."

Again, the sun came out as Raph smiled. He stepped forward and kneeled in front of Indy and laid his arms along the tops of Indy's thighs. Riah pushed through the surrounding group and stood at her twin's side. She laid one hand on Indy's shoulder and the other on her brother's. Riah nodded to Raph, who shut his eyes and began.

Everyone inhaled and froze.

No one said a word.

The weak winter sun warmed the tin roof as it creaked in protest. Birds called. Cars passed on the street outside. How could the world be so ordinary when something so amazing... life changing... extraordinary was happening.

It was wrong.

But Raph was right.

He could help.

And he was.

We could see the movement under the pants covering Indy's legs. His spine straightened.

Raph's face scrunched in concentration, his efforts forcing a sheen to cover his skin. The fire from his violet armour sparked and bled into Indy's blue. Joy, shock, amazement and celebration burst from Indy in a roar.

Raph scooted back and stood. He smiled weakly as Riah threw her arms around him and he leaned into her. Dan and I rushed forward in case Raph was going to collapse. I got down on my knees next to him. "You okay little man?"

He nodded, wiped his forehead with his sleeve then looked at Indy with a tired smile. "How do you feel?"

Indy was gasping, his knuckles white from gripping the arms of his chair. He looked at Iza.

Her eyes were wide and dry. The question on her face was silently being screamed around the warehouse. "Well?"

Cautiously, Indy lifted one leg from the footrest and placed it on the ground.

Iza's gasp was echoed by everyone in the room. Almost everyone. I wasn't really shocked at all. I had come to believe my little brother could do anything through the Light.

Iza stood and took hold of the handles of the chair, so that when Indy tried to stand he wouldn't tip.

With both feet firmly on the ground, Indy pushed his body up and stood.

Yep, you heard me.

Stood.

Then fell flat on his face.

The world stopped spinning and time paused as we waited to see what would happen.

Indy rolled onto his back and howled with laughter then looked to Dan who was frozen... into an ice statue... just like I was. "Don't just stand there gawping, bro, help me up."

Springing into action, Dan raced over and helped Indy get back up on his feet.

Time hiccupped again.

Indy got his balance, then took a step. Then another. And another. He wobbled a bit at first, but it wasn't long before he found his balance. He began to jog around the group who gasped and cried and hugged each other. But soon everything was drowned out by Indy's howls of victory and laughter.

He sped in, captured Iza in a hold, swung her around and kissed her. She wrapped herself around him and kissed him back... soundly.

Then they were both on the ground.

Indy's legs had given out under them both.

They made an effort to untangle themselves... which was kind of impossible with Indy's laughter and Iza's blinding tears. Eventually with everyone's help—which was actually more hindrance—they both made it back to standing, and hugging... everyone.

Every.

One.

No one missed out on being engulfed in an embrace by... everyone.

But Indy didn't try to pick Iza up again. Which was probably for the best.

He was so tall. He stood a head taller than Iza. I couldn't take my eyes off him.

So strong, whole and tall.

Did I mention he was tall?

And broad.

I hadn't noticed how broad his shoulders were when I looked down at him in his chair.

And now I looked up at him, he was huge.

Thanks that he's on our team.

I returned to Dan's side to watch Indy take off and was soon swallowed in a hug as my friend released his own emotion at seeing his brother restored to wholeness.

Energy was bursting out of Indy as fire danced along his armour. He turned to wink at Dan, who nodded in return, kissed the top of my head and took off. Dan chased Indy as he disappeared out onto the street like a bolt of lightning... wobbly lightning, who tripped and clung to the front gate as he gathered his feet back under him before launching out onto the street.

25

MARCUS: HARD PILL TO SWALLOW

Val slapped the young bull on the cheek. She could have put him on his butt. She could have broken his jaw. But instead, she danced out of his reach as Indy stumbled past her, and patted his face. Firmly. Again.

"You are not ready to challenge me. Go back to training with Marcus or Dan. Kait would be good for you to work with too."

The lad spluttered and spat. He turned around and came at her again. His rage and exhaustion rendered him dumb as bait and blind as a bat. He came back, swinging wild and wide. Val didn't even bother to move her feet; she merely swayed to the side and slapped him on the rear as his momentum kept him turning as he passed her.

He growled.

Val's face became a mask, all congeniality gone. "I mean it, Indy. Back off and cool down."

This was going to hurt. But the boy put his brain on hold and led with rage. What had started out as a cocky challenge ended up turning sour. He couldn't see that there was a dead cat on the line, and he was about to join it. He was dumb enough to come at her again. But it would be the last thing he did... well, for the rest of the day.

In the blink of an eye, she had him flat out. Her knee in his diaphragm and a blade—very real and very Seen—to his throat. "I told you, enough."

An eel out of water, he was gasping and gulping for air.

"You will find that humility is like a wonderful dessert." Her tone had turned conversational, despite Indy's grand distress. "It's best served a little each day. If you have it all at once it will make you sick. Sick and sorry." A flick of her wrist and the blade had disappeared back into thin air. She eased off his chest, rolled back to standing and held out her hand.

He did think about it. But in the end, he accepted. She held fast and pulled him close. "Time for you to pull your head in, get back in the boat and grow up." She said it quiet enough that it didn't carry to the crowd that had gathered around the edges.

She walked off. Training was done for today.

"Come on, lad." I handed Indy a towel and pointed to the corridor leading to the Common Room. "Shower, then debrief in five minutes. Dan, I expect you there as well."

"Why? What did I do?" He was like a five-year-old.

"Nothing... yet. But if you don't show up in five minutes, we'll reassess the situation."

They headed off together, grumbling about how tough life was, like a couple of gossipy old goats. But it was me intention. At least this way, Indy had an ally.

Dan placed a hot cup of coffee on the table in front of his brother as he joined us in the Common Room.

"Twik," Indy grumbled under his breath.

Dan froze, his hand still grasping the mug. "You better be talking about me, bro. Because if you're referring to Val, things are going to get ugly."

The two boys glared at each other like young bullocks facing off in a paddock.

"Settle." *Give me strength and wisdom here.* "You know Kait said trouble is coming?" Indy flashed his eyes to me. "And don't even think of saying anything about me Kait... boy." I needed to get this back on track and not get distracted. I inhaled something kin to calm and continued. "It's pretty obvious you're struggling, lad. We're trying to help you to make sure you're safe when the attack comes."

He didn't say a word. He glared daggers at me for a moment, then unbridled the raging beast in his chest with a sigh. He seemed to find something intriguing at the bottom of his cup of coffee. His fingers absently brushing over the scabs that had taken up permanent residence on his elbows from all the random falls. His armour was weaker, his discipline had evaporated, and his relationships had gone to pot. All since getting his legs back.

"Time to make some choices, lad. Are you in the Light or not? Currently, it looks like you've come to the party for the presents and now you got what you want, you've scarpered."

His head dropped lower.

Dan slammed his own coffee on the table, black gold spilling out unnoticed. "Oh, for frack's sake. Toughen up princess. You think you're the only one who's hurting, confused, or been fracked by life?" I wasn't expecting Dan's tirade, but it looked like he had a boil that needed lancing, so I let the pus flow.

"Newsflash, Indy. Life. Sucks." Dan ran his hands through his sweaty hair. "You think you're the only one who had skrat happen? Look around. Everyone here has had skrat happen. Then look closer. Cause you're the only kret who's had things fixed."

Me boy was yelling now, but did a good job of reigning it in. "Poor Indy, he lost his friends and family. Poor Indy, his dad was killed in front of him. Poor Indy lost his legs. Poor Indy found a kick-butt amazing girl to stand by him. Poor Indy has a roof over his head and a safe place to live. Poor Indy gets just what he needs from frack knows where every single day of his frackingly pathetic life. And now poor fracking Indy got his legs back and he wants to run away." Dan stepped away—he'd been inching closer to a subdued Indigo and had ended up standing over him. Rage was boiling out of his eyeballs and venom was spewing from his mouth. The lad had a full head of steam and there was no stopping him now.

"Well, you know what? I liked you a hell of a lot better without them. Cause somehow, in the process of growing legs, you lost your balls. Toughen the frack up. Stop feeling so fracking sorry for your-self. When you gonna realise none of this is about you? Here's another newsflash: You. Indigo. Are not the centre of the fracking universe.

"Are you in or out? Make up your mind. If you're in, get over your-self and get on board. If you're out, get out. Skitch off. This sitting-in-the-middle is a waste of bleeding time. And a burden to everyone else. Hell, even Hiro has stronger armour than you."

Indy refused to lift his head. He gave nothing back to Dan to lock onto. Didn't matter how much me lad raved, Indy wouldn't block. It was like shadow boxing. "Damn you, Indy. Damn you to hell."

"Careful, Dan. Them words is asking for trouble. You apologise now and make amends." I doubted he realised he'd crossed the line, but it was past time to reel this in.

He shot fire at me, then nodded. "Yeah. You're right." He was silent for a moment, then continued. "I'm glad you're in the Light. I'm glad you've got your legs back. When you're ready to man-up, come see me." He nodded to me, but without another word he left the room.

I let the temperature cool and the words hit home. Silence was a welcome guest and the three of us kept each other company as I enjoyed me coffee. Whilst Indy did his best to drown in his.

RAPHAEL: THE WHEELS FALL OFF

"What are you doing Riah?"

My sister turned to me and glared.

I had just come from the kitchen and the garden, looking for her. I knew Val would be leaving soon on her daily outing and Riah had not done her jobs. Again. I knew I was covering for her. A lot. But there were still some things I really needed her to do. I found her on the verandah under the trees with Lily and Amber. My sister was curled up in a chair wrapped up in an old padded quilt cover, her attention glued to her new friends as Lily was telling them some story.

"You haven't done any of your chores… again. And I have been held up. I cannot do everything Ri."

She just raised her shoulder and flicked her chin.

Oh dear. Oh dear. Oh… dear.

No sooner had I thought it than I saw it. Val poked her head out of Warehouse One and scanned the yard. Her face was set in fury and her eyes were narrowed to lasers.

Oh dear.

Her scan of the yard stopped on me, and at my gasp her eyes became dangerous slits.

Taking the long way round, making sure to stay under the cover of the trees, she marched to the cabins. The air rippled in her wake. Thankfully Marcus had been alerted and dashed out behind her.

"Are you ready to go, Sariah?" Val wasn't yelly. Val didn't get yelly, except in battle when we needed to hear her orders. Right now, Val was the opposite. And very, very scary.

Riah lifted her chin and gave a half-shrug.

Oh dear.

Marcus arrived on Val's heels and scanned the scene. I saw a slight widening of his eyes before he shook it off. "So, hey everyone. How's it hanging?"

Val's voice was ice. "Sariah was just about to explain why none of her chores are done... again."

Oh dear.

I had warned my sister. I had been trying to cover for her. But I thought I was keeping it a secret so she would not get in trouble.

"And she was also going to explain why it's okay for her to allow others to do her work for her." Val turned her scary eyes to me and quirked an eyebrow.

Oh dear.

"Come on now, Val. Don't be too harsh on her. She's just trying to find her place and settle in." Marcus tried to smooth the stormy sea. But when Val turned her quirked eyebrow to him, his Adam's apple bobbed like a raft in a washing machine.

"For eight months?"

Marcus threw his hands in the air in a sign of surrender. "We'll work something out, won't we, Riah?" He nodded at her.

My sister turned on her big, doe-brown eyes, blinked a few times and nodded.

"See?" Marcus was nodding like a bobble-head doll.

But then, my silly sister quirked her own eyebrow at Val and did not bother trying to hide the hint of a victory smile.

Val sighed and gave the impression of giving up the battle. "Okay then, if that's how you'd like it to be. I can work with that." She looked to Marcus, who quickly wiped his brow. "You are now responsible for

Sariah's training. And making sure her lessons and chores are done, every day at the right time."

"Sure, Val, we can do that. Can't we Riah?"

Wide innocent eyes nodded back.

"And you, young lady, are accountable for your actions and inactions." She turned to go but stopped. "Oh. And since Sariah won't be coming into the city with me anymore"—Val made sure to acknowledge the shocked look on Sariah's face before she continued—"you can take her to get a training bra. It's well overdue and we were going to go shopping for one today."

Sariah jumped forward and the quilt dropped from her shoulders. Like magnets, everyone's eyes were drawn to her developing chest under her sleep shirt and couldn't help but see the flood of fire consume every inch of visible skin on her body.

Marcus gasped. Then choked. He made several attempts to speak but, before he could, Val had left. Not before she shared a hint of a victory smile over her shoulder at Sariah's expense though.

Lily, who had been sitting silently, watching the whole scene unfold, erupted in laughter and ruffled Sariah's hair before departing for her turn in the garden. "She got you there, Squirt."

Oh dear.

I made my way back to the kitchen in a daze. Skirting the shadows by instinct, I tried to calm my breathing and think what I had to do today and all the things that had to be done. I had not done my schoolwork for a long time. And I had stopped helping the others with their letters and numbers. We were all working in the garden, and I was teaching them planting schedules, recipes and quantities, hoping that might be enough.

I was worried when Kait found out she would be very angry. But thankfully she was not checking, so that helped me not worry so much.

I traced my fingers over the scars in my hands to help calm me and remind me of my victories, but I had forgotten about the burns. I had become clumsy in the kitchen and now had new scars to add to my collection. But these were not scars of victory. Rather, they were signs of failures. I had made mistakes and become clumsy. I had to try harder.

"Where shall we put this load?" Joko and Hiro had come into the Common Room. The benches and tables were full of bottles and jars we were filling with jams and chutneys for the Canal Markets, Good to Go and Kazi's parents' cafe. The sink was full of soapy water and the burn on my palm was stinging.

All I could do was stare. Their arms were full of produce. But they had not brushed the soil or trimmed the greenery off. Jordan trailed behind them, dragging baby beetroots by the stems, their wispy tips ghosting tracks in the dirt trail left by Joko and Hiro. I could not think past the list of things I had to do. And struggled not to get frustrated that Riah was supposed to show them how to, and check that they had cleaned the produce first before bringing it in.

"I am afraid we are not ready for more produce yet. And because we do not have the fridge space it is hard for us to store it and keep it fresh." I gently wiped my wrinkled hands. "Did Riah harvest this lot?"

I do not know why, but Joko thought that was an invitation to come further into the room and dump his load on a clean table, next to the sterilised jars. "Riah has left us in charge."

"What about Amina, or Genni, or Amber, or Lil—"

"We know what we are doing. We do not need Riah anymore. She has handed things over to us." Joko's nostrils flared and he looked an awful lot like his mother.

Tired tears pushed at my eyelids. I was not ungrateful. I was happy that we were achieving so much. But I just felt like it was all a bit too much. And I just could not face another argument, or more hostility, or more work, or more... anything. Especially since there was a whisper whipping around the Factory that we should have our own markets now that we were producing so much.

The ladies were getting braver going out in their new disguises. And Indy had started gathering his supplies later in the day and not being secretive when he went out. Now that he had legs, and Dan by his side, he went out heaps and did not seem to care if he got into fights. Even though he still kept falling over.

I looked from the mud on the floor to the dirty vegetables on the table mixed in and around our prepared jars and the tired tears pushed even harder.

"We've got more to bring in."

"No!" I did not mean to yell. But I could not deal with one more thing. Taking a deep breath, I worked very hard to clear the red haze from my veins. "Please do not bring in any more. We are not ready."

"But we have a pile more wait—"

"Hi everyone, we saw these outside and thought we'd bring them in." Tomiko walked in behind Kazi, who had another pile of veggies in her lap. At least this lot looked like they had been brushed off. From the edges of the red haze crowding my vision I noticed Vashti and Shauna move to the overflowing table to try to bring order to the chaos, whilst Aiko was tied to the big pot on the stove, stirring conserve. I was so grateful for them. They knew what to do without having to have the obvious pointed out.

I was still trying to catch my breath and hold the tired tears at bay when Ben walked in behind Tomiko and Kazi. Ben never came to the Factory during the day. He always worked at the cafe. But there he stood, behind his wife's shoulder. His plain appearance contrasted against her bright apple-green armour. I was so confused. Light was still pouring in through the window and we had not yet prepared lunch, so it definitely was not afternoon.

My tired brain was still trying to understand why the three of them were in the kitchen when Tomiko approached me and squatted down next to Kazi's chair. "Raph, we were wondering if we could ask you something." She flicked her eyes over her shoulder to Ben who was now holding the back of Kazi's wheelchair. He looked back at her and shook his head. Suddenly, all concerns about the veggies, mud and mess disappeared.

"Of course, is everything okay?" Everyone in the room had gone silent and all eyes focused on our little group.

"Yes. I mean no. I mean"—Tomiko's eyes dropped and focused on Kazi's legs—"we were wondering if you could fix Kazi."

I stared at Tomiko, waiting for her to explain. "Fix Kazi's what?"

"Kazi. Can you please try to fix Kazi." Tomiko's voice dropped to a whisper. Ben's jaw clenched and Kazi stared at her fingers that were knotted in her shirt.

"But Kazi is not broken." I looked to each of them again, trying very hard to understand.

Ben cleared his throat. "Tomi, love, you don't have to do this."

Tomiko stood. She looked at her husband, and through gritted teeth, and many tears, she confronted him. "I have to do what I can. To make it right. To fix things. This is my fault." Her hand flew to the side, pointing to Kazi's legs.

Realisation flushed through my brain. I had never seen Kazi as not having legs. I had always seen her as just Kazi. It was different to Indy because he and Dan had talked about how he used to have legs. Kazi had never had the use of hers. "I don't know." I looked at my friend, but she would not lift her eyes. "I think it is different."

Tomiko reached out and took my hand. "Could you… would you… please try?"

"I will have to ask the Light. You know it is not me who can heal. It is Him."

Kazi's eyes were focused on the mess she was making of her shirt. She had not said anything. I called her name and finally she looked at me. Her gaze, glossy and red-rimmed, curled my heart. "What do you want, Kazi?" She just shrugged and went back to her twisted clothing. I looked to her parents. Ben just kept shaking his head, his eyes pools of sadness, as he looked at Tomiko. Tomiko, red-faced, teeth clenched, was drilling holes in my conscience.

I whispered, "But it is not up to me."

Tomiko breathed deeply through her nose, exhaled through her mouth and yelled at me with her eyes. After a pause, in a low voice she asked, "Well, do you think you could ask the Light and see what He says? Please?"

I nodded. "Of course." I was a bit scared of Tomiko and I wasn't sure what Kazi wanted. I felt lost. I usually had Riah with me when I did something like this. Or Val. She would know what to do.

Please help me.

I looked around the room and my eyes rested on Vashti. She smiled and came to my side. Kneeling down next to me, she took my hand. "Would you like me to petition the Light with you?" Her smile chased some of my uncertainty away and brought a sense of warmth to my rapidly beating heart. I just nodded and turned to face her. Vashti took both of my hands in hers. "I am here. Ask."

What is you plan for Kazi? Do you want to give her legs? I cannot feel the pressure in my heart to heal her. Is it because I am so tired? So busy? Please let me know what you want for her and tell me how to help. I just do not know what to do.

I did not receive a definite answer. I didn't even receive a vague answer... or a feeling... or an idea... of anything. There was a void. Nothing. Emptiness. There wasn't even warmth. Not even cold. Just nothing. But I did feel the warmth of Vashti's hands. I looked up at her and she smiled, giving me a small nod. I leaned in and whispered in her ear. "I am not hearing anything. Are you?"

She gently shook her head and whispered back. "Let's give it one more try."

Once again, I went back to the Light.

What do you want me to do? Could you please make it really clear, because I am not sure and I really want to help. And Tomiko is a bit scary, and Kazi is my friend, and Ben looks sad, and I'm just so tired, and I do not know what to do. Everything hurts, and... and... please tell me what to do.

Nothing.

I opened my eyes and looked at Vashti. She must have seen the despair on my face. She pulled me into a hug and stroked my back. "It's alright. Follow the Light and all will be well."

"But He has not given me any instructions."

"Well?" Tomiko stood over me. "What did He say?"

I did not want to lie. I did not want to disappoint her. Or Kazi. But how could I tell her I had not heard anything. Nothing to indicate a "Yes". But then, I had not heard, "No" either. "I can give it a go. But I normally have Riah with me. She helps with her Badge."

"I will lend you mine instead. If you would like?" Vashti's eyes were warm and I found myself sad-smiling in return.

"Thank you." Turning to Kazi, I asked, "Before I can do this, I have to ask your permission. Do you want me to try to help? I do not know if anything will happen, but I need you to say if you want me to try."

Kazi did not speak, but still with the tears running down her cheeks and with a sniff, she nodded. I stepped closer and kneeled down in front of her so I could lay both arms along her legs. I felt one of Vashti's hands on my shoulder and snuck a peek to see she had the other one on Kazi's. I nodded.

I saw that Aiko had moved to Joko and Hiro and picked Jordan up and carried him on her hip. Everyone was very quiet.

I breathed slowly and deeply. I tried to push the Factory and all the jobs I had to do from my mind and focus only on the Light. It was hard pushing through not only the distractions but my fatigue too. I could not let Kazi down. If it was the Light's will for her to have use of her legs, I had to do my bit. Gritting my teeth, I ducked my head lower and forced myself to focus only on the Light.

Kazi was surrounded by bars and pillars of darkness. She was in chains and held down. The chains were not pinned to any point in the past. They were piled on top of her.

It was like walking into the strongest wind. I tucked my head lower. I had to make it past the pillars and squeeze through the bars. Then, finally, ask the Light to lift the chains.

Please help me.

One foot in front of the other, I made ground. Each centimetre I crept forward, digging my toes into shifting sand. I was so tired and had so far to go. The Light filled me and I could see my armour blaze within my vision. I would keep going. The Light was with me. He would do the work. I just had to get there. Toe by toe, I made ground. Once I had passed the boundaries, screams and hissing filled my head. But I could not allow them to distract me. I had to focus on the Light. I had to bring the Light to the chains that bound my friend. If the Light wanted her free, He would lift the chains. But I had to get there first.

Wind continued to tear at me. Screams continued to fill my head. But I stood. I hung on as the Light lifted the links weighing Kazi down. My focus wavered, but He was close. I dropped to my knees. My heart was galloping, my breaths were coming hard and shallow. I had to hang on. I watched, and willed the Light to move the chains. There were only a few to go. But there was nothing to cling to. He was almost done. I could feel my purchase failing. I was being pushed back. My knees leaving deep gouges in the flying sand. Clawing my fingers through the loose ground I grabbed for anything to help me hold on for just that bit longer. Gritting my teeth, I fought on. I could feel the sweat running rivers down my face and back. Sand blasted my skin raw.

Not long. Not long. Not long.

Just as the last chain lifted, I caved in. I could not hold any longer. In my vision, my kneeling form collapsed onto Kazi's lap. From within her chair, she embraced me, Light bursting out from cracks spiderwebbing over her skin. Everything went black. And silent. Blissful silence. Then... nothing.

* * *

"What is the meaning of this?"

"What's wrong? What's happened?"

"How long has he been like this?"

Voices, yelling and arguing brought me out of my wonderful rest. I could not hold in my groan. "Stop. Stop it." I tried to roll into a ball, to shut the world out. "Please, stop." I couldn't move because I was held in a vice.

"Enough." Val barked and everything fell silent. I kept my eyes shut; it took too much energy to even think about opening them. But I was jostled as I felt myself rising and being carried. "Family meeting. Here. Two hours. No excuses."

"Kazi?" I snuggled into the chest that carried me, protected me from the onslaught of the yelling and fighting. "Kazi? How is—"

"Kazi is well, Raphael. Rest." Val's words were enough, I let myself retreat back into the peace in the safety of her arms.

27

MARCUS: SLAP DOWN

Val landed lightly over the brick wall—our shortcut to the canal nature strip—and prowled her way to the Common Room. Right on time. And whilst it did me heart happy to see her free from sporting all the Dark Lord's blades like a pincushion, at this particular point in time I wouldn't have minded her having a bit of a handicap. One little bit. Instead of those blades buried deep in her flesh, they now flashed and sparked, catching the Light, as they were strapped to all available space over her armour.

I'd also like to say she looked happy to be home. But rather, she looked like she'd been hunting demon hearts for lunch. Or sport. Or a spot of fun. Her grimace had me regretting every bad thing I'd ever done, thought to do, or imagined I might have done. Even if I hadn't actually done it. I was feeling very guilty.

The laser beams of her eyes cut to the rest of us through the window, hunkering down in the Common Room pretending not to cower. Adding to our pending doom, the door opened very quietly. Our communal gulp was audible.

"Right." Val stripped each one of us to the core and I was ready to start apologising and confessing. I wasn't quite sure what for, yet, but that was immaterial. We'd been called to a family meeting, and we were all here. Except Raph. I hoped he had a good excuse. The rest of us were ready to be served our butts for butter.

Very quietly yet clear as a bell, she started. "We have all failed and this is our opportunity to see how. And make sure it does not happen again." Each of us were hung, drawn and quartered in turn. "There are, and will be, no excuses."

There was a string of dead cats on the line and obviously five more were about to join them. Six. Raph stumbled into the room. Frackety skrat, he looked like the duck's guts. He dragged his feet to her side and took a seat. Before I could make comment, Val spoke, her eyes raking Raph. "I'll begin." She dropped her eyes and looked at her hands. Neither escaped her inspection, she rolled them, pushed a thumb into each palm, then lifted her chin. "I knew what was going on, but delayed intervening because I was hoping those involved would take responsibility and act with integrity." She quietly inhaled, breathed out slowly, then straightened her spine. "I had not factored in Kazi, nor the toll it would take. That caught me off guard. That's not an excuse. I am, in part, responsible." With Raph nestled at her side, she leaned over and laid a soft kiss on his head.

I could feel me shoulders drop, and the tension ease. Thank the Light that was over—I thought we were all in for a roasting. But then Val lifted her eyes, and the tension snapped back and grabbed me by the nethers. This was just the beginning.

Val went on to explain that our Raph had been doing his work in the kitchen helping to prepare meals, and clean up afterwards, teaching the ladies to cook what we'd grown. He'd also been researching how to pickle and preserve excess food for storage and sale. Then experimenting with the ladies so there was a constant supply. He had also taken over responsibility for the garden, the watering schedule, and the chickens.

Me eyes flicked to Riah and nausea tainted by guilt started rising. But Val didn't stop. She then went on to point out that Raph had also taken on laundry duties for our family and teaching the other kids what he could of reading and writing, because no one was around to wash or teach. The guilt turned to shame as me eyes travelled over Tessa, and Kait—who was still clinging to that... baby.

Did she stop there? No. Of course she didn't. She also explained that Raph hadn't felt he could ask for help because he didn't want to be a nuisance. He had been invited to join us boys for our "teach and talk under the trees", but had to turn it down because he was too busy doing everyone else's chores. Instead of inquiring why he'd refused our invitation, his refusal had been accepted then ignored. The shame and guilt turned to acidic bile and I was sure I was going to be sick.

Yet still she went on. The knife going deeper with every sweep of her sword. "Then, when Kazi, the one person here who actually offers to help him carry his ill-gotten load, asks for help—with the support of Tomiko and Ben—what is he going to do? Where is he going to go for assistance? Where are the people who know him and know what he needs in these situations? Nowhere.

"Vashti stepped in to support him. And the Light worked another miracle through him." The gasp around the room silenced her momentarily. "But not the one they were expecting. A bigger one. And"—she waited for quiet—"the Light is about to perform another miracle of healing."

I'll admit I'm not the sharpest tool in the kit. I looked around to see who else was ill or injured.

Val groaned and shook her head. Her disgust was not quite as palpable as her anger, but it was up there. Thankfully, I wasn't the only clueless one in the box. I snuck a scope of the room and realised we'd been joined by... everyone. Everyone but Kazi, Tomi and Ben... and Genni. Me gut full of shame swamped me soul. We were being dressed down with an audience. All of whom were as clueless as I was.

"This family." It was more of a bark than an explanation. "Just because we are doing what the Light has called us to do, and we are where the Light wants us to be, doesn't mean we can neglect the bless-ings the Light has laid on our lives." I heard her teeth grind from across the room. It was good that I was out of reach. But it did put me in direct line of sight. Actually, there was no safe place right now.

"Always." Her lasers slashed us all again. I was very close to being flayed to the core. "Always. In everything. Light first. Family second. Work third."

"But they are family." Dear Lord. The boy was either as oblivious as the fog that surrounded him, or as brave as a rooster. Raph pulled his upper body away from Val so he could face her. "We are to ask if people need help and if they say yes, we must help them."

In a blink of Raph's confused eye, the whole of Val's demeanour changed. Her body softened, her eyes pooled, and her hand rested on Raph's cheek. "Yes." She smiled. "And no." I'm sure the rest of us disappeared from their conversation, we were just eavesdropping interlopers. But, sure as houses, I wasn't leaving.

"Who is always first?" Val asked quietly.

"The Light."

"Correct. Who do we get everything—our Badges, supplies, strength, purpose, family—from?"

"The Light."

"Correct. And who do we consult on everything?"

"The Light."

"Correct. And who does the Light love, purpose and have a job for?"

Raph smiled. "Everyone."

"Correct." She returned his smile. "Even you."

His face screwed up and his head gave the slightest shake. "I know this, Val. That is why I have been very excited to try out how much my Badge can do."

"But Raph, if you have worn yourself out running around doing everyone else's job, how will you have the strength you need to do what you have been given to do... by the Light? You pushed yourself past your boundary to help Kazi. What would have happened if you had been too tired—too worn out from doing everyone else's jobs—to do *your* job, use *your* Badge effectively for Kazi? No one else can do what you do how you do it. If you are too burned out to fulfil *your* purpose, how would that give glory to the Light?"

The boy was trying to come to terms with what Val was saying, but before he could voice his opinion, she continued. "And how is it fair to everyone else?" She looked around the room. "How are they going to explore, improve their Badges, and get experience, if you jump in and do their job for them?"

Raph's head dropped. Val had a gift of kicking—literally and metaphorically—everyone in the guts. Poor kid. Me parental hackles were rising and I was on the verge of intervening on his behalf, when her no-longer soft, pooling eyes cut to me. "You might want to ask yourself where those feelings have been for the past eight months."

I kept forgetting her Badge of Seeing. It wasn't a constant, but bleeding heck, it could be jolly inconvenient at times. It was a stare-down of epic proportions, minus any brotherly-sisterly feelings.

How dare you accuse me of that? She had wounded me in public and I was speechless.

Her eyes flicked to Sariah. *You have two children! How dare you throw one under a bus for the other?*

Flashes and memories of all the times I had made excuses for Riah flickered through me brain, not even thinking that it had been Raph who'd been left to pick up the slack. I had never seen Val so angry. At me. Thankfully, it rendered her speechless as well. I would have been destroyed if she'd voiced *that* truth to the room. I was wounded, furious and justly accused. Wasn't even aware I was on the move before she nailed me again.

Sit the frack down. We're not finished.

Val turned back to Raph, made an effort to breathe out the rage, then gently lifted his chin. "We're all human, and we all make mistakes. But mate, how are people going to know you need help, if you don't ask? I'd like to think we are all super-aware of each other"—again she eyeballed the room—"and that's something we're going to work on. But what's the first rule in first aid?"

The lad's head tilted like a confused pup. "Check for danger before entering the scene."

"Correct. Why?"

"So you..." Raph dropped his head again and mumbled, "don't become another casualty."

"Correct." She pulled him in for a hug, then, with hands on his shoulders, held him at arm's length. "You are a first responder. You are the one who has the best read on what's going on in here"—she tapped his head—"and in here"—she laid a hand over his heart. "When things aren't right, you take steps to make it right. First ask...?"—she tilted her head and lifted an eyebrow.

"The Light."

"Correct. Then, who else can you ask?"

"You."

"And?"

Me boy looked straight at me. Then passed to Dan. I was officially a broken man. Me heart was carnaged: its splatter coated the insides of me ribcage. But Raph didn't stop at Dan either—his eyes moved to Tessa. They didn't even stop as his gaze passed over Kait, then rested on his sister. Riah's face was awash with tears. Her hands were tangled together, marbled white and red. He then came back to Val and confirmed, "My family."

Val's voice broke on the word, "Correct." He was then smothered in her embrace whilst me sister, Valerie, did a very poor job of hiding her tears pouring from her cracked heart into his mess of hair. Seems I wasn't the only one with parental hackles. "For my part in this, I am sorry. I have failed you by not stepping in sooner to stop the nonsense. I am proud of you and what you have achieved"—she took a deep shuddering breath—"and how, despite your exhaustion, by sheer force of will, you have brought a new beginning to Kazi through the Light."

Once the jiggle had started, not even Val could contain him. "Is she healed? Can she walk?"

Val paused and pinned the boy like an insect on a square of foam. "Kazi is still in her chair. Her spine is no different. Yet, through your love for her, a bigger miracle has been worked. Kazi's heart has opened and she is now in the Light."

He was silent. His face a circus of emotions. Then slowly he nodded. "I am sorry that Tomiko will be upset. I hope that Kazi will forgive me. But, Val, I do not think the Light felt there was anything wrong with her. She is not broken or needing to be fixed." Then the sun broke out from his smile. "I am happy she is in the Light now, though. I cannot wait to see what colour she is."

I could see the cogs turning in his head, thinking things through. No doubt already working out what would come next. What lessons to teach her, to show her about the Light. The lad had already moved on. Forgiven us all for letting him down and moved on to planning his next saving grace.

But *I* couldn't move on till I'd put me house in order. "Raph"—both Val and the boy looked at me, as I dropped to a knee and placed a hand on his shoulder—"I let you down. And I'm sorry."

I swear the kid was too good for this life when he just looked at me and beamed. "It is okay Marcus, you were very busy with Dan and Indy and B—"

"No excuses, Raphael." I looked to Val. Her eyes narrowed, but she gave the slightest nod. Raph squeaked as I hauled him against me chest and wrapped him in me arms. Then, holding him out so I could look him in the eye, I said me piece. "Of the primary jobs the Light has dealt me, family is the highest. It's with pride I think of you as me boy; me son. And I let you down." I took me own steadying breath to push back the tears. "I am so very sorry. I want you to know you can always come to me. I will always do what I can to help. I may not always have the answers, but you can bet your bippy, I'll do me best to figure them out... with your help."

Relief washed over me as, with glassy eyes, me boy returned me hug. We were going to be alright. However, I did catch Val's eye over Raph's shoulder. That wound may take a bit longer to mend.

A tap on the shoulder had me turning to see a queue formed behind me. Seems I wasn't the only one who was feeling the need to make things right. I scooted out of the way and let the others say their piece. But, once again, me heart was cracked as I saw me beautiful wife sitting in the corner of the room, looking at but not seeing the child playing in her lap. Her shoulders were slumped and there was no life in her eyes.

Lord, only you know what's going on there. You know the distance and pain—the abyss between us.

It wasn't an excuse. But the Light knew part of the reason I'd been spending so much time away with the lads was because I didn't know what to do. I'd lost me wife to a babe. She'd set an immovable barrier between us and I didn't know how to get through or around it. Or if she even wanted me to. There was no room in her life for anyone else. Seems she'd finally got what she'd always wanted and I was no longer… necessary? Important? Seen?

I knew the others saw me full of bluster, but without me Kait, I had no core. I was just that: an anchorless, rudderless, bag of hot air. I knew I had the Light. I had me kids. For good or bad I had me sister, Val. But Kait? Kait was me home.

2 8

KAITLYN: SHATTERED HEARTS

There was a canyon in the pit of my stomach and every time I thought about what I'd done, my soul poured through. I was losing myself in the shame and guilt and didn't know how to make it stop or to make the pain go away.

As if outside myself, observing from the corner of the ceiling, I saw my hand play with the blonde curls of the angel on my lap. I couldn't feel. Couldn't think. Couldn't see any way out of this black hole. She had been my special blessing. A gift. A reward.

Oh Lord, I was going to be sick. I could not hold the numbness at bay. Nausea flooded my soul like a king tide. I was powerless against it. My vision blurred and from far off, a wild animal keened. I clung to Dawn and rocked her. What else could a mother do?

Mother.

A word that stripped, sliced and slayed my heart.

Mother.

A cruel joke. A wicked temptress whom I had followed to my demise.

I had been so desperate to be a mother, I'd neglected my children.

The keening grew louder. The wild animal came in for the kill. I willed it to hurry up and finish me off.

Let me die. I am so ashamed. And so very, very sorry. I have been blind and selfish, self-seeking, self-entered, self... self... oh, Lord, take me now. Please.

I don't know how long I sat, but eventually realised the wild beast had passed me by. And, damn the creature, it had left me both alive and tortured. There wasn't even a wound I could show for my pain. I became aware I was surrounded by a presence. Chairs pulled up close to mine. Arms wrapped around me. Someone standing behind. Company and warmth, neither of which I deserved. Couldn't they see? I deserved... needed to suffer.

Then Vashti's voice settled over the room like a comforting, weighted blanket. "Hormones are a powerful thing. A scary thing. I see the joy and the fight and the love in the mothers. But that was not in me when Micah was born." Her story was like a salve, allowing me to breathe outside of myself for a moment. To slacken the dread that strangled me.

"I had been donated to the Temple as a baby, offered to men as a child, impregnated by a stranger at sixteen and cast out to the streets by my family nineteen years ago. The Temple stripped me of choices and stole all hope. I had nothing. Knew nothing. Was nothing. I had..." —she shook her head—"nothing. When my baby was born there was no milk and fewer emotions. I was a used up, empty husk, sacrificed and thrown on the trash pile. When Micah died from malnutrition shortly after he was born, I had even less." Vashti was no longer in the room with us. Her memory had taken her hostage as she was hauled over the coals of her past.

"I tried to end it. Life was too hard." She raised her eyes to the window. "And what was there left to live for? I was too tired, too weak, too incompetent, too sick... too... hungry. But I couldn't even do that right." She shook her head again and inspected her hands, still lost in her past. "One night I stirred and felt a presence sitting next to me. She was murmuring. I couldn't understand what she was saying. But she was weeping. As soon as she realised I was awake she stopped. It was then I became aware of a warmth enfolding me and a softness under my head. I shifted and she helped me sit. When I was propped up by the wall, still wrapped in her blanket, on the ground next to her, she offered me food... just a little... and water. She told me to rest. So, after she helped me to get comfortable again, I did." Vashti hugged herself like the blanket in her memory.

"In the early-morning light I woke again after truly sleeping, and she was still there. No longer murmuring, just softly weeping like a little fountain. I shifted again and looked up at her. She smiled at me and said, 'Thank you.' I hadn't said a word. She brushed her face and said it again. With the warmest, glistening eyes. 'Thank you.'

"She offered me more food and water and we sat quietly as the sun rose, offering warmth from outside as well as in. She told me a bit of her story. I think it was pretty obvious she knew mine—I was still a mess from Micah's birth—she just kept saying thank you. Before she left that day, she made me promise that I'd meet her again. She said she needed me.

"She. Needed. Me." The softest of smiles ghosted across Vashti's face.

"And that's how it started. Every couple of days, I'd come into the suburbs and she'd bring food, clothing, water and toiletries. And we would sit. Not really talk. Just sit. She said it's a powerful thing to sit in the company of shared experience."

I was pulled out of Vashti's past as I felt the pressure of Helen's arms—emblazoned in orangey-yellow armour—hold me firmly. Vashti's attention landed on me, and her sad smile drew me back into her story. "Because nobody could know the utter devastation of loss, the pain of emptiness, the inability to give, take, share... could participate in the hollowness of isolation as one who has survived a similar experience."

Vashti looked to Helen. Who sat sheltered under Kerm's wing, as she, in turn, nestled me. Her eyes wet mirrors. "I still need you," Helen said.

After a pregnant pause Vashti continued. "When Iza and Indy found the others and brought them back here, Helen brought me here and the others let me stay."

From somewhere in the room Lottie coughed and barked, not

quite hiding the hitch in her voice. "Of course we let you stay girl, you're one of us. And, as it turns out, we need you too. Glad the black dog didn't keep you down."

With the grace inherent in everything she did, Vashti moved over to Lottie, kissed her cheek, then returned to the pot of tea she'd made and glided out of the room holding two steaming cups. I watched as she skirted the property under the shade of the trees and made her way to the cabins where Genni was wrapped in her cocoon of a "bad day", locked away from the world. And from Dawn.

I could feel the world's eyes focus on the child, now sleeping and content in my arms. My heart shattered like frozen glass and pierced every single raw nerve. For the girl in the hut who couldn't love the baby she had. And for me, who couldn't have the baby I loved.

Marcus's gentle voice drew me from my depths. "Kait. Love, you've got to stop hogging the baby. It's time she went to be with her ma."

He was right. I knew it. To my core I felt the truth of his words. But still the hooks were buried deep. "But she didn't want her baby. I tried. She just kept turning away. Dawn would cry and cry and cry." Oh Lord, the memory of her desperate calls still caused a visceral response in me. "I couldn't bear it. Genni didn't want her baby. What was I supposed to do? Let her starve? Let her little heart crack because she wasn't wanted? It's not Dawn's fault her mother didn't want her. Wasn't in a position to love and care for her. But I could." I felt the door to truth slam shut. Nothing was taking this child from me.

Marcus gave up speaking to me and turned to the room at large. "It's just not right. What's wrong with Genni? Is she ill?" He faced Lottie, almost begging. "Does she need medicine? Can we get her something? A doctor? Tell me what she needs, and I'll see to it."

Lottie's rough voice was gentle. "Nah mate, not much a doctor can do for that."

He forged on. "We've got to do something; a child should be with her ma."

I didn't even think, I just became aware that I'd clutched Dawn closer to my chest.

"Kait, darlin', I love you true—"

"But I love her, and she needs me." Couldn't he see? If he loved me, he would understand.

"She's not yours. You've got to give her back." Marcus's pleading bounced off my slammed door. What was wrong with me? I knew he was right. Why couldn't I let this child go? It was a war within, and I was losing. "But Genni wouldn't even get out of bed."

"Wouldn't. Didn't. Wasn't. Listen to yourself Kait. It's all past tense. Look around. Genni is out now. Participating. But maybe she needs more incentive to get up. To eat and... I don't know... do stuff. If she had to care for her child—if she had something to live for, to fight for —then it wouldn't be so easy to give up.

"Kait, you know better than anyone. Sometimes you just need something to fight for, something to force you to get up each day. If you make it too easy, you take away her reason to live. For goodness' sake Kait, you're a nurse. You know this!" His voice rose as his patience fled. Yelling. Marcus never yelled at me.

"Vashti's right." Helen's quiet voice brought reason. "The mind is a powerful and scary thing." She stood and, taking Kerm's hand, they quietly followed Vashti's path to their own private gate and left the premises.

Help me please. Help Genni, help me. Help me do what's right for Dawn. And my own family.

I should have known Marcus wouldn't back down or walk away. "What are you going to do when we leave? You can't take her with us. She needs to be here with her family. Her ma. Are you going to stay?" His voice broke.

Indy's voice broke into our pain. "What do you mean, you're leaving?" I hadn't even realised he was in the room.

"Well, we're not staying, lad."

"When? All of you? Dan too? Why? Why do you have to leave? You can stay, there's enough room."

"Indy, we're only here to help you, open some doors, show you a different way. We're taking up valuable room that you could be using to help others who really need it. We're here until you don't need us. You were all doing a top-notch job before we arrived. We are just pointing you in the right direction so you can do a good job, better." I could hear Marcus trying to be reasonable, but even now, I knew he'd not given up on me or let our argument rest.

"Well, how long are you staying for then?"

"It's hard to tell. But when the time is right, we'll be heading off. Dan and Tessa are adults and can make up their own minds. But Kait?" Marcus paused. It was the final straw. The rawness of his question and his genuine uncertainty as to whether I would choose Dawn over him tore through the wall.

Then it really hit me. I already had. Over my rock, my core, my love, over the children the Light had blessed me with, and over my sister. I had turned my back on them all for this child, who wasn't, couldn't be, mine.

He continued, "And me, Val and the twins will move on when we've done our job, to the next place the Light calls us. And we'll start all over again."

I stood and turned my back on everyone, wiped my face on my shoulder and left the room, skirted the wall under the shade of the trees and walked up onto the verandah of the cabins where Genni spent the day pinned down by the "Black Dog".

29

RAPHAEL: HOLIDAY

My life had burst into one big holiday. One day I could not see past my toes, the next I was living my dream.

"For goodness' sake, Kait. Fight, damn it." I flinched as Val lost her temper with Kait. Again. Even though training had been better for me since I was not so tired, it was another story for Kait who had lost her spark. Ever since she had given Dawn back to Genni, she had been a shadow.

But not at training. At training she was a solid chunk of fleshy concrete, absorbing everything, evading nothing. Refusing to defend herself—all kicks and hits scored marks on her body somewhere. She did not even try to block.

Over the past month the world had changed in so many ways. Even though Kait was locked in autumny-winter, for me spring had arrived both inside my soul and out in the world. And just like our garden beds were divided into different sections, my heart was divided into many boxes.

The box Kazi lived in was a summer breeze. For a month now she had been learning about the Light, her armour a soft pink. I had felt sick that I had failed her, but over these past weeks, a feeling had germinated that she had not been the one driving for change. Tomiko had not been back to the Factory since that day. Ben dropped Kazi off and picked her up. She made it clear to her parents she wanted to come round. So, I just kept treating her as I always had, and she seemed happy with that. She was a bit awkward with Indy and his legs, but since he was hardly here anymore, she was more focused on helping me with my chores and Riah in the garden, now that my sister was back in the swing of things.

At first, I had been worried. Riah and Kazi had never really been friendly. But, after our family conference, Riah was getting on better with everyone. So, now, the box in my heart where Riah lived was as vast and deep and moody as the sea.

I flinched at the sound of steel colliding with concrete. One of Val's knives—a Seen one—skidded across the warehouse floor.

"Did you just throw a weapon at me wife?"

"I wasn't trying to hit her." Val's glare cut from Marcus back to Kait. "Just trying to wake her up."

I felt Riah come closer and bump my shoulder. *Should we do something?*

I turned to face her. *We can try?*

Hand in hand we edged our way over to our warring adults but stopped in our tracks when Val's icy eyes landed on us. "And what do you two think you're doing?"

I felt a bit silly. I had raised my hand to demonstrate what I was planning. But when Val continued to be a glacier, I let it drop and tried my words. "Helping?"

"Well, unless you can help her grow a backbone, I wouldn't bother wasting your time." I could not remember ever seeing Val so angry. I was not scared… well, not really. I knew she would not hurt me… us. But we gave her lots of space on our way to Kait.

Kait's box in my heart was frosted over with thick, impenetrable, blurry glass. Her eyes were dead and sadness leaked out of her like a sieve. I did not think she even saw us, but together we laid our hands on her. It reminded me of the morning after our birthday party and Tessa had come home. She had been lost and sad and broken, like a mess of tiny, fractured twigs. One strong breath, and she would have fallen apart. But Kait already had.

I checked with Riah. She felt the same. We both moved in to hug her.

Please let her feel our love. Please lend her our warmth. I know I can't put her pieces back together, but you can. Lend her my strength. Show her my heart.

I squeezed my eyes shut and made a picture of all my happy memories. Of the times Kait had held me, taught me, laughed with me. Of the times she had helped me ride the Dragon and find my way through the red mist. Of the times she had been the calm in my storm. Her box in my heart took up a lot of room. She meant so much to me. And I loved her very much. I knew she was sad about losing Dawn, but she would always be my mother. And I really hoped that, one day, Riah and I would be enough for her. As her children.

I knew it was not really healing. And sharing my thoughts with people other than Riah was not my Badge. But I pushed all my memories and feelings from my head and willed them into hers. And to help it along, I squeezed Kait really, really hard in my arms. But I was forced to let go when she dropped to her knees and, with quiet sobs, she drew Riah and me in for a very tight hug of her own. Kait was not the only one crying.

"I am so very sorry." It was a whisper, but because her face was between ours, we heard it loud and clear. "I have let you guys down and I can't forgive myself. I am so, so sorry."

We pulled apart a little and Riah wiped Kait's face: soft brown feathers over gaunt white cheeks. Over and over, caring, caressing, calming. I felt Riah's badge of Peace flooding with every stroke. She then pulled their foreheads together as they breathed the same sorrowful air. Sharing grief, brokenness and love.

I felt the shift. It was audible. A ravaged scar on the landscape, rent by an earthquake, came back together. Re-joined. Whole. Not as it was before, a bit mismatched, rugged and rough. But healed, sewn tight, the scar line thick and strong.

They both turned to look at me and I was hit by a wall. I would have staggered backwards if they had not been both holding me in a vice. Without saying a word, they both spoke volumes.

Boundless love. Overwhelming grief. Desperate repentance. Hunger for forgiveness.

I thought we had gone over this. I thought I had made myself clear. I could not understand why they both kept longing for what I had already given. Why could they not accept my word and believe that I had forgiven them and moved on? And to be perfectly honest, I started to feel a bit like Val.

Frustration burbled away deep in my gut. I did not want to make things worse, so I took a deep breath and levered myself out of their hold. "I have already told you. Both." I tried to imitate Val's icy glare. "I have already forgiven you. Both. It is time to move on. If you cannot accept my forgiveness, I will take it back and give it to someone else." Of course this was a silly statement. But I was not doing a satisfactory job of keeping the frustration at a simmer. And I hoped by saying such nonsense they would realise just how silly they were being.

Dan's voice broke the spell. "Okay LM, I've got your buckets. It's time to go."

Joy washed the annoyance away and I swivelled out of the claustrophobic pity-party. It was time to hit the streets with Val and Dan. Which reminded me. I spun to face my sister again.

I have forgiven you for being lazy. I have forgiven you for leaving me in a heap. But I am not sure I can forgive you for keeping the secret of what you were doing in the city from me. We do not keep secrets, sister.

Val made me promise not to tell.

I know you, Riah. No one makes you do anything. You chose to keep this from me. I am still angry about it.

She did not even try to respond or hold my glare. It was Dan's arm around my shoulders that swung me away and capped the hurt. "You ready to make some music, my man?" Like a switch flicking, the sunshine flooded back into my mind at the thought of what the rest of today held. With his guitar over his shoulder, Dan handed me my buckets and we went to meet Val at the ladder set up against the compound wall. It was now our official secret entrance to the outside world.

My grin was as unstoppable as Dan's humming as we made our way to Serendipity. Since the day of the Family Meeting, I had taken Riah's place on the trips to the city. I could not draw like her, but, as Dan liked to say, I could "hold a beat". Living with Riah since before I was born, I had been around and aware of music my whole life. It was just as much a current in my blood as it was in hers. And to be offered a space to share that was exhilarating.

"How many sets are you here for today, LM?" Missy, the owner and head chef of Serendipity, met us at the door. She was leaning against the frame with a glint in her deep-brown, almost black eyes.

Val answered from over my shoulder. "Just the one. We've got an appointment."

"Sweet." Then Missy pulled away from the door and revealed what she had been hiding in the shadows behind her back. "Saw this old thing in a charity shop and thought of you."

My buckets clattered to the ground as I reached out and took hold of the drum. It had a stretched leather top and was like a cut off kind of funnel. She also brought out a stool, just like Dan's. "Figured if you were going to be a regular we needed to get you set up properly."

Val chuffed and gave me a gentle push from behind to respond. I had not been able to stop running my hands over the worn leather, absorbing the inherent warmth and hum of the instrument. "Thank you." It was only a whisper, but Missy winked and nodded before heading back inside the restaurant.

Since it was a beautiful spring morning, Missy had organised us outside in order to draw people into her restaurant. Dan had tuned and was ready to go and let me experiment with my new drum. The icing on the cake was when he did not shush me when I quietly joined in with his singing. I knew I was not Riah, but when the music took over I did not have the power to resist. And on such a beautiful day, I did not even try.

In a matter of moments our first set had finished, and Val was itching to get going. I was torn. I really wanted to go with her to her appointment. But I also really wanted to stay and play. It helped knowing we would be back tomorrow. "Thank you for the use of your drum, Missy. It has a great sound."

"Nah, LM, it's your drum and *you* make it sing. Take it with you if you want?"

She could have asked me if I wanted to keep breathing. Of course I wanted to take it with me. I could not wait to show the others. I went to thank her properly, but my body took over and I was hugging her before I had thought whether that was appropriate or not—as Marcus had been explaining. But he was not here, and I was hoping Val would not tell.

Val winked. My secret was safe. "Come on Raph, we've got places to go and people to see."

I wiggled out of Missy's hold and tried very hard not to skip along the street by Val's side. I found it interesting that my opinion of this city was controlled by my emotions. In our early days here, I had not been a fan of Laodicea. But today, the sun bouncing off the walls of the glass buildings to join in a dance with the water of the canals and aqueducts mirrored my feelings. The smell of vehicle exhaust constantly blending with perfumes, food and coffee as we progressed past shop fronts through the city was not cloying, but exciting. But maybe that was more to do with where we were going and who we were going to meet.

The vibrations raking my body were not controllable, containable or able to be hidden. I snuck a glimpse at Val. She smiled and pressed the button for the lift. Her armour was zinging as much as mine was by the time the doors pinged and opened.

"Hello my dear friends. It is… heartening to see you this fine day."

"Felix." I dropped my drum on the carpet and launched myself at him. He tried to hold me at a distance, but then gave up and woodenly patted my back. I jiggled and held tighter until he sighed. His arms softened, came round and gave a brief but real hug. I pulled back. "You are improving, Felix. But we shall keep working on it."

Val barked out a laugh. "Bet you didn't see hugging on the curriculum."

"My dear woman, if I had, I may have had to turn you down nine months ago when you initiated my tutelage." Felix's orange armour glowed like the impenetrable sun. His sword hilt, like a battle flag, rose above his right shoulder. "So, aside from hugging"—with warm eyes he nodded at me—"what is on the agenda for today? Oh, and just so you know, Fleur is otherwise occupied, but Marlene will be dropping by for a spell once she has finished her errands."

"Uncle Felix?" He stopped and gave me his attention. "Why are you a secret?"

He looked to Val, then back at me. "My dear boy, where to start? First, I am not a... secret for nefarious reasons." He looked to Val, she nodded. I was not adept at reading their secret language yet. Felix continued. "One day all will be revealed. I have, in fact, been involved with the group at the Factory since before they were in situ. They are unaware. Presently, you and your family are helping them transition from dependent and without hope, to independent with a future without outside assistance. Both Valarie and I agreed that a sense of... self-realised achievement is the foundation for the continued success of the endeavour Izabaal and Indigo have established."

As I chewed over what he had said and what it meant, Val crossed the room, removed her tattered copy of *The Way* from her messenger bag, and laid it on a table set with the makings for morning tea. She explained how the next one-and-a-half hours would be spent: training, sparring—hand to hand and sword work—and continuing Felix's education of living in the Light.

"But not before a cup of tea and an update on life at the Factory." Felix lifted an eyebrow and tilted his head at me. "How is your young friend Kazi coming along? Has she started sword work yet?"

We filled him in on my friend's progress and how Tomiko had still not returned, the gardens, chickens, baking, markets and updates on everyone. Val even told Uncle Felix about her frustrations with Kait.

But then it was Val's turn. "What news from Philadelphia? Jonathan?"

"Ah, my dear friend Jonathan and the... dichotomy that is Philadelphia." Felix placed his cup back on the table and leaned into the embrace of his chair. His eyes were focused outside the wall of windows and his eyes were sad. "The Gerent's inexhaustible funds still gush into the fledgling city and they remain on schedule for a full... grand recovery by the end of the year. No expense has been spared. Truly, he is a... generous ruler. Why his focus is solely trained on Philadelphia and none of the other nine cities devastated by the quake is... perplexing." Felix swung his heavy eyes back to Val. "But the people? They are crushed. Money cannot mend that kind of trauma. And Jonathan? More... traumatised than most. I am worried."

"What can be done? That isn't already being done, of course." Val was leaning forward, her forearms resting on her knees.

"Only the Light knows. It is... frustrating to be quite so... inadequate. Yesterday I chaired a meeting with representatives from the other cities in the accord, in the heart of the rebuilt CBD. It was encouraging to see Philadelphia's Community rising from the ashes. But... all is not well within the rank and file." He shook his head, his shoulders sagged and his eyes were weighty with grief.

Val stood. "There is only one thing for it." She had our attention. "We fight." And even more so when she drew her sword, challenging my uncle.

He pirouetted from his chair, pulling his own sword in one smooth movement. My heart cheered—and may have even hooted—as I watched just how wonderful a swordsman Uncle Felix was becoming.

30

DANIEL: THE BURN

E ven though it was spring, the nights were still long and the days were still cool. And I was burning. Tessa was different now. She had more spunk and swagger. She'd had huge success teaching the girls hand to hand and about the Light and *The Way*, designing clothes for them and altering clothes from Good to Go for the rest of us. Each month she went off with Helen to the Canal Markets and was bringing in money from things she had created as well as selling produce from what everyone else had made. She was fully involved in organising our own Silver Scale Markets. She was skilling up in all areas and she'd rediscovered her joy.

I was making an effort to hang out with her every day, searching for moments to connect, but it wasn't enough. She wasn't playing hard to get, but she sure as hell was being elusive. Not obviously so. I mean, she was playing nice, and was approachable, but she wasn't taking hints. Any hints. At all.

I knew she wasn't dumb. We'd made our peace and we were good. To a point. We were friendly but we weren't friends. *Friends* friends. And I kind of think that maybe that's what I really wanted. But I wasn't sure that was what she wanted. She wasn't giving me any signals and it was seriously doing my head in. I had to find a way to be with her alone, see if I could pick up a read, get an idea of what she was thinking.

And I had to do it soon. I was finding this huge factory too small and the group of people too close. Tessa's sunshine was burning me up from the inside out and I didn't know what to do about it. I'd been talking to Marcus. He'd suggested I run more, or work out more, or I find other things to occupy my mind. He then suggested that if none of that worked, I could make time to hang out with her. Like, actually ask her to meet up with me at a specific time and place. So that was my plan.

She'd finished up for the morning and I was ready—desperate—to make this work. I was almost set to go. I had changed into my running gear and could tell by the pattern and weight of the footsteps coming down the hallway she'd finished her session. "Hey Tessa, you ready?"

"Almost, just give me a sec." She bolted past my door and went into hers next along. She was already in her gear and looking hot... as in good... and temperature. I mean she *had* just been training with the girls.

I waited for her in the hallway. I could hear the chatter of the crew growing in the Common Room as everyone came in for lunch. The smells were enough to make me second-think my idea. But then Tessa bounced out of her room. Tight black leggings, oversized dark-blue hoodie and her crazy white hair tied back in a knot. She'd been growing it. And I loved it. Her sunshine-yellow armour gave off enough light to blind me. All thought of... everything... fled my brain.

In my excitement, I darted out of the shadows, frightening the life out of her. As she stumbled, I snagged her and pinned her to my chest with the excuse of stopping her falling on her face.

"I don't need rescuing, Dan." There was steel in her voice, but it was buried deep under breathy laughter.

That was a good sign. Wasn't it? "I don't want to rescue you, Tessa. I want to hold you. And..." *Frugly, fritting, frudge. Do I tell her?*

"What, Dan? What is it exactly you want?"

Skrat. What should I say? What would not make me sound like a complete fool and hopelessly desperate. Cause I kind of was. Could she cope with that?

Tessa shook her head, then started to back out of my arms.

Skrat. Skrat... skrat. "Kiss you? A lot?"

"Are you sure about that?"

"Which part? That I want to kiss you? Or do lots of it? Or that I really want to kiss you? A lot." *Yeah, that's me, real smooth.* The hitch at the end of my question helped like a bucket of ice water.

Tessa tapped her chin with her finger and looked me over—as much as she could this close in a darkened hallway—and slowly nodded her head.

"Is that a yes? Or are you thinking? Or, are you just absolutely sure, beyond a doubt, that I'm a complete idio—"

She silenced the ramble by grabbing the back of my head and pulling me into the sweetest kiss in the history of the universe. If I'd known she hated rambling enough to kiss me in order to shut me up, I would have tried it sooner. As it was, I was just a truckload of relieved: that I could stop talking, that I was kissing Tessa... and Tessa was kissing me back.

It started playful, but by the time Indy interrupted us, I had her up against the wall and we were breathing hard.

"Hey guys, glad I found you. What'cha doing?"

I put Tessa back down on the floor and she blushed, coughed and straightened her jumper.

I breathed. Deeply. Then turned. "We're just heading out for a run."

"Great, I'll join you, yeh?"

Great? Yeah, nah. Since he'd been having trouble with Iza, Indy'd been sticking like skrat on my shoe. He didn't seem to see that at times—like now—he was a bit—like a tonne—of a third wheel. But how do you tell a guy he's not wanted? Especially when he's been kicked to the curb.

"Um. Well..." I turned to Tessa.

She beamed up at me, reached up on her toes and kissed my cheek, then took my hand and turned to my lost friend. "We're going on a date, Indy. And we've never been on one before. So, I'm very excited." She walked over to him still holding my hand and reached her other hand and cupped his cheek. "We love you, and love your company, but this time it's just us." Tugging my hand, she then pulled me down the hallway out into the warehouse and we hit the driveway running.

Brilliant. She was just brilliant. I couldn't have done that. I loved this new Tessa; she was so confident and knew exactly what to do and say. She buzzed with life and light and energy. She was like a mozzy-zapper drawing me in, irresistible and lethal. But I kind of didn't care what the consequences were right now. I just wanted to sign up to her buzz.

We started off at an easy pace, skirting the outer wall of the Factory, then took the bikeway that ran alongside the canal. Ten months ago, when she'd exploded from the gates after losing her skrat with Carley and Lily, she'd been unfit, angry and at war... with me. Now we were in harmony, keeping rhythm even though we didn't speak, didn't touch, just worked away side by side. It was so easy. For the first time in forever my heart kicked at a peaceful beat.

All was good in the world. I was fit, healthy, fed. But it was more. I had people to go home to and I had purpose: they depended on me. I had a job to do. I was part of a team. But it was more. I had a partner. She was one of my best friends. Well, apart from... Indy?

You know what?

I think that perhaps she was.

Tessa wasn't a bloke; it was different than having a bro friend. I think I finally got what she had been talking about.

It stopped me in my tracks. I almost tripped.

"What's wrong?" Tessa spun and came back. The sun caught hold of highlights in her hair. The tie she used was useless to tame that beautifully wild beast. Tendrils broke free and danced with the breeze. It was as animated and beautiful as she was, when she wasn't trying hard to be someone else.

I couldn't help myself; I took a curl and wrapped it around my finger.

She cupped my cheek. Just like she had with Indy. But with me, she smiled. From the heart. "You okay?"

"I get it now."

"What?"

"You're my best friend. I mean, my *Best Friend*. There is no one else I prefer being with than you. Not just because you're a chick and you're hot—"

"Why doesn't that sound like a compliment?"

"No, listen. I get what you're saying, it's not just physical attraction. There is that." I looked at her, swallowed and forged on before I got distracted... again. "But it's more. You're oil on my choppy water."

"I'm oil? What's with all the compliments today?"

She wasn't really annoyed. The predator bird was nowhere in sight.

I ran my hand over her cheek and down her neck to her shoulder and arm, then took her hand. "Tessa. You know what I mean. I just realised. My heart stops searching when you're around. Not just around, but aware of me. Wherever you are, whatever you're doing. When you become aware of me, I feel it. My heart... exhales."

I almost fell as Tessa launched herself at me. She was my own living breastplate: her arms around my neck, her legs around my waist.

"So... that was a good thing to say?"

Her head nodded in my shoulder.

I held her little, firm, perfect body close and inhaled. "I just don't know why you put up with me."

It was the arctic wind that changed the scene. She dropped like lead and punched my arm. It wasn't too hard. I was still standing. "What?"

"What do you mean, what?"

"Whaaat? I don't know what to say cause I feel whatever comes out of my mouth will be the wrong thing."

"How can you say that?"

The way I saw it, I had a fifty-fifty chance of stuffing up. She either meant the "what" bit or the "putting up with me" bit?

Who was I kidding? No matter what I said now I was going to stuff up.

I tried silence.

"Well?"

Didn't work. "I'm confused."

She took pity on me. "How can you ask why I'd put up with you?"

"Well, come on Tessa. Seriously, I still skitch you off heaps. I see things differently—"

"Like not seeing mess. At. All."

"Well yeah, I guess. And my safety parameters—and by that I mean, my desire to experience life—are set *a bit further afield* than yours. And I—"

"Just shut up and kiss me."

Okay, that I could do. So, I did.

As dates went, I think we did alright. We finished our run along the canal and made our way back to the Factory in time for a late lunch. The others had cleaned everything up but left the fixings out for us. "So… um… you wanna do that again sometime?"

"What? Eat lunch? Yeah, I like lunch." She laughed at my groan then her eyes softened. "Yeah, I'd like to do that again sometime."

She had me in such a mess. I wanted to jump right in. But then I also wanted to do things right, like Marcus had been telling me, to lay a solid foundation. Get the basics right first. So I was going to do things right and court her, showing her the best version of me. And make her fall as hard for me as I had—once again—fallen for her.

"If you can rearrange your schedule, do you want to come into the city with Val, Raph and me… one day… soon…?" Okay, so, I was ready to go slow but I didn't want to wait for ever. "Tomorrow?"

She laughed, then studied her shoes. A pink glow—my pink glow, the one only I could create in her—bloomed from her cheeks. That, right there. I did that. I was king of the world.

No. Wait. I don't mean that. You know what I mean, hey? You're King of the world. Totally. But right now, I'm feeling right up there. I mean, you did this. You listened. You moved. You, like, did a miracle and… thanks. You are totally rocking the whole Light thing and, thanks. Just… thanks.

Tessa looked up and from under her eyelashes she nodded. "I'd like that."

Yep. Totally rocking it.

31

KAITLYN: LIGHT'S LIKE THAT

"Who's got the unpicker?"

I wouldn't go so far as to say it was a feral growl, but it was not far off. Iza was in a foul mood. In the eleven or so months since we'd been here, through all the manure we'd survived, I had never seen her in such a state. Her composure had completely dissolved.

"I have a spare here." Tessa dug through her overflowing box of bits and passed one over. We'd just arrived back from Good to Go with a new load of clothes and fabrics. I had escorted Tessa, Iza and Carley over the wall and through the shadows to do their weekly pickings from the new stock. Even though they were wearing their adapted style of clothing that mostly covered their scales, we still made sure they went out with a guard. The girls combed through everything and selected items they wanted to alter, mend or adapt.

We had a huge table set up in an old room of Warehouse Two—the Veggie Garden shed. The room had large windows to the front car park making it light, bright and airy. We'd pulled the desks from the office in Warehouse One and set them up along one wall. These now were home to Tessa's sewing machine plus two others. At the end of the room, holding pride of place, was Kerm's knitting machine. Early on, he'd taught the girls how to use it and it had saved our buttooshies through winter.

But for now, the main table was covered in a pile of clothes, mostly men's, to be adapted into the girls' new unique style. But also for the menfolk. And some women's items as well... for me... and Helen. She loved it. We both did.

Iza's mood had been deteriorating rapidly. Considering how bad things had been when we first arrived, I didn't think she was capable of this level of angst. When things had been bad, and continued to be so for quite some time, she remained calm. Now things were good, her calm had headed for the hills.

We needed to sort this out. Everyone was avoiding her, which was a major problem because she was the heart of this place. When she was off, everything was off. It was time to call a spade a spade. "What's wrong Iza?"

"I lost my pick."

"No, I mean what's wrong with you?"

"Nothing."

So, it was going to be like that. I passed Dawn to Carley. It had taken me a while to reconnect with the child. I knew I had made a complete mess of... everything. In the end I had not helped anyone, least of all Genni and Dawn. But praise the Light, Genni and I had come to an arrangement. She was still plagued by the Black Dog, so each day she filled a shift with the garden team—it was where she found the most peace—and during this time, I would watch over Dawn.

The precious child had been confused, grieved and lost. It broke my heart anew. Every day. But I knew it was my penance, and I had to make things right. And I honestly believed, thanks to the Light and the gracious forgiveness of my family—old and new—I was doing so. Which brought me back to Iza.

Not only had I been neglecting my own precious kids, I'd been neglecting my responsibilities here at the Factory. Iza was my concern. And it was well past time I confronted her on this tangled problem, whatever it was. "Iza." I waited till the girl looked at me. "We can do this the easy way, or we can do this the hard way."

She shot me with the accusation. "What!"

The hard way it was, bless her.

I wasn't too upset about that. I was still coming to terms with my own angst, and a girl could always do with a good fight to rid the system of those particular frustrations.

I gave Carley the nod. With Dawn balanced on her hip, she tidied her area, gathered Jordan and left the room, quietly but firmly shutting the door behind her.

"You can either start talking and telling me what the problem is. Or I will start guessing, making assumptions and then start lecturing you on how you can fix each and every one of my misinformed notions." I paused to let that sink in.

"I've told you Kait, nothing is wrong. Stop hassling me." She spun her chair away from me and was confronted by a solid wall.

A terse-faced Tessa sat with her arms crossed, giving me her full support. "I'm calling skrat, Iza. I don't for a second think you're fooling yourself. And you're definitely not fooling us. And we're sick of it."

Iza rolled her chair back so she wasn't surrounded by the enemy. Her eyes bounced between us. "Well... if you don't like it you can leave."

I tried to hold back my scoff. Well, not really. But a girl had appearances to maintain. "Is that what you really want? Because we will. You just say the word and we'll hightail it right out of here." Calling her bluff brought her up short. "But don't think it's only us who will leave. We're not the only ones tired of your tantrums. So, you can either sort it out, or get ready to be left out in the cold. Your call."

She went a paler shade of shocked.

"I'm serious. We did not come here to cause trouble or a divide." I held up my hand. "I confess, again, that I made a serious error of judgment. I have and will continue to apologise for my error. But, from the bottom of my heart, I swear to you in all honesty we came here to help. If our welcome or usefulness has run out, we will go."

Iza's terrorised gaze flicked from me to Tessa, who just stared grim-faced back at her.

That's my girl. Hold her in and block her escape.

"Please," it was a whispered croak, "I don't want to be alone."

My heart cracked a smidgen, but not enough to back down. "But don't you see? You already are. Whatever's eating you up is keeping you at arm's length from everyone. Even the kids are scared of you."

She swallowed loudly. Then the tears came. I wasn't overly worried but nor did I feel a great deal of success, yet. Iza was truly gifted with the tears. "You're all leaving me behind. You're all doing this"—her hand flapped vaguely towards the cavern of Warehouse One—"thing. They've all changed. Not just little things, but big things too. It's changed everything. I don't know where I stand." She was silent for a while. Then the colour returned to her face. Not a soft healthy glow, but a fierce, raging, pomegranate-red. *Buckle your seatbelt girl, here we go.*

"It's all this Light... business. It's His fault. Everything was fine until you came along and started changing everyone. It's ruined everything." Her hands were clenched and she threw them on the table. "Dan. It's all Dan's fault. He was the one who started talking to Indy about the Light. I wish he'd never come here."

Oh sweetheart, if you weren't so tied up with your own problems you would know you had just declared war on my girl here. And true to form, Tessa took the bait. "Hey. Don't go blaming your problems on Dan. It's not his fault. He's been doing everything he can to hel—"

"Tessa." Her armour was crackling with fire. "Calm, sweetheart. We'll sort this." I tried to get between their locked horns. "Iza, Dan is not responsible for the changes in Indy. That is Indy's doing. He has made his choice and now he's working out what that means and what that's going to look like."

Iza threw her arms in the air and stood. "I don't even know him anymore. And if that's what the Light does, then I definitely don't want any part in it." Iza had worked her way to yelling and stepped back further, creating a bigger distance between us. She began pacing like a caged tiger.

I gave her space and time to pound out her frustrations then re-entered the battle. "Sweet girl, this is not about Indy."

"Of course it is. I thought you were supposed to be smart, Kait. This has everything to do with Indy. I can't live without him and, now he's changed, I can't live with him. It's all the Light's fault."

I calmly and slowly repeated myself. "This has nothing, to do, with Indy." Then went for the jugular. "This is, all, about you."

She froze. The glare of pure rage she shot revealed the truth. I had poked the bear real good. But I had a bit of the bear myself. So, I served it up hot, hard and silent.

Honey, you are way *out of your depth. Back down. Listen up. Get ready to learn.*

With a yell she released her fury and went back to wearing tracks in the concrete floor.

I gave her another moment to work out some of the bloodlust, then went in for the kill, confronting her with the blatant truth she'd been working so hard to deny. "How do you think you met Indy that first night on the bridge? Chance? What about the house here that just happened to be unlocked? Coincidence? It's a Soteria House. Any of us could get in without a key. Others can't. Didn't you ever wonder why you were safe in that hut for *seven* years? You do know there are people out there looking for you? Don't you?"

Actually, I didn't know that. Until, with utter certainty in my spirit, I did. But before I gave it further thought, I continued. "Did you ever question why your heart picked it over your sense? There are no amenities in that building, but the cabins and the Warehouse are fully fitted out. It would have been so much easier for Indy if you had picked the office in Warehouse One where he could easily use the bathroom without having to hide in the bushes to get there. No. You just happened to pick the only place on this premises where no preda-tors could get in. And you didn't even know you were being watched over, shielded and guarded all this time."

Again, I gave all of that a chance to sink in, then continued. "What about Indy walking? Or the fact that no matter how much—or how little—food Indy brings back from... who knows where... there is always enough for everyone? Creative cooking? I don't think so. What about when you were healed? We know it was more than just the injuries from that night. Should I go on?"

"No." She'd returned to her chair, the fight gone out of her. "I am glad he has his legs back." Talk about a one-track mind! Of all I had just laid out, that is what she went back to. At least she was giving us insight as to what the real problem was. "I really am, Kait, but he's not careful anymore. He isn't staying hidden and he's leaving the Factory in the daylight. He's bringing danger to us. We aren't safe, with him behaving this way. People now know we're here. I don't know if people are still looking for me, as such. But as Greyscales"—she spat the word—"we are all in danger.

"I love Helen and Kerm, you know that, but even they come and go in the middle of the day. My sisters walk around and the children aren't being careful anymore. No one cares that we have to stay hidden. How can I keep everyone safe if no one can be bothered keeping the rules? Damn it, even Mina's changed. It's all the Light's fault." She was right about it all. Especially Mina—the woman was still as prickly as a briar, but she could have a civil conversation with Marcus without overt derision. A miracle was working its way through her soul.

I asked her quietly. "Do you believe in the Other?"

She just nodded her head.

That was a good start. The girl was drowning in a storm of denial. But at least she could acknowledge all the evidence that had been right in front of her eyes from the beginning. "This is not about anyone else but you. How you respond has nothing to do with anyone else but you. If Indy wants to keep acting irresponsibly—"

"He's not irresponsible." Despite the stewing angst and frustration, Iza's loyalty to her man was unwavering. Well, at least when someone else said something less than glowing.

"He's not being particularly wise at the moment. Regardless of what he is trying to work out and come to terms with. And"—I waited for her to look at me—"as you have already pointed out, he is being a bit thoughtless in regards to everyone's safety... and his own duties." I raced on before she could start arguing again. "But his choices are on him. And he will wear the consequences. Just the way your choices will come back to settle upon you." Again, I let her mull over that for a while.

"Do you remember Tessa's party shortly after we arrived?"

She nodded.

"Do you remember things happening that you didn't understand?"

Again, the nod.

"What's going on inside this Factory is nothing compared to what's coming. It's been coming for a while, and it's why the Light sent us. Those demons came because your family started making a choice for the Light. Now, most have had their eyes opened and accepted the invitation. Something big is coming. The Light is holding it back until we have had time to teach everyone how to fight. But they are coming."

Her eyes widened and again she paled.

"I am telling you this so you can make an informed choice. Regardless of what you believe and how you feel about Indy. The Dark is coming, and they are looking for souls. Every day we train so your family can defend themselves and fight back. But what about you, Iza? You have no armour. You have no sword. You are as blind and helpless as a baby. What will you do when they come, and you are the only one here who can't defend herself? This is far bigger than you and Indy, Iza. This is far greater than every single person here. We came to help you all get ready. But the choice is yours."

3 2

IZABAAL: FLY AWAY

I had heard the laughing and joking outside the door before he came in. So why did he make an effort to be quiet opening the door and shutting it? What did he think? After all these years, had this cabin, all of a sudden, magically become a soundproof room? I gritted my teeth and tried to breathe through the frustration.

He'd been for another run and then decided to spend even more quality time with Dan before showering and coming to bed. The heat of his body—his presence—crept ahead of him across the room and brushed my cheeks. Or it may have been my rising anger. For eight years we'd had a routine: retire together, rise together. But for several months things had been changing.

Change.

Everything was changing.

He *was* silent now. I sensed more than heard as he crossed the room, pulled back the blankets and climbed in. His arm wrapped around my middle, his hand on my stomach where it lived every night, pulling me close. My back pressed against his front. I sighed and snuggled his body in the mattress, making a nest for himself, but stopped when he felt my body tense and roll away.

"What? What's wrong?"

Stupid tears started leaking. I tried to hide them but couldn't help the sniffle. I was tired. I was hurting and confused. My rock had shifted. My point of reference—my anchor—gone. And out of the cracks it left behind, the tears came.

"Frack, Iza. Again? What now?" Indy rolled out of bed. I could hear his feet pacing in a circle. And all of a sudden, our little room which had always been big enough for the three of us—him, me and his chair—was now too small for the two of us.

I was angry at myself for being weak. I was angry at him for not understanding. I climbed out of bed and pushed the tears down. Normally when I wanted to speak to Indy eye to eye, I sat on the side of the bed. Now, more than ever, the change was hammered home as he towered over me. I stood, clenched my fists, and readied myself for a fight.

But even then I had to crane my head back to look at him. I kept forgetting how tall he was. It reminded me of the first night we met on the bridge over eight years ago. He'd unfolded himself from the shadows and stretched his arms above him. I couldn't then—and I couldn't now—get over the immensity of him. Tall, wide, powerful. Full of energy. Even then, when he had been defeated, he still buzzed with energy. He was a lot of man.

Now he looked down at me. "You scared of me, Iza? Is that it?"

I took too long to answer. I knew it. But was I? Scared?

Before I finished thinking, he continued. "You know Amina is wrong, don't you." It wasn't a question. "I am a man. A fully capable, hungry, male." The heat of his glare and anger dried my tears. "For eight years I've kept my promise. I am not going to touch you—take or give—until the day you ask."

I knew he was right. I remembered that first night we met on the bridge—when he had stepped out of the shadows I'd been over-whelmed by the size of him. He made me a promise that night: he would not touch me in the manner priestesses were used to until the day I asked... very politely. Then, and only then, would he consider it. If I was lucky. I had laughed.

Later, I had to look for another place for us to stay. I'd warned

Indy I couldn't go out without a Keeper, or in the daylight. He hadn't understood. I scoured the streets looking for a shelter to move to. My scales were seen and the crowds wanted their piece of me. I managed to escape, but I was a mess. I'd warned Indy I couldn't go out without a Keeper, or in the daylight. He hadn't understood. That night was the first night we'd shared a bed. I'd crawled under his covers and rolled to the wall, leaving space for him to arrange himself behind me. I was pressed up against him, my body bruised, battered, swollen and hurting all over. I felt safe in Indy's arms.

But then in his sleep his body had responded to me.

I froze. I needed to escape. The desire to climb over his broken body and run was driven by blind panic. I had to get away from him. But where could I go and what could I do? We'd only been together for a few months. I lay pinned to his chest and forced myself to breathe and wait. Eventually it passed.

Never once had he acted on it. I knew Amina was wrong. Indy wasn't impotent. He was trustworthy, dependable, loving and faithful. He was everything. "Yes, Indy. I know Amina is wrong."

It hadn't been the last time it'd happened. And it didn't just happen when he was asleep. Never once had he acted on it. And for eight years we'd both pretended it wasn't a truth. For eight years I'd trusted him. What was the difference now? There had never been anything *disabled* about Indy. He was fully capable in or out of the chair. I guess the true strength of a man is demonstrated in what he chooses *not* to do, and the promises he chooses to keep.

For eight years I'd trusted him. What was the difference now?

I knew I shouldn't be scared, but he was intimidating, nonetheless. "It's just a lot to get used to, Indy. The change. It's a lot. And you're not here. You're gone all the time. I don't see you anymore. Things for you might have changed. But for us they haven't. We're still locked in and the prison walls seem a lot closer now that you're gone."

"What do you want me to do Izabaal? Go back to the chair? Kick this gift horse in the teeth, be disabled for the rest of my life? Not take this opportunity with both hands? Is that what you want?"

"No, of course not. But don't for a minute try to tell me, in or out of the chair, there is anything you haven't been able to do if you wanted to. Except run. Now that's all you ever want to do. Run. Run away. Run from here. Run from us. Run from me. Of course I don't want you back in the chair, Indy. But I want you back in my life."

"But what about my life? I've put everything on hold for you guys. For you. And now I have the chance to catch up on all that I couldn't do before. I have the chance to discover all that I've lost."

He could have stuck me with a knife and it wouldn't have hurt as much. I thought he was here for love. Because he loved me. Turns out I was the disabled one all along. Not only was I a prisoner to my scales, I was blind as well. "Well, Indy, you can go. You know you're not needed to get supplies for us anymore. We're growing our own food. We're making our own clothes. Producing goods to sell and make money. In just over a week, we start our own markets. We're good. So, congratulations. Job done. Your ties are cut."

"What do you mean?"

"I'm giving you a free pass; I'm cutting all ties and responsibilities. You don't have to be here anymore. I can see you want out. You want your freedom. So, now you have it."

"Are you saying you don't want me anymore?"

"Of course I want you, Indy. I love you. But I don't want you here with me out of obligation. Because you have to look after us. I want you only if you want to be here with me and my family and all the ugliness and mess that entails. The fights, the brutalities; the reality, warts and all. But if you don't want that, you don't want me. And if you don't *want* me, I don't want you. I love you, I need you, but I don't want you unless you want the whole package.

"You've got your legs, you've got your friends, you've got your god and now you've got your freedom."

Inside, the whole time my mind was on repeat, *please don't go, please don't go, please don't go, choose me.*

"There's the door, Indy."

Please don't go.

It kept cycling in a loop, right up until the door closed and all I heard were his footsteps taking him away.

33

INDIGO: FAREWELL

"Come with me, man, let's ditch this place and go, yeh?" It was a clear night, cool but not cold, half-moon lit. Perfect. It was hand-made for running.

"And where exactly would we go?" Dan sat in the shadows at the back wall of our cabin, looking to the skies. Office lights dotted the skyrises in the city. The occasional car made its way across the bridge. There was a heaviness about him. Maybe it was in the night. Or, maybe, it was in me.

"I don't know. Anywhere. We'd be free. Just like old times. Don't you just want to get away, shake off the responsibility? Have a life without this crowd to carry and these things to worry about?" The lie didn't take long to take its revenge. A blazing blade immediately gutted me and almost brought me to my knees as I thought of my boys. And Kazi. Even Dawn. I would miss them. I'd miss the girls too… I guess. But if Dan came with me, it wouldn't be so bad.

"And what part of the 'old times' do you think I'm looking back on and getting nostalgic about? Seriously Indy, that life was hell."

"Don't you ever just want to be free? Free from the responsibility? Free to come and go? To not come back? Do your own thing… be your own person? Not be tied down or chained up?"

"Indy, I lived that life for seven years. It was seven years of hell. I had no one. I had nowhere and nothing." With his elbows on his raised knees, he shook his head and ran his fingers through his hair.

"But you'd have me, this time."

His head shot up and with wide, unblinking eyes he stared at me. "Mate, I love you like a brother. And no matter what, you'll always be my brother. But I have found something more... more important than my freedom. It's not a perfect family and it's sure as frack not easy. But I wake up each morning and know I'm needed. I have a job to do. And if I'm not doing it, it won't get done; no one else can do what I do like I can. I have a role here—a place, a purpose."

The earth was shifting beneath me. It was like hands on the clock speeding ahead... or the earth spinning away from me. Everything was moving forward as a unit. But I was frozen in place watching everything and everyone move away. Even if I wanted to go with them, I couldn't. My feet were stuck. "But you're leaving me. You're leaving me again."

Dan's voice came out through gritted teeth. "No, Indy. You left." He shook his head again and groaned. "Listen"—he shifted his butt on the tarmac to look at me fully—"you have to do what's right for you. But staying with my family, going where they go, is right for me. Yes, we'll move on. I don't know where that'll be, or what we'll be doing, or what that'll look like. But you'll always have me as a brother. I will always be there if you need me. But these people need me every day. And I need Tessa. I love her and I am going to show her she is worth fighting for and working for. I've got to show her that I'm committed to her, and I am there for her regardless of what that looks like. I've already jeopardised that once. I'm not going to do it again."

"So you're just going to be hauled around like a whipped dog, yeh?" I tried to make it a joke, but even I heard the bitterness in my voice.

"After my seven years as a lone wolf, I'd pick a whipped dog any day. And I'm not a whipped dog. If I choose to stay, choose to be, choose to work, I'm making a choice. And, for me, it's the right choice.

"So, mate, I can't and won't tell you what to do. I can't tell you what's right and wrong. I wish you all the luck in the world. But I

228

think you're a bleeding fool. I don't know if the door here will always be open when you decide to come back—and you *will* once you've experienced life out there alone. Right now, you have no idea just how completely stupid you're being." He growled at me. Yep. Growled. Then clenched his teeth and fists. I didn't think he was going to hit me, but I got ready for it just in case. But, just as quickly, it faded and he continued. "If you're not welcomed here when the time comes, you're always welcome with me. Come look for me. You'll find me."

I couldn't believe Dan's choice. I'd always thought he'd have my back. That our family tie was thicker than any other. He continued speaking, but in all honesty, I tuned him out. All I heard him say was he'd picked a chick—one he wasn't even committed to—over me. He'd shut me out.

The next thing I knew, he'd stood and was shaking my shoulder to get my attention. When he had it, he looked me in the eye. "But don't take too long. We don't know how long we're here for." He punched me hard.

"What the frack." The Kret.

"One day you're going to grow the frack up and stop running away." With that he turned away. Like he couldn't look at me any longer.

The fracking princess. I'd offered him the opportunity to come with me. I'd let him know what I was doing. No one was forcing him to stay. He just chose to let me go. Alone. Again. So, I did. I left his sorry butt in the car park and scarpered over the wall and fell flat on my face. Damn legs still let me down. But I didn't care. They were good enough to be out of that bleeding chair. I didn't need it anymore. And I didn't need that sorry lot in there either.

The lie still burned all the way through my heart.

34

DANIEL: TELLING IT LIKE IT IS

I could not believe Indy was making the biggest mistake of his life. And since I'd been with him for a significant part of that life, doing significantly stupid things, that was saying a lot. I got that he was feeling useless. He wasn't into gardening, or cooking... or sewing. He didn't need to protect his family nearly as much now Lily had come off the street and the women were all getting better at defending themselves. He still went out every day for supplies but came back with fewer and fewer things as we needed less from the outside.

He was struggling to find his place. His purpose. I'd never claimed to be super smart, but the way I saw it, he wasn't going to find his purpose out there. He needed to be here with his family to work that out. And check in with the Light.

Can you smack him around some, please? Bring him to his senses? I don't want him hurt more, but I figure sometimes you gotta reach the end before you learn there's nowhere else to go. So, I'm kinda scared to ask, but... I know you love him... and you'll watch out for him... so can you please do whatever it takes to break him? Then rebuild him in a way he fits... finds his purpose and bring him home where he belongs? Please?

I was beat. We'd been flat-out prepping everything for the markets. And now my brother had just kinda kicked me to the curb. The kret.

Under the cover of night, I stepped away from the back wall of the hut and looked up to the clear sky.

You know, sometimes it all kinda feels a bit too hard. Like we're swimming through set concrete. I know you know the end game. But, man, some days just do my head in more than others. I know you know that too. But I'm just kinda putting it out there.

To be honest, my biggest knot was Tessa. I'd got to the point where I couldn't sleep… or think… for thinking about her. I'd go for a run to punish myself physically before turning in—it was the only way I could sleep—but then I was too tired. Crazy, I know. Too tired to sleep. Everywhere I went, she was there. Every time I looked around, she was there. More amazing than ever. Stronger. Brighter. More alive than ever. I'd been courting her. Trying to be the best version of myself. To prove I was different; worthy. But we weren't going anywhere. Nothing was happening. I don't mean *happening* happening. I mean between us… progressing. And things had kind of cooled because of it.

What am I gonna do? How do I make it right?

The night was too beautiful to turn in yet. I wandered over to Warehouse One and slid down the wall and spent time chilling out with the Light, taking in the magnificence of the sky.

You really are that big, aren't you?

I breathed in the freshness of the night, the metal behind my back chilling my spine while the tarmac warmed my butt. Sounds from the city ebbed and flowed across the canal and over the wall, offering quiet background music. The metal of the surrounding buildings cracked and popped as the temperature cooled. The evening breeze carried the scents of the neighbourhood. I breathed them in deeply, trying to discern each one.

I saw movement in the shadows. Someone was coming out from under the trees by the wall and making their way across to me.

Tessa.

She stopped in front of me. "May I join you?"

"Be my guest."

She slid down the wall next to me and joined me in contemplating the stars. "Whipped dog, hey?"

"You heard that?" *Skrat.* I was madly replaying my conversation with Indy, trying to remember what I'd said and if I'd hung myself out to dry any further in her eyes. I was still trying to figure out how she'd weigh up what I'd said when she interrupted my thoughts.

"I miss you, Dan."

Time stopped. Emotion rose up inside me like a hungry beast ready to consume me. I couldn't speak. To hide my response to her four simple words, I dropped my head between my knees and tried to breathe through the tears. Yeah. Not proud. I was exhausted, okay?

She rubbed her hand over my back and pulled me close until I got myself under control.

I brushed my face along my arms, then sat up. "I've missed you too." I swivelled a bit to face her. We were both in the dark but the moon and reflected city lights was just enough to see her. To read her. "What do you want to do?"

She tilted her head at me.

I took her hands. "Tess. Do you want us to figure this out? To work *us* out?" I hurt like hell, but there was no point trying to smash jigsaw pieces into a puzzle they weren't made for. But she'd given me hope. After hearing me bare my soul to Indy, she'd still come over.

She lifted her eyes. The deep, dark pools of sadness rocked me. I inhaled as deep as I could before I drowned. I watched her swallow. She bit her lip. She tried to twist her hands out of mine, but I held firm.

And there it was. I was not only drowning, I was being cast adrift.

Frack. I'd blown it. I'd waited too long, hadn't tried hard enough and now I'd completely missed the boat.

I was so far down the pit of misery I almost missed her whisper. "Do you?"

"Frac— I mean, yes, Tessa. I really do."

The pools in her eyes brimmed and her bottom lip disappeared again. Then she nodded.

"What? What is that? Is that a yes you want us to work? Or ..."—I swallowed and nodded—"right now Tessa, I need crystal-clear confirmation. No ambiguity. Okay? You gotta spell it out for me, tell me exactly what you need."

She nodded again. It caused twin rivers to leak down her cheeks.

I couldn't take it. She was so small and broken. How could this be? The girl had beaten demons, she'd bested Amina—a freaking Amazon twice her size. She'd transformed every woman in this Factory, giving them a new lease on life. She'd helped bring Carley and Lily—of all people—into the Light. How could she be this fragile? I couldn't help myself. I pulled her over and wrapped her in my arms, willing my strength into her. My fortress had room for her. I could make her safe, damn it. She had to know that... feel that.

She sagged into me as her body shook. Her arms tucked into my front and her fists clenched my shirt. I waited until she had ridden the tide. Her body rose and fell with a cleansing breath.

"Do you need another towel?" It worked—she huffed and swatted my leg. "Seriously, Tessa. Honey, I need words. I've been busting my gut trying to show you I can be better. But I don't know where I stand. Do you want to make this work?"

"Yes." Again with the whispering. But for now, it was enough.

"Okay... alright... we can do this." I breathed deeply till my heart slowed down. "Right. In Sodom we made a pact." I sat up and tilted her away so I could read her face. See her response. "We were going to tell each other when we did something wrong. We shook on it."

Help me here. This is so fracking hard. A bit of help would be really cool right now. Please!

"So"—deep breaths—"you go first. How'd I stuff up?" I was kind of hoping it was going to be like a sticking plaster, rip the thing off as fast as possible. I tensed myself and waited for the verdict.

Tessa huffed out a little laugh and shook her head at me. Then the humour drained from her face. "First." Skrat, that meant there was a list. I gave myself a pep talk. I could do this. I nodded and she continued. "I meant it when I said I missed you. It's like you're trying too hard to be someone I don't know. I want... you. The old you. The you

I fell in love with. Not this… socially acceptable, squeaky-clean version of you."

Internally I collapsed. Possibly outwardly, too. It was like being allowed out of those ridiculous skinny jeans she used to try to make me wear. "That, I can do." The relief gave me confidence to keep going. "What's next?"

"You know I make mistakes, all the time. Literally. All. The. Time." She dropped her head and gave it a shake. "I stuff everything up. Are you sure you want to do this with me?"

I nodded.

Another deep inhale then she continued. "If you want us to work, you've got to accept that I'm not perfect."

I waited.

Nothing.

"And…?"

"What do you mean, 'and'?"

"And… what? What else. Be normal, accept you're not perfect and…?"

"That's it." Her eyes were wide and clear.

I ran my hands through my hair. "Words, remember Tessa. What the frack does that mean?"

"It means, Daniel, that I make mistakes. I am going to continue to stuff up, break, ruin, damage and generally destroy everything at some point. I will continue to let you down, disappoint you and hurt you. I don't want to"—tears threatened again—"I seriously don't want to," she whispered, "but I will."

I stared at her blankly. How could she believe that? "No you don't… you won—"

"Yes, I will. And you are going to do the same to me." She took my hands in hers. "Don't you see? I can't be everything you want or need me to be. And you're lying to yourself trying to become that person for me. I don't want to need rescuing. Sometimes, I need to rescue myself. And sometimes I'm going to fail. And then I need to know you're going to be there."

"So, what are you saying?"

"That I love you, just as you are. And I need you to love me, just as I am. I need you to keep taking me back, when I stuff up. When I fail." She leaned back against the wall. "I was on a crazy learning curve, and I slipped. I am not proud of how far I fell. But the hardest thing of all is that you locked me out. If you can't accept that I'm flawed now, at the outset, I can't do this... us." She lifted her hand to my cheek. "I couldn't survive that again."

"You seriously saying you love the real me? The messy, gutter-rat thief who skitches you off."

"Dan, that is where you were. That is not who you are. We've both moved on. Were you even listening?"

"Yeah, I heard. No shutting you out. Got it. Leave the key out under the mat. I can do that. But do you promise to come home?"

"What?"

"Do you, Tessa, promise to always come home after you leave me?"

"Oh." She gulped. "Yes, Dan. I promise to come home. Always."

"Because, Tessa, that's what I need. I want you to fly. I want you to go as far and as high as you want, reach for the stars and claim each one. But"—I pinned her with my bleeding heart—"I want you to take me with you. Go anywhere you want to, but always come home to me." I swallowed the lump in my throat. "I need to be a priority. I need to know that whatever you're doing, wherever you're going, I'm with you and you're for me." I pushed the last words out in a whisper. Damn it. I was not going to cry again. Frack it.

Tessa leapt onto my lap and surrounded me like a blanket. Her arms around me like a vice, her legs over my lap like a brace. Her wild white hair smothered me, and I breathed her in. Grateful that she couldn't see my face.

Leaning back, she looked at me closely. Damn. Then spoke solemnly. "I promise you, Dan, that I will always make you a priority. Except"—sparks of mischief kindled in her eyes as I tensed—"for the Light. Him first, then you."

The ogre I had been piggybacking for the last twelve months climbed down and finally switched off. I couldn't remember the last time I could actually breathe. Hiding the tears that threatened to betray me, I closed my eyes and exhaled in relief. Soft delicious butterfly kisses whispered as Tessa touched, tested and teased my lips.

"I promise you, Tessa, to always leave the light on, the key out, and the door unlocked, for you. And only you, for always." Wrapping my hand around the back of her neck I pulled her head down and kissed her. It was a pact. We were sealing a deal: deep, searching, belonging.

And best thing of all, she kissed me back. And more. Her small, lithe, perfect body fit over mine, not only like a cloak, but a well-fitted, glove-like cloak. She ran her hand madly through my hair and her body pushed into and brushed up against mine. Things went from good to, "Whoa, there Tessa. Give me a sec."

She stilled, settled in my lap, then breathed. "You okay?"

Oh God, help me here.

I pictured Marcus standing over me.

It helped.

I then pictured Kait.

Better.

Then I pictured Val.

It was like a cooling shower.

Then I pictured all three with their swords drawn and it was like a bucket of ice.

Thanks!

Breathing slowly, I eased Tessa off my lap. "We should go for a walk." I hoped she didn't notice the squeak in my voice. But her giggle killed that and the twinkle in her eyes revealed she knew the damage she'd caused. "You little minx. I'll get you for that." I croaked out.

She laughed and jumped up. "Come on."

I took her hand then swung her around and tucked her under my arm. "Slow down for a sec, okay." She laughed again but wrapped her arm around my waist and went at my pace. "So, Tessa, when we're introduced, we're not 'Friends', okay?"

She reached up and pulled me down to kiss my cheek. "Okay, we're enemies." I pinched her. "Well, what are we, Dan?"

"What do you want to be?"

"I don't know?"

"What do you mean you don't know?"

"Well, girlfriend/boyfriend seems so teenager-y." We walked on. "Maybe since I'm older than you, I could be your coug—"

I growled, "Don't say it." We walked on for a while in silence. "Would you be my girl?"

"Sure." She smiled. "And you can be my boy."

"Boy?"

"Okay... man. Better?'

"Much. Thanks."

35

IZABAAL: BROKEN

The paper-thin wall holding back the void dissolved. Despair rose from the pit and consumed me. I had been running from the ache my whole life. Indy had been the only thing holding it at bay. And now he was gone. As was my last defence. Gone. All gone.

THE WEIGHT of emptiness paralysed me.

He was my everything. I had loved him with all I had and given him everything that was in me. But it was not enough. I was not enough. He'd taken it all... and left.

"Now you know and understand my pain and the ache in My heart."

Everything in me froze. My focus was electrified away from my suffering. A voice had spoken *in* my head. In the silence... true quietness, I strained to hear. Did I imagine that?

"I have loved you with all my heart, Izabel. I have provided, protected and poured my love out for you. And still, you reject me."

The racing of my pulse drummed through my mind. "Who are you?"

"I am, have been, and will always be, the Light. I am love."

"The Lig—" Before I could finish the thought, images raced

through my mind: meeting Indy, being sheltered at the hospital, having a home to go to afterwards, my mother, finding our hut—the Light's house for us, the Factory. Then a kaleidoscope of faces— people who had been brought into my life to help. Images flashing past my mind's eye.

The air rushed from my lungs. The bed caught me as I collapsed. The weight of love—overwhelming, incomprehensible love—pounded and pinned me to the mattress. I couldn't move, breathe or think of anything except the love forcing its way into every nerve and cell of my being.

And pain. I felt His pain that His gift—He Himself—had not been seen, heard, or accepted. His love had been rejected. Just like my pain of being rejected by Indy. But one hundred times worse. A thousand.

It was too much. My brain refused to function, my limbs dead, useless weight. A wild, animalistic keening slowly made its way through the barrage. Something was wounded. Was it His pain?

Stop, stop, I can't... too much... I can't...

Eventually, sense returned. Rough hands shook my inert body. "Izabaal, what? What is it my girl?"

Voices were making their way through the wailing. "What's wrong with her? Amina? Do something. Someone find Indy."

His name was all it took to drive me back into the depths of the void. But the love pursued me relentlessly. There was no escape.

"He has gone." Amina's voice confirming the truth sealed my fate.

I was hoisted up and pinned to a firm body, arms wrapped around me, holding me together. The keening continued as I was hauled across a lap and embraced. Once again, I became blind, deaf, unreceptive to everything except the pressure of the love and pain pouring into an insatiable vacuum; a black hole that consumed everything; a bottomless pit. There was a war tearing my body apart and ripping my soul to shreds. The emptiness was pushing against the love. The love was filling and forcing the barrenness back. I was not strong enough to contain the battle. I was only mortal, a broken, fragile vessel. I could not contain the force.

Make it stop. Please. Help.

A gentle voice snuck in underneath the battle. A song. A lullaby. It was a switch, bringing with it memories of being rocked to sleep in Amina's arms. Safety. Love. Amina. I clung to the memory. Soon the battle abated, and Amina's voice became clearer, offering me a lifeline out of the chaos.

The wailing quietened. The picture became clearer. A divan swathed in rivers of fabric: purple, blue and gold. Always purple, blue and gold. Curtains of sheer gauze giving the illusion of privacy. Hiding away from the worshippers, the Keepers and the acolytes, curled in Amina's lap, she held me, rocked me, kissed my hair and sung. A young girl herself, at times her words were flowered with tears. Other times frustration. Occasionally fear. But always love.

The haunting lullaby returned calm and equilibrium. The keening softened to quiet sobs, but still my body lay limp in her arms. Totally spent. Rendered useless and incapable by love. The void no longer pursued me. I was filled to overflowing with the love of the Light and Amina.

He saw me. Not just the scales, not just the outer shell. But me. Inside. My fears, my joy. What was important to me was important to Him, purely because He loved me. He understood the ache in my heart caused by Indy's rejection. Because my rejection mirrored the pain in Him.

The weight of my grief shattered my heart. *I am so very sorry. Please... please forgive me.*

"Izabel, do you want to come home? Do you want to take your rightful place in my family?"

Yes Lord.

"Then you must demolish your wall of pride and stop fighting me. Let me in. Acknowledge that I am the only one who can repair and restore you; I am the only one who can fill the void in your life. Choose me and I will always remain true in you. Turn to me and join me in the battle to bring Light into the darkness, beginning first in you then into all the world."

He understood my battle and along with Amina wept for what had happened to me at the Temple. He wept for all of us. He burned in pure rage because of what was happening there. He challenged me to step back out on the ledge and trust Him. To be His instrument to bring the suffering to an end. But more. He wanted me to work with Him to bring the Temple to an end.

The love that now dwelled within me transformed into passion. A simmering passion to set His daughters free. All of us, at the Temple and here at the Factory, He wanted to set us, His cherished children, free. He invited me to step into the role He had been creating for me from the start. The one Amina had been helping to craft. And how could I refuse? It had been the cry of my heart all these years.

"Izabel, will you trust me? Will you stand with me as I bring this abomination to an end? My daughter, I love you. Will you stand in me and step into the role you were created for?"

Again, a rapid succession of images, flashes of memory, times I'd turned my back, slammed the door, and refused to heed His call raced through my mind's eye. He had been pursuing me for years. And now I was at a crossroad. Would I walk away for good? Or was it time to come home?

I opened my eyes and a wonder surrounded me. Amina, Vashti, Aiko, Shauna... everyone, even sweet Amber, all stood encased in shimmering light. Different hues, but a halo of... armour? encased each one. I had noticed the change in their scales. Instead of dead grey that absorbed light, each one of them had the most vibrant, glorious silver, reflecting light from every source. But now I could see more. "Amina? What is this?" I dragged my leaden hand and brushed my fingers across her cheek. It went straight through the halo. I watched my fingers sink and rest on her skin. Looking into her tearing, smiling eyes I was speechless with wonder.

"Finally, you have met our Father, my girl."

"Mina, it was..." Closing my eyes, I felt a blanket of peace resting heavily over my spent body, calming my fractured mind. "...intense."

They all laughed. It was joyous.

Slowly I sat up, sliding off Amina's lap, and took in the wonder of my sisters as they surrounded me. In the corner I saw Sariah and Raphael. Peeking through the door, Tessa and Dan. I had heard his conversation with Indy. His eyes held a world of pain for me. I managed a smile.

Are you still there?

"Always, my child."

Will he be alright?

"I am with him."

Will he come back?

"Izabel, I love you. I will always be with you. In me you can do all things."

You will watch over him?

"Always."

I love him so much.

"As I love you, I love him also."

A memory of the weight of His Love pressed into me. *Thank you.*

"Alright lass, enough of this. Time to tell us what this carry on is all about. Wailing like a banshee in the middle of the night." Lottie dragged out what had been our only chair and plonked herself down. Her weight was decreasing with regular exercise, but still she clung to those wretched cigarette butts.

"I met the Light."

"'Bout time you came to your senses. But I still don't understand what all the caterwauling was about? You woke the neighbourhood."

Tessa piped up from the doorway. "Indy's gone."

Lottie huffed. "Well, that's nothing new."

"For good." Dan hammered the last nail in the coffin.

Gasps and shudders rattled around the room.

I glanced at Dan. "The door is open for him when he returns." I sat up and took Amina's hand and looked at my family. My incredible, beautiful family. Each one of them precious in my heart and in our Father's eyes. And on cue, water started cascading from my eyes. "I love you all so much."

Lottie rasped, "Alright lass, calm down and take a breath."

"Oh, beautiful Lottie." I did, in fact, take a huge breath and bring my emotions under control. "I have met the Light. He has shown... demonstrated in a very decisive manner His love for me... for us. I found... find it a bit overwhelming. But"—I took my time looking around the room, making eye contact with every single one of my family—"regardless of whether Indy comes home or not, I have a job to do. I would be very grateful if you would join me." Again, gasps rebounded around the walls of our crowded hut. Amina squeezed my hand and lifted it so I could see what they had all just witnessed. Beautiful, rose-gold armour spread itself all over me. A visible demonstration of His love.

"Oh. My. Word. Even her armour is perfect and beautiful." Tessa tried to make it a joke, but I could hear an edge of desperation in her voice.

Everyone laughed until Dan's whisper ghosted through the group. "Almost as beautiful and perfect as you, Contessa."

"Right you are, then, young lady, what's this job you've got to do and how can we help?" Marcus, squeezed into a corner with Kait, moved the attention away from his kids.

I sat up tall. I would have stood, but there was no room. Breathed deeply.

Are you sure about this? Did I hear you correctly?

"Yes, my daughter. I want you to stand with me as I free your sisters."

"Right then." Again, I looked around the room and decided to focus on Marcus. "He wants us to bring down the Temple of Ashera."

Silence exploded throughout the room.

ACT 3: RESTORED

36

CONTESSA: SILVERSCALE MARKETS

It was the first day of the new year. We'd been here almost twelve months to the day, and we were ready. So ready. And I agreed with Iza, I didn't think it was a good idea to have the markets inside the Factory. We were too vulnerable. Marcus had suggested we move our operation to the grass verge edging the bike path beside the canal, under the trees. It was well-worn from where we'd all been meeting in our little groups for "secret business".

For the past two weeks the kids had been walking the concrete path with Riah's chalks, advertising for our big day. Kerm and Helen had put flyers in their shop, as had Ben at the cafe, and Missy at Serendipity. Ben, Helen and Kerm had lent us some tables and we'd covered them with gorgeous old bedspreads and sheets we'd bought from Good to Go. Shauna and Kazi had arranged some of their glorious flowers in old jars and spaced them along the trestles. Clothing racks, also borrowed from Good to Go, displayed a selection of our clothes. On another table we had a variety of vegetables and eggs.

It all looked so perfect.

Riah and Hiro had drawn amazing artwork all over the path and on the low walls of the canals. Jordan had contributed stick figures.

The sun was out and the sky was clear. And Dan and Val had somehow jumped through all the hoops required to get us a permit to have a stall this morning. Sadly, the only thing missing was Indy.

Thankfully, Tomi had gotten over herself and was back in the swing of life at the Factory. She and Ben had donated flour so Raph, Vashti, Shauna and Aiko could bake. There were plates, boxes and containers full of yummy scones, biscuits, pikelets and cakes. All beautifully decorated and presented. Their table also held jars of jams, chutneys and pickles. The whole arrangement was seriously stunning.

"Where do you want me?" Dan had arrived with his guitar and a chair.

I just looked at him.

He blushed.

"Enough of that, you two." We hadn't told anyone of the new level of commitment we'd agreed to. But I was sure it was obvious. We weren't hiding it; we just hadn't got round to telling, that's all. Kait squinted her knowy eyes at us, then pointed to a space at the end of the last table under the trees. It was still cool, but as the day heated up it would be a beautiful place to sit.

Joko followed with another chair and Riah's guitar.

"You playing drums today, Raph?" Marcus arrived in their wake with a third chair and Raph's special drum. He was a pretty easygoing kid. Except when it came to that drum. No one was allowed to use it. But on a good day, you might be able to look at it.

He couldn't help the bounce. Always trying to act cool and grown up but, today, Raph's excitement was volcanic. He kind of covered it up by racing over to retrieve the chair and drum from Marcus.

Within moments my heart was melting again as Dan started playing. Raph soon joined in, and Riah came running out of nowhere to tune up and play along.

Once again, I was blown away and had trouble focusing on what I was supposed to be doing. When they played, I became all kinds of jelly. Simple as that. They took my mind and sent it away on the breeze.

The good news was that I wasn't the only one. A group who'd

finished setting up raced to the grassy area next to them and started dancing. I quickly finished preparing our clothes stall and joined them and, until we had any visitors, I joined Dan and Raph's singing.

The sun was warming the concrete path and shadows played along the canal. The birds in the trees above chirped and chattered and the smell of coffee finished the perfection. Kait and Iza came around the bend carrying trays of coffee plungers and mugs for everyone. Ben flew by to drop Kazi and Tomi off and to wish us luck before going home to open the cafe.

I was on such a high I was in danger of flying away.

Then our first customer came. I felt like Raph, trying to hide my excitement behind a mask of semi-professionalism. One turned into a trickle, and before long we started to believe this might actually work. Dan had invited Missy and the Serendipity crew. And some regulars of Good to Go came by and chatted to Helen. We were doing so well we were almost out of jams. Next time, if we could figure out how, I'd love to find a way to serve coffee and drinks. Oh. And put some tables and chairs around under the trees so people could sit and listen to the music and eat our baking while they lingered.

I looked around at our large family. The women's dead grey scales all transformed to beautiful silver, reflecting the colour of their thickening armour. Even Amber's scales, which had never turned grey, now shone in glorious silver, the goddess's colours reduced to a dim hue.

Thank you for this glorious day. And this glorious success.

But then the music stopped. I looked over to the path and my heart fell.

"Hey, where you been, twik? I've missed you."

Lily's arm flew in an arc and dislodged the man's hand. Dan, Marcus, Raph, Sariah... everyone really, even the customers, stopped and stepped closer. Lily had the situation under control... sort of. But we wanted to show our support. I was super excited when customers joined our side of the conflict. Even though the women were covered as much as possible, it was still obvious that their beautiful silver scales used to be grey.

"I no longer work the streets. You'll have to go elsewhere. Please leave." Lily's voice was fierce, but still, I could hear the tremor. I knew she'd suffered under Axel, and I guess there was nothing like an "up close and personal" with your past to bring back the memories.

The guy looked around the group and saw a selection of Silver-scales... and Iza. He puffed his chest out and started walking toward her but was met by a sea of people. "No." Marcus was at the front. "If you're wanting to buy some jams or veggies, we can help you. But that's all that we're selling. So"—Marcus shifted his body and opened a way to the path—"if you're not interested in the produce, we've nothing for you."

The guy didn't move.

"Thanks for stopping by. Have a nice day." The words were pleasant, the tone wasn't.

The guy didn't move.

The air crackled. I wasn't scared. I mean, I could probably take this guy down all by myself. But this was what we'd been expecting, and it would put a real dampener on a beautiful morning.

Finally, he turned to leave. We all exhaled. Then he threw a sneaky swing at Marcus. Who was ready for it. It turned into a minor scuffle. I could tell Marcus was pulling punches—he didn't want to destroy the guy, he just wanted him to leave.

Which he eventually did.

With lots of swearing.

And promises to his return with his mates.

Empty threats.

I hoped.

Kait took Lily under her wing and decided they needed to check on a few things back in the Factory. With the two of them gone, a murmur began weaving through the small crowd who had witnessed the unpleasant scene. It was only a matter of time before gossip would spread like wildfire. Our first market would go down in local news as a minor confrontation rather than the huge success it represented.

I grabbed a handful of boxes holding scones and cupcakes and walked through the small gathering of shoppers. "Thank you so much for stopping by today. Please take a sample of our baking to share with your family and friends. We would love to see you back here next fortnight for our next market."

That seemed to do the trick. People moved on with a smile and happy chatter. Choruses of, "Wasn't this great?" and, "What lovely produce," drifted along the footpath.

As they moved off there was a lull in business, so we all took the opportunity to congratulate ourselves on dealing with the drama and diverting chaos.

Until chaos came back with his mates.

A large gathering of unfriendly mates.

With weapons.

Oh Lord. Please help us. Why couldn't they just leave us alone?

Tomi and Kerm gathered the children—including a resistant Riah and a nervous Raph—and herded the women in an attempt to get them back into the safety of the Factory. The rest of us ran interference trying to give them time. But as a consequence, we were outnumbered. Our five to their fifteen or so. Well, this was a great endorsement of our first attempt at outing the Silverscales and mixing with the community.

I looked around madly, trying to get a handle on the situation, and I couldn't believe my eyes. We weren't alone. A number of people who had stopped by to support us had stuck around. And Missy from Serendipity had her phone out. She was holding it up, aiming it at us like some kind of weapon. Without taking her eyes from the screen, she yelled out. "Just wanted to let you all know I'm filming this."

Really? I mean… really? Some people were just too insensitive.

"And I have a great shot of all your faces. Yep. All fifteen of your ugly mugs coming up and accosting these five innocent people holding a stall on the canal. Just outside the old factory. A great stall by the way." She just kept talking into her phone as she panned it around the group, talking about all the things we'd had on sale, filming the products that were still displayed. Her phone came to rest on me. Eeeks. But her dialogue rolled straight over the top of my churning stomach. "That's right. Fifteen of you big ugly brutes who are threatening these five people. Three of whom are women, and one, just a slip of a girl."

I think that was me she was referring to.

I started to see red. I mean, seriously, why couldn't people see me for more than just a simple, useless girl?

Dan reached out and gently grasped my wrist before I went on the attack. "Just watch," he breathed in my ear, and goosebumps cart-wheeled down to my toes. And all of a sudden, I was very happy that I was "just" a girl.

Missy continued, "So, just thought I'd let you know that you're all on film before you do anything else."

By now, a number of other people had their phones out and were doing exactly the same thing. Except Helen, who was actually talking on hers.

We were at an impasse.

The fuming men were held captive by the cameras. People filming were glued to the spot, waiting for them to do something. No new customers could make it through the barrier of warring sides.

I think the term was stalemate.

Or piggy in the middle.

More like five piggies stuck in the muddy middle.

But then, a new group of people walked around the end of the factory wall and approached us.

Wearing uniforms.

And guns.

Not that they had them out or anything.

Then there was movement. The fifteen hostiles took off and the pent-up air that had been holding me upright escaped and I sagged like a rag doll.

The Enforcers walked among the group, and everyone was very keen to spend their two cents worth of information. One came toward us and looked us over. I tried to think of what we would look like through his eyes.

"You folk okay?"

We couldn't have looked too bad. In Sodom, our appearance alone would have got us in trouble with the Enforcers.

Val stepped forward. "Thank you for stopping by. We appreciate your help. We're fine now that they're gone."

Who was this woman and what had she done with Val? Val could have probably taken them all on by herself. With the five of us, it wouldn't have been too much of a problem at all. A bit messy—and bad advertising—but we could have managed.

The Enforcer looked over the five of us again, his eyes lingering on Kait. "Glad we could be of assistance." He then looked at the stall and the products we had laid out. "You got a permit for this?" He was holding a jar of chutney, but I'm pretty sure he was referring to the stall.

Dan retrieved the paper from his back pocket and handed it over. Not finding fault, the Enforcer handed it back, nodding. "Alright then." He looked back at Kait, then to the chutney before placing it back on the table.

He was acting weird, and I was worried he was going to find a way to make more trouble. Maybe that's what Val had been doing—making him feel like the hero so he would leave us alone. I raced over, picked up the jar he'd been playing with, along with several others, and handed them over. Putting on my best demure, "simple girl" smile, I looked up at him. "Please accept these as a token of our thanks." I gave a bit of a flutter to my eyelashes, until Dan stepped up behind me and thrust out his hand.

"Yeah, we really appreciate it." He then threw his arm around my shoulder.

The Enforcer just stared at us, at the jars in his hand and stacked up his arm, then back at Kait who was now wrapped in one of Marcus's arms. "Happy to help." He turned to go, then stopped. "Hey, aren't you Kait from Eye on Laodicea?"

Twice in a blink of an eye I was exhaling tension.

She smiled and told him yes.

He blushed. "Can I have your autograph?"

I turned into Dan's side to hide my giggle. But when I saw

Marcus's face I had to bite my tongue to hold in my laugh. Cool as ever, Kait signed a napkin and invited him to return with his family in a fortnight's time. He nodded and moved back to his crew.

After that, the market was pretty much over. Except Missy had kept filming. When the enforcers left, showing that they had given us support, and we were in the right, she signed off. "So, like I said. These brilliant markets are operating fortnightly by the canal at the Old Factory. They have awesome stuff so come by and check it out. Then pop over the bridge to Serendipity for a coffee afterward."

"Publicity hog," Dan muttered as he went over to embrace and thank her.

"That was gold, hey. That'll get you customers, no worries. You coming by, tomorrow?"

Oh. My. Word. "Wait, what? Are you going to post that? All of that?"

She smiled. "No. That was live." She winked, then threw over her shoulder, "See you tomorrow."

37

INDIGO: HOME FIRES BURNING

"What are you doing here?" Ben tucked the tea towel he'd been polishing cutlery with into the ties of his apron.

Good question. What was I doing here? Skitched if I knew. "I was wondering if I could camp out for a while?" I'd tried two weeks on the streets, and I was ashamed to admit I'd got soft and lost my edge. I couldn't do it, eh. I was exhausted, hungry and stank to high heavens.

"No."

"No?" Ben had always been here for me. "What do you mean, no?"

"You have a home and somewhere to 'camp'. You have a horde of a family worried sick about you, and I will not help you hide any longer. I might stretch you a feed… and a shower, if you're on your way back. But if you're heading back out to the streets, you're on your own and you can go. Now."

I just stared at him.

Arms crossed over his massive chest, ham-leg arms bulging, he didn't move.

"Go?" He was pitching me out?

"If you're heading home to sort your skrat out, I'll feed you first. But it might help you bargain your way back in if you go back looking as hopeless as you do now." He made no secret of looking me over. "I could be doing you a favour."

I then looked at my reflection in the counter glass. It had only been two weeks, but yeah-nah, I wasn't pretty.

"But you better make your mind up quick. I'm heading over to help out. I just need to wait for our mutual friend."

"What? You're taking her there? Are you mad?"

"Well, you haven't been here to give her updates and she's beside herself with worry. The Factory has been plastered all over the internet for the past two days." He shook his head. "But you'd know that if you'd stuck around long enough to help them for their big day."

"Why? What's happened?" Iza.

Help them be alright. Please.

"Seriously? You have the nerve to ask me that after you took off and left them to fend for themselves?" He shook his head again. "I've known you for years now, lad. But never have I been disappointed in you. Until now."

"Just tell me, would you? What's happened? Is she okay?" I swear if he didn't tell me soon, I'd strangle the guy.

"So, you're telling me you've decided to care?"

"Oh, for frack's sake." I spun and bolted back to the Factory. I didn't slow or think until I had made it back to the compound. The gates were open and there were people milling on the tarmac in front of our hut and Warehouse One. Strangers. Inside my home.

"Iza." People turned to look at me. Obviously an unremarkable piece of junk washed in from the street, I held no interest. I was dismissed. As one, the crowd turned back to the closed doors of Warehouse One.

"Iza." Seeing red, I pushed my way through. They paid attention when I happened to shove some people out of the way to get in. Some guy was at the front with a camera. A TV camera.

I ran straight up to our cabin and barged in. She wasn't there. Back on the porch, I released the rage that I couldn't hold in any longer. "For frack's sake. Iza? Where the hell are you?" I launched myself over the railing into a group of people and forced my way through to the side door of the Common Room in Warehouse One. "Iza? Are you okay? Where the frack are you?"

The door was locked.

"I'm gonna fracking kill someone."

I couldn't get in.

"Frack. I'm gonna kill…"

I couldn't get to her.

I started pounding on the door.

"Iza!"

Fists. Feet. Swearing, swinging away. "Where the frack is Iza?"

The door gave way and I fell into the Common Room. Frantic. No time to waste. I searched all the faces. Until at last I saw her.

Leaping tables and throwing chairs out of the way I made my way to her.

I had no control left.

Running my hands all over her body, turning her around and inspecting her for any wounds.

Nothing.

She was okay.

My knees buckled and I fell to the floor clinging to her legs, the emotion escaping like an out-of-control steam roller till I was flattened. Completely. Empty.

She was okay.

Oh God, oh God, oh God. She's okay.

Slowly her arms came around me and held me to her stomach and caressed my head. I knew she was crying.

"I'm so sorry. Oh God, Iza. Forgive me. I love you. I need you. Please forgive me. Tell me you forgive me. Let me come home to you? Please Iza? I'll do anything. But please, please forgive me." I was going to be sick.

Gently she eased my head back so she could look at my face and I became aware of three things. She was encased in soft, rose-gold armour, she was smiling, and my heart was exploding. It hurt so damned much. How the hell could I have been so stupid? Damn it. I was so fracking angry with myself.

"Welcome home, my love."

Sobbing like a bleeding loon, I didn't care who heard or saw it. I was a fracking mess over this woman.

"I am not happy with you. But I love you and this is your home." She pressed me to her body again, cradling my head.

I circled my arms tighter around her and buried my face in her stomach. Once I had managed to calm enough to drag in a deep breath, letting the anger and worry and fear ebb, her hands took a firmer hold of my hair and with a bit more force she tilted my head back and looked me in the eye. Her smile gone. "But I promise you, Indigo, if you ever… think of leaving me again… think long and hard. Because you will not be welcome back."

I stood and gently took her face and kissed her, hoping she could feel my vow and the depth of my love.

"Right." Lottie's bark broke through the haze I was floating away on. "Now we've got that sorted, go and have a shower. You stink. Then we can work out what we're going to do about the skrat-show going on out there." There were just too many questions. How could there have been so many changes in such a short time?

I brushed my face on my arm and looked around the room. The crowded room. "What the hell is going on?"

Iza couldn't help herself. "Indigo, language. And Lottie's right. Please go and shower."

Before anyone could answer there was a knock at the door. "Kaitie, darling, are you in there?"

"Georgie!" Kait and Raph yelled in unison. Riah was jumping up and down. Kait opened the door to reveal two men and a woman holding a camera. "Griff? Lucy? Quick everyone, inside." She ushered the newcomers into the room as the crowd behind them surged.

38

KAITLYN: REUNION

"Darling. How are you?" Georgie pulled out of my embrace and looked around the room, his eyes sparkling as he dissected the group. But before I could think or process what he was doing here, hands grabbed me and I was smothered by a solid, yummy-smelling chest. "We've missed you. Are you okay?" It took me a while to respond to Griff's gruff question. I could see the emotion bubbling away behind his eyes. My heart turned to caramel, and I hugged him back.

Then between us all we filled Indy, Georgie, Griff and Lucy in on what had happened and where we found ourselves.

"Darling, I saw you online against those gad-awful fellows who looked ready to eat you alive. Not that they could, of course. But, still, dramatic, with a capital What's My Girl Doing? We've missed you so much." I was dragged into another embrace, and I let myself be held as I tried to comfort my beautiful friend.

"We figured something was up, and we want to help. There's more here, isn't there?" Griff looked around the room, his shrewd eyes absorbing all the information: Silverscales, children, and Iza. "Right. Skrat's about to hit the fan, so we'll do a piece. Human interest. Put it out on our regular channels. People know you and you've built rapport. We'll get in first and strike fast." Pulling a tablety-phone device from his pocket, Griff was already making plans and calling people.

"What about the Overseer? You're planning to use the Community's resources to not only help these women, but us. He hates us." I appreciated their efforts, but this was either not going to work or it was going to backfire and leave these guys wounded.

Griff pulled his phone away from his ear. "The fool will have no idea. And we have Felix's full endorsement." Then he was back to his phone conversation. I still felt unsure. This could land my beautiful friends in hot water.

Georgie took over as Griff worked his magic behind the scenes. "Right. Everyone, this is what I would like. Moth—"

"Izabel."

"Check. Izabel, if you're happy to help, I'd like to interview you fir—"

"With Indigo."

"Check. Then, ladies"—Georgie studied the room. I knew from experience he was looking at his subjects, the lighting and the background—"I'd love to hear your story next." He was a bit distracted. From experience, I knew he had already worked out his angle and the path the interviews would take. He was looking for the edge, the hook.

"I've got the location, Georgie." He, Griff and Lucy all stared at me. I led the group to the garden in Warehouse Two with everyone in our wake. The three newcomers stopped and turned to stone, their eyes devouring our garden. It was beautiful: rows of vegetables, flowers, and our chicken pen. The whole scene was full of living colour, vivid scents and excited sound. Insects buzzed and weaved, appearing and disappearing through lush leaves and over bursting flowers as they worshipped the garden. Open mouthed, our three guests turned first to me, then to the group who'd followed us out. Everyone was brimming with pride. And so they should be. They'd toiled faithfully and relentlessly to produce this work of art.

And once again, Georgie was hugging me. "Perfect darling. Perfect.

Check. Then, Kaitie, when we've heard from all the women and Indigo, I'll put you in to bring it home."

"Georgie." Raph had worked his way to the front of the group. His voice cracking, he coughed and tried again. "Georgie. I'd like to share my story too."

"No." I don't know whose denial was the loudest. Marcus, Val's or mine. We didn't mean to frighten him, but he was cowering before us.

Georgie took over. "Darling boy. You are so brave." The man stopped to give Raph a one-armed hug. "But what your family was very bad at telling you, is that they want to protect you. You, and the other kids here—they don't want people in this city knowing who and where you are. Do you remember how horrible it was at school? How everyone picked on you and my girl?"

Raph nodded.

"There are going to be people who are not happy with our story. Now, these beautiful women"—he looked at the group—"have lived with that scorn for a long time. This piece is about showing them for the amazing women they are. To highlight their individuality and tenacity. To show the world that they are human beings who deserve basic human rights, at the very least. But I want to show that, because of how they have been treated, they deserve so much more. They are survivors and victors."

I knew the cunning man was working to bring the Silverscales on board. This had stopped being about Raph.

"I know you and Sariah are heroes. But this is about these incredible women."

Raph nodded and gave Georgie a hug before moving back towards the other kids.

Once the ladies had heard Georgie's plan they were all desperate to share their side of the story. Lucy had been on the hunt for background and lighting levels and called the kids to help her set the scene with garden tools and leftover vegetables from the stall, and then went through checking camera angles and placement of reflectors.

Georgie had finished his interview with Izabel and a showered, socially acceptable Indigo, and was now working his way through a conversation with the ladies. First, he interviewed Shauna, Vashti, Aiko and Tomiko. Lottie was not interested. She said she was not going to help the cause in any positive way by getting in front of a camera. Then Georgie spent some time getting to know Carley, Lily, Genni and Amber. And then it was my turn.

Please let this be the right thing to do. Please let me say the right things. I just want to share your love to Laodicea, show them how much you love them and our new family. Please give me the words to say.

"So Kait, about twelve months ago, you disappeared off the face of the earth. Tell us, what have you been up to?"

Like a tap, I let the story pour out of me. A few times I had to stop for a tissue break. When I thought about how these women had been treated, I was overcome.

Thank you for what you've done here. Thank you for how you've allowed us to be a part of it.

And so it was that the world was introduced to the Silverscales.

39

IZABEL: RECKONING

We were back in the Common Room, now that our stories had been shared. Georgie and his people were still interviewing Kait.

It was a solemn moment. After this, there was no going back. No staying hidden. Not only had we let ourselves be seen at the markets, we were going to be broadcast across the city. Possibly the world.

It was a solemn moment. What had we done?

Are you sure this is the right thing to do? Will my family be safe?

"*Be at peace, Izabel, all will be well. I am with you always. This is my plan for you.*"

The crowd outside was growing, and swamping a van trying to get through the horde. It was utter madness. But then I recognised the van as Ben's. Naturally he would want to remove Tomiko and Kazi from the horrendous mess of a day.

He drove up to the Common Room then raced around to the passenger door and helped a woman to alight. A woman I had not seen for eight years—one whom I had never wanted to see again. Ben shielded her from the crowd and ushered her into our presence, firmly closing the door behind him, shutting the chaos outside.

"Mother? What on earth are you doing here... with Ben?"

Thoughts were gridlocked in my mind. Two separate parts of my life had collided—behind my back, apparently.

My mother, in teal armour, dashed across the room as soon as she was through the door. "Indy, my darling. Are you alright? I have been so worried."

Again, I was stunned. Too confused to think or make rational connections. Not only had she not acknowledged me, my mother was wearing armour and hugging my soulmate.

I pinched myself. Doubtless I was still asleep. This was all a dream. Surely.

"Sorry Audette. I didn't mean to make you worry, yeh?"

"What was I to think? The television reporting horrible stories. Not being able to get in touch. I just had to come here and see for myself." Her French accent and her natural beauty had everyone enthralled. She turned and looked around, taking in the gaping audience for the first time. "Hello everyone. It is a pleasure to finally make your acquaintance. Of course, I believe I could pick you each out from all that I have been told. But to see your beautiful faces brings me such joy." Her French accent and her natural beauty had everyone enthralled. Her smile caressed the gathering.

Kait and the others came back into the Common Room, but I had no room in my frying brain to acknowledge them.

"Stop. Just. Stop. Enough. I cannot think. Mother, what are you doing here and how do you know... all this... my family?"

I looked to Ben, then Indy, then back to my mother. "Is this some kind of a joke?" I looked around the room. Does anyone know what's going on?" Mina shifted. "Mina? What do you know of this?" Her eyes flicked to Indy. "Enough. Someone tell me what is going on. Now."

"Well, my darling, you see..." Mother hesitated. She looked to Indy, whose shoulders had slumped. He gave her a nod before collapsing into the chair nearest him. She continued, "I was so worried about you and Indy when you had been cast adrift from rehabilitation. I needed to make sure you were going to be alright. So Indy and I made an arrangement."

I just stared at her, waiting for more information. But she was silent. "And?"

"And I am very happy to see you are alright." She looked around the room and looked at all the girls. "It has all been worth it. Knowing you are all safe and well."

Kazi wheeled her chair through our growing group and quietly embraced my mother in an awkward side lean from her chair. Audette squatted to embrace her fully. "Hello, ma cherie. How are you?" Nervous in the large crowd, Kazi just nodded. "It is so good to see this new chair fits you well and"—she held Kazi at arm's length—"your beautiful armour. It still makes my heart sing."

I was confident now that this was all an illusion. Mother knew Kazi. And more confounding was the fact that Kazi knew Mother well enough to embrace her... in a crowd.

"Okay. Time out." I couldn't process any more. But before I could even begin to pull threads of a plan or idea together there was more commotion from outside. The crowd was growing, and I suspect becoming impatient after Ben and Mother had been welcomed into our fold.

"I've had enough." Indy stood and strode to the exit. "Come on, we don't have to put up with this."

I could not take one more ounce of... anything. "Who else is here? What more do they want?"

"No... just the trespassers. Time to show them the door. I'm—"

"We're." Marcus stood beside him. His family and most of mine joined him.

"—going to ask them to leave," Indy finished his sentence.

"Interesting timing, Indigo." He was right to prefer an angry mob over me. Things were not going to be pretty or pleasant when I got to the bottom of this.

"Iza, I will be straight back and will help sort this out, when our guests have left." And with that, he left the room. Everyone else hot on his heels.

Cowards.

"As much as I would love to stay and see this reunion unfold,

Shauna and I are going to get the kids washed up and ready for dinner." For the first time in my life, I believed I had just witnessed Lottie flee a fight.

I was left in the dining room with my mother. She was standing by the window watching the scene outside. Ignoring me. "Mother?"

With her eyes locked on the window she absently answered. "Yes dear?"

"Please explain."

She exhaled and physically deflated. Then turned her head to look at me, and I was shocked to see how much she had aged. She came to the table near me, pulled out a chair and invited me to join her.

"It has never been easy, Izabaal."

"Izabel."

She turned her head to inspect me.

"It is the name the Light gave me. I have decided to adopt it."

"Yes. I can see that." She studied my armour and, as always, reached out to touch me. To caress me. It was a ritual we went through. I would freeze. Her hand would drop.

"Easy? You think my life has been easy?" I couldn't believe her. Her ignorance was phenomenal.

"No. Not for a moment. My darling." Her eyes watered. "I do not believe life is supposed to be easy. But I have fought to give you life. And for these past eight years, to keep you safe. I could never give you easy, but I have worked hard to make you safe."

The wheels started turning. Fogginess lifted. How could I have not seen it. "You! You are the contact. You are the one who has been supplying all our needs."

Her silence was all the confirmation I needed.

"Why? Why would you not let Indy tell me?"

At this she actually scoffed. "Because we all know your stubbornness is legendary. If I had allowed Indy to tell you, the many times he asked, I am confident you would not have accepted any more help. And then what? Not only you and Indy, but each one of these women and children would have gone without. You would have rather starved than receive my help. So I made sure that no one told you."

"No one? How many people know this has been going on? How many people have been lying to me?"

"At first it was just Indy. But then he had that terrible accident in the alley. The morning Ben saved him. After that, I could not bear the thought of him going out and endangering himself. So Ben suggested I meet Indy there, at the cafe. He would pass on the information of what you needed, I would get the supplies, meet him before light at the cafe, catch up on the news and leave to get back home before Alain knew I had gone. So, of course Tomiko and Kazi know. And Amina too. She would come and give me updates as well."

"Amina? Amina knew, and never told me she was going behind my back?"

"But, my darling, did you not know? From the day you were taken to the Temple Amina has been keeping me updated on your welfare. I was so grateful to be back in touch with her after Uriah was killed. And to get to know Banjoko."

"All along?" Now I was truly speechless. "Amina? Behind my back?"

"My darling, you do not understand. I have loved you with a love that consumes me. But you have rejected me your whole life."

"Love me? Love! How can you say that? If you had loved me, how could you let that man give me to the Temple?"

"I did it to protect you."

"Protect me from what?"

It wasn't a yell, but emotion burst from her. "From your father."

"What do you mean?"

"He was… is… ambitious. He always wanted fame, power and wealth. At first, when we met in medical school, I believed him when he said he wanted to change the world, to make it better, to bring healing and ease the suffering. Our hearts were the same. We both chased… believed the same things.

"But when we came to this place, he started mixing with people I did not know, I did not like. He changed. Our successes were never sufficient, our advancements never enough. And when you came along, he saw you as an opportunity."

"But why did you let him give me to the Temple?"

"Because I had no choice." It was half cry, half yell. She stood and ran her hands through her immaculate hair, causing choppy waves through its sleek perfection.

"Of course you had a choice. You could have said no."

"You do not understand. I was trapped. I did everything I could to keep you alive. He wanted to sacrifice you to the goddess. I convinced him to let you live."

"What? What do you mean, sacrifice?"

"It is an old practice his new friends told him about. To sacrifice his firstborn for the power and success he craved."

"Sacrifice?"

"Apparently there is a rite. An ancient ritual where leaders would offer their firstborn to the goddess as a blood sacrifice. This, then, would give them power and ensure their success. It is not common these days, but there is provision at the Temple for this… offering."

"I don't believe you. I lived there and never saw or heard of such things."

My mother looked at me. Straight in the eye. Instantly, I felt like a child. Her perfect, congenial veil was removed and once again I was ignorant, naive about the world's harsh truths. Time stopped until eventually her mask slipped back into place. "I could not let him take you from me. I thought if you were an offering to the goddess, a living offering, you would be safe from him. Even now, he is hunting you. Every day you have been away from the Temple, he has not stopped his search. But I have made it so he cannot touch you. He will never hurt you again. And I made equally sure he had no other children… by me, that he could use in this way."

"But why didn't you just take me and run? You have money. You are independent, you don't need him."

"I am ashamed. I knew the work we were doing was changing the world, we were making a difference, making lives better. And I believed you would be safe and well cared for."

"I was a slave." It was my turn to screech and yell. "Abused by men, to make money for men and to be discarded by men. How is that safe?"

"Because you were out of your father's reach, whilst still beneficial to him. You cannot understand how powerful and vindictive he is. I was trapped. But not anymore. I have found the Light. I have accepted His love and forgiveness for what I have done. Since then, I have been freed from Alain. He has no hold over me because you are safe."

"What about your work?'

"Of this I am most ashamed. I only learned of it after you left with Indigo. Even though I was able to stop him sacrificing you, he still made a deal with Ashera. His medical genius dried up the day you left the Temple. I swear I had no idea. But that is why I have been doing everything I can to protect you and keep you safe and hidden from him all these years.

"The work, the advancements, the help we were able to provide... all of it, if it was at the hands of the Dark Lord and your suffering, I wanted no part in it. I have been learning about the Light. I believe He has great plans for you. I am here to support you in any way you will accept." She twitched the corner of her mouth, but her eyes were filled with years of sadness. "I may never forgive myself. But now I have come to join you in the fight."

I just stared. Seeing without seeing. Overwhelmed. All this time, she had been providing for us... me. All these years, checking up with Amina then Indy.

My friends... family going behind my back, keeping me in the dark so that, what? I wouldn't die and take everyone with me? Did they really believe I was that stubborn... that selfish? It was a rude awakening. All of it. That maybe my mother was right, that my family didn't trust me, and that perhaps they were right, too. Even now it galled that she had been behind the scenes.

One by one, everyone began coming back into the room. It was time to start preparing for dinner. I hadn't moved. I couldn't. Everything today had been too much.

40

MARCUS: CLEANSING WOUNDS

The following day we put together a low-key dinner celebrating the twins' twelfth birthday. Despite all the fuss and fiasco, it was agreed the milestone should still go ahead, but equally important to keep it simple. We needed to give the collective worry a juicy bone to gnaw on. They were lost sheep without their shepherdess. Iza was in shock, no two ways about it. Everyone was skirting around her, silent. Like she was a timebomb waiting to go off. How bad would the fallout be? This wouldn't do. That video was out doing its thing in the ether. Georgie and Griff would soon release their interviews. Any moment now, the whole world was going to be sucked through a whirlpool, starting here.

I looked to Val, then Kait. *This won't do. Attack is coming and they're prime for the plucking.*

Val took charge. *Time to catch all the little foxes before the battle.* Moving to the centre of the room she started. "Listen up everyone. The crowds are out and the gates are locked. But tonight, after dinner, we'll set a guard. Three hours apiece." She weighed up the room. "Sariah and I will go first." The girl's eyes grew to saucers. Val then hitched her chin to me. "Marcus and Kait next, followed by Amina and Indy. Tessa and Dan take the final shift, 2.00-5.00 am." Her indigo armour sparked and flashed. The time was coming, and a fight was on the horizon.

She addressed Vashti and Aiko. "Ladies, might be best if everyone stays in here while dinner is prepared." Then she spoke to the room. "Tonight, and for the next few days, I would prefer it if everyone travelled in pairs, at least."

Walking over to Izabel she had a few quiet words, then nodded. "Izabel asked us to join her in her quest to bring down the Temple. That battle has begun. She is now going to petition the Light on our behalf." Iza squeaked. My menace of a sister winked and continued, "But first, is there anyone who wants to mend a wound, repair or restore a relationship?" Val looked around the silent, vibrating room.

No one moved. It was a big ask. But then me Kait stepped forward.

"I know it was five months ago now. But I want to first, thank the Light, and thank you all for your understanding and grace when I caused a rift between Genni and Dawn." We all looked to where the two sat. Genni held the toddler in her lap. Both smiled and when Genni nodded, Kait continued. "I am ashamed of how I let my ache and thorn tear this family apart. But I am grateful and humbled by how you have all forgiven me and welcomed me back with open arms." The last was a hoarse whisper. Then she turned to me. "But most of all, I am sorry for what I did to you. To us. I am so very sorr—"

She couldn't finish the end of her sentence because the emotion had stolen her voice. But mainly because she was pressed so hard to me chest, if I didn't let her go soon, I suspect she would not be able to breathe. But first, I had to wait till me own emotion let go of me tongue. "Loved you then, love you still. Always have, always will." I then released her—just enough to get air—and pulled her out of the spotlight and kept her hidden under me wing.

The room was in shock. I guess none of them had experienced a cleansing before. It was like Russian roulette. Everyone looked around to see who was next, scared it would be them. But you could have wiped me clean with a feather when Amina stepped forward and looked to Izabaal... Izabel. Her eyes darted around the room, then she shuffled—I don't think I could ever remember seeing that woman shuffle, but there it was—closer to the girl… woman she saw as her daughter. "I stepped down from the High Priestess throne for you. And I was happy to do this." She flicked her eyes to Audette. The women shared a sad smile. "Uriah had been brought to the Temple by his boss and associates. He found it… distasteful. But we met and he returned. Over time we fell in love and"—her eyes now flicked to Lottie who nodded—"I fell pregnant. He made plans and prepared a place for me with his people in Benin. I would be free, and we would live in safety to raise Banjoko." She swallowed loudly.

Even though this was supposed to be a time of clearing the decks, none of us was going to stop this woman finally sharing her story. Especially when she honoured us by doing it surrounded by family. And that she included us in that classification.

"He had prepared everything. The girls helped by covering for me as I made my escape. But someone told the Keepers. When Uriah came for me, they stepped out of the shadows and took him from me."

Amina stopped to breathe a heavy sigh. She gritted her teeth and continued. "They took him. And they beat him. Just like they beat your father"—she looked to Indigo. "He stayed with me and fought for us. So I could escape."

Tears not only ran down her face, they pushed their way into her words. "I ran to protect Joko. To protect our unborn child…" It was too much for her now, she had to stop. We all held our breath until she spoke again. "And I let him die for us." Anger sparked across her eyes, but then it was gone.

She turned to Indy. "Each time I look… looked at you, I felt that pain. The never-ending ache that my man died. That they took him from me." Brokenness engulfed her. "Each time I look… looked at you, I saw my own guilt. Of running away. For that, I am sorry."

Amina now turned to face me. "When I saw men, I knew what was in their heart. I lived my life feeding their desires. They took everything from me. Even though you helped us, I convicted you of having the same heart. I have fed that hate. I would not, could not be at peace with you." She looked from me to Dan. "For that, I am sorry."

I was speechless. Looking to Joko sitting in the shadows with his friends, I realised the boy was eleven now. All this time, the woman had been chained to a pillar of grief and dieting on bitter herbs. But today, she'd dropped her guard and drawn back the curtain to her soul. I had to respond. I knew I'd get it wrong. Possibly throw a bucket of acid on her wound. Yet I wanted to let her know we saw her.

"Amina. You... women... all women are a gift. A blessing. You... women... make life worth living. Women in me life are cherished." Dan and Indy grunted in agreement. "The low-life krets who did what they did to you and your man"—I looked to all the women in the room—"who did this to you, and your children, are no men. They are animals. No. Not animals—mindless, selfish, plinter-krets."

"Marcus, language please." At Iza's wide eyes and shocked response to me tirade, some of the gravity shifted.

"Sorry Iza." I turned back to Amina. She was trying to compose herself. Joko had come to stand by her, his arms around her waist, her arm tight around his shoulders. I held out me hand to her but was nudged aside when Indy came in and hugged her. Since neither of them were exactly touchy-feely, it was more than a tad awkward.

Val murmured from the sidelines. "Hey Raph, I think they need some lessons from a natural." She winked at him, and he blushed. The rest of us laughed as Indy released Amina. And breathed a relieved sigh when she didn't drop him to the floor for touching her.

"A miracle indeed." Apparently, me inside voice had spoken out loud. Amina speared me with unreadable eyes, and nodded her head once, shook me hand, then took Joko with her back to the sidelines next to Val. Her red armour ablaze with Light.

Val gave her a quick embrace then stepped back into the ring. None of us escaped her inspection. Slowly she nodded. "Thank you for your honesty and courage for sharing"—she nodded to Amina, then Kait, acknowledging their armour, which flashed and sparked. "The rest of you, spend time in the Light. Seek out the ones you have to restore yourselves to and make peace. Get rid of anything that is blocking the Light and weakening your armour. We go into battle soon. Now is the time to prepare." Again, she gave the room a once-over with her Seeing eyes, then turned to Iza and gave a nod before stepping back.

"What?" It was more of a squark than a challenge.

"Now is the time for you to petition the Light for us, on our behalf, as we prepare to step into the battle the Light has called you to lead." Val was quiet, calm and as soft as a granite boulder.

"What? Now? Aloud? In front of everyone?" It was like Val had asked her to walk a tightrope naked across the city. I didn't think the girl's system could take much more. "But I've only just met Him, and I don't know what to say."

"Good one, Iza, when have you ever not known what to say, yeh?" Indy pulled her close and kissed the top of her head. Taking her hand between his two. "How about I start off for you?"

Hope dawned on her face and she looked to Val. "Is he allowed to do that?"

Val threw the girl a lifeline and smiled at Indy. "Take it away."

He closed his eyes, cleared his throat and began. "Hey, I just want to thank you for Iza. I'm stoked that you have brought her in to the Light and even happier that she finally gave up and let you in, and me back in too." She hit his leg. "Anyway, I also want to thank you for the best group of people ever and the best family a guy could have, yeh? Also, thanks for Audette and what she's done for us over the years. And Helen and Kerm. You were a bit sneaky there. Which was sweet-as, but finding out they were with you... Vashti too, from the start was cool, yeh?

"Thanks for Dan and his crew. For every one of them and how they've helped us. Thanks for every sister and child you have brought here for us to get to know. For Amina and her sacrifice, for bringing her home to us. Thanks for Ben and Tomi and Kazi. And for my legs. Thanks, I mean, how can we say just a simple thanks, but the way you fixed Iza that night, then used Little Dude to fix me and... yeah-nah, words just can't say.

"I want to say how sorry I am for ditching these guys... Iza... when she... they needed me most. I'm sorry to them, but most of all, I'm sorry to you, eh. I just have to figure out what you want from me here. So, a bit of help would be sweet-as."

The boy was like a tap... a broken tap, it was all bubbling out of him like he didn't know how or where to go next, he was all over the place like a headless chook. There was no one else in the room. Like Kait and Amina, he was having his turn of airing his dirty laundry. Never in our times sitting under the trees had he ever spoken so openly. But it was all good. So I just sat back and let his gratitude wash over the whole room. Because every single word he said was spot on. When the tap ran dry, he sat up, shook his head and came back to us.

"Right. Yeah, so"—he looked to Iza—"your turn."

Her blue eyes paled and I heard her gulp from across the room.

"You'll be fine." Indy dropped his eyes to lock with hers. "Yeh?"

Iza looked around, nodded, then shut us all out by closing her eyes. It took her a couple of goes, but in the end, she cleared her throat and started. "Hello?" She gulped again. "Um... I guess I just want to say, um... thank you?" She paused. "I mean, this is all so new and so... much. I've been living in the dark all my life"—a puff of a laugh escaped—"literally and figuratively. Your Light is... a shock... and sharp. It is beautiful, don't get me wrong, but it still burns my eyes and... my skin... it burns—no, not burns—tingles. It is like I have overdosed on something... and I am scared of what will happen, of what I will do... of what you will do... and ask of me.

"I want to trust you. But it's all so new. And, not-new. I am becoming aware of hints... memories of your presence... and presents. Like waking from a dream, I am trying to grab hold of them. But like water, they're slipping through my fingers. All that's left is the feeling of what was. Then a buzz... a warming vibration begins from my heart outwards. It's true. Not a dream. And then I remember all the people"—and like the 10.30 express from Zoar, the tears came—"and the things, and the opportunities and... everything."

The girl had to stop for a while to get herself back under control. I snuck a peek and watched as Indy wrapped her in his arms and offered her his shirt to wipe her face. It must be a thing with these lads. I was impressed, but glad me Kait was not one for tears—I was not thinking I'd be so ready to do the same. Eventually, Iza had her horses back in harness and she was off again.

"Thank you for being patient with me and bringing me into your Light. Thank you for allowing me to be part of this... fight, this... cry of my heart. Thank you that you have brought all these people here with the same desire. With skills and experience and all that we need. I am not sure what to expect, except this: it will be big... bigger than I can imagine. And it will be costly." The girl paused to inhale a shaky breath.

"But I do trust you. I trust that you have called me into a battle you plan to win. You have allowed me to be part of that. Thank you for sharing your fire with me. It burns. Rages. Consumes me with a desire to bring the Temple and all of it to the ground. But more than that. I want it destroyed. Demolished. Desecrated. So nothing will ever stand in its place again. Let it be a warning to all who see the scar: all life is precious and to be treasured." Her fists were clenched. Her chin was high. Fire literally crackled along her armour. And passion infused her words.

She breathed heavily through her nose and wrestled composure back into her petition. "So we will now prepare as Val has instructed. We will wait for the Word you will give to Kait. And we will be ready for when you lead us into battle. We don't know what that will look like, but we trust you to guide, protect and bring about a victory and rescue our sisters."

Nodding her head, Iza stopped. Opened her eyes and was reminded she had an audience. Instantly she blushed and dropped her head. Indy tucked her back under his wing and looked around the room.

We all looked back.

He grinned like a Cheshire cat and made a point of going back to petitioning.

We followed his lead.

"Anyway, before we knock off for the night, I was going to ask you another favour. I know it doesn't seem right after all the cool stuff you've already done. But, you know, Marcus said I should ask. So here

I am, asking. I know you already know her, but Iza is not only the glue here in our family. And the heart of our family. She's the glue that holds my heart together. And since her biological dad is an utter kret —no apologies for that, you know it's true—and Iza has accepted you as her new dad, I thought I should ask you first and see if it was okay with you."

An edge had entered the room and we were all sliding along it waiting to see where this was going.

"And, since I'm still not too sure how this"—his hand flicked between himself and the ceiling—"works, it'd be really cool if you could make it crystal what you think? That would be sweet as well."

We all waited in the silence with him.

"Right, then. Sweet-as. So, now… I was kind of hoping you might help me when I ask and, kind of nudge her to say yes. Cheers, thanks a lot."

Indy opened his eyes and saw we'd all leaned closer. And every single one of us, Iza included, were staring wide-eyed at him. "Oh, hey everyone." Now it was his turn to wear a slight crimson blush, darkening his skin to a deeper shade.

"Well?" Lottie was not waiting for anyone. She wanted to know what we all wanted to know.

Indy nodded, then looked to Iza. And breathed. Several times.

"Oh, for the love of all that's good, get on with it. Ask her." Lottie seemed to be on a timecard.

Indy turned his body, "Izabaal—"

"Izabel."

"What?"

"Well, it's what the Light called me, and I kind of like it, so I've decided to keep it."

"Right." He took another deep breath. "Izabel—"

"You've already said that bit. Get on with it, we want to eat."

Indy glared at Lottie. "Izabel"—then swung his focus back to the woman in front of him—"I love you. I know we kind of promised not to say that. But with all that I am and all that I have, I love you. I am ashamed to say it took me running away to hammer the truth home.

With or without legs, there is nowhere else I want to be. With or without purpose, you are who I *want* to be with. I knew it before I left, but for some idiotic reason I thought I could live without you. I am hoping that you will not only forgive me, and allow me back into our home, but you would also accept"—he bent down and undid his shoes and handed them to her—"these."

"Indy, I do love you, I do forgive you, and you are welcome home. I have told you that. But"—her head turned away and her nose wrinkled—"I don't know what you want me to do with your smelly shoes."

"No more running, Iza. Unless you're by my side. Izabel, I want to be with you, and for you, and yours for always."

On cue, Iza's eyes pooled, overflowed and cascaded. This girl could cry like none other I knew. She sniffed, and tilted her head, then a smile sparkled through her saturated eyes. "Yes. As long as you take your shoes back."

Indy crowed like a rooster. His grin split his face in two. He looked to Dan. "She said yes."

Iza stilled. "What exactly have I said yes to, Indy?"

"Well, marrying me, of course."

The room exploded into cheers. And everyone embraced Indy, slapping his back and congratulating him.

Except Iza.

She froze.

Audette made her way over and crouched next to her daughter, her hands stroking the girl's head and embracing her. Eventually the room came back to them.

"Iza?" It was a whisper. Fear smothered Indy's voice. "You did say yes, didn't you? You do want to marry me, don't you?"

Iza looked to her mother and allowed the woman to embrace her.

Audette whispered in her ear. The two looked at each other as Audette wiped the tears from Iza's face, kissed her daughter's cheeks, and smiled.

Iza inhaled. Turned to face her family, studied everyone's faces, then looked at Indy and then his bare feet. She smiled. "Yes, Indy. I said yes."

The previous eruption paled into insignificance at this. Kids were squealing and jumping up and down. The women were embracing and crying. Dan was slapping his friend on his back. I looked over to Tessa, me precious girl, and was glad to see genuine happiness in her quiet smile. Her time would come. But now it was time to celebrate. To make memories before the battle. Because as sure as dollars to dash, the battle was coming.

41

MARCUS: CLEARING THE DECKS

Nine o'clock and it was our turn at the watch. Kait and I had used the space leading up to it to go for a walk. We made it back to the Factory and caught a glimpse of Sariah wrapped tightly around Val—she was like mould trying to work her way through the woman's pores.

"I guess they've finally made their peace." Can't say that I wasn't with the cow and fiddle about that. I wasn't too sure I was up for this teenager parenting jag. One year. Just one more year and she would be a teen. I was doomed.

Kait saw me watching. "You did good, Bear."

"I don't know. She's growing so fast. Seems to me she's aging faster than Raph. I just don't understand girls and feel as sharp as a marble when it comes to doing what's best for her... them."

It took me a while to realise the silence between us was loaded. Racking me brain, I tried to figure out what the problem might be. But I was just too tired and didn't want to be second-guessing with Kait. "What is it?" Her silence continued and me calm started packing its bags. "Kait?"

"Hey guys. All's quiet out there for now." Val approached with her arm around Riah's shoulders. The girl was smiling from the inside out, her red armour glinting in the moonlight. "We'll fix some supper and then turn in." She paused for a beat, looked between us, nodded, then led Sariah to the dining room.

Okay. Whatever it is, could you help me get it right with Kait. I need us to be good. You know how much. So, please, help us out here.

After watching Val and Riah disappear into the building, I turned to see me Kait with her hands wrapped around her middle and the streetlights reflecting off her watery eyes.

Oh no, oh no... no. "Kait, you've got me worried, love. Talk to me." I ran me hands up and down her arms, begging. "Please. Don't shut me out."

She exhaled. "I'm so sorry."

With that, me calm walked out the door and took reason with it.

She saw me face and spoke into my growing panic. "I've let you down. I've let everyone down. You, Val, Tessa..." She let out a sob. "The kids." She fell into me arms and I hugged her tight. Me heart was still beating so fast, preparing myself for the worst. But I waited for her to fill in the blanks.

"We're good. Aren't we?" A cold took hold of me spine and started pulling it out through me toes. "Aren't we?"

Kait dropped her head. But didn't say a word. Not one word.

"Kait?"

Nothing.

Oh, dear Lord. Me world went from saddled and steady to bolting to the horizon, with me left on me butt in the dust. "Kait? Please? Give me something."

"My greatest crime was against you. Can you forgive me, Marcus?" Oh Lord, she was using me first name. This was serious.

"Well, Kait, first you'd better tell me what you've done, and then, whatever it is, we'll sort it out."

She pulled back from me arms, confusion replacing her grief. "What do you think I've done?"

"I don't know Kait, but I'm worried. You're awful upset and... I have no idea what's going on and... I just don't know."

"I left you to deal with everything... everything. The kids, the

Factory, Indy and Dan, training… Sariah… everything, while I…" The tears and a sob put a halt to her words. I pulled her close again and rubbed her back. Whatever it was, I needed to hear. Truth be, I'd forgive her anything. But I was always waiting for the other shoe to drop. Breathing in a watery breath, she continued. "While I abandoned you all for Dawn."

Me knees almost collapsed with relief. Me own tears may have welled. And I may have said me prayer of thanks out loud.

Again, she pulled back. Her confusion tinged with accusation. "What did you think I was apologising for?"

Desperately trying to find me balance after flipping belly up, I just shook me head. "Kait, that thing with Dawn is done. Dusted. Gone. So I had no idea what you were apologising for. I knew you felt bad about it. But I understand completely. It killed me to see your pain and the love you were drowning in. Do you not think I didn't feel it myself? Do you not think it kills me that I can't be giving you kids?"

"But you were expecting something else, weren't you?" That tinge had turned into a full tint.

"I didn't know what to expect. Give me a break here, Kait. This has not been our best year and I'm still feeling a bit like a pig on ice."

"I cannot believe you are still hanging onto that."

I shook me head. "What? Please do tell, Miss Kettle, what pot would I be hanging on to? Help me out here. *Your* dance with Dawn is water under the bridge. *I've* moved on. I am a simple man, Kait, and I am as lost as a needle right now."

"Trust, Marcus. We're talking about trust."

"What? How did you get to that from there?" I could not believe we could be on two completely different tracks. I walked away to get some air and try to juggle me words and thoughts into sense. I came back to her. "Look at me, Kait." I waited. "I mean, really, look at me." I threw me arms out to the sides and turned a circle. "What have I got? Nothing. No education. No security. I've no money. I can't house you, support you, give you the clothes and lifestyle you've enjoyed here in Laodicea. But I know we've reconciled to that. The Light has called us and set us on that path. But Kait, despite all that, I can't give you what you really want. What you need. I can't give you a family."

She opened her mouth to speak, but I rode right over the top of her. "Now, look at you. I mean, I look at you every single day of me blessed life. And then pinch myself. What twisted reality allowed a bloke like me to be with an angel like you? You are… I can't even think of a word worthy of your beauty. Inside and out. I know why they snapped you up for "Eye on Laodicea". Because they saw what I see every day. Your intelligence, your wit, your passion and compassion. Your genuine interest in everyone around you, everyone in your world. And that's where people want to be, Kait. In your world, because that is where the sun shines warmest and truest. Your love of the Light radiates out of you and transforms you to reveal His love to us. And I get to have that every day. And a bloke like me has to ask, how?"

"So, when you come to me and apologise with such brokenness, I've got to be thinking, finally, she's woken up and seen the truth. I'm not good enough for her."

Me beautiful wife stepped close to me, swung her arm back and slapped me soundly across the shoulder. Me initial reaction was shock, closely followed by gratitude it wasn't a closed fist. "You finished?"

Gobsmacked. Here I was, pouring me heart out, and she bleeding well hits me.

"How dare you?" The fire in her eyes was pulsing down her arms and sparking off the hilt of her sword poking over her left shoulder.

"Pardon?"

"How dare you insult the both of us with such drivel."

"Pardon?"

"First, you say I'm intelligent then accuse me of being ignorant and blind. That I can't see the truth of who and what you are, Marcus. We have been together for twenty-five years. Do you think that I am so incapable of thinking for myself that for *twenty-five years* I have been blind to the truth of who you are? Of my current circumstances? That I am so weak that if I did not want to be here"—her arm swept around the Factory—"with you, and my family, that I couldn't make it on my own? Are you suggesting that I am incapable of taking care of myself if I chose to do so?"

"What? No... Kait. How...?"

"Marcus. For heaven's sake. How long are you going to keep looking at yourself through that broken lens?" She clenched her teeth and fists and closed her eyes, breathing through her nose... loudly. Then she opened her eyes. *Damn it man, I love you.* "Why can you not trust me? My judgement? My lens?" *I see you, Marcus. And I love you. I am proud of you. I have faith in you. You are my hero.*

Me breath and everything else holding me up took off like a bat at twilight. She'd been saying the same message for... twenty-five years.

"Don't you ever doubt me. My love is true. Nothing is holding me here... to you"—she stopped at my gasp—"but my choice. I chose you. I choose you every day. That's what love is, Marcus. It is me choosing you despite our imperfections. That is why I am apologising. That is why I am so very sorry. I chose Dawn over you and over the kids. I thought she was the answer to the ache. But she isn't. You are. Val is. The twins are. Dan and Tessa are. I am sorry that I became narrow-minded and self-absorbed and left you to carry the load alone."

"Well, I've stuffed up again. Doesn't seem I can open me mouth but to change me feet." I opened me arms and she came home. "Forgive me, Kait. But love, I still can't see it." She tensed. "Settle your petals, I'm not arguing with you. But seriously, I don't doubt you Kait, I just don't understand. But I'll be honest with you, I'd be happy to have your help with Sariah. That girl is way beyond me skillset."

She pulled away and lifted her hands to me face and caressed me cheeks. And smiled. *Are we good, Bear?*

Loved you then, love you still. Always have, always will.

She smiled from the corners of her eyes to the depths of me heart. "War is coming, Bear. Soon. Iza was the key, and the pieces are all now in place. We don't have long, and we have to make sure we're good. You and me. Please, Marcus Joseph"—the use of Abbot's name-gift inspired me and grounded me like a tent peg on a flagpole—"don't let the Dark Lord's lies weaken our bond. Do not let his gnarly, spiteful fingers get between us. The Light is our solid ground and anchor, but you, my dearest Bear of a man, are my soul-love. You know all my weaknesses, and the ways I let you down. But never doubt my love."

What else was there to say? I took hold of me beautiful, intelligent, powerful wife and kissed her until she was weak at the knees. She clung to me as I set her aright. "Yep"—me chest seemed to grow two sizes—"still got it." She gave me arm a playful slap. "Come on, me girl, we've got work to do." I took her hand in mine as we set off to check the perimeter.

4 2

INDIGO: PLAYING NICE

"So, you will marry my girl."

Here it came. I gritted my teeth and waited.

"You are good for her."

Yeah, nah... what? "What did you say?"

She smiled. Well, I think it was a smile. I'd never seen one on Amina before, so I couldn't be sure. But there was a non-lethal light in her eye as we passed under a streetlight on our patrol. So, I chose to believe it was genuine. "You give her claws."

"Oh no, Amina. That's all you."

A noise escaped her lungs. It might have been a huff. A chuckle, even. If it wasn't, at least it wasn't skitched off.

"Yes, but you give her reason to use them."

Right. I was hoping that was a good thing? Since our awkward truce, I wasn't going to stoke her fire any more than I had to. By which I mean, I didn't want to, but for the last eight years just being present and breathing had stoked Amina's skitch. Her nose-flaring, eye-scalding, word-scathing fire. And as much as my actions had proved otherwise lately, I was not a complete idiot. So I shut up.

The silence was good as we continued our rounds. Comfortable.

Until it wasn't.

Amina was agitated. Edgy-agitated. So, going against my better judgement, I opened the door. "Spit it out." Then winced at my choice of words.

Again, with the huff noise. "You are a good man, Indigo."

I waited for the back-handed comment that would wipe the compliment away. After several long moments I had to release my breath. "And?"

"You want more compliments from me, my boy? Do not push your luck."

At last I could relax. I knew this wasn't some alien inhabiting my sister's body. "Thank the frack for that. You had me worried, Amina."

"Do not let her hear you speak this way."

"I know, I know. But seriously, you had me worried. I am not used to nice Amina. Good to know you're still in there... somewhere." I shoulder bumped her—gently—to show her I was kidding... kind of.

Again, the silence came and we resumed our patrol. Comfortable in each other's company. Then her words sank in and I was the one who became agitated. "Thanks. That means a lot." I couldn't help being swamped by the memories of our time here at the Factory. Things were about to change. Frack that. They already had. Irreversible change. For good or bad, who could tell? But I was sure of one thing. Not only would I always have Iza in my life, I would always have Amina too. "Thanks for being there for her. I mean, from the very beginning. Thanks for fighting for her... and watching over her."

She nodded. Didn't say anything, but after a while I heard her sniff. When I looked at her, she turned her head away and wiped her face on her shoulder.

Frack. Crying. What the frack am I supposed to do?

I slipped my arm around her shoulder.

She froze. Then looked at me through old-Amina eyes and very slowly shook her head. Twice. Then narrowed her glare until I very slowly retracted my arm, thankful it was still attached to my body. Once I was all clear, she hitched her chin once and we continued our patrol.

The silence was not quite so comfortable until it was.

"We good, Amina?"

"We are good, my boy."

43

CONTESSA: YES

I was in a most wonderful place of peace, and calm, and all kinds of lovely, but something was tugging at me. Pulling me away. "No, I won't go."

Instantly I was awake. Something was in our room. I looked over to where Val and Sariah lay on their cots. Nothing moved except the gentle rise and fall of their sleeping bodies. I sniffed the air. Had I missed the sulphur? Turning my head gently, not to give my awareness away, I scanned the room. There was enough of a night-light glow coming through the window for me to make out a body.

A human.

A male human body.

Someone had slipped past the guard and they were in here looking for a Silverscale, or Iza...

He leaned over me.

And. Kissed. My. Lips.

No flopping way.

I let fly with a punch and caught him in the face. Got him good, too.

"Frack."

"Dan? Oh no. Oh. Oh. Dan, I'm so sorry. Are you okay?" He didn't answer. I jumped up on the edge of my cot to get a closer look. He just stood there, breathing deeply, holding his face. But my cot tipped and the whole thing rolled, throwing me at Dan's chest. I grabbed at him wildly so I didn't end up on my butt on the floor.

Val growled from the shadows. "Nice work, team."

A pillow came out of nowhere and smashed me in the back of the head. Sariah was equally impressed.

"Oh. My. Word. I am so sorry. How bad is it?"

"Come on, I've got the kettle on." With his free hand, he grabbed my arm to pull me out of the room.

"Wait, I'm not dressed."

"Tessa, I'm warning you, get your gear and get out of here before you wake up the whole Factory." Just so you know, Val was really good in an emergency. Like, if a real intruder had broken in, she would be all over it like chutney on toast. But wake Val up for no good reason, and, well... not so good.

I scrambled through our cupboards and grabbed my clothes, then ducked out of the room with Dan. He went on to the Common Room while I raced to the bathroom to get dressed. And clean my teeth. Because. You know. Morning... or seriously early—middle of the night—breath.

I threw everything on as fast as I could, one-handed, whilst brushing like a mad woman, then raced to the Common Room. Dan was leaning over the bench, his head hanging low, waiting for the kettle to boil. "I really am sorry." He didn't turn. "Dan? Let me look." I stopped by the freezer and got some ice and wrapped it in a cloth, then stepped between his arms and forced him to take a step back. A very red cheek and an eye being forced shut due to swelling. "Oh. Poor man. Sit." I forced him to sit in a chair and gently laid the ice on his cheek bone.

He still hadn't said anything.

I was beginning to get worried.

But the kettle clicked off. Grabbing his hand and putting it over the ice, I hopped off his lap and made the coffee, giving him time to decide if he was going to talk to me again.

Ever.

I could feel him tracking me. Every move I made, his eyes burned a hole in my back. When I returned to him with two cups of plunger coffee, his one good eye continued to burn me to a crisp. "Can I have a look?"

He slowly lowered the ice and all I could do was grimace. "What can I do? How can I make things better? I am so sorry. But seriously, Dan, I did warn you." I pointed to myself—"Stuff up." How many times could I apologise before he responded?

He pulled me forward until I bumped the chair with my knees between his open legs. He lifted his hand and ran it up my arm, then curled it behind my neck and gently pulled me down. And very softly kissed me. "Just for the record, the door is still open. And"—he kissed me again—"good morning, Tessa."

Oh. My heart kind of puddled. "Good morning, Dan." Pulling a chair up in front of him, I took his beautiful, injured face in my hands and very, very gently kissed his bruising eye and his swollen cheek. "I am so sorry. Can you forgive me? I thought you were someone breaking in."

His arms came around me and held me in place. "I forgive you. And I'm glad you're not defenceless. But next time, I might just throw something at you from the door."

"Oh. I wouldn't mind being woken up by a kiss. Just as long as I know it's you."

"Right. So, throw something at you, then come in for a kiss."

"Perfect."

"Um, Tessa?" His hands were making circles on my back and totally distracting me. I just smiled in response. "Are you going to wear this on watch? I mean, I don't mind…"

I looked down at myself. I was wearing the birthday present Marcus had brought back from Ephesus for Sariah twelve months ago. It was inside out, but you could still read the backward message: "Kiss my royal buttooshie." It really said a lot that I could fit into an eleven-year-old's T-shirt. "Oh."

"Hey guys, you're up." Indy walked into the Common Room with

Amina on his heels. He laughed. "Nice shirt." Then he looked at Dan. "Nice face."

Amina raised her eyebrows but didn't say anything. She shoulder-bumped Indy.

Yep.

Shoulder.

Bumped.

And he was still standing afterwards.

Then she turned and left the room, making her way back to her cabin.

I eased myself out of Dan's hold and ran from the room. "I'll be right back."

They both laughed. But that could have been because I almost ran into the closed door. I managed to hear Indy before I disappeared. "What's happened to Tessa? You kryptonite to her epic cat skills?"

Properly dressed and coffees in hand, we made it out of the Common Room in one piece. Indy had reported that there had been no disturbances, and all was quiet on their last circuit of the Factory. We decided to do our own loop and then stop for a while by the side gate.

The night was crystal clear and the sky was putting on a show with the stars. It was hard to see past the glow of the city, but if I turned and looked out over the suburbs, I could make out pinpricks of light. The early hours of summer's morning sent a shiver through me. My coffee was gone and I'd not thought to bring a warm jacket.

Dan stepped behind and wrapped his arms around me, tucking my head under his chin. I snuggled deep and was comforted on every level.

Thank you for bringing him back to me.

Since he couldn't see my face, and he held me secure, I felt it was a safe time to bring up the question that had been eating away at me. "The other night, when Indy asked you to leave with him, and you said no. You also said that when it's time to leave here, you'd go?"

He turned me around in his arms so I faced him. I couldn't see his face in the shadows, but when he spoke his voice was a whisper. "You seem pretty tight here with Iza, and the girls, and the markets, and… everything. What will you do? When the Light calls the others out to somewhere else?"

"I kind of get the feeling that's not too far off. That our time at the Factory is almost over."

"You too, huh?" Dan's voice was still a quiet whisper, as soft and unreadable as the shadows.

"Yeah, and from what Iza's decided, I figure things are going to turn all kinds of ugly before we're done."

I felt him pin me with his eyes. "You worried?"

"No. Yes. Maybe?"

Dan pulled me in and wrapped me in behind his wall and I felt safe enough to continue. "There's been things in Laodicea I've loved. And things I've hated. But I've learned." I pulled back. "I feel I've grown. You know, not just with skills, but grown up, too. Laodicea has changed me. And for better or worse, I like it." Again, he waited. "But they're my family and when it's time, I'll go with them." It was time for laying our cards on the table. "But Indy is back now. For good. Will you stay here with him?"

He held me at arm's length. "What? Are you serious? Indy?" The whisper was well and truly forgotten. "The guy's my mate and my brother, but he's not my life, Tessa."

Even though I couldn't see them, all the stars shone a million times brighter. "So, do you still plan on coming with us?"

"Listen, it was me who got hit in the head just now, not you. Don't you remember what I said the other night? Whatever you're doing, wherever you're going, I want to be with you."

"But that was when Indy had taken off. Now he's back."

"Tessa. The other night I asked you to make me a priority. What I didn't say was that you are already mine… after the Light." I heard the smile in his voice at using my own words back at me. "Indy has his life here. I'm stoked we've caught up. But he's on his path and I'm on mine. I'm sure we'll stay in touch. But this is not my home. He is not my priority. He's not my *best Friend*, Tessa." Dan bent his head forward into a shaft of light. His smouldering eyes kind of melted me into another puddle of happy.

"Oh. Okay. That's good to know." It was my turn to whisper.

And then he kissed me.

The chill of the morning evaporated under Dan's hands and mouth. Soon I was a senseless jellyfish puddle of bliss. Until he pulled away and coughed. Gently laying his hands on my shoulders, Dan created a distance. Breathing deeply, he bent down and picked up our empty cups. "Here, you take these back to the Common Room. I'll circle round the southern perimeter and meet up with you at Warehouse One for another circuit. He lowered his lips to mine for the softest kiss, then gently ushered me in the direction of the main door and awkwardly took himself off the other way.

44

RAPHAEL: TWIN SPEAK

"Come on. It is starting, and you are going to miss out." Joko was at the door of the Common Room, leaning in from the hallway. From before sun-up we had been preparing for the ceremony. Vashti, Shauna, Aiko and I had been cooking all day. But the ladies had gone a while ago to be with Izabel as she prepared. I was alone in the kitchen finishing up the cleaning.

"I am almost ready. But we cannot have everyone come here for the meal afterwards with all of these dirty dishes." We had all been busy today. And I understood. I was happy to help. But I was very tired of washing dishes. I knew I was supposed to ask for help. And I would have, if there had been anyone around to ask. There was still a bit to do, and we had run out of time.

I looked around the room and was proud of all the things we had achieved. The tables were overflowing with food. The smell of baking, desserts, and flower arrangements mingled in the air. Audette and Dan had brought many ingredients, but Audette had also brought a cake. It was huge and a work of art. Just like her. Not that she was huge, but she was beautiful. Just like her daughter. I walked through the tables to make sure everything was just right. That the food was covered and nothing was missing.

But enough gloating, I still had dishes to do. I turned back to the sink and stopped. "Riah, what are you doing here?"

She didn't face me; she just kept her hands busy in the sink.

"I thought you were tied-up finishing all the flowers and decorations."

She shrugged.

"And hanging out with your friends."

She shrugged again.

"And getting ready for the ceremony."

She didn't bother responding, she just kept washing up. I was not going to argue. Even though we had made up and Sariah had gone back to doing her share of the work, it had been a long time since my sister had actually gone out of her way to help me with my chores. Standing beside her, I started drying and putting things away. We did not have long but I would be ashamed if people came into my kitchen for a meal and there were dirty dishes in the sink or drying dishes on the rack.

We got into a rhythm and soon the work was done. I grabbed all the cloths, gave the benches a final wipe, surveyed the room and, satisfied, bolted for the door. There was time to throw everything in the laundry basket and throw on a clean shirt. If I was quick.

I spun and bounced off Riah. She was blocking the door. "Move, Riah, I don't have time." She was already dressed.

Like a pillar of bronze, she was rooted to the spot.

"Alright, you take the washing so I can get changed." I pushed the pile in my arms into her and it dropped to the floor. I loved my sister... sometimes. But today I was struggling to find patience with her. I released a sigh and counted to three. I would have counted to ten, but there was no time.

"What do you want, Riah? I have been working very hard to do my bit. I am late and I am dirty. I do not have time to have a shower, I only have time to—"

I was wrapped in a fierce embrace. It hurt. But then, I guessed my sister was hurting too. Instantly I was on alert. "Riah, what is wrong? What has happened? What do you need?" I tried to get out of her hold to look at her so I could see what she wanted to say. But she tightened her grasp. "Um. Ri, you are... um... hurting me." I did my training every day just like everyone else. But still my sister was stronger. She dropped her arms and her head. And sniffed. She was crying. Riah never cried. She got angry, but hardly ever teary. But then she looked at me.

"Oh, Riah. I love you too." She normally used her hands to speak to me, but today it was all in her eyes: grief, pleading, pain.

"Yes, I forgive you, Riah. Have we not already covered this? Please, I am going to miss the wedding."

And now the anger came. Shaking her head like a dog with a snake. Her pointer finger flicking between us.

I stopped. "Yes. I understand. You are welcome, Riah. You are my sister. But you are more. You are my twin. My second half. It has been good here, to make new friends. To do new things. But whatever we do, wherever we are, Sariah, you are my soul's nest. Always."

She made a new symbol but immediately I recognised it. A soul nest. *Always.*

Always.

Dan interrupted us. "Come on you two, get a move on. Val and Amina have just got back with a bloke who's gonna do the ceremony. He's chatting with Indy and Iza now."

Riah madly flicked her hands around and Dan nodded. "Yeah, if you're quick, Raph, you have time to jump through the shower. Riah, go tell them they gotta wait ten"—he looked at me with an eyebrow raised in question; I nodded—"minutes."

Riah took off down the hall one way. I ran the other.

45

IZABEL: THE WEDDING

"*Remember, my daughter Izabel, I love you.*"
The Light's weight gently pressed into me and stopped me flying away. I was on a wild ride... like I had taken that step off the bridge eight years ago, but instead of falling into the canal below, I had been swept away on a whim... in a dream.

"I have you and hold you in my hands, no matter what."

His presence thrummed through my body like an embrace. His rose-gold armour around me pulsed with His power and protection. It had only been a few days, but for the first time in my life, the emptiness that had been haunting and hounding me was gone. Cauterised. Completely.

Thank you. Thank you for... all of it. How can I put into words how I feel? Help me understand my mother's betrayal. Help me see the truth behind her actions. I want to believe her. But I don't know if I can.

"Izabel." Val quietly pulled me from my musing. My sisters and mothers—both of them, Amina and Audette—were fussing around me. I was the eye of their storm. "I have brought a minister of the Light who is happy to marry you and Indy." She squatted before me and took my hands in hers—calloused, cracked and secure. "I know we've spoken of this, but it will ensure in the eyes of everyone—the Light and the law—your union is legal and binding."

This woman was such an odd mix. So very tough and strong… and scary. But compassionate, loving and thoughtful. I had not had too much to do with her personally over the past year. Val had spent most of her time with Amina, then taking off into the city each day. But I decided, then and there, I would change that and make an effort to get to know her and her secret. She radiated confidence and peace. I was still not used to seeing her in armour. The deepest, beautiful bluish-purple, swirling with patterns, sharp angles that gave off fierce intent. Not to mention the knives.

She called my name again and brought me back to the present. "Are you happy to proceed?"

"Oh, yes. Yes, of course. Thank you."

"Since we would like him to officiate, and he is a member of the Community, I have brought a representative of the Community here in Laodicea as well. I hope you don't mind. He won't interfere."

"Um, sure, I guess. I cannot see how our wedding is of interest to him, but he is very welcome to join us." My sisters had finished their fussing, and calm came to the room. I thought of how each had come to join us and how they had added their own essence to our family. This was a celebration for all of us, not just Indy and me.

"And one more thing. Kait's friends, Georgie and Griff have asked if you would mind if they took some photos and footage." At my alarm, she raced on. "For you only. Not to be published or shared, but so you have a record of today to look back on later. But it's up to you. I will tell them no if you'd rather not."

"Please pass on my thanks, that is a wonderful gift."

She nodded and left the room to pass on the message and let everyone know it was time to begin.

I stood and looked in a mirror that Kerm had brought over for the making and fitting of my dress. Not only was I now encased in my beautiful armour, Kerm, the stunningly gifted man, had made me a dress in the same colour, a simple, flowing gown with a short train. I noted, like my sisters, my scales had started to change. The goddess's colours had faded, and my scales had taken on a translucent silver. Not only did they reflect the colour of my armour, they picked up every hue and shimmered like a rainbow. Kerm's masterpiece made the most of showing off my transformation.

I stood and took the flowers Sariah and my sisters had grown, wrapped in a dress Tessa and Kerm had designed and made, encased in armour of the Light's love, and readied myself to meet the man who was prepared to commit the rest of his life to me. We would be surrounded by family, old and new, and we would celebrate over a meal Raphael and my other sisters had made. I was overwhelmed with love and peace.

Each of my sisters went before me out the door, kissing me as they passed. Val smiled and held the door open for me to join everyone so that I could marry my soul partner. It was no surprise that the tears were cascading, and it was all I could do to hold back the sobs. But when I saw both Mother and Amina at the door, ready to escort me through the gathering, it was too much. Both embraced me, and Val passed me a cloth to wipe my face. We were a huddle of indigo, red, teal and rose-gold. And within that hug I felt it; the knot of pain towards my mother started to loosen.

Thank you.

Dan, Sariah and Raphael played music that pulled me back under control, and when Tessa joined Dan in a song, it was my cue to move. The three of us made our way through my gathered family and came to a stop in front of Indy. His eyes shimmered with his own tears, his smile radiating love. I have no idea where he had found them, but he, Dan and Marcus were wearing beautiful suits. I ran my hand down his lapel and smoothed my hand over his chest. He took my fingers and kissed them.

More tears fell and, before we could proceed, I needed to once again take some time to wipe my eyes. Indy pulled me close and held me until I brought the emotion under control. It was here in his arms that I was transported. Heaven opened and a song, so pure and joyous, heartbreakingly perfect, washed over and through the Garden Shed.

By the stillness of Indy's heart pressed against my ear, I guess it stopped him too.

I turned and was rendered speechless when I saw Sariah, standing beside her brother, holding his hand, singing. Her face was lifted to the ceiling and her armour blazed as she lifted a song of praise to the Light and a gift of blessing upon us all.

When it ended, the warehouse rang in silence, the echo drifting through every cavity of my soul, ringing with truth in its purest form. She looked to Raphael who was openly wearing tears and embraced him. Then looked to Indy and me, smiled a brief smile and flicked her hand as if to say, "Get on with it."

Once again, I was wiping tears from my eyes, but for the first time ever I felt my mind nestled—anchored—at one with my soul. I was overwhelmingly embraced. I turned to Indy, and the Shepherd of the Light began the ceremony. His words were beautiful and I was so grateful to Val for organising this gift. "Indigo, I believe you have something you wanted to say to Izabel?"

Indy turned and took both my hands, once I'd passed my bouquet to Lily. "Izabel, from the moment I first met you on the bridge, you had my heart. Each day we have journeyed from that point, you have had more and more of me till I am nothing, I have nothing left to give. You already have all of me. But I promise, for the rest of my life your heart is safe with me. I will continue to be the wall that holds the world out when you need it, the company to walk you through it when you want it, and the place for you to come home to for as long as I live. Iza, would you do me the very great honour of being my"—his voice broke, he coughed and tried again—"my wife."

Of course I couldn't see a thing because I was crying so much. But I nodded.

"What was that? We didn't hear you," Marcus called from the group. Everyone laughed.

"I said—"

The large sliding doors to Warehouse One screamed in protest as they were ripped open. "There they are. Get them."

Everyone was on their feet and creating a wall around us. I still couldn't see. Not only from the tears but the crowd as well.

A large, bald man stormed into the building, waving pieces of paper in the air like a weapon. "You have no right to be on this premises. And you have no right to be here." He pointed his meaty finger at me.

"I beg your pardon, who are—" Mother was interrupted.

"Overseer, how... nice of you to be here." A tall, thin man stepped out from beside Val. "And Alain, what a surprise."

Oh no. Father was here. Before I could register what was going on, the large man was yelling again. "Felix! I should have known I would find you mixed up in this mess."

"Mess? I would say the contrary. It has been an... exquisite service... until now. What seems to be the problem?" I didn't know who this man was, but Raphael and Sariah had gravitated to his side. And Marcus stood behind one of his shoulders, and Dan and Tessa the other. Val and Kait were edging their way in front of the twins. Their whole family had him flanked.

"To begin with, you are all trespassing. This is private property. As we speak, a councillor is contacting the owners of this property and informing them of the infringement."

On cue, two phones rang within the group. Mother's and this man, Felix's. "Excuse me Overseer, I suspect that might be the councillor now." He took the call, muttered a few words and looked over his shoulder to my mother, nodded, then looked back to the irate accuser. "Right, now that's sorted. What else seems to be the problem?"

"You?" The large man spat. "You own this property?"

"Not solely. I have a partner."

Behind the Overseer and my father, a new crowd of people arrived. Enforcers.

Now it was my father's turn to ruin proceedings. "I believe you have something here that doesn't belong to you."

Mother spoke up. "What are you talking about, Alain? This has nothing to do with you. What are you doing here? Be gone you... little man."

Father sneered with such venom, I felt a surge of protection—and pride—towards my mother. Amina, Indy, Ben, Tomi and I all moved to surround her. To protect her from the vileness of my father. "You betrayed our work. You betrayed this city. And what is worse you betrayed me, you weak, pathetic woman. She was the price we paid for greatness. She is the key to the glory. Standing here, with them"— he glared at my sisters, then my new family—"you have disgraced yourself."

In that moment, I felt an ocean of pride for my birth mother. She stepped forward from within the group of us trying to protect her, and marched up to my father and stood toe to toe with him. In her heels, she met him eye to eye. "On the contrary, Alain, today I have the greatest honour of all. I stand among champions, beside my daughter who has succeeded against the odds, against your wishes and your best attempts to find and destroy her. To know she is safe and happy is my greatest reward and my truest success."

"Enforcers, take her." The warehouse erupted in cries of anguish and disbelief until my father quietened everyone with a shout. "You cannot stop them." He too waved papers in the air. "Izabaal was contracted to the Temple. That contract has not been terminated. She is still their property to be returned immediately."

I yelled at my father. "I terminate the contract." How dare he come in here and attempt to ruin my day. Ruin my life. Again.

"You can't. You are the asset."

"Well, I terminate the contract," Mother interjected, and tried to intercept the Enforcers.

"You can't because both our names are on the contract. Both of us need to terminate. If she were a Greyscale... or married." Father looked to the Shepherd. "Is she married?"

The poor man looked ashen. We all knew the truth. He shook his head and tried to speak but father rode over the top of his attempts. "Then she is still the property of the Temple."

"And so is this one." A Temple Keeper had been camouflaged within the crowd of Enforcers. Now he held Amber by the wrist.

"Please, no." Kait had approached one of the Enforcers and was speaking rapidly.

He looked at her, his face a mirror of sadness, but shook his head. He pushed past her and came toward me. Indy stood in front of me and everyone else gathered round trying to create a barricade.

The lead Enforcer, the man we'd met at the markets, looked through the crowd and into my eyes. "I'm so sorry, but it's the law."

Indy was ropeable. "Over my dead body."

The poor man was as helpless as we were. "Step aside, son, they are within their rights."

"She is a human being. What about her rights?"

"Those rights were sold to the Temple. She has none, now. Step aside. I don't want to hurt you or anyone else."

I could see Indy was not going to move.

Please help us. What do we do?

"Trust me. All will be well. I have everything under control. Go with them. I will be with you."

I drew a shuddering breath. "It's okay, Indy, step aside. I will go with them."

"What? Are you mad? No Iza, you can't."

"Indy, my love." I stepped through my family and held his face in my hands. "It is not for long. I promise." I kissed his cheeks, his jaw clenched like steel underneath. Then, with my head held high I walked through the stunned, silent group, my armour wrapped firmly around me. As I approached my father and mother, I kissed my mother. "For what you have done, I thank you. With all that I am, I love you. All will be well."

The Keeper raised his hand to take hold of me. "You"—I glared at him with all the anger and hurt that was swirling beneath my thin layer of sureness—"do not touch me. You do not lay a hand on me. You do not even look at me." He faltered for a minute before dropping his hand and leading the way out of the warehouse. I gathered Amber under my arm and the two of us were placed in a van and taken back to the Temple of Ashera.

It appeared the battle had begun.

46

KAITLYN: FALL OUT

It was like the aftermath of an atomic bomb. The van holding Iza and Amber drove out and we were incapable of doing anything to stop them taking our sisters. Before we could pull ourselves together, the Overseer stepped out of the shadows. I had forgotten he was there.

"Felix, this is the last straw in a long line of offences. As of right now, you are fired."

Could this day get any worse? I was at a loss to think. Everything had turned inside out and upside down.

"May I ask what... specifically would be the reason for my dismissal? Would it be that I own property under my own name? Is it that I am attending the wedding of friends? I'm afraid I am at a loss as to what I have done to deserve termination."

"I don't care what the reason is. I will come up with something. Do not think your business track record will save you this time."

"But Overseer, that is my role... Administrator of the Community of Light in Laodicea. Running the business and looking out for the best interests of the Community is what I have been employed to do, and anyone who would care to investigate will see I have gone above and beyond the expectations that were presented to me when I began."

"Irrelevant! I have had—"

"So, you are saying that my track record and success at the job I have been employed to do, and the successful management of the team and the business of the Community over the past fourteen years, is not a good enough reason for me to keep my job?"

"Right now, Felix, I don't care how good you are at your job. I don't like you and I will see you gone."

"Well then, I believe I will have a good case for… unfair dismissal. Thank you for clarifying."

"Do not play games with me, Felix, you forget I have good friends in high places. You cannot succeed. The law can't save you this time."

"And… cut." From the side of the warehouse, Griffin caught everyone's attention. "Georgie, did you get all that?"

Georgie grunted.

"Good, I think that's a wrap. Unless there is anything else you would like to add, Overseer?"

The Overseer's face mutated from an enraged-red to an apoplectic-fit aubergine-purple. He could not speak. Or breathe.

"I'll take that as a no. I believe the team are ready to receive the tape. We'll drop it off on our way to the station."

"Griff?" Georgie kept looking up, then back through the lens of the camera. "Why does everyone look different through the lens?"

Georgie moved aside to let Griff see. Now it was both their turns to be shocked. "Kait, why are you surrounded by a green halo?" Griff rubbed his eyes and kept checking the camera. But Georgie's constant tapping grabbed his attention.

"It's not just through the lens." Georgie's eyes bulged as he looked around the warehouse and looked at every single one of us in our armour.

"Kait. Please explain." The Overseer forgotten, Griff struggled to come to terms with their introduction to the Light.

"Okay. Everyone just breathe." I turned and addressed the family at large who were still reeling from the loss of Iza and Amber. "I have received Word. The battle has begun. Do not fear. Iza and Amber are where they need to be. For now. The Light is beginning the work He had already told Iza about." I made my way over to Indy, Amina and Audette, huddled in a shell-shocked group.

The Overseer blustered and spluttered. "Do not walk away from me, woman. I have not finished."

I glanced at him over my shoulder, raised an eyebrow and turned back to my friends. "It will be hard for them. But they will be home soon. A day? Two at most. The Light has asked that we trust Him and allow His plan to unfold. I suggest we go through to the Common Room and discuss a plan of attack as we eat some food. We will petition the Light for Amber and Iza and we will ask for guidance and wisdom."

The Overseer yelled, "I will not be ignored!" And right on cue, a car arrived and pulled into the open door of Warehouse One. Three men stepped out, the stench of demon dripping from them.

"Ah, I do believe your... cavalry have arrived, Overseer?" Felix withdrew his sword and swung it in arcs, limbering up, looking far more proficient than he was a year ago. "Have you come for practise, lads?"

Sariah and Val drew their swords as well. Raph raised his hands, palms out.

"Looking good, Felix, you ready to go fishing in a barrel? Pity there aren't more to go around." Marcus drew his sword and went to stand beside his friend.

"Yes, well"—he used his eyes to indicate the twins and Val—"these three are very... proficient teachers. However, I must give credit where credit is due. The opportunity to practise on these three"—his eyes bored into the newcomers—"has been equally beneficial." Felix stepped forward, inviting the three to engage.

They looked around and saw a warehouse full of armour and declined. One of them spoke. "You'll keep. You all will. We've got her back now. And you should see what we're doing to her." The other two sneered as they looked to Indy. "Hope you said goodbye, boy. You'll never see her again."

Another added, "Well, looking so pretty, that is."

"You weren't man enough to keep her. You're not man enough to have her," the third sneered, then the three of them bundled the Overseer into the car and took off.

"And now you've met the rest of the High Council: Raymond, Nyle and Edward." Felix re-sheathed his sword.

Georgie may have whimpered. With their new sight, they would have seen the whole show. "What is that God-awful smell?"

I walked back to Griffin and Georgie and embraced them both. They flinched. "All will be well. Come sit with us and we will explain. And formulate a battle plan."

"The video," Georgie managed to splutter.

Felix joined me. "I have phoned a courier; they are on the way. The station is expecting it and they will air it this evening. But before we release it"—Felix turned to speak with Indy—"I understand this was to be a private video of your wedding for your family memories. I am asking permission for us to use this to stir support for not only Iza and Amber, but for all the women and girls at the Temple. I believe this is part of the Light's plan. But I won't proceed unless you give me permission."

Indy looked to Georgie. "How much did you get on film?"

"From the moment those beautiful women entered the warehouse, as that mirage of a woman followed, up until just now when the Overseer shot himself in the foot." Georgie didn't even try to hide his glee.

Indy stopped and reflected.

We all did.

"Riah!" She was filmed singing. What would that mean for her? I looked to Val and Marcus. "What do we do?"

"Riah, me love, what do you want? Shall we ask them to cut it out, or are you happy for people to hear you sing?"

She shrugged her shoulders.

Val made an executive decision. "Cut her out." Then the tide rose and swept everything along.

Back in the business of what he knew best, Georgie's experience and genius snapped back into place. "Missy's video—that's gone viral, with the interest piece we put together that was aired last night—not only on the internet but mainstream as well, plus this piece. Add the fact that Kait is well known and loved, Iza was the Jewel of Laodicea, if we add this video as well…" Georgie and Griff closed ranks and started planning and plotting. "We'll need to edit it a bit. Polish. Bring out Indy and Iza's story. The Silverscales. They're hot. No one has seen anything like it. They'll want more."

Griff was nodding, hands on hips, scowling in concentration. "We'll bring in the self-sufficiency. Having to live in hiding, but not too much. Subtle. Let it play in the background. It will help sway opinion. People will want to know. This place will need better protection." Griff turned. "Felix, can we help with that?"

"I was just thinking of that myself, Griffin. I will ring Marlene momentarily. But before I do," Felix addressed everyone still standing in shock, "naturally, we want to continue to do everything in our power to protect you." He nodded to Audette who was too shocked to respond. "But we won't do anything without your permission. If Griffin and Georgie believe this will help procure Izabel and Amber's release, I believe them. But conversely, it will reveal you to the world. I know this is new to many of you, but Audette and I have been working with you, behind the scenes, for the past eight years to keep you hidden and safe. I have believed this *was* the best action. However, times have changed, and I believe secrecy is no longer the way forward. Not only for Izabel and Amber's safety, but for you all. But, as always, the decision is yours."

Amina clapped Indy on the back. Her rage had settled to a volcanic roar. Through gritted teeth she addressed Indy alone. But it was impossible not to hear her. Her vow rang to the rafters. "I think this is best. It is what we should do. What do you think? You and me. We go to get them back. Get them all. But, if these two"—without looking she threw her thumb over her shoulder at Georgie and Griff— "say this will help, I say yes." Breathing through her tears of rage, Amina put both hands on Indy's shoulders. "We will fight for them. For all of them. We will bring them home. All my daughters. We bring them *all* home."

She dropped her head for a few beats, then continued as tears streamed down her cheeks. "You and me, we will fight every one of them in the Temple. But if we do not have to fight the whole city to get there, this is good. Do you think?"

Indy's blue armour was engulfed in black flames. Seething. He nodded once to Amina. Then to Felix once more. "But you better do it quick, hey, cause I'm not waiting. Sorry Kait, I'm not eating again till my wife is by my side, yeh?"

Another car drove into the warehouse. Felix walked to meet it, calling Georgie and Griffin with him. "If you want to work on the tape, do it on the way. The studio is expecting you. Marlene has brought some equipment I believe you will be able to utilise."

The woman herself exited the car, as always an exquisite vision in ornate emerald armour. She held the door as Georgie and Griffin discussed working enroute. Once they had left, she turned to Felix. "Hello, dear." Then to Val. "What's the plan?"

47

KAITLYN: WAR COUNCIL

Marcus addressed the group but looked only at Indy when he spoke. "Listen, son. You could fly out of here now, full of steam and bubbles, and you'd achieve diddly squat. We don't willy-nilly flounder into a battle half-cocked without our heads. We're going to get them back. But we need to make a plan. Felix, how long till that film goes live?"

"It is scheduled for the six o'clock news. It will be their lead story." Felix flicked his wrist, glancing at his watch. "We have an hour. However, I would suggest we... give people the opportunity to digest the news and then quantify their reaction."

At this, Indy growled, clenched his fists and started pacing.

Felix hurried on. "I am suggesting thirty to forty minutes at most. Then we go and start the swell, inviting people to join. Giving them a focal point for their... righteous indignation."

"Right. One-hour-forty, tops. Everyone into the Common Room. We plan, we fuel up, we petition the Light." Marcus looked at me. "You say you've had another Word, Kait?"

I beamed and nodded.

We stumbled through the hallway to the Common Room where

Marcus started directing traffic again. "Lottie, Shauna and Genni, will you stay with the kids and guard them here?"

"No." Shauna stood. "I'll fight at the Temple." Her declaration opened the meeting.

"Excellent. Val, I'll hand over to you for the plan of attack, and Dan, go shut that bleeding gate. And lock it. We don't need anyone else driving in here this evening." Just as he spoke a small red car darted through the gate. "Bleeding heck. Get out there now!"

"It's Fleur. Her timing as always is… impeccable." Felix smiled at his friend as Marcus fumed.

Once Fleur was inside and a quick introduction was made, Val stood.

The room quietened as she looked around, making eye contact with everyone. But none were more surprised than the kids when she addressed them first.

"Joko, Kazi and Hiro, I need you to do a very important job."

The three looked at each other then moved forward, nodding.

"You know what's going on and you know we're going to go and get Iza and Amber back. We'll get them all. Do you understand?"

Again, the three nodded.

"Good. But I need your help. We will fight better at the Temple if we know our home is safe. I want you three on guard duty. Kazi at the main gate—"

"But they will see her?" Tomiko grasped her daughter's shoulders.

"They already have, love." Ben joined them, an arm around Tomi's shoulders and a hand covering hers as it rested on Kazi's shoulder. "It's time to come out of hiding. Kazi too."

Tomiko swallowed her lips and squeezed her husband's hand but didn't argue.

Val continued. "Right. Joko and Hiro, I want you on the walls. Joko, eyes on the road running south-east. Hiro, eyes west." She waited until they both nodded. "Very soon, people are going to start arriving. If they have armour, let them in. If they don't, don't. Got it?" She waited for their nods. "If you have any doubt, check with your guard." She then acknowledged the three Warriors standing together at the back of the room who each dipped their chins in response.

"After we're gone, others may come... in armour. Please tell them where we are and ask them to meet us. Can you do that?"

"Yes, Val, you can trust us." Joko took up the role of spokesperson.

"Good. I knew I could count on you three." She pulled the trio into a huddle and quietly petitioned the Light over them and for them. "Questions?"

"No, Val. We can do this. You just bring Iza and Amber home." Kazi was doing her best to hide her tears.

"They are in the Light. He will take care of everything... and He will let us help. But we need you guys here helping as well. Okay? Off you go."

The whole room held their breath as the kids filed out. As soon as they had passed her, Val tapped Dan on the shoulder and used her chin to indicate the window. "Open the window." Then flicked her gaze to the fence and the gate. *Eyes on the kids.* "Open the window. "Tessa, door."

Both Dan and Tessa positioned themselves so they were still in the room listening to the plans, but had eyes watching the youngsters from afar.

"Are they going to be okay? What if the attack comes here?" Tomiko had held it together until Kazi was out of earshot. Her hands were making knots in Ben's shirt.

Val looked to me and I was overjoyed that I could report on the Word I had heard. "They will be safe. The Dark Lord is aware of the focus building at the Temple and that is where he is pouring out his resources. The Light is sending more Warriors here, to be sure. But the Factory is off-limits for the battle."

"But how can you be sure?" Aiko, also speaking up now that her son was out patrolling the perimeter from on top of the wall.

"Because the Light has said so."

"But—"

"The Dark cannot overstep the boundary the Light has set. If the Light says here and no further, then that is as far as the Dark goes. He has told me the Factory is safe, so it will be. The only trouble here is making sure those kids are made to feel useful and kept busy." I looked to my thoughtful sister and knew what she was doing. "But Val has seen to that."

Kerm spoke up from the corner of the room. "I'll stay. They will get bored soon enough, but I think I can think of enough things to keep them occupied."

Helen whispered to her husband, but it carried around the room. "Are you sure?"

He smiled. "I believe the Light has more use for me here. You go and lend your sword." Helen leaned in and wrapped her arms around her husband's side.

"Good. Now, the rest of you. Any here who do not want to come?" She waited and again made eye contact with everyone around the room. "There is no shame in staying behind. I will tell you now, those of you who come with us are about to see the truth like you've never seen it—or probably ever wanted to see it. You are all ready and able to cope, but if you are scared, you are free to stay."

"Come on already, are we done? Can we go?" Indy was up and pacing. His body barely contained his fury.

Val stalked over and stood in his path. He was so consumed he didn't even see her till they were toe-to-toe. She spoke quietly. "If you do not get yourself under control, you will not be coming with us."

He began to protest but she steamrolled right over the top of him with her lethally quiet words.

"I understand you are angry and in pain. I understand you are frustrated. But if you can't get your skrat together you will not be coming." Again, he tried to protest. "I will personally knock you out, tie you up and leave you here where you can wait it out, if you cannot put all of that emotion in a box somehow. I will not have you jeopardise *my* mission and endanger *my* family by your immaturity and lack of self-control."

We all knew it wasn't an idle threat. She could and she would, in a heartbeat. When it came to battling, Val was both a details and a big picture kind of gal. Add to that, she'd been itching for a fight for about a year and she was pretty amped up herself. Not that you'd notice if you didn't know her. It was all about the fire in her eyes. And that her indigo armour was a blazing inferno, with each and every one of the mass of knives attached to her crackling like lightning. I guess that's where she kept *her* emotion. It also helped give her message impact.

Indy nodded and stepped away. But Val wasn't finished. She turned her laser eyes onto Amina. "That goes for you, too."

Amina ground her teeth and narrowed her eyes. She'd seen Indy being taught a lesson by Val, early on, after he got his legs back. I don't think she was keen to attempt to take her on as well. She nodded.

Val then eyeballed the room. I guess she was gauging the mood and looking for any other lapses of control. "Hear me, all of you. We *will* go to the Temple. We *will* face the hordes of hell. We *will* find Iza and Amber. And we *will* bring them home. I guarantee this because the Light has said it will be so." She paused to let it sink in.

"I can also guarantee there *will* be casualties. There may be loss. We are not playing games, people. We train and work hard every day because we are at war. You have been sheltered and protected, living behind a veil, blind to the truths that surround us. But you are about to come face to face with the Dark Lord, for we are storming his lair. You will also experience the power and the reach of the Light. Stand firm in Him and keep his Law on your lips and allow your body to fall into the rhythm of the known—the disciplines, the routines—we practise every day. Allow it to take over; it is why we train. It will save your life."

Again, she paused to eyeball the room. "Anyone wanting to stay here and help prepare for our return?" No one moved.

"Right." She rolled her shoulders and moved back to stand in front of the window. Glancing outside, her eyes flicked to the wall and the gate, then turned back to the room. "Marcus, Kait, and I will be the head of the spear. Helen, Vashti, and Audette will be left flank. Felix, Marlene and Fleur the right. Our job is to break through the ranks and get Dan, Tessa and Sariah inside. Indy"—she paused until she was confident she had his full attention—"you do not engage the enemy.

Do not get distracted. These guys will get you in and cover you so you can find the girls. Understood?"

Again, he nodded.

Val turned to me. "Any Word on where they are?"

I was overflowing with joy that the Light had blessed me with my Badge again. "They're in a dark room, no windows, one door."

"I know where that is," Lily piped up. "It's the naughty priestess room: the Vault. For when you form an opinion." A hostile murmur bubbled through the room. It seemed a lot of these women knew of the naughty priestess room. "I can show you the way."

Val didn't respond, she just stared at Lily. I suspect she was getting a read on her; trying to See her. In the past she'd proved to be a tad flaky.

Lily's voice was edged with desperation. "I can do it, Val, I promise."

Tessa spoke up from the doorway. "I'll watch over her."

"Done. Lily, all you need to do is show the others where the room is. The fighting will be thickest in there. I can't guarantee you'll come out unscathed. Are you sure?"

Lily gulped, then, with wide eyes, she bobbed her head.

"Val"—I snagged her attention—"they're going to need Raph."

My sister was not a woman who swore, but through her clenched teeth and behind her eyes, I saw a litany of fury and profanity.

Sariah moved up beside her brother. Marcus's face had drained of colour. Even Felix started gravitating toward our boy.

Reining in that slight demonstration of emotion, Val looked at me. "Is that from Him? Or a nurse's assessment?" It wasn't harsh, she was just getting facts.

"From Him, dear heart."

"It is alright. I will go." Raph smiled and lifted his hands. "If I need to, I will just hang on and petition the Light, like last time... and the time before that."

Val dropped her head and exhaled. "Alright. Our job is to get these guys into the Temple and cover them, drawing as much attention to us as possible." She turned to Dan. "You get in, follow Lily's directions, get Raph and Indy to the girls and get them all out."

An alien noise disrupted the silence. "It's Georgie"—Felix pulled a mobile phone from his ear and shared the news—"the video is going live now. He said to give it forty minutes at least. He and the teams have spread the word via their networks, and… spammed? The social channels. He believes after the story runs he should be able to start… 'whipping up a frenzy' within half an hour. He suggested, for best results, we should arrive shortly after the… hubbub has begun." He hung up and returned the phone to his pocket. "Well, that sounds… promising."

Val nodded, then addressed the group of women who had been huddled in the outer rim, silently standing at the back of the room waiting for their orders. "You five will sit in behind the spearhead. Amina, Aiko and Carley form one group, Shauna and Tomiko another. There will be fighting but we'll do our best to make it minimal. We'll funnel all hostages through to you. Your job is to secure any who want to leave. There will be crowds waiting—they'll help."

Audette spoke up. "I will ring the hospital and have a team on standby. I can also arrange for some ambulances to be waiting at the scene with medics."

"Thank you." Again, Val looked around the room. "Anything else?"

Ben stepped forward. "Yes, actually." He sized Val up. "I may not know exactly what you're talking about, or what the hell is really going on here, but I'm not an idiot and I'm not chopped liver. I can help."

Some of the tension in the room escaped through the crack of Val's laugh. "Too right, Ben. You don't have the sight… yet. There will be a lot of stuff going on you can't see. But if you want in—"

"Bleeding oath I do. Hardly gonna let my wife go off and be a hero without me, am I? What can I do?"

"Okay." Val looked over the group again, making adjustments. "Pairs. Carley and Aiko, Amina work with Shauna, Ben with Tomiko. One cover, one fight. Get them out. Questions?"

There were none.

"Can we go now, Val?" Indy was straining, trying to be patient, but the boy was beside himself.

"Indigo, what part of forty minutes do you not understand?" She shook her head, but the quirk at the corner of her mouth was at least an acknowledgement that he was trying. "Now we eat and petition the Light."

"Eat! Are you cat-skrat crazy?"

All humour was sucked dry in a heartbeat.

Again, Val's voice dropped. "*You* are going to eat. *You* are going to petition the Light. *You* are going to prepare like I tell you to prepare, or *you* are not coming."

"I can't eat, I can't even look at the food, eh?" Indy was now close to tears of frustration.

"Take the food and stick it in your mouth and chew. I don't care if it's like straw, I don't care if you have to grit your teeth to stop it coming back up. You need the fuel. I am not asking you to enjoy it, I am telling you to eat it. No one who fights with me fights on an empty stomach."

"Or a full bladder, isn't that right Val?" Raph's squeaking voice piped up in all earnestness.

The smile was back. "That's right, LM." It was enough to once again bring a small degree of levity to the room. "Dan, Sariah, Raph? Would you play for us while we petition the Light: for Iza and Amber while they wait; for the other priestesses and acolytes; and for us?"

As they went to get their instruments, Vashti, Aiko and Shauna handed out food.

48

IZABEL: INFERNO

Being back here at the Temple made me physically ill. It was like I had been transported back to when I was a child: robbed of all choices, stripped of all rights, reduced to someone else's property. Led to places I didn't want to be, dressed in clothing that repulsed me and given to men whom I abhorred. The cloying smell of incense blended with the scent of fear from the women and scorn from the Keepers. It was enough to turn the wafting veils of gauze fabrics—all in the goddess's colours—into a prison.

"I am with you. I love you. I have heard the cry of my daughters and it is time to set them free. Stay in me and I will win this victory for all of you."

Nausea threatened to overwhelm me, but I refused to show a weakened facade to the minders. They may have brought me back, but they were going to regret it.

Please show me what to do. And please, watch over Indy, protect Amber and help me.

Warmth pulsed through my armour, adding steel to my spine. I was being led through the halls of the Temple to a chorus of gasps. "Mother? Is that you? Amber?" Alyssa—the latest High Priestess—stepped out of the growing crowd lining the corridors of the Temple.

"We heard whispers they'd found you. Before that, we believed you were dead."

I stopped and waited for my sisters to gather around. My Keepers were not happy. One went to grab me and pull me onwards. "Do not touch me. I have already warned you. I am here, but I am not fodder for your feedlot." I turned to the growing gathering. "I am here for a short time only. I have come to take you home with me. When the call comes, be ready."

At this the Keeper grabbed me roughly. I used the tactics Kait and Tessa had taught me. It was sickeningly obvious I was still a beginner and I allowed myself a brief moment of regret for not taking them up on the offer of training earlier. But still, I was able to catch my guard by surprise and force him to unhand me... assertively. "I said, do not touch me." Again, gasps rang through the Temple.

I had fought back.

Of course, this was only an invitation to be punished. But my goal had been achieved; the women had heard my message. And more importantly, they had seen me stand up to the guards. It was only minimal, but it was a start—before I was knocked to the ground and hauled to the Vault: the holding cell for disagreeable priestesses.

Sitting in the small, dark room, with no food or water, hidden from prying and judging eyes, I let the tears fall. This was my wedding day. And my beautiful dress had been torn and stained. Tonight was the night I was going to celebrate with my family and be with my husband. When I first escaped from this hell, I swore I would never lie with another man. Ever. But for eight years Indy had faithfully demonstrated his love, patience and self-control. After our wedding, tonight, I was going to lie with my husband.

I promise you, no matter what it takes, I will not be given to a worshipper. Well, they may give me, but I will not be had.

It would earn me more beatings, but I would stand fast. I would not be meat in the Temple's abattoir ever again.

My face hurt where the guard had hit me. Normally they went for body hits—the back, or anywhere down the left side where our scales hid the bruises—but never on the face. They didn't want to put off the punters. Maybe this would work to my advantage.

I didn't have long to wait. They had worked fast to start the payback for the years I had gone missing. Scrambling up and arranging my dress, I remembered who I was, whose daughter I was and whose wife I was going to be. I no longer needed my imaginary priestess cloak, I had my beautiful armour. I was summoned by a new guard. And I was ready. Having my warning once again ignored I disengaged his hand from my arm. Only to be met by his fist. Becoming a thorn in their side was proving to be a painful exercise.

Once again, I was dragged to my old chambers—Alyssa's now—tossed inside and told to prepare for my worshipper. Oh, I would prepare. Walking to an open space on a lush rug, I loosened my arms, breathed deeply, released the fear and anger, and began working through a set. My body easily fell into the motion of the well-practised pattern. My body hurt as I stretched and moved, but I was able to push past it and get into the movement and rhythm.

I did not stop when my Keeper brought a man into the room. Locking my eyes first on the guard then the "worshipper", I continued working through my set.

The punter laughed. Until he swore. He had stepped in close, and I had merely sped up my movements and defended myself against his advances. The guard came forward and I did the same. This was not merely an "unhanding". This was me defending my body and my right to say no.

After his initial shock, the punter started yelling and came at me again. I kept going through the sequence of the set. But each time one of them approached, I sped up and met them. Even though they could not see or feel my armour, I felt it protecting me to some degree. I knew I would feel the pain of each hit and slap later, but for now my arms and legs were like steel, I was doing my best to give as good as I got.

By now my guard was yelling too; his protests brought reinforcements.

But it brought Amber as well. I couldn't hide my relief and pride as she ducked through the growing crowd and stood by my side. She had been learning from Tessa for much longer than me and just her presence bolstered my confidence. But then she spoke in a very loud voice. I knew the message was for our sisters as they too gathered, whilst remaining hidden in the shadows. "You do not own us anymore. We are not your slaves. We are free women and you cannot—" A guard rushed forward and tried to silence her. When he lay inert at her feet, she continued. "You cannot control us and use us for your gain. We refuse."

By this stage, most of the guards had arrived. Amber and I stood side by side. The large bed I was supposed to entertain my worshipper on was at our back. We fought as hard as we could and, I am proud to say, I injured a few. Amber injured more. But it was not enough. She was dragged away, and I was pinned down.

Each of my arms was secured by a Keeper, two more grabbed my legs. Another locked my head in place. Fury erupted out of me. Screaming. Struggling. Biting and clawing. Any movement I could gain I used for my advantage. My blood boiled and rang in my ears. It almost covered the shouts and swearing in the room. But when someone slashed my beautiful wedding dress up the middle, leaving me bare from toe to chin I lost all rational thought and allowed the rage its head and gave it complete control.

More men came and pinned me down. Every cell of my body strained. I managed to free one leg and I used it to kick someone in the chest. More men came and poured on top of me pinning me down, securing me, immobilising me. A gag had been placed over my mouth. Tears, spit and snot cascaded down my face and pooled in my ears and hair. I was in danger of both suffocating and drowning in my own fluids. My body was a rigid plank. Seething with pure hatred I had finally been locked down.

One of my captors yelled over his shoulder. "Quick, we've got her."

I watched through squinted, teary eyes as they parted and allowed the worshipper to approach. Even though my head was pinned, and my mouth was gagged, I growled and threw every curse word I could remember Indy using throughout our lives together.

"Are you sick? Not like this. For frack's sake, you guys are whacked in the head. Let her go, for frack's sake. Let the poor woman go." The worshipper, shocked into action, tried to pull the Keepers off me. They resisted but, not having anyone to do the deed, they started releasing the strength of their hold.

I leaped into action. As soon as their grips loosened, I started fighting all over again. With an arm and a leg free I made as much damage as I could before I was knocked unconscious.

49

IZABEL: THE VAULT

Of three things I was sure, of four I was confident. Thin, sinewy arms embraced me. A hauntingly familiar tune wisped through my ears. Shouts and chanting yells pulsed from outside the Temple. And hundreds of pairs of red eyes glared at me from the shadows.

Was I dreaming?

"Shh, I have you."

"Amber?" My voice cracked.

"I'm here, Izabel."

I tried to raise my arm to point. To question. To be proved wrong. But I hurt too much to move.

"Lie still, something is happening. I don't know what. But I can imagine. Our family might be coming to get us."

"The noise..." The chanting still echoed through to us from outside, but there were yells and shouts of distress from inside as well.

"It started a little while ago and hasn't stopped. It just keeps growing louder."

"Are you hurt?"

"I'm not too bad. I've been hurt worse at the Temple."

"Amber?"

"Yes Iza."

"Are there eyes… hundreds of eyes, watching us?"

"Yes Iza."

"Who are they?"

"I think it's the Dark. I'm not sure. But it seems when I sing the songs Dan sings, and when I say snippets of *The Way* I remember from classes, they stay back."

It was all too much—the pain, the confusion, the anger. My vision became blurry and the red eyes around us shimmered through my tears.

As consciousness continued to return, so did my memory of what had happened and what they had done to me… to us.

"Did they get to you, sweetheart? Did they hurt you?"

"Not like they tried to hurt you. I will be fine."

Tears of self-pity turned to tears of anger. "They ruined my dress."

"We'll make you a new one."

"We shouldn't have to. They've taken everything from us. And it was not enough that we were living quietly, unobtrusively. They had to come in and take our lives from us… again." I tried to sit up, but all my muscles screamed in protest and the pain in my head boomed in time with the chanting from outside. "Is there any water?"

Amber just huffed. "Did you forget we're at the Temple? We're in the Vault. There's nothing here but you, me and our audience."

Even gritting my teeth hurt. But I was not going to take this lying down again. I was no longer a priestess. I had rights. "Can you help me up, please?"

I was ashamed of the amount of groaning I made, but I figured with all the noise outside no one would hear. I had to pause a few times, waiting for the waves of nausea to pass. When I was upright against the wall, I tried easing myself around to the door. Even though my body was in pain, my head was the biggest problem. Each time I moved I had to focus to stop vomiting. And to make the room stop spinning.

"It's locked. I've tried it." Amber walked at my shoulder, holding me.

I couldn't answer, I was scared I would be sick. But Amber patiently accompanied me as I shuffled around the perimeter of the room to confirm her discovery.

A beast stepped out of the shadows and stood in front of us. The shock was too much. My stomach ejected itself all over the creature.

It swore.

The others laughed.

And I slid back down the wall and passed out again.

50

DANIEL: THE RESCUE

Finally, we were on the move. Indy jogged to the truck and fumbled with the latch in a hurry to get moving. No one could ever accuse the old bus of being classy, but it proved its worth in how much it could carry. Amina, Aiko, Carley, Ben and Tomiko said a rushed farewell to their kids. Kazi was positioned next to the gate with Jordan on her lap, ready to roll it back in place once we'd left.

I looked to the walls and noted the Warriors of Light standing guard. I knew the kids were going to be alright. But climbing into the back of the truck heading to a big battle in the city had too many triggers reminding me of our big showdown in Sodom. And I was struck with memories of losing Abbot. There was no guarantee we would all come home.

But just as I was back then, most of the people joining us were completely ignorant of what lay ahead, of what they were about to be confronted by.

Please watch over us... them... us. Help us. Keep us in You and... just please keep everyone safe.

Kait and Val locked us in, and Marcus drove us out. Indy and Amina were too amped to sit. They stood and paced. Until the lurching became too much, that was. Then, they just clung onto the walls and seethed.

"Sit down. The battle will come soon enough. You'll burn out before we even get there." Ben sat seemingly relaxed against the side wall.

Indy was still spitting chips. "What? What do you know about it?"

"A lot actually, son. This is not my first rodeo. And even though I can't see whatever's going on out there, battle's battle."

"Do you want to see, Ben?" Raph sat opposite him and was bathed in a beam of light coming through the window from the opposite wall.

Everyone was silent, holding their breath, waiting. The rattle and hum of the truck the only noise.

"Well, lad. I've been asking myself the same question."

Tomiko leaned in closer to her husband and gripped his arm but remained silent. Her eyes huge and hopeful.

"Do you not realise there is a world happening around us that you cannot see? Do you not acknowledge that someone Other healed Indy?"

"Well, it's not that easy."

"Abbot used to say, the journey of a lifetime starts with a single choice. But not making that choice when the time is right, is like trying to dam a mighty river with twigs."

Ben's laugh had a hard edge. "I'd say twigs was about right, lad."

"If you like, I could ask the Light to chat with you and you can work it out with Him. He really is very nice, you know."

At this everyone in the truck laughed and Ben looked around, lost. I guess he felt the sting of being the only one who didn't get the joke. "Alright mate. How about you do that. And when this is all over, maybe He and I can sit down and have a... chat." Now he was the only one laughing. Poor Ben, he really didn't understand. That's actually what it was like. Well, not the initial meeting. Mine anyway. Or Iza's by the sound of it. But afterwards it was.

Immediately, Raph got up and went to sit by Ben's side and laid his scarred hands on the man's shoulders.

"What are you doing, Raph?" Ben didn't push the boy away, but he was clearly uncomfortable.

Raph didn't respond. His head was down, and his lips were going ten to the dozen.

Tomiko clung to Ben's arm, her eyes squeezed shut, her head nodding and bobbing side to side.

"Raphael. What are you doi—" Ben's eye's flew open. Then his jaw dropped. Tears swam and he turned to stone. His Adam's apple bobbed furiously, then he dropped his head between his knees, his shoulders shaking gently. He remained like that for some time. We all waited silently, and I would have bet money... if I had any... we were all petitioning the Light on Ben's behalf.

Eventually, Ben inhaled a deep watery breath and quietly sighed. "Yes." Nodding his head he whispered, "Yes." Then he stilled, his head resting on his arms crossed over his bent legs. Tomiko wrapped her arm over his back and pulled him close, her eyes sparkling. "Thank you, Raph."

"Oh. It was not me. It was the Light. He said it was about time Ben stopped fighting the wrong enemy. And, He said, He did not want Ben going into this battle with his eyes blind, his ears clogged and unarmed. He said Ben would understand." Before anyone could respond, Raph continued talking to Tomiko. "He also said it is time you let it go. Kazi's injury at birth was not your fault. He wants you to stop carrying an imagined burden. Kazi is loved and whole. She is where and who she needs to be. He wants you to be at peace and move on."

Tomiko gasped and Ben pulled her close. "I've been trying to tell you the same thing for ten years." He wiped his face along his arm and looked at Raph. "Thank—" His eyes locked on Raph, then he looked around the truck. Everyone's armour was glinting in flashes of street-lights and the glow breaking through the windows from the city.

Indy stepped over and clapped him on the back. "Welcome, brother. Glad to finally have you aboard." Indy held out his hand and Ben just stared at it. Then back up and over Indy's armour. Mouth open, eyes popping out of his head.

But then he saw his wife.

Time to get us back in the game. We didn't have long, and we were heading into battle with a complete newb. Not ideal, but better than a blind man.

A little help here, please?

I breathed out and did my best to copy Val. "Listen up, team. Val has given us orders. We each know the play, but I want to prepare you... scrap that. I can't. There is nothing I can do to prepare you for what you're about to encounter. So, I strongly suggest whatever you do, whatever you see, remember the Light is bigger, gnarlier, and stronger than anything you are going to witness or experience tonight. Just stay in the Light. Just keep talking to Him."

"And, I might add," Felix spoke up, "some very good advice someone told me once—and it happened to save me... twice, when I had very limited experience and knowledge of the situation"—he slid his sword out from the sheath down his back—"draw that thing on your back and aim the pointy end out. Anything that comes close, stick it... demonic that is. Although, I don't believe it will do too much damage to anything that isn't... Other. So, if in doubt, just point and stick." He gave his sword a bit of a flourish and smiled.

"Good advice." He nodded in response to my compliment. "You been practising, Felix." This time he couldn't hide his smile. And when he looked at the twins and winked, Riah's face split in the widest grin I'd seen on her since her birthday. Neither of the twins had left his side since he'd shown up, if they could help it. He didn't seem to mind. He even rested his left hand on Raph's shoulder.

We travelled through the city. It wasn't a particularly long drive and as we neared the Temple Mount, Kait yelled through the "hole in the wall" leading through to the cab. "Hang on everyone!" Instead of going through the car park entrance we normally used to access the Temple, Marcus took us straight up the guts of the avenue, over the kerb and up to paved paths and gardens in the huge square fronting each of the three main Temples.

We'd heard the chanting of the mob before we arrived. But when we broke over the kerb and up onto the square their cheers could be heard over the roar and strain of the old engine. In the back we were all clinging to the windows to see what was happening. As we approached, the crowd parted, so Marcus drove the truck right up into the middle of the square.

Val jumped out and came round to let us out. As soon as the back roller door was up, the crowd went wild. Georgie and Griff had done their job well. People were pointing and yelling when they saw Indy, and the Silverscales. It was seriously weird. Going from being in hiding to being celebrities was a surreal trip.

Val, Marcus and Kait made a bit of a human barricade to help us get the ladies out of the back and over to the Temple. The look on Val's face helped. People were tripping over themselves to get out of her way. We just followed in her wake.

When we arrived at the steps of the Temple of Ashera, she stopped. We had been arranging ourselves in our pre-arranged formation as we made our way over. Val flicked her glance over each shoulder checking we were ready. Looking behind, she saw the Silverscales… and Ben. One eyebrow rose, she smiled and nodded to him. "Welcome."

She then flicked her chin up, calling the twins, Tessa and me to her. "You guys good?"

Raph was holding Riah's hand. "Yes Val, we are good. It is a bit exciting. I cannot wait to see what the Light does here. I have never liked this place."

Val went down on one knee before them and embraced each one. "Eyes on the Light, guys. Love you."

Marcus dropped a kiss on each of their heads and Kait couldn't stop her arms snaking around us all.

Riah leaned into my side. I ruffled her hair—she still hated it, but she knew I loved her. I quickly pumped Tessa's hand twice. She returned the gesture with a quick kiss on my cheek. With Raph, Indy and Lily behind us, the three of us were ready.

Val went back to the head of the spear after giving everyone in her crew one more check. The mob filling the square quietened. Waiting.

They stood back a way, not sure what to expect. But the energy in the air was electric.

"We have come to claim Izabel and Amber who were wrongfully taken from our family... their home." Her voice rang and echoed around the colonnade.

There was no response.

She waited a beat of ten.

She drew her sword.

We all followed suit.

"We have come to claim our family members. If you do not bring them out, unharmed, we will come in and retrieve them."

She waited again.

It was at this point I realised the Keepers and Guards were kind of frelcked. The Temple had been designed to allow maximum access for maximum business. There were no gates, doors or defensible walls. There was nothing stopping us just going in and getting Iza and Amber.

Except the hordes of hell who started spewing out from the portico and down the front steps.

Marcus's grumble ghosted to me on the breeze. "It's like the night we arrived. When Hell vomited its spawn, angry as a swarm of wet wolves."

Gasps and cries flared behind us, but they were drowned out by Val's roar. "For the Light. For His victory. For His glory." Knives flew from her hand.

Whether the crowd could see it or not, they erupted in fury.

"Here we go, guys, stay with us." I had to hope Indy and Lily stuck in behind. I knew Raph knew what to do. But with the battle joined, Tessa and Riah's blades flying either side of me, I only had eyes for what was in front. We had to move in behind Felix, Marlene and Fleur and get through the arches on the right. Lily had told us that was the most direct route to where we needed to be.

The three in front of us were seriously lethal, and before long had made a path for us to break through. "Go, dear, we'll cover your back," Marlene yelled as we made our move.

"Lily? Which way?"

"S-straight ahead."

We ran into a space and waited for Lily to call out directions. "Focus, Lily, where's the Vault."

She shook her head then nodded. "Let me." She dashed past us.

"No. Get behind." I managed to grab the fabric of her cowl and pull her back. I pulled her too hard and she landed on her butt. Where her head had been, a hand full of deadly talons swiped thin air. Riah pierced its exposed armpit and dispatched it. Lily scrambled out of the way as the body started dissolving into a puddle of tar. "Stay behind. Just tell us. Where next?"

She couldn't speak but pointed a shaking finger.

"Indy, Raph, get her up. We've got to keep moving."

At every turn, behind each corner, was an ambush. It was the most obvious tactic. They knew what we wanted and where we were going. They just had to wait for us to arrive. We were holding our own, but it was slow and hard going. Thankfully our personal Warriors were covering our backs. We didn't have to worry about what was behind, below or above. However, the further we went into the inner sanctum of the Temple, the darker it became. Reflected light bounced off the white marble floors and sandstone walls. But no lights were lit. No candles burned in the sconces. We were heading further into the Dark's lair and the way was literally getting harder to see.

Tessa puffed in a brief lull. "How much further?"

"Not too far. Just around the next bend."

The hallways were wide, which made it easier for us to fight abreast, but the marble floors became slippery after a few kills. With a trail of dissolving bodies behind us, and the final turn in front, I thought it was our last opportunity to have a brief breather before the final push. No doubt they had something special waiting for us.

We don't know what's around the corner, but you do. You have what it takes for us to get them out. Show me what to do. Help me lead my team to save them.

Keeping close to the wall, I crept to the corner then slid to the floor and, on my stomach, peeked around the corner.

It was empty.

"Are you sure this is where the Vault is?"

Lily raced forward, Indy hot on her heels.

"Careful, it could be a trap," I growled.

But Indy didn't stop. He raced through the open door and his legs gave way. From the floor he yelled back, "It's empty. Frack. Where the frack are they?" He hauled himself up and punched the wall, then released the most primal, broken cry of pain and frustration. "Iza!"

My ears rang and my heart broke for my brother.

But then we all froze.

"Did you hear that?" Tessa was off and running. "Come on. It's her."

We darted through corridors, listening to Iza's yells as they gradually got louder and easier to follow.

"Oh no," Lily cried. "We're heading to the Forbidden Place."

"Iza." Indy was beside himself. "Iza, we're coming."

I am ashamed to say I dropped all precaution as we ran for our lives… for Iza's life, following Lily's lead through to the bowels of the Temple.

Iza's scream split the darkness. "Father, no!"

"I should have done this years ago. It would have saved me a lifetime of trouble."

There was more scuffling and the sound of skin hitting skin and another cry. "Don't you hurt her." Iza was no longer pleading. Anger infused her voice. "Amber, run."

We neared a door and Lily was visibly shaking, she could barely control her limbs.

"What? What is it?" I grabbed her by the shoulders and gave her a gentle shake.

She couldn't speak. She covered her mouth with one hand, pointed to the door in front of us with her other and just kept shaking her head. She was useless. Incapable of helping us at this point. I motioned everyone to be still and silent. Forcing the group to just hold. Breathe. Think.

There was more huffing and slapping. Iza yelled, "Run, Amber!"

"Okay. We're up against two kinds of enemy here. Indy, you and I will take the humans. The rest of you take the demons. If there are too many humans, Tessa, you lend us a hand. If there are too many demons, I'll help you guys." Everyone nodded. "I'm just going to see what we're up against so we're not running in blind." Puffing hard and readying weapons, they nodded as I snuck forward and peeked through the open door to see what we were up against.

Frack.

51

CONTESSA: SACRIFICES

Dan pulled his head back and leaned against the wall. But in the flickering light breaking through the open doorway it was plain as day things weren't good. He shut his eyes for a moment then silently made his way back to us. "A dude, probably Iza's dad, and one Guard. Everyone else must be fighting out the front. There's a handful of demons getting off on what's going on. Humanoids." He looked at me because he knew how much they gave me the creeps.

"Change of plan. Tessa and Riah, make a move on the demons first whilst they're distracted. There's only five. Lily, see what you can do to help them if needed. Remember your training and you'll be fine. As soon as you're free, check on Amber."

He turned to Indy. "You and me take her dad. We'll go wolf on him. You come in the front and get his attention. He knows you, doesn't he?"

"I'm guessing if he didn't before, he does now, after what was on the telly and the wedding. But yeah, I'd say he'd remember me."

"Good. Go in the front and skitch him off. Get him 'all eyes on you'. I won't need long. I'll circle round behind, take the guard, then come in and take him from behi—"

"No. I take him."

"Whatever, as long as someone takes him. I'll only need a minute to take out the guard." Dan moved closer to Indy and locked eyes with him. "I'm going to ask you to do the hardest thing you've ever done." Indy stilled. We all did. "Do not look at Iza. Just get in there and skitch her dad off. It won't take long. Five minutes max. Then you can have at him. Then we get Iza and Amber and run. Okay? I need you to focus on her dad. Please."

Indy paled. But nodded.

"Alright, we ready?" He cast a quick glance to Raph and gave the smallest of nods. Raph knew why he was here and what he had to do. Best that Dan hadn't drawn attention to him or his target: Iza. It would not have helped the others. When we all nodded, Dan led us into hell's heart.

Please help, please help, please help, please help... please.

Indy entered the room and true to his word, he went straight for Iza's dad.

"What are yo—" The man's eyes bugged out of his head and spit flew out of his mouth. "You." The man was so angry, I wouldn't have been surprised if there was venom in his saliva. "You caused all of this." He was holding a short, curved knife, and when he saw Indy, he raised it and charged him.

I was worried for Indy, but we had other things to worry about... far more things. Dan had been wrong about the number, but not what they were doing. Six. Not five. Six humanoids were standing around, salivating over what was going on in the room. They were so focused on feeding off the disgusting feralness, it helped Riah and me take out two before the others knew what was going on. I watched Dan come round the wall and with one quick hit to the head, the guard crumpled.

Then quickly taking in the scene: Indy and Iza's dad going toe-to-toe, Raph leaning over Iza, Lily hyperventilating in a heap next to Amber, and Riah and I taking on the four remaining humanoids. Dan altered his plan to lend us a hand and between the three of us we managed to dispatch them without too much trouble. We had been practising working as a trio and we were getting way good.

Thankfully, Lily had snapped out of her hysterics long enough to try to rouse Amber. Checking the enemy was taken care of and our Warrior Guard were stationed around the wall holding any others at bay, I glanced over to Indy and Iza's dad. Both men were enraged... fully frontal lobe—all brawn and absolutely no brain. But it looked like Iza's dad had flipped into fully nuts-o-crazy.

Then, and only then did I allow myself to look at Iza. Raph was standing still with his eyes shut. His hands resting on her shoulder. Dan was madly fighting with the ties. "A little help here, guys." It was enough to snap me out of my trance. I stumbled over and helped release her feet. Every centimetre of her naked body was bruised and battered. Her beautiful face was swollen and bleeding. Her wedding dress was nowhere to be seen and she had been laid out, strapped to a huge block of stone. She was whimpering and shivering.

Riah came over. I saw her swallow, her eyes wide and unseeing. I suspected she was having trouble not remembering her own suffering. I put my arm around her shoulder and tried to turn her away. She struggled against me just enough to stop me turning her. With one hand holding my arm in place around her shoulders, she moved to the edge of the slab. Then placed both of her hands on Iza's leg, shut her eyes, and did her thing. Within seconds, with both twins working on her, Iza had stopped whimpering and shivering. She was still a mess, but obviously a tad more comfortable.

Iza's dad must have seen that we'd unstrapped his daughter. He yelled and went berserk. Coming at us with that knife raised, aimed at the back of Raph's head. Raph was so deep in the process of healing, he had no idea what was going on around him. Dan was securing the guard; Lily was with Amber; and there was a mountainous stone slab between Iza's dad and us. "Raph." I knew screaming wasn't going to help, but I was helpless.

But as his opponent had shifted his focus, Indy now had Iza in his line of sight. He released a bestial roar and threw himself at Iza's dad. Tackling him to the ground and then proceeded to beat the skrat out of him. The man stopped fighting. And protesting. And moving. And still Indy punched away.

Dan flew at his friend to get him off. To stop him. But Indy was possessed. Dan couldn't budge him. Indy started hitting him as well. *Possessed.* "Riah, quick." I grabbed her and pulled her around to the other side of the altar. "Use your Badge on Indy. Quick." Indy had gotten a few good hits on his friend, forcing Dan to retreat. On his hands and knees, shaking his head, Dan was out of the game. And Indy was back pounding Iza's dad's inert body.

Riah closed her eyes and it wasn't long before the rage fell away from Indy's pummelling. He still swung away, but with less passion. Then he stopped. Sitting astride Alain's unconscious body. His head hanging. Fists bleeding. Completely spent. But still.

"Indy?" All of us looked to the stone altar. Iza still lay flat on her back, but her head was turned, looking for him. She called him again, tears in her voice. "Indy? Are you here?"

Dan stood next to her, swaying slightly, trying to get out of his shirt to lay it across her body. Indy climbed to his feet and dragged himself to her side. Iza lifted her hand and he took it. His eyes travelled over her body. He gently lifted the shirt to see the damage underneath.

"Don't look, my love. It won't help." The words slurred out of her swollen mouth.

Raph still stood in a trance at her shoulder, and Iza lifted her hand and laid it on Indy's cheek. Still holding her hand, he dropped his forehead on hers and wept.

Lily spoke up from the floor. "We need to get them out of here. They both need help. Audette will have ambulances waiting and we need to get them to the hospital."

Riah laid a hand on Raph's shoulder and moments later he came back to us. "Iza had some internal damage, I have tried to heal the worst of it. She also has concussion. But I think none of her bones are broken. I think we can move her." He looked around, nodding. Then looked at Iza and immediately took his shirt off to help cover her. His face a deep shade of red.

Iza smiled at him. "It's like the first night we met all over again. When you healed me before."

338

Raph couldn't look at her, he just handed her his shirt.

I went to help Lily get Amber up, but she was having trouble standing. So, we settled her against the side of the altar as we made an attempt to dress Iza with the shirts of Indy, Dan and Raph. Indy then picked Iza up and carried her from the room, Dan put his arm around Amber and half carried her, and Lily navigated. I took point and Sariah watched our tail as we got our girls out of there.

We had done it. I mean, I knew we weren't out of the Temple yet. But we had done it.

Thank you.

They were safe now. No one could take them again once Indy and Iza were married. But what about Amber... and the others? "Wait. Lily, is there somewhere they keep the records? The contracts?"

Indy growled, "Tessa, we don't have time."

"You go ahead, guys, Riah will keep guard. But we have to stop this ever happening again." I tried to make him see.

"It's okay. We passed the office on the way in." Lily once again raced to the front to lead us out. I wasn't confident it was all over, so I grabbed her shoulder and indicated she should walk behind me.

"Let's go quietly, huh? And carefully. We're not out of the woods yet." Dan gave me the nod and we continued. Lily pointing the way.

We came to what was obviously the office. Desks, bookcases and filing cabinets decorated the room. There was plush carpet on the floor and dark, ornate furniture spotted around the room. There were no external windows, but a soft glow came from a desk lamp. We didn't have time for stealth now. I searched the walls beside the door for the switch and flooded the room with light.

In the corner a man stood in front of an open safe. He froze with his hands full of cash. "What are you doing here? You can't be here; this is a private office."

Still holding Amber up, Dan didn't waste time. "The files, where are they?"

The man spluttered and protested some more.

"Look man, keep the money, we don't want it. We want the files." Laying Amber gently in a chair, with Raph and Riah standing guard either side of her, Dan stalked to the man. He was tired, on edge and wanted to get out of here. But understood how important it was to destroy those contracts.

The man wasn't a guard or a Keeper, as the women called them. This guy seemed purely administrative.

"And I can keep the money?"

Dan nodded. "Where are the contracts and files on the women?"

"Women? What women?"

It was Lily's turn to growl. "The Assets."

"Oh." With a hand full of cash, he pointed to the wall behind us. Banks of filing cabinets stood in rows.

I couldn't hide my groan. There were so many. So. Flopping. Many.

"Open them." Dan didn't seem put off.

The man hesitated, but when Dan stepped even closer, the guy stuffed his handful of cash in the bag at his feet then waddled over. He withdrew a chain from his pocket and sorted through the keys at the end.

Indy had had enough. "For frack's sake. Hurry up." Iza murmured something and he quietened.

The cabinets were unlocked. "Riah, shut the door. And lock it. Everyone, help. Pull out all the drawers. Middle row out on the floor, top and bottom drawers just open. Lily, find something to light this lot with."

She raced to the desks and started searching drawers. Indy clung to Iza and stood next to Amber while the three of us attacked the cabinets. Starting at one end, Dan yanked out each middle drawer and tossed it on the floor. I ran along opening the top drawers. Raph and Riah worked around the obstacle course Dan was creating, sliding open the bottom row of drawers.

"Got it." Lily returned, grinning, with a lighter and three bottles of incense oil.

"Perfect." Undoing the caps, we doused the open drawers and then lit each one. "Let's go."

It wasn't guaranteed to work, but it was something. Hopefully it would do enough damage to protect the women.

We were back in the hallway, smoke following in our wake.

"Stop. Stop. The fire. The money." The guy in the office was left making a decision between his life and his fortune. We left him to it and made for the light and fresh air waiting for us outside.

We continued to race, Lily directing from behind my shoulder. Gradually, the light became brighter and the air sweeter. But from behind a billowing cloud of black smoke chased us. Soon, we didn't need Lily's directions. Yelling and shouting pulled us to the outside where another battle waited for us.

Through my muddled mind, I realised it wasn't yelling, it was cheering.

They must have won.

We were going to make it.

I let myself believe for the first time.

We were actually going to make it.

I lost focus and ended up on my butt after bouncing off the rear end of a gigantor. It had appeared out of nowhere. And now it stared down at me, acid drooling from its many rows of needle teeth. Lack of reason and intelligence stared back at me from its dull eyes.

Whilst humanoids creeped me out, gigantors frightened the living goodness out of me.

Please help. Please help. Please help.

"Tessa. Move." Dan's scream woke me up and got me moving as its paw came down at me. I threw myself back, flat on the floor. The move saved my life. But the ends of its talons sliced me open. Fire exploded through my whole body. Hands grabbed my shoulders and I was dragged back. I couldn't hold in the scream. Agony ripped through my gut where its claws had sliced me open.

Dan bellowed, "Raph. Quick."

All I could do was grit my teeth and try to blank out the pain. It worked. I was conscious of hands gently laid on me and then nothing.

RAPHAEL: TIME TO SHINE

Riah and I worked very quickly to do what we could for Tessa. Indy sat Iza on the floor, next to Amber who was quietly petitioning the Light under her breath. We pulled Tessa over by them and asked them to watch over her. Lily was whiter than her namesake and trembling like a leaf. Silently, I asked Riah to use her Badge on the four of them. It took a few moments, but I think it worked. Or, at least, it seemed to.

We had very little time. Indy and Dan were left by themselves, trying to take down the gigantor. It was just like the one in Ebony's library in Sodom. It had been very hard to kill. It had taken everyone's efforts... everyone but mine. I had been too scared. But now? I was still scared, but I knew for a fact that Dan and Indy could not fight this beast alone. Riah and I had to help.

Of course my twin knew what I was thinking. Very quickly, she squeezed my hand twice, then we turned to see how we could work alongside the others. Dan and Indy were taking turns at running in from opposite sides trying to attack as the other distracted it. Like they did with Izabel's father. They were keeping it occupied, but they were not achieving anything apart from making it angry. Very angry.

Thick black smoke started billowing out behind us. Iza, Amber and

Lily were staying as low as they could and edging their way into the open, gently bringing Tessa with them. But the space between the smoke and the demon was getting squeezier.

Surely there was more on fire than the office we lit. There was just too much of the thick, tar-like cloud.

I saw Riah size the gigantor up. I knew, like me, she was remembering how Val had killed the one in Sodom. But she was not as strong as Val. We didn't have Val's knives. And this one was not crippled with Marcus's sword lodged in its hip. Or Kait's sword in its eye.

"Riah, you are fast and light and very good with your sword. I am fast and light and can use my hands."

She glared at me with squinty eyes. She knew what I was thinking and did not like it. But there was no other way and no time. We had to do what we could to help.

"We are not like the others, Riah. We do not have what they have. But we have what we have. You can either help me, or I will go by myself."

She shook her head, then nodded.

We made our way over to where Indy and Dan were tiring, but desperately trying to find a weak spot in the demon's defences.

I tried to get Dan's attention. In the end I got Indy's. I tried to explain what I was thinking. He did not understand. Riah gave up and bumped my shoulder. We would just go when we saw an opening and an opportunity. We neared the beast. Riah would go first. I would follow.

Indy ran in, but his legs gave out and he fell to his knees. Dan darted in and started waving his sword, trying to give Indy time to get back up. The beast reared as Dan managed to connect his blade with its underbelly. It then swooped down to try to swipe him. It was our chance. We took off as fast as we could. Riah leaping onto its back. Me in her wake. She dropped her legs around its neck and stuck her sword into the first soft spot she could find. Seconds later I sat behind her, my hands sliding either side of her waist, coming to rest on its head. And with all I had in me I petitioned the Light.

It screamed and bellowed. My ears went deaf with the noise. I felt scraping down my legs, but I gripped tighter around the outside of Riah as she clung to her sword lodged in its eye. With my eyes shut I did not see anything except the explosion of Light in my mind. I heard nothing but the pulsing of my heartbeat. My one thought was to hang on and petition the Light. To stay in the Light. I kept saying over and over.

All *for the Light. Victory* in *the Light. Glory* for *the Light.*

Hands tried to pry my fingers off the demon's brow, but I hung on.

"It's okay, Raph. You can let go now." Val broke through my offensive.

Slowly, I unclenched my lids and looked around. The tar-black smoke was pouring out over the top of us, stinging my throat and blurring my vision, but through it all I could just make out some figures.

We were surrounded.

53

MARCUS: HOLDING IT TOGETHER

"Get those rubberneckers out of here, now." Bleeding heck, some of these people were dead from the neck up. "Bring the ambulances up to the front steps, as close as you can." I could not believe what these crazy kids had done. I could not believe me eyes when I saw them riding the kret of a gigantor. A. Gigantor. What the frack were they thinking? If they survived this, I would personally kill them. Each of them. Several times over. One at a time.

And Dan and Indy. Thinking they could take it on by themselves. Just the two of them and Indy hardly trained. I'd skin them alive. We'd seen them and not been able to get to them. A last wave had kept us separated. But watching me kids was enough to release me inner berserker and make short work of everything standing between us.

And Tessa. Oh Lord... I just couldn't think. Not me girl. She had to be alright. "Where the hell are those ambulances?"

Vashti pushed her way through the crowd that was spreading onto the threshold of the burning Temple. "They're on their way, but they can't get through the people."

"I'm not waiting." Val stood, with Riah in her arms. "Marcus, get Raph." She looked around, her assessing eyes running over the group. "Dan, can you walk?" He grunted but was already on his way to Tessa.

He bent down, preparing to carry her. "Indy, get Iza. Lily help Amber. We're moving out. Now. Kait, clear a path. The rest of you help her. We stop for no one. Go." Her rage was exploding out of every pore.

By this stage, our whole crew had finished checking all the women rescued from the Temple were with medical professionals and being cared for.

I gently lifted me boy into me arms and did me best not to break down sobbing. He'd done it again. He'd thrown himself onto the fire to save the others. But now wasn't the time to consider how close we'd come to losing them. Losing them all. No. Not now. I'd be as useless as a carpet fitter's ladder if I didn't get myself under control.

By the time we had our kids ready, everyone had all arrived and we were ready to move. The Silverscales, Ben, Felix, Marlene, Fleur, and Helen formed a barrier around us and me Kait spearheaded the way out. One look at her face—and Val's knives in each hand—had people scrambling over themselves to get out of the way.

"Over here." Audette had organised more ambulances and had her medical team on standby. But when she saw her daughter, she screamed. It was the catalyst that brought everyone's attention to us. The crowd froze. As those in front descended the stairs, the wounded behind them were exposed. I didn't think much of it, I was just heading to the medical teams to get me kids checked out and to get us out of the bleeding smoke.

But even I turned when I heard the collective gasp. The only two left on the top step were Indy and Iza. Iza spoke to Indy and he put her down. She was an absolute bleeding mess. Her face puffy and swollen, cuts and bruises all over her. She wore a man's—Indy's—shirt around her top, Dan and Raph's wrapped around her waist. It was only earlier this evening that her and Indy's image had been plastered across all screens: beautiful, pure and joyous in their wedding gear. The contrast slapped ignorance out of the park.

Audette was sobbing and pushing her way through the crowd to get to her daughter. But she stopped when Iza lifted her voice. "This has to stop." Cameras and phones were held up recording the scene. "No more. What goes on in this place has to stop. The men running the business behind the Temple front have robbed, ruined and raped your daughters long enough."

Black clouds continued to spew out of the halls behind her. I don't know what those kids had done, but there was going to be a hell of a lot of damage. Especially since no one seemed to be in a mind to put it out.

Iza still had everyone's attention. Standing on the steps of the once-great Temple, toxic black smoke billowing a backdrop to her battered body, on display as the shirts draped around her flapped open in the night's warm breeze. With Indy by her side, his naked, bleeding torso exposed, she continued. "Let this place and the evil within it die today, for good. This place is an abomination and the Light has seen it cleansed. He has said, no more." With her chin up and her back ramrod straight, she finished her message and allowed Indy to guide and half-carry her down the stairs. They made an imposing impression.

By now, along with the rest of the city, Amina had seen Iza, left the rest of her charges and raced to climb the stairs alongside Audette. Both women sliding to the wrong side of sanity. Hugging Indy and Iza. Eventually Indy managed to persuade them to allow him to get Iza to one of the waiting ambulances.

She'd done it. She'd set out to bring down the Temple, and... we'd done it. I was happy for her. And the women. And that she and Amber were safe and walking. But enough of the theatrics. Me kids were unconscious and in need of medical treatment. I was very close to losing me grip, so I covered it up by yelling, "Someone help me kids. Now."

A team raced across the remaining space and tried to take Raph from me arms. "No. You show me where to put him, I'll take him." Val was beside me and the fury in her face was enough to have the medicos turning and pointing to a makeshift first aid set-up.

I gently laid Raph on a table but kept a hold of his hand. Kait came and wrapped an arm around me shoulder as we watched Val lay Riah down. Next Dan brought Tessa over, placed her on a table, then immediately crumpled to the ground beside her gurney.

"Dan." Kait was by his side in a heartbeat. "Dan, what's happened?" Kait wouldn't let anyone near him, she was running her hands all over him, trying to find a wound or the cause of his collapse.

"He took a few hits to the head in the Sacrificial Chamber." Lily made her way over with Amber.

"The... what?" Kait asked.

"Her dad was going to sacrifice Iza. Amber was trying to fight him off. The others arrived just in time. But Indy got a bit carried away when he saw the shape Iza was in," Lily said.

Kait was still trying to make the sense of it. "But how was Dan involved?"

Amber chipped in. "It was time to go. We needed to get Iza out, but Indy went ballistic. Alain was not moving. But Indy kept going. Dan tried to pull him off and, well, Indy wasn't in his right mind. He didn't mean to. It wasn't on purpose." She fought to hold onto her tears. "Will he be okay? He... they saved us. Alain was going to kill Iza and me. But they saved us. And then we burned the office." Her breathing became fast and shallow. "And then that... attacked Tessa, and the twins—" Amber swayed on her feet and fell into the arms of a medic who had raced to grab her when he saw her spiralling.

"The hospital is on standby. Let's get everyone loaded up and move them out." Audette had re-saddled her swim and abandoned the sink. "More ambulances are on their way."

Out of the chaos, Felix approached and looked at the wounded. I noted he was sporting a matching set of his own battle badges. "What about Alain? I have not seen him... emerge."

Audette turned on my friend, her face twisted in rage. "Did you hear what he was going to do to my daughter?"

"Yes, I did, Audette, and he will stand trial. But my dear friend, you have sworn an oath."

"If there is someone who is available, send them to look for bodies. I am too busy. If you care so much, Felix, you go."

Me friend made his way over, but I am not sure he saw me. "Oh, I do believe I am needed here, Audette. I'm sure we can... rustle up someone, at some point." Me good friend looked down at the table where Riah lay and ever so gently took Raph's other hand. "I am far too busy."

Before the first batch of ambulances loaded with priestesses and girls could exit the area, a cavalcade of cars sped across the square. The crowd were screaming and jumping out of the way. The next thing we knew, the fleet had strategically placed themselves in front of every exit and possible escape route. Seemed we weren't out of the woods yet.

Val was up and running, putting herself between the newcomers and our wounded family. She yelled. "To me." All of us who were still conscious and capable were instantly on guard, taking our positions behind her. "Audette, get the next load of people ready to go. We'll try to make a path through."

I looked up and me blood chilled. After six months driving that thing around, I would recognise that particular car anywhere. The Overseer fell over himself trying to get out of the car. With arms waving, mouth blustering. Spit flying, his face obscured by rage.

I had to trust Audette and the others to do what they did best and get on and do what I did best.

Be with me kids. Make them better. Please. Give us the strength to keep fighting, to just... keep... going until we can rest.

"What are you doing? Get those whores back into that building." The Overseer's podgy finger stabbed the air in the direction of the Temple.

Felix pulled up next to me and responded. "That building?" As one, we turned to see the Temple—or what we could see of the Temple, the few parts that weren't obscured behind billowing clouds of black smoke—and the red glow from the windows within.

Shaking me head in disbelief, I looked back and turned to ice. The Overseer now stood in front of not only his three personal demons, but the crest of a new wave from hell.

Oh Lord, help us.

With a calm I didn't feel, Felix continued to engage the Overseer. "It is heartening to see how the Community's representative is here to help these poor souls... personally, be restored to their"—he looked to the Temple again—"home." Never in me life had I ever encountered such a master of sarcasm. With Felix it was an art. It may well have been a Badge. If ever one existed.

The roar of rage echoed around the vast square in direct contrast to Felix's calm. I was also aware in my periphery of cameras being picked up, of ears pricking and eyes turned. All attention was back on us and the scene the Overseer was creating.

"Paint the dragon, Felix." Val spoke from the corner of her mouth. But I suspect Felix was totally aware of the situation and didn't need Val's prompt.

Felix gave her a whisker of a nod and continued goading the Overseer. "Oh, so you're not here to help?"

The Overseer's scream drew a chuckle from Val. I'm not sure if it was an intended barb, but regardless, it was a red rag to a bull. "You." The Overseer was practically frothing at the mouth when he turned his focus on Val.

Me sister turned on the "innocent simple girl" act, which was hard to believe, especially when she stood encased in the fiercest armour— hidden by an armoury of knives—I'd ever seen in me life. The Overseer didn't believe it either. But that was not the point. The crowd ate it up.

And that wasn't all. Bodies coloured by the Light's armour emerged from the gathering around the scene and came to stand behind Felix, and consequently us. More and more they came, until a rainbow army stood behind us: true Community members. Led by the swell, other Unseeing members of the mob came as well.

Soon, the Seen standing behind us almost outnumbered the Unseen standing across from us. Of course the crowd, most of them, had no idea. They just thought they were making a stand against a madman.

"Enough, my petsss."

Oh, here we go. The Dark Lord had just shown up at the party.

Those standing behind us, who could See, drew their swords. The Warriors of Light closed ranks. I threw a look over me shoulder to check the kids were still covered and protected. Knowing they were safe, I loosened me shoulders and prepared for round two.

He stalked along the open space between us, his hands behind his back, but still we could hear the faint echo of a singular hand's clapping. He stopped in front of Valarie. "Hello again, my dearessst Valarrrie."

Val didn't respond, but she did drop her eyes.

"Your cubsss have grown clawsss." He looked at us all, stopping a bit longer on Felix, then the crowd standing behind us. I don't know what he was looking at and I sure as boxes was not going to turn my back on him to check it out. Bringing his focus back to us, he rolled his head on his neck, then looked back at her. His eyes travelling over her body, a sneer masking his face. He then turned to the Overseer and his minions.

Even though the Overseer's armour was faint as ruled lines, he had enough Sight to know who and what faced him. Turns out the man did have an ounce of sense in his oversized head; he dropped his eyes and quaked.

Speaking to no one in particular, the Dark Lord raised his voice. "Where isss my pawn?"

Silence followed.

Then gasps and cries tumbled over one another in the crowd as all of us, Seeing and Unseeing, watched as Alain's inert form levitated toward us through the diminishing clouds of smoke.

"Payment isss due. The termsss of our agreement are ssstill unmet." He then sought out Izabel in the crowd and raised an eyebrow at her. "And look unlikely to be filled any time sssoon."

You can bet your bippy I would not like to be in Alain's shoes, dead or alive. Nor would I like to be standing on that side of this face-off. Or even on our side without armour.

"Your time isss up." I didn't know if Alain was still alive, but either way, he was about to meet the consequences of his choices and make the payment for the deal he'd struck.

The Dark Lord turned to leave. The still-levitating body followed him. "Take that one withthth you." His hand flicked toward the Overseer, who was bundled back into a car which fled the square. And then all of hell's horde turned to face us.

Oh, dear Lord, please give me stren—

Me petition was drawn and quartered as the brightest light that'd ever burned me eyes exploded across the night sky. Hisses, spits, groans and squeals had me forcing me watering eyes open. What was coming for us now? Me gob was well and truly smacked as arrows from Heaven split the night and cauterised the enemy.

I LOOKED from the carnage in front of me to me sister, then back. And in that time, the square was surrounded by Warriors of Light. The first ranks standing shoulder to shoulder, swords drawn, closing off any escape. Behind them, circling in chariots of fire, another rank of Warriors faced the enemy with spears held high. Above us, mounted on eagles, each the size of a gigantor, another rank of Warriors circled, flaming arrows notched in bows primed and aimed at the flood of Darkness confronting us.

Joy eclipsed hope, and relief washed me soul clean. I'd always known we weren't alone, but the evidence to support me belief was currently rendering me speachless. The wall of Warriors who had stood between the wounded and the battle moved forward to incorporate us within their protection.

I had to cover me ears as the snarling, shrieking and screaming of the enemy, now trapped, escalated as a spear from heaven landed in the space in front of us. "The Star of Laodicea," Val yelled over the din, grinning.

Such was the bloke's confidence, he'd landed facing us, not the enemy. His eyes travelled over us all. He smiled and nodded, a pleased look on his face. Then looked to Val, a glint in his eye mirroring the one I often saw in hers. He nodded again then turned, and with a battle cry in a language I didn't understand proceeded to lead his troops in flushing the square clean.

One by one, those who were in a state to do so came from behind to stand beside us for a front-row advantage. It was a scene I would never forget. The Warriors systematically worked their way through the horde, not allowing any to escape. They waged until every element of Darkness was removed. Warring until the sky was crystal clear, and the air was pure as the Light Himself.

Only then did any stand at ease. The infantry was first to depart. The horsemen retreated next. And finally, after broadening their circling and confirming the coast was clear, the eagle riders withdrew. The Star of Laodicea turned once again to face us. He sheathed both swords over his shoulders. When he spoke, you could have knocked me down with a whisper, but I drew myself together quick smart—I would'na missed this for the world. "I have a message"—his eyes encompassed the Seeing. "Well done, faithful. You have fought well."

He looked to Val, "The Lord is with you, mighty warrior."

To Felix, me and the rest of me family he said, "He is pleased with you. Now is a time to rest, recover and prepare. For there is an arduous journey before you."

Then he singled Dan out. "Remember your dream."

And he was gone like he had arrived, a spear of Light returning to the heavens.

Finally, it was over.

Then a scream split the night. I turned to find me sister, Val, on her knees, with a number of knife hilts sticking out of various joints.

I was almost sick.

Val was.

5 4

INDIGO: TIME'S UP

Audette had outdone herself. After footage from tonight was splattered over the networks, Alain and the Overseer had lost their power. And she'd come out a hero. Her support of Iza, who was now a local legend, meant access-all-areas—medically speaking.

Which was sweet-as, because at the hospital all the women from the Temple, the Silverscales, and every other member of our team were being treated in the "penthouse"—private use of the top floor of the hospital. Currently we were all in one large room with lounge suites and couches for our guests. Each bed had a curtain that could be pulled for privacy.

Apparently, it was nothing new for that sick frack, the Dark Lord, to use Val as a pincushion. Something Raph's wonder-hands couldn't heal. That kind of blew my mind, yeh? All that skrat he'd done, and he couldn't pull out a few knives. Val was on another floor being submerged in a stinking-hot tub of water. Seemed her crew knew what to do and that was the only thing that helped. They were going to take her to a private room next door to our shared ward when she'd got a handle on the pain. Whatever the frack that meant.

Raph had been able to work some of his Light-powered wonder on Iza and Tessa, but they were being kept in for observation. Dan's concussion was being observed. I still couldn't believe I'd done that to him. Made me sick to think about it. So he too was kept in and woken every hour. And let me tell you, he was not impressed. After doing the 2.00 am watch with Tessa, then a full day of wedding prep, then a whole night of battle, the guy was an aggro zombie and wanted his flecking sleep.

The twins had come round after their shock. Their acid burns from demon blood and wounds from its talons were being handled by the burns and skin specialists. This was when the medicos had their own dose of shock, because they got to witness the miracle that was Raph. He'd got to Riah, Dan and me first. We still hurt, but we'd live, and heal pretty quickly—but have some pretty cool scars to show for it. The kid just kept blowing me away. I'd only suffered a few stripes from where I'd scored a lashing from the demon, and that was bad enough. Raph was covered in scars. Not only on his hands with a fresh batch of burns, but all down his legs where the beast had raked him.

I still couldn't believe what those two did. Climbed on the bleeding thing's back and stuck a sword in its eye. What on earth put that fool idea in their head? But I had to admit, it worked. Dan and me weren't making any impact on the kret at all. Just skitching it off, whilst poking around trying to find its weak spot.

It was only when Riah stuck it in the eye that we both ran in and sliced it up the middle. Just in the nick of time, too. It had grabbed hold of Raph's leg and was going to rip the kid in half. But it became distracted when its innards were collecting in a pool at its feet. Not knowing which wound to protect, it threw Riah off with the swipe of one claw and tried to hold its guts in with the other. Not long after that, it started dissolving. Val hurdled its body and tried like a woman possessed to get Raph to release his hold before he was left lying in a pool of acidic tar.

Tessa's gut was healing. Puffy red stripes ran across her stomach. The marks matched the scars down Dan's back. They'd had to treat him sitting beside her bed. He wouldn't leave her until she woke up. Even then, they'd pulled a gurney up next to her and allowed them to share the space.

Amber had been checked over and, considering most of her wounds were superficial, she'd been allowed to go home. Same with Lily.

Marcus and Kait formed a vigil around their four kids. Only ever leaving the room one at a time.

Marcus was still too skitched to speak civilly or to make much sense. "Wait! Why on earth didn't you wait? Or send someone to get us? What were you thinking? You could have been killed." He'd have his rant, march around the room, breathe deeply with his hands on his hips, eyeballing each of them, then draw a shuddery breath and leave the room for five minutes. He'd then come back in and go to each bed and declare his undying, unconditional love to each of them. Embrace his wife. Sit silently for a few moments then get up and do it all again.

Kait just moved from one body to the next, kissing them and fussing over blankets. Asking if they needed anything, if they were warm enough, then leave the room for her own emotional breakdown.

It was exhausting.

Marcus stood. "What were yo—"

"Enough already." I just couldn't take another bout of his ranting. "Give it a rest. We get that you were worried, yeh? We get that you may have done things differently. But please."

He spun and glared at me, ready to take me on. Then he really looked and saw Iza trying to rest beside me, and he softened.

"Sorry mate. I just…"

"I know." I ran my thumb over Iza's knuckles as her fingers entwined in mine. "I know." I couldn't look at Iza… still. We'd all seen her dad… float… levitate… fracking fly out of the Temple. If others hadn't confirmed it, I'd have been sure I was going mad. The office clerk didn't make it out. His official cause of death would probably be smoke inhalation. But seriously, it should have gone down as stupidity… and greed. Blind greed. I still didn't know about Alain. Was he dead? Did I kill him? Was it the smoke? I just couldn't be sure. I mean, I wasn't upset that he was gone. But to think I may have done a permanent job of it… that was a step too far.

Oh Lord, was it me? I mean, I kind of don't want to know. But then I kind of do. I am sorry. I'm not sorry... but I am. If you know what I mean. And I guess you do. I'm just so sorry.

I fell back into a trance, remembering how we'd found Iza. Tied up to the altar. Her dad a crazed frack with that crazy-butt knife. I was that close to losing her. I couldn't help the downward spiral. My thoughts were eating me alive. It didn't help that I was sitting here by her bed, in the same hospital where it all started. When the roles had been reversed. "I think I know how you felt." When she looked at me through her blackened eyes, I explained. "That first night... here, at the hospital. You sat by me and... I suspect you might have felt hopeless. Felt responsible, and helpless."

"But Indy, you're not responsible for this. My father is."

"Yeah, nah, just like you weren't responsible for a drunk driver? But I am. I didn't stop them taking you. I didn't get to you in time. I..." The grief welled up like flock of angry vultures and stole everything. I couldn't speak. I couldn't think. I couldn't breathe. The sobs consumed me. I gently wrapped my arms and head around her broken body and had no control as the swarm plucked me clean.

The burns from the demon blood burned like a banshee, but the pain was good. It helped me feel like I was paying my penance.

All the while, Iza ran her hands over my head and back, careful to avoid my wounds. I was completely helpless. From the moment those krets had shown up this morning... yesterday morning... to now. She was wounded and hurting and there was nothing I could do to help. "If I could change places with you, I would. I'd take all your pain. I'd take it all from you if I could."

Iza's face was sheening from tears. I didn't have to see to know, I heard it in her voice. "Oh Indy. Don't you see? It was my battle to fight. I was the only one who could. It was my path to tread, and Indy" —she waited till I sat up and was looking at her properly—"I won. We. Won. We did it. The Temple is finished." At the pride bursting from her eyes, and the skrat-eating grin spreading from ear to ear, reopening the split in her lip, I couldn't help but return her smile.

"Yes sweetheart, you—"

"We."

"We did it. But you gotta stop smiling"—I focused on the trickle of blood dripping off her chin—"or that lip will never heal."

She laughed as I handed her a tissue. "We've come so far, haven't we?" She looked around the room, tearing up again. "We've saved them." Looked me straight in the eye. "You and me, Indy. We saved them all." Her tears ramped up to a sob. I climbed up onto her bed and lay beside her and held her as she released all her emotion. Just like it had always been. Her and me against the world. With a bit of help, granted. But, at the heart of it, Iza and me. I wrapped her into my body and became the wall shutting out the world, protecting her in our cave.

"Indy?" Marcus shook my shoulder gently.

"Huh, yeah?" I looked up and saw that the room was full of people. Our family and friends. And they'd brought food from our party from yesterday morning. From our wedding. Was it really only yesterday?

But I had her back now. With me where she belonged. Where I belonged... And so was our whole family. "Where's the minister?"

Everyone laughed until they realised I was serious. I turned to Iza. "I know it's not ideal, and you're not wearing your nice dress." She was now cleaned and wearing a blue smock thing, but she had not let them take our shirts away. I knew she was going to keep them forever. She wasn't a hoarder, but tokens... trophies were important to her. "And you don't have your flowers. And you're kind of beaten to a pulp and lying in hospital. But Iza, will you marry me? Now? Before anything or anyone else comes along and tries to stop us? Or take you away again?"

Felix spoke up. "There is a Shepherd... delegated to the hospital. If Iza is in agreement I can speak to him and ask if he would come up and perform the ceremony? But I do believe, after the damage done in the Temple, and since Audette has verbally revoked the contract, no one can interrupt your wedding ceremony again? If you would rather wait?"

I turned to study Iza and tried to gauge her response. As always, my girl was a cut above everyone else. She wasn't just the Jewel of Laodicea; she was my jewel. "No."

My heart stopped, until I remembered my last question. "No, not wait? Or no, wait?"

Causing another trickle of blood to run down her chin, Iza smiled again and said, "No, not wait. Yes, I will marry you. Now."

And so it was, lying in a hospital bed together, her bruised silver scales wrapped in my scarred black hands, surrounded by our family —old and new—we waited for someone to hunt the Shepherd down. Someone had bought flowers from the hospital's florist and given them to all the women and a huge bunch to Iza.

But when it came time to find something else for her to wear, Iza dug her feet in and demanded to wear the filthy, smoke-stenched, ill-fitting shirts. However, she did agree to keep the clean hospital gown on underneath. "Do you not realise what these shirts represent? Do you not know how precious they are? Not only the gift of them and what they cost, but the men who gave them to me? I could not think of finer clothes to be married in." She reached out her hand and invited Raph over. The kid was blushing like a beet. She pulled him close and kissed his cheek. "I would not be here today without you. From the moment I met you to this very minute, you have been saving me, picking me up and putting me back together. Thank you. It is an honour to wear your shirt."

At this the kid was tearing up and incapable of speech. His sister came up to rescue him. But Iza stopped her. "Sariah. What...? I cannot even start to find the words to explain how..." Iza shook her head and pulled Sariah close. Now it was Riah's time to cry. "Sariah, all I can say is thank you. For so much. For your bravery beyond your years, for the gift of your song and Peace, for how you have become my sister, for saving me. When I grow up, I hope to be half the woman you are."

The twins stepped back as Iza called Dan over. "The brother of my soon-to-be husband makes us family. It is an honour to know you. For what you have done for me, for Indy and for the both of us, I will forever be in your debt. Thank you."

She pulled him close and went to kiss his cheek, but seriously?

That was my wife. Or she would be if we could get through all of this carry-on. "That's enough. You can step back now," I mock-growled at my brother.

Everyone laughed. But Dan, the sneaky kret, dived in and kissed her on the lips instead.

"Step away from my wife." I was only partly joking.

Dan winked at me. "Not yours yet, mate."

"And she's not yours." Tessa stepped up with a raised eyebrow and hooked her arm through Dan's elbow. Again, everyone laughed.

"Tessa…" Again, Iza was lost for words. Both girls were crying by now, so they just hugged. It was a relief when the Shepherd finally showed.

"Okay, folks, I believe someone wants me to marry them?"

EPILOGUES

55

KAITLYN: ABBOT'S LETTERS

"You know he'd be so proud, dear heart." I pulled up a chair next to Val and her in the open space beside the garden in Warehouse Two. Comforted by the fact that even when the walls came down, the garden would remain. The work we'd done here would remain when we started the "arduous journey" ahead of us.

Marcus came up beside me and pulled up his own chair. We basked in the glory of the garden, the children playing and the new members of the Factory community marvelling at the wonders of their new home. "Who'd be proud of what?"

I knew he was not nearly as dense as he made out sometimes, but really? "Really?"

Val huffed a chuckle and pulled the lightweight blanket tighter around her shoulders. "Abbot. I was just thinking of him and what he'd think of the twins and how'd they've used what he gave them to produce this bounty almost two years later. Not only in the garden but within the whole community. All that they have achieved."

"Not just the twins, dear heart. You as well. You are a bit of a sly one. Training Felix and not letting on."

She chuckled again. "I couldn't leave him new to his armour and cast adrift. And we agreed, the people here had to win their own victory to achieve true freedom." Then she sighed. "I think it's time."

"For what? To leave?" Marcus leaned forward in his chair so he could see Val on my other side.

Again, she smiled at him. "Soon, yes. But I think it's time to give them" —she nodded at Tessa and Dan as they came in from a run, hand in hand, and ambled over to greet the twins who were busy showing the new ladies around the garden—"Abbot's letters. They've come so far and I think they're ready. He knew exactly what he was doing when he gave them each the other's rings. He knew what was ahead of them from the moment Dan entered our house in Sodom. And I think now is when he would want them to read his heart message for them. What do you think?"

The three of us sat back and watched our four children. I took Bear and Val's hands as they sat either side of me and pumped them both twice. They returned the double squeeze that was the twins' sign for "I love you". We were in agreement.

***

Tessa, dear heart,

Please excuse an old man's folly, but I wish to give you this gift. And why would I bequeath you a man's ring, the ring my mother presented to my father? First and foremost, my hope is it will be a reminder and a symbol of the commitment and the love the Light has for you.

I have noted at times that Daniel refers to you as Contessa. The name means countess—nobility. And, as the daughter of the High King of Heaven, so you are. Remember this: you are beautiful because you are loved, you are whole because of Who loves you, and your value rests in the heart of the One who loves you for eternity: your Father, the Light. No thing and no one can change this. It is an absolute.

Your badge of Joy has warmed my tiring, worn heart over the past year. I grieve not to be part of your future journey, yet I give thanks I

363

was able to share this time with you, witnessing your transformation from broken to glorious.

My prayer for you, dear girl, is that you continue to humbly submit yourself to His wise ministrations, His immense power and passionate love. Whilst you are loved just as you are, you are loved too much to be left as you are. Continue to allow his love to flow through you, restoring, strengthening and shaping you as He continues to rejoice in you.

If at some point you choose to walk with a helpmate, please ensure they are of the same ilk as your Heavenly Father, who loves, cherishes and sees you for the wondrous creation you are.

In Him, in Light and Love,

Abbot

***

Daniel, my dear boy,

It gave me great joy to see you step into the Light. Some would suggest that now the Unseen has been revealed, the way before you is a clear path. Whilst I would agree, I would also like to suggest that rather than singular, your path is now a continual crossroad.

Previously there has only been one way—that of the Darkness. But with your choice to come into the Light comes "choice" every step of the way. Make no mistake, my boy, you are at war. But then again, you always have been. Previously, like us all, you were at war with the Light. Now you are at war with the Dark and his dominion: the world.

However, it has been my experience of living in the Light to never go without. And, whilst I lived in isolation, never was I alone. Please accept this gift of the rings my father presented to my mother as a symbol of companionship, a reminder that you too are no longer alone.

They are of great wealth: sentimental and financial. My hope is that they will serve several purposes. First, a reminder of your lifelong companionship with the Light, in the Light, and for the Light. Secondly, if you find yourself in need of finances, use them to meet your needs. And finally, if in time you find your helpmate, I hope you might consider presenting these to her, knowing it is with the greatest joy I have been able to contribute in some way to your journey.

In Him, in Light and Love,

Abbot

5 6

DANIEL: GIFT GIVING

It was the middle of autumn and just over three months since the battle. Kait and Marcus had returned from their three weeks' holiday in a flash apartment here in Laodicea—organised and paid for by Felix. And Indy and Iza had returned from their honeymoon in France—organised, paid for and accompanied by Audette.

Sunshine warmed the air circulating through the wide-open doors of Warehouse One and out through the veggie garden roof. We'd set up a huge table in the middle of the space. The chairs round the outside were slowly filling, as more and more of our guests arrived. I'd rounded up the kids who were finishing off the decorations. "Quick, she'll be back soon, and you know she'll be skitched when she finds out what we've done. We'd bleeding-well better be ready so we can take cover if needs be."

Joko paused. "But Dan, it is a birthday party, why will she be upset?"

"Because it's Val. And she's in pain. She hates a fuss, and she hates being incapacitated. Plus, she thinks it's a farewell party for us heading to Philadelphia. When she finds out we've misled her, she'll be super skitched. Come on, hurry up, guys." My nerves were electrified, and it had nothing to do with Val's party. Today was the day. I'd been putting a bit of extra money away to get things just right. This morning I had picked it up and now I was going to be sick. Not really. But yeah, really.

We'd just received a text from Felix, so Raph, Vashti, Shauna and Aiko were transporting platters of food to the table. Sariah, Kazi, Genni and Amber were fussing over final flower arrangements... everywhere. It was all systems go because we were running out of time.

I was running out of time.

"It's them. They're here. They're here," Jordan squealed from his lookout next to Lottie at the front gate. He'd been so hyped, now he'd done his job he ran in circles screaming, "She's here, she's here." Lottie tried to wrestle him to safety before Felix pulled into the car park. We'd reserved a spot for him right next to the doors so Val wouldn't have to walk too far. She'd hate it, but she'd just have to deal.

Hopefully her hydrotherapy would have her mellowed out so she wouldn't crack heads when she found out what we'd done. But that was highly unlikely.

Jordan's siren call had alerted everyone—and the neighbourhood—so we were all in position when Felix pulled up, got out and raced around to open her door. Seeing us, she froze. Her eyes narrowed. She looked past us into the warehouse, then back to Felix. "What have you done?"

Tessa who was tucked under my arm couldn't hold back her giggle. It was the straw that started the cascade of laughter.

When it calmed, Felix responded. "My dear woman, I merely drove you to the hospital, waited until you were finished, then drove you home." He handed her her cane. Fire shot from her eyes and consumed him. Well, if Val had had her way, it would have. As it was, Felix just held her gaze and smiled without moving a muscle. It was a gift.

Val wanted to refuse the cane, but she couldn't, so with ill grace she took it and limped through the crowd, then pulled up short when she saw what lay in front of her. She stopped and tried to turn but the knives lodged in her major joints stopped her. Raph was beaming and trying really hard not to jiggle. Riah was silently clapping her hands and the rest of us were beaming. Front and centre was the most spectacular cake I'd ever seen. In indigo icing it read, "Happy Birthday, Legend. We love you."

The fire in her eyes was extinguished by a watery veil. Val tried to cough to cover her emotion, but Kait ran forward and embraced her and helped her hide the tears. Then Marcus threw his two bits in. "Hurry up and let's eat before the demons come and ruin everything." A nervous titter circled the group, but it got everyone moving and we all took our seats.

As had become our habit, all talk soon turned to the future plans of the Factory. Blueprints had been drawn up for townhouses to accommodate all survivors from the Temple. The veggie garden would stay where it was, but everything else would be pulled down and rebuilt. There would be gardens, play equipment, an art space and an industrial kitchen.

Val was able to fade into the background, her favourite spot, and Indy stepped into the limelight—his favourite spot. "While you are all here, Iza and I just wanted to, once again, thank you all for your part in making all of this possible… not just the party, but the future of the Factory." He reached down and took Iza's hand. "We also wanted to let you know that in about six months, we're going to have a bab—"

Roars and cheers overrode the end of his proclamation. Tessa and I had already known, along with Audette and Mina. And whilst everyone was busy fussing and congratulating the couple, I pushed back in my chair, turned toward Tessa and took her hand.

Help me please. Make this come out right. Please.

"Tessa?"

She gave me her attention and smiled.

This had seemed a lot easier when I practised it. I should have written it down.

"What is it, Dan? Are you okay?"

"Yes. No… Yes?"

She tilted her head. "Dan?"

"I love you, Tessa."

"Yes, Dan, I know. What's wrong?"

"Nothing's wrong, I just wanted to tell you I love yo—"

"Are you sick? You're white and your hands are sweating." She half-stood and started looking around for Kait.

"No." I didn't mean to yell. "I'm not sick. I just… needed to tell you that I love you."

"Oh. My. Word. Are you dying?"

"What? No." But I kind of felt like I was. And sick. I was going to be sick.

"Dan, you're green. Are you sure?"

"Yes." *No.* By this stage the whole crowd were silent and looking at us. So, dying was probably a good thing. I looked around the room and decided now was not the best time. I'd wait till there wasn't an audience.

But Marcus barked from across the room. "Don't stop now, lad. Finish what you started."

I shut my eyes and tried to stop the nausea overwhelming me. Tessa reached out and rubbed my back. "Dan, what's wrong?"

Time to do this. I could do this. I looked up, swallowed my bile and started reciting my speech. I would not stop for anyone. "Tessa, I love you. You are my best friend. You are the sunshine to my day and the warmth to my soul. Your joy is my joy, and your laughter is my elixir. Tessa, I love yo—"

"You've already said that bit."

"Shut up, Lottie." Indy laughed from somewhere in the vicinity.

Don't stop. Don't stop. Don't stop.

"—you. I have already promised that you, apart from the Light, are my priority. I have already promised to always leave the light on, the key out, and the door unlocked, for you. And only you, for always. You have already promised to make me a priority and to take me with you even when we're apart."

Tessa had turned to a statue. Her mouth was wide open and tears were glistening in her eyes.

Don't stop. Don't stop. Don't stop.

"So, in light of all that, I was wondering if you"—I gulped—"would make it permanent?" I'd done it. I'd got it out. I could breathe again.

Tessa screwed up her face. "What?"

"What do you mean, 'what'?"

Marcus barked, "Use the word and give her the gift."

"Oh. Fralk." I fumbled in my pocket and freed the little box that had been burning a hole in my leg all morning. I got down on one knee, flicked the little lid open and asked, "Marry m—?"

I hadn't even finished my proposal and I was wearing my Tessa-cloak. I was now on both knees with Tessa wrapped so tightly around my neck I could hardly breathe. Again, there were deafening cheers and whoops. I pulled back and looked her in the eye. "Words, Tessa. You gotta use your words." I figured it was a yes, but she still hadn't said it.

She nodded and with her watery yes I could finally breathe again. I slipped the ring Abbot had given me—freshly cleaned, dark blue stones sitting in a circle around a now-sparkling diamond, re-banded—from the box and slipped it on her finger. Finally, she was mine and all the world could see it for themselves.

AFTERWORD

A note to my readers

Thank you so much for joining me on the third leg of this adventure into the Light. I hope you have enjoyed getting to know more of the family and a bit more of the backstory as much as I have. This book and these people are as real to me as my family, and it is a pleasure to bring them to life on the page and share them with you.

If you have enjoyed this book, please consider leaving a review. It would inspire others to pick it up, as well as encourage me to write some more. Although, that's not too hard to do.

To keep up to date with more books in the series and other news, sign up to my newsletter at

donitabundy.com

db

BROKEN RESTORATION PLAYLIST

Broken Restoration theme: Bye Bye Babylon — *Elevation Worship*
    Valerie: Rebels — *Influence Music*
    Isabel: Wild Hearts Can't be Broken — *Pink*
    Indigo: Feeling Good — *Michael Bublé*
    Contessa: Rebuilder — *Carrollton*
    Daniel: True Companion — *Marc Cohn*
    Kaitlyn: Storyteller — *Morgan Harper Nichols, Jamie Grace*
    Marcus: Darling — *Needtobreathe*
    Raphael: Your Hands — *J.J. Heller*
    Sariah: Gratitude — *Brandon Lake*
    Family: Loved — *Fresh Life Worship*
    Silverscales: Peace — *Harvest*

ACKNOWLEDGEMENTS

To begin with, I think it needs to be said that, to date, due to many forces pushing, pulling and deconstructing, this has been the hardest book to write. Which is why, even more than ever, I would like to acknowledge and give thanks for those who support me and have patience with me and "that writerly thing I do".

To my family and support crew, thank you:

Belinda Pollard, my friend, sister-in-arms, and editor, whose wisdom, life experience and oodles of patience helped me cross number three off the list.

Alix Kwan, the most amazing proofreader of all time, thank you for carving time out of your very busy life to help continue the dream. Your work ensures we can let the story have its head and not be held hostage by typos.

Ella Green and Lee Cawthray, the most wonderful cheer squad in the history of the universe. Ever.

For my Beta Reader Crew, who fronted up for another round of wading through the outworking of my at times chaotic mind, ensuring order in the lives of those who live within these pages:
- Ella Green
- Lee Cawthray
- Belinda Pollard
- Bethany McKenna.

The Somerset Writers Group: a more diverse, caring, supportive crew of creative geniuses would be hard to find.

To my family at our own Soteria House: for your constant prayers, support and encouragement, thank you.

To my mum, always in the wings, always encouraging, always supportive. I couldn't have got this one over the line without you. Thank you.

And finally, and most importantly, I give thanks to the Light, whose story I believe this is. Whilst it is told through the lens of my life experiences, it continues to be inspired, carried and created in His strength alone. My prayer remains, dear reader, that you find inspiration, challenge and encouragement to keep journeying the incredible adventure in, and with, the Light.

ABOUT THE AUTHOR

Donita Bundy lives in the Somerset Shire (Queensland, not England) with her husband, two boys, her socially inappropriate cat and irrepressible red dog. She loves creating images with words and, when she's not writing, her camera. Eating chocolate, hanging out with the wallabies and walking the aforementioned red dog are a close second.

To connect, follow her blog, listen to the podcast, check out the gallery or just keep up to date with what's going on, go to her website and sign up to the newsletter at

donitabundy.com

ALSO BY DONITA BUNDY

ARMOUR OF LIGHT SERIES

BOOK 1: DANGEROUS SALVATION

What if your saviour was more dangerous than your enemy?

Lonely and living on the streets, forced to steal clothes to survive another bitter winter, Daniel has an encounter that turns his world upside-down.

Confronted by two strangers who tell him things about himself that no human could possibly know, Daniel is offered a choice: to stay where he is and face the dangers of the street, or accept the invitation of a warm bed, a family... and to join their war.

Can he trust the safety this "family" appears to offer? Or will he give in to the temptations of the Dark Lord?

He must make a decision. Fast.

ISBN:

Print: 978-0-6487423-0-8

Ebook-EPUB: 978-0-6487823-1-5

BOOK 2: BLINDING REVELATION

What if the Unseen was more blinding than the Seen?

The crew have survived the chaos and hardships of Sodom to arrive in Laodicea's lap of luxury. A city ahead of its time: beautiful, pristine and enemy-free. It is the perfect place to rest, recover and regroup.

But all is not what it seems.

Something sinister lurks beneath the sterile exterior of the golden city.

How will the refugees from Sodom adjust to life in this foreign city?

With no common enemy to fight, what will hold them together?

Is this place heaven on earth, or is it the threshold of hell?

ISBN:

Print 978-0-6487823-3-9

Ebook-EPUB 978-0-6487823-4-6

BOOK 4: HUMBLE INSURRECTION - *COMING SOON.*

ALSO BY DONITA BUNDY